APARTMENTAL EVIL

Gabriel James

This book is a work of fiction. Names, characters, places, and incidents are products of the author's imagination or are used fictitiously. Any resemblance to actual events or locales or persons, living or dead, is entirely coincidental.

ISBN- 13: 978-0-9898647-0-1

ISBN-10: 0989864707

Front cover artwork by Gabriel James.

Printed in the U.S.A.

I dedicate this book to my loving wife Katie. Despite my crazy pursuits, she still loves and supports me. (As long as I don't accidentally blow up the house.)

To my three nephews, who remind me of what it is like to be a kid again.

And to Susan, who reminds me that there are still kind people out there...somewhere. Maybe they are hiding under a rock or something?

Contents

Prologue

It was a dark and stormy night. Lightning flashed and the sky lit up for a few seconds. You could hear the howling sounds as the wind was starting to pick up. It was clear that a thunderstorm was on the way. Tonight was a bit different. It just felt like something unnatural was in the air. Loud thunder echoed in the distance. That was the signal that told most living creatures it was time to seek shelter.

Up in the heavens above, there was one evil creature hovering directly above the apartment complex. The creature's tattered robe whipped about as the wind blew. Its eyes glowed like icy blue embers in the darkness. When lightning flashed, its ancient face was revealed for a moment. The creature came here for one sole purpose and that was to feed. It floated slowly downward, like a rotten leaf in the wind, to the apartment complex below. It could feed off of anyone but people that have committed villainous acts always gave off a taste that was unequal to anything else it had ever known. The creature had his eye on one man in particular. From the shadows, he waited patiently for an opportune time to strike. But unfortunately for this man, that time was going to be tonight.

The monster gracefully landed on the slanted rooftop. Cold rain was pouring down now. The roof was slick from the water but not to this shadowy thing that was neither dead nor truly alive. The rain did not bother this creature since it wasn't completely physical. It came from one of those dark corners of someone's mind where the evilest things lurked. The monster slowly crawled, head first, down the side of the building. It had no fears of being seen by mortal eyes. When the lightning flashed its shape glowed slightly for an instant and then it would become transparent again. It had waited with intense anticipation for the savory feast that was to come. A few unfortunate souls it had fed upon but it had not had a meal that was going to be as satisfying as this one. This man's evil deeds gave off a smell that made him quite irresistible.

The dark thing moved to the third floor window. It slipped through the window and manifested in the shadowy confines of the closet where it sat there patiently waiting.

After an hour, the man finally arrived. He walked into the room quickly and sat on the bed. The creature's wait was finally over. The man slowly rolled up his sleeve and started to tie off his arm. He had a small wooden box with him that he slowly opened and pulled out three filled syringes.

The creature already knew that this man was a drug dealer and an addict. It was one of the reasons that brought the monster here. He quickly tied his arm off looking for a vein to inject into. He was slightly trembling in anticipation. With the circulation in his arm being cut off, it brought his veins closer to the surface of his skin. He slowly took the syringe in his right hand. He stared at it for a few seconds grinning and knew that

6

this was going to make everything feel better. It was going to make all the pain go away. Without hesitating he took the syringe and plunged it deep into an artery while he pushed the plunger all the way down. The creature in the closet knew the feeling all too well. He too had cravings and desires that he was anxiously waiting to satisfy.

After a few minutes the man leaned back on the bed. The drugs were in full effect now. As he lay there, he happened to turn his head towards the closet. He squinted his eyes as they tried to focus on something that was lingering in the darkness. The man had suspected that something was trying to harm him, but he had no proof until now.

"I see you demon. I see you hiding in the corner." The man said as he came in and out of conscious. His mind was trying to decide if this was a drug induced hallucination or if this was real. The monster knew it had been seen and there was no point in hiding anymore. The creature wickedly smiled as it moved out of the complete darkness towards the bed. The drugs left the man temporarily paralyzed.

"Ar...Ar...Are you HIM? Are you Death? Ha..Have...Have you come to carry me away?" His words were slurred as he tried to talk.

The living darkness stood by him on the side of the bed now. All was quiet in the room except for the sound of his breathing. The man started to laugh and cry at the same time. "Th..This is impossible. You're not REAL. YOU ARE NOT REAL!" He shouted.

The demon grabbed the man by his shirt collar. He lifted the man like a rag doll and effortlessly pulled him close to his face to look him right in the eyes. "*I am REAL!*" The creature shouted in a deep demonic voice.

7

The man could barely lift his head but he looked directly at the creature. Even in the man's present condition he instantly recognized the face of his tormentor. "So it's you. I always knew you were evil from the first time I saw you. What did I do to deserve this?" The man said in a whisper as he was unable to fight back or run.

The creature's waiting was over. He was ready to feed. There was no chance of escape for the man now.

"*You will not escape me again, my little morsel. You know what you did. I am going to drink your life and watch you wither...*" The creature whispered in the man's ear as it placed its blackened hand above its head. The man felt an unnatural coldness spread inside his body. He knew his soul was about to be violently ripped apart. He shuddered in terror. The creature slowly opened its soul devouring mouth. After a moment of silence the draining ritual was about to began.

All of a sudden there was a knocking at the front door. Both the man and the demon turned their heads towards the sound.

Knock. Knock . Knock. "Hello anyone home?" someone shouted from the front door.

The demon's face twisted in rage. As the man was held in the demon's death grip he managed to let out a small laugh. He smiled mockingly back at the demon. "What are you going to do now? Kill us both...

Part One:

Moving Day

Chapter 1

The mind of Jack. Friday May 31.

It was a warm sunny day in May. I was extremely excited because for me, it was moving day. I was driving a rented moving truck to my new apartment. The sun reflecting off the white paint of the hood was blinding. The outside looked new but looking at the mileage I could see that it had spent some time on the road. It sure was different sitting this high from the ground. It was much bigger then my small economy sized car that I was used to driving. However, my car did get good gas mileage. Being this far off the ground made a person feel powerful. I am the king of the road. The engine slowly rattled and roared to life when I gave it gas. I was not sure if it was going to make it to my new place. It sure seemed to strain to get up smaller hills. I thought I might have to get out and push. I could hear the sounds of my clothes and items shifting in the back of the truck. A hard knot formed in the pit of my stomach. In my head I could picture opening the back door and seeing all of my belongings shattered and broken.

As I drove, I thought about how funny it was that a person who has never driven a very large moving truck could walk in and get behind the wheel without any training. I nearly hit at least 5 cars and I had to yell out the windows sorry a few times. I only got flicked off one time so I considered that a successful trip. "Good old St. Louis drivers." I said.

My friend Dave and some of my family were helping me move into my new place. They were going to meet me there. I hope they are ready to do some heavy lifting. Even though I am strong, my back can only take so much punishment. I was on the third floor which is the top floor. That was a fact I purposely omitted when I told everyone I needed help. If I told them, all of a sudden, they would have had "special" events going on that they had trouble naming when questioned about what that event might be. I wanted to get a room on the bottom floor but the leasing office said those usually go to the elderly and handicap people. At least the third floor had more privacy and was less likely to get flooded since no one lives above me.

I just graduated from college a month ago. I earned a bachelor degree in Graphic Design. I was extremely lucky to find a job right out of college. That does not seem to happen that much now with the economy not being so great. I had done an internship over the last year at a design firm and they offered me a job when I graduated. It also helped that I was friends with the son of the owner of the business so he was willing to give me a shot.

I finally saw the blue sign of the apartments. Northfield Grove Apartments. This is the place. I made a left and I heard some low hanging branches scrape the side of the truck as I pulled in. Ahh, it is just a scratch. I hope. I had to stop by the office to pick up my keys. I parked and went inside. The office manager was there. She was a large older woman and she dressed like she was from the seventies. When I talked to her I couldn't help but notice that she was missing some teeth on her bottom jaw. She seemed somewhat friendly though. I signed the paperwork and she handed me my key.

"Welcome to Northfield Grove Apartments. Your room is toward the back of the complex on the right side. One of our maintenance staff will be dropping off your washer and dryer sometime in the afternoon. If they are not there by 4, call me and I will see that it is taken care of." She said.

"Wonderful. That sounds great. Now for the fun part. Unloading." I said as I left the office.

The buildings were all tan and brown in color. They must have had new siding put up recently because it looked fairly new for a place that's been here for 30 years. The buildings were shaped like three giant rectangles with a pool in the middle of two of them. In the front section the pool was across the street by the office. There were thirty six apartments on each side of the rectangle.

I finally found the section where my apartment was located. The numbers on these building were not in any particular order and did not make any sense. They were 5804, then 2506, then 3547, and on and on like that. Maybe I was not seeing the pattern. Here we are. I pulled the truck in backwards so we could unload right onto the sidewalk.

"This is it." I said. I got out of the truck and opened the back. Everything looked moved and jittered but still in one piece, as far as I could tell.

"Nice driving back there. I think all the paint has peeled off the side of the truck. I like how you nearly ran the blue car off the road. That was awesome." Dave said.

"My driving is still way better than yours. Hey, why don't you grab a box here and start unloading. I am in M at that one over there" I said in return.

Everyone started grabbing boxes and walking up the stairs. I grabbed a box and walked up the three flights of stairs. I am physically fit but I was already winded and tired. I pulled out my key and unlocked my door. The apartment looked clean. It had new carpet and clean white walls. There were a few cut marks on the countertops but that was the only problem I could spot.

I was so excited. This was my first real place. It sure beat my tiny college dorm room. For some reason I always got stuck with a foreign exchange student for a roommate. It was difficult since most of them spoke very little English and I had to act out with my hands to communicate. It was also better than living with my parents who had their own peculiar rules that they made me live by.

Everything was going smoothly until we got to the couch. I grabbed one end and Dave grabbed the other. We started walking to the stairway. The first flight of stairs was easy. When we got to the second flight we had to push half the couch outside of the railings and hold on so it did not fall. There was not much room to maneuver. We pushed and shoved its way up to the third floor. After we got it into the door I threw the cushions on it and passed out.

"Com'on man. Get up. We still have to get the mattress and table tops." Dave said.

"Yeah I know. I am going."

The mattress was the most difficult since it barely fit in the stairway. On one side it was just barely able to fit up the stairs on the other side it was way too long. We managed to move that to the top. That was most of the

13

big heavy things. We all kept moving boxes and bringing my stuff up.

I saw the final box in the very back of the truck. I walked to the back and my footsteps echoed through the emptiness. My legs and back rejoiced. I was extremely sweaty and exhausted. The sweat stains on my shirt went from my neck to my stomach. I am starting to look like my dad. As I moved to the very back of the truck to get the final box I heard something coming up the ramp. I thought it was Dave. I turned around slowly. A giant tan German Sheppard was standing at the opening. It was sniffing the ground.

"Hey puppy. Where's your momma?" I said in my most friendly tone.

The dog's ears went straight up and the hair on his back stood up. I stood still and watched its body tense up. Its brown eyes focused intently on me. Its top lip curled up into a menacing snarl revealing sharp teeth. A deep growl slowly thundered from its mouth. I was no longer getting a friendly vibe. I noticed how very sharp its teeth looked. They looked like little white daggers that were ready to tear at my flesh.

I really felt that this dog was going to bite me. I stood frozen. The sweat and heat I was feeling earlier was gone. The happy feelings of the day evaporated leaving only terror behind. My first instinct was to run but the only way out was blocked. My grip on the last box tightened. I might have to use it as a shield. I quickly thought maybe I could still try to run by the dog. In my mind I was having flashbacks of something I saw on tv about police canine unit training. They always show the guy with the padded suit running from the dog. The dog always catches up to him, clamps down on his arm, and then pulls him to the ground. When he takes off the suit later he is actually unharmed. It sure would be nice to have one of those suits right now.

14

I started yelling every dog command I could think of "SIT. LAY DOWN. FETCH. GO GET YOUR STICK. BAD DOG. BAD DOG. ROLL OVER, WHERES YOUR TOYS? HELP? ANYTHING."

The dog started to close in on me. I was boxed in the corner. I could see drool coming from its mouth now. Being in the empty truck made the barking seem like thunder. The entrance to the truck seemed to move further away from me as the barking got louder.

Surely, someone helping me move would see this and help me. Hopefully they notice that I have been in the truck for some time.

I started to yell "HELP! SOMEONE HELP ME!!!!" I know yelling for help isn't manly unless you are being attacked by a shark but I did it anyways. Suddenly I heard someone yelling something.

"Ellie. Ellie. Ellie there you are. Get over here." The dog barked at me one more time, turned and walked down the ramp as if nothing happened. The danger I felt dissipated. My mind went from fear quickly to anger. I slowly walked to the opening of the truck. I was a little shaken up and kind of pissed off.

I got to the front and there was a women standing there. She was in her early twenties. Her hair was brown and blonde streaked. She wore heavy perfume but smelled heavenly.

"Hey you need to keep your dog on a leash! She nearly bit me!" I said.

"Oh I am so sorry. I am so sorry. She took off out the door before I could get the leash on her. Did she bite you or anything?" She said with a concerned look on her tan face.

"No she didn't bite me." I said angrily.

15

She was kneeling down and the dog was licking her face. She rubbed her tummy and the dog seemed happy. The anger the dog showed toward me was gone. In a baby voice she said "Ellie likes her tummy rubbed doesn't she. She wouldn't hurt anyone. She has never done that to anyone before I swear. She likes you. Tell the handsome man you like him." The dog looked at me and growled again.

"Like hell she does." I said.

"Oh, hey, where are my manners. Are you moving in? My name is Nichole. Most people call me Nikki or Nicks for short. I live in the next apartment over on the bottom floor. I am going to college but I live with my parents. Sadly, my dad lost his job two years ago and then they lost their house and we ended up here. What's your story?"

"Well, my name is Jack. I just graduated college a month ago. I have a degree in graphic design. The design firm that I work at is located close to here. Before, I was driving an hour to work and an hour going home. It was getting old pretty quick having to sit in traffic on 270."

"Oh yeah, I have a few friends that are majoring in graphic design. They seem to like it. I am trying to become a teacher. I only have a few classes left. I am taking a few summer classes. I enjoy working with kids. Hey, you look hot, I mean thirsty. Do you want something to drink? A soda or water?"

"Sure anything cold sounds great." I said.

"BRB." She said. "Ellie, Stay." She walked down the sidewalk and turned into the next breezeway. Ellie sat on the ground and stared me down the whole time. I could hear mini growls coming from her. I decided to take a break and I sat down on the back of the truck.

16

There were some onlookers. I noticed one man in particular who was walking nearby. He was slender and muscular. He was wearing a dark grey hooded jacket and holey jeans. I thought it was a bit odd to have a coat on since it was about eighty degrees outside. His coat was weathered and had a black tree printed on the center of his chest. The sleeves where his hands came out were all tattered and torn. He had his hood on and sunglasses. I never actually saw what the top of his face looked like. His eyes were hidden behind his sunglasses. I could only see the long black hair that grew on his chin. It made his face look like it came to a point. He was carrying a dirty grey bucket and had a grabber he was using to pick up trash. I guess he worked here. I could vaguely hear him humming a song even from this distance.

Nicki came out carrying a cold bottle of water for me. "Here you go. So which apartment are you moving into exactly?"

"6520 M. At the very top." I said as I quickly drank the whole bottle of water in one great big gulp. The water was cool and refreshing. I sat the empty bottle down at the edge of the truck.

"That apartment has been vacant for a few months. I hung out a few times in that apartment before. I was good friends with the guy who lived there."

As I moved my hand I accidentally knocked the empty bottle on the ground. I didn't move to pick it up. Nikki said in a kind voice "Hey, are you going to pick that up?"

"I will in a minute." I said.

Nikki looked around quickly. Her eyes darted back and forth like she was expecting something to happen. I didn't know what she was doing. Her body turned back and forth as she looked quickly in every direction. Her head jerked side to side. The big smile she was wearing was turning to a look of panic. Then her eyes stopped and focused on the man in gray. He was standing quite a bit away up the street. He was definitely out of range to hear what we were saying. I noticed the man in gray had also stopped what he was doing and he was now intently looking at us for some reason. I could not see his eyes but I still felt the presence of his gaze quite intently. He was certainly watching us now.

She said more sternly now "Please, Just listen to me. Just pick up the bottle."

I looked into her eyes and I saw fear. Her eyes were starting to get glassy and teary. I looked at her like she was crazy. My eyebrows bent down and my cheeks curled up. I slowly shook my head side to side. I was confused about what she was afraid off.

"Hey what's a matter? " I looked at her, then at the man up the street. "Are you afraid of that guy or something?" I said in a calm but firm voice. Right after I said that, I felt something in my head or more specifically in the back of my mind. It was cold at first. The only thing I could compare it to was if an unknown presence was invading my mind and stabbing me with icy needles of pain. I was in such agony I had to grab the back of my head. I shook my head back and forth. I then ran my hand through my hair in case maybe I was stung by something and this was a new level of pain I have not experienced before now.

The pain was getting to a point that I could not fight it. I looked directly at the man in grey. He stood still as a statue. I think I saw a flash of blue light behind his sunglasses. Nikki took action and bent down and picked up the bottle. I never looked away from his face. "Sorry." Nikki yelled while she shook the bottle at his direction.

I think I saw his head move ever so slightly in a nodding fashion. The corner of his mouth curled up in the smallest of grins. He slowly turned and walked away in the other direction.

Nikki looked at me like she knew what had happened. "I told you so. That did not feel good did it? I told you to just pick up the bottle."

"What just happened? It felt like my mind was being stabbed by ice. Who is that guy?" I said

"That's the keeper of the grounds. He works here. I think his real name is Max. Don't ask me how he knows things, he just does. He knows everything that happens here. He did that mind thing to one of my friends who lived here and she went up to talk to him. He said that he didn't know what she was talking about. He laughed and said really that sure seems pretty fucking crazy and then he kept walking. She yelled at him a different time to make it stop and after that it only seemed to get worse. She thought that she was going crazy and she moved out shortly after. It kept happening to her over and over. It kept happening even at night to the point she was afraid to go to sleep. She firmly believed he was doing it. I know it seems crazy and there is no way to prove it."

"So that happened before. Are you sure that I am not having a stroke or something?" I said

"You are too young to have a stroke idiot." Dave said.

I turned around and he was standing there. He said "I was wondering what was taking you so long so I looked out the window and I saw that dog jump into the truck. I got my camera phone out and recorded you. I heard you screaming help like a little girl. Wait a minute, who do I sound like Help, help me. I am a little girl. I

19

already put the video on the net. That was some funny shit."

"Glad I could entertain you asshole. That was awesome that you decided to video tape me instead of getting that dog away. Where are my manners? This is my now ex-friend Dave from work and this is Nikki from across the way." I said.

"Pleased to meet you. Is this the big bad wolf?" Dave said as he pointed at Ellie.

"Yes, her name is Ellie. Be careful." I said.

He went right over there and started to pet her. Ellie was licking his face and shaking hands with him. She rolled over and let him rub her belly. I looked over in disbelief.

"She's not so tough. She is just a big teddy bear." Dave said.

"Anyways, do you hang out around here often? Maybe we can hang out some time. I would like to find out more about that Max guy." I said to Nikki.

"I am going to give you some advice. Stay away from that guy. Don't even say his name. Whatever you do, do not let him in your apartment. Do not do anything that might upset him. I personally try to avoid him when I am out walking my dog." She said in a whispered voice.

"I think I will stick to your suggestions. "I said

"Well I gotta be going. I have to get ready for work. I work part time at that quick shop at the corner. You seem like an ok person. If you want to hang out sometime I live right over there in apartment B. Well, it was nice meeting you. Sorry about my dog trying to bite your leg off. Really, really sorry. Come on Ellie lets go home." The dog hopped up gave me a woof and then trotted off.

"Hey no problem. I didn't need that leg anyways. That's cool. Maybe we can hang out sometime. "I waved good bye as she walked away. She smiled and turned the corner into her breezeway. She seems pleasant I thought. I hope I see more of her.

"I hate to see you go but I sure like to watch you walk away. She is kinda cute. I would totally do her. I am glad to see that you are making new friends." Dave said jokingly. We turned around and walked up to my apartment.

After a few hours of unpacking I waved good bye to my helpers and looked at the big mess that lay before me. My apartment was stacked to the ceiling with boxes. The only carpet I saw was in carefully made walkways. I had to climb over and squeeze through areas. I started to unpack some of my boxes. I thought the kitchen would be a good place to start. I found the boxes with kitchen marked on them and I started pulling out utensils and the pans. It went pretty quick. Then I heard a knock on the door.

"Coming." I yelled. I tried to stand up and make my way around some boxes to the door. I slowly looked out the peep hole. There were two guys standing out there.

"Who are you?" I said through the door

"Maintenance. We are here to deliver your washer and dryer." He said.

I opened the door. There was a large heavy set man standing there. He had short grey hair. He had a stained tee shirt on and his gut was sticking out of the bottom of it. I looked over and the man in grey was with him. I stared at them nervously.

"How are you doing? Did you get moved in alright? We are maintenance here. My name is Jim and this is Max. We have your washer and dryer. "Jim said in a friendly tone.

In my head I quickly remembered the warning Nikki gave me. I was hesitant to letting them in. They had my appliances so they were legit. I opened the door wider. I began making a path for them to bring the washer in. They stood at the doorway. Max had the washer on a dolly. He tilted the washer back ward and he started forward but he suddenly stopped when he got to the doorframe. He stopped as if he hit an invisible barrier. Jim yelled down the hall to me. "We can't come in unless we are formally invited to enter by the owner of the apartment. You have to verbally say that we can come in. It's just some silly rule the office made us start doing. One time we went in unannounced and someone fired shots at us because they thought we were burglars. When we got to that apartment we knocked hard and yelled maintenance a hundred times. This guy was rumored to have been a hard core drug dealer. I think he thought we were the police or someone coming to take his drugs. Anyway, so he popped out from the back room and started to fire down the hallway. We were lucky that no bullets hit us."

"That is a silly rule. Isn't that the same rule that applies to vampires? They can't come in unless invited." I looked right at Max when I said that. He grinned.

Both guys started laughing like crazy. "I think you have seen too much Twit-light bro. So you are saying we look like vampires. What was that guy's name Tedward Callen or something like that? Have you ever seen a fat vampire or a tan one? " Jim said laughingly.

I looked at them and said "Ok. Ok good point." I really hesitated and then I said it. "Ok, I formally invite you to come in." My stomach got tight. In my head I was thinking that IS exactly what a vampire would say to get invited in. I COULD see a vampire playing dumb and coming up with some scheme just like this to get inside. I felt like I did something bad. Somewhere in my heart I knew I just messed up, really, really, messed up. It was like the barrier that was holding them back broke. The sturdy dam that held the water back cracked and the dark water came through. They pulled the dolly with the washer on it down the hall. It looked white and used. It had some scrapes on it. Then they went back out and got the tan dryer that was equally beat up and hung it on the wall. Max stood back while Jim, who was fat and muscular at the same time, lifted the heavy dryer and attached it to the wall himself.

I kept an eye on Max the whole time. He did not speak. He had glasses and a hood on the whole time.

Jim asked if I knew how to use the washer? He said these were a little different since they were not pre installed. You have to pull this hose through this hole in the wall and then hook it to the sink.

"I am a little upset because the display room that the office agent showed me did not have the washer hooked up. This is totally ghetto." I said.

Jim said "Yeah I know. This is the old school way of doing things. I know it looks beat up but these old metal ones hold up a lot better than the new ones with plastic parts. They don't ever show that to people when they move in. Just remember to push this lip down on this hose or it will not hook up right to the sink. When you turn on the sink it will spray water everywhere and flood the people underneath you. One time I had an emergency call to come to an apartment where they had the hose attached to the sink with a hundred rubber bands. When I walked into the bathroom it was like a sprinkler spraying water everywhere and they flooded everyone beneath them."

"That would be horrible. Good thing I am on the top floor." I said.

"Alright, looks like we are done here. You are all set. Remember there dryers are small so you can only put in one pair of jeans and it takes a long time to dry. "Jim said.

"Good to know." I said.

They started to walk toward the door. Max was pushing the dolly. They quickly exited the apartment.

"Just in case you are vampires you are uninvited to come back in." I said laughingly.

"Sure we are. Welcome to Northfield Grove. Well have a good one." Jim chuckled. Max was already walking the dolly down the stairs. I watched them walk away. I started to slowly close the door then Max said something to Jim. I am not sure but I vaguely heard him say "Should we tell him. No, He will find out on his own." My head felt weird again. Not as painful as before but definitely something. I think I heard the sound of cold laughter in the back of my mind.

Chapter 2

The mind of Jack. Monday June 3.

My alarm clock went off. It was early in the morning. I had finished some of my unpacking. Ow, my back and legs were really sore. I slowly moved out of bed and into the shower. The hot water felt soothing to my body. My arms were tired as well and it felt like a real strain to put my arms above my head to wash my hair. I got out of the shower and got ready for work. Then, I ate breakfast and was on my way. I went out to my car and got in. I always bring a soda with me to drink on my way to work. I noticed I had a half full soda already in the cup holder. I needed a place to put my new soda. I sneakily looked around to see if that Max guy was around. Coast is clear. It was about 7:30 and most people don't start work until 8 so I didn't think Max would see me. I am going to set this soda can on the ground and see what happens. That Max jerk can't tell me what to do. Casually I opened my car door. I looked back and forth to see if anyone was watching me. Still keeping my eyes peeled I slowly set the can on the ground as if I was expecting something to happen. I heard the metallic sound of my can touching the asphalt.

Clink. I smiled. I looked around like someone was going to pop out of the bushes and yell at me or something. "Looks like I win Max." I said with a grin on my face. I quickly shut my car door and drove off as if I just committed a bank robbery. If this was a game of chess, this would be moving that first pawn across the board. I drove out of the apartments and headed to work.

I got to work and started my day as usual. I had to design a logo for this skateboarding company. I started drawing out a few ideas and then started to bring then to life on the computer. After a few hours I went to lunch. Time seems to fly when you are having fun. When I came back Dave stopped by my cubicle.

"Hey man. What's up bra? So did you hook up with that chick? She seemed nice." Dave said.

"Yeah, I banged the shit out of her. Actually, no. We didn't do that. We just met. No, I didn't see her again after she went to her apartment. You and her dog seemed to hit it off. Maybe I should set you up with Ellie." I said as I laughed.

He grabbed his sides. "Ha. Ha. That is sidesplitting." He said mockingly. "You are not funny. So are you going to see her sometime? See if she has some cute friends that want to do something. "Dave said.

"Why would I ever want any of them to meet you? I saw my dog attack video that you posted on the internet. It has already gotten 156 hits. I thought you were joking about putting it on the internet." I said.

"If you get that girls last name I will do some internet stalking for you. I will get you all the juicy details you want. "He said.

"No, that's not necessary. I could just go and talk to her next time I see her."I said.

"That's one way to do it. Not the very fun way. I could just go online, type her name and find out every little detail with the click of a button."He said.

"No don't do that. Anyways, I need to get back to work I have to finish this by the end of the day."I said.

"Ok, that's koo. Talk to you later Jack." Dave said.

I went back to work. A few more hours passed and it was time to go home. I got in my car and started driving. When I got home I looked around to see if my soda can from earlier was there. It was gone. The grounds people probably picked it up or it blew away to some dirty corner. I started to walk to my door. When I got to the bottom of the stairway I felt something drip into my hair. I rubbed my hand through my hair. Eww! It felt sticky and thick like syrup. "What the hell." My first thought was maybe someone set trash outside their door and it was leaking down. I started to walk up the stairs. It's not coming from the second floor so I continued to the third floor. Then it hit me. Whatever is leaking is coming from where my door is. What is going to be at my door? I started to take the stairs two at a time. When I got there my door was covered with brown soda and the door knob was sticky. There on my doorstep was the soda can I dropped on the street earlier that morning.

"Dammit." I said out loud.

Using my fingertips I slowly touched the doorknob and turned the knob. I quickly went in and scrubbed my hand clean. I was mad. I grabbed the first towel I found and wiped the dried soda off the door. My anger eventually subsided. "Good one Max." I said quietly to myself.

I sat down and ate dinner. After that I decided to do some exploring around the property. It was also a good way to get some exercise. I started walking. As I walked I noticed all the different things people had on their balconies. It gave me some ideas on how I wanted to decorate my own. There were a lot of people walking their dogs. I try to not make eye contact because they may want me to stop and pet their dog or something. One lady ran her chubby little dog right up to me. It had to have been the fattest Yorkie I have ever seen.

"My dog Bunny wants you to pet her." She said.

"I can't stop walking because I am working out. I want to keep that heart rate up." I walked right by her. I could tell she was not going to give up. She needed to lay off the caffeine. She was probably about fifty so I knew she would not be able to keep up. Hopefully.

"I am walking with you if you don't mind." She said.

"My name is Jamie and I live over there. Are you new here? "She said.

"My name is Jack. Yes I am new. I live toward the back on the right side." I started walking faster. She started to follow me but here dog stopped to smell something so she stopped.

"Well welcome to the apartments. I hope to see you again Jack." She yelled as I walked quickly away.

"You bet. Nice meeting you." I said. I kept walking.

I walked around the property. It was the beginning of summer. The grass was green. The trees and flowers were in bloom. I followed the sidewalks. They were broken in bits and weeds were growing through the cracks in some areas. There were some kids jumping the curbs and doing tricks on their skateboards. I use to be good on a skateboard. I could do a few tricks but that was when I was younger and could bounce back quicker after taking a fall. Now if I did that I would have all kinds of broken bones. It was funny to see kids now wearing helmets. When I was younger no one wore helmets and we did all kinds of dangerous things.

I rounded the corner. There was a laundry room there. I glanced in through the window. It had a wall of washers and a row of dryers. They looked like they were from the eighties. They did look to be normal size and much bigger than the ones in my apartment. It takes my dryer two cycles to dry a few shirts.

There was a fenced in area on the side of the property. I wasn't sure what it was for. From far away it looked like it had a teeter totter, a hoop, and a small house. I had noticed it had a new white plastic fence. There were three large cartoon pictures of dogs along the outside of it. When I got closer I realized what it was by the strong smell. A dog park. I remembered a few years ago on the internet there was an article that said the number one amenity that people living in apartments wanted was a dog park. A pool was second on the list. I guess that is because at any age a person can have a dog but not everyone likes to go swimming. The choice for a dog park seems like a good idea at first but they clearly did not think that all the way through. I know the dog owners probably thought this would be great for their dogs to run around and play in. Get some exercise. Maybe if this area was bigger it might not have been as bad. The whole area was a stinking mud pit. All the grass in there was dead. The green grass inside the fence had turned yellowish brown. Every dog that entered marked his territory by urinating on everything. The whole area had a lovely aroma. There was dog crap everywhere. Obviously, picking up after your dog was a rule but it was not enforced. I was considering getting a dog but I would not take it here. I felt like I needed to spray myself with some disinfectant just for being close to the entrance. I turned around and walked in the other direction.

I walked to the center of the court yard and saw a pool. There was a seven foot tall plastic fence going around it. It looked clean. The pool water was crystal blue. No one was in it so I went and put my hand in. It felt warm. I only like to swim if the water feels like bathwater. The temperature usually has to be a hundred degrees for a few days to heat the water up to my standards. If it is cold, my teeth start chattering uncontrollably and it is not a pretty sight. I checked out the sign and it said the pool opens at ten and closes at nine. Good to know. I went back to my apartment to watch some television.

A week went by. Nothing weird happened. I finally finished setting up my apartment. I couldn't stop thinking about that girl I met when I moved in. I thought she said she was working at the nearby quick shop. I had to get some gas and some snacks so I thought why not make a trip. I fixed my hair, put on some deodorant, brushed my teeth and put on one of my nicest shirts. That sure is a lot of work to just run to the quick shop for some candy and soda. I jumped in my car and I was off. I slowly drove by the front to see if she was working. I thought I saw her. I got out and went in.

The smell of cooking hot dogs and other meats hit my nose. There were two people standing in line. I looked at the person behind the counter and it was her. I casually walked the store deciding what I wanted and I tried to look cool doing it. I stopped at the chocolate. I knew girls loved chocolate so it was always a good choice. You can never go wrong with chocolate. I looked at the alcohol as well. I grabbed a pack of beer. Now this is a party, chocolate and beer. I made my way up to the register. There she was. I had to say something cool so I started with "Hey."

"Hey to you." She said as she rang me out.

"I have not seen you around the apartments. Have you been hiding out?" I said.

"Yeah I have been busy with school and work. This is a lot of beer here. Are you planning to drink this yourself? " She said.

"No this beer is not all for me. I am throwing a house warming party so I needed some drinks." That was the best answer I could come up with on the spot.

"Oh yeah, and you did not invite me." She said.

"You are totally invited. Ellie is not invited. What time do you get off of work?" I said.

"I get off at nine but I have to eat and change first."

"Yeah that's cool. Well if you change and come over I can fix you something to eat." I said.

"Ok cool I will be over then." She said

"I can't wait." I started walking out and I looked back to wave good bye and ran straight into the door. BUF! I ran right into the glass. She was laughing.

"I thought it opened out ward." I yelled awkwardly. I jumped into my car and thought that went well except for that end part. It was 6:30 and she got off at 9:00. I better hurry home and get cleaning.

I went back to my place and started to clean like crazy. I had to pick up my clothes and clean all my dirty dishes. I had let them pile up for a few days. I had to clean up and arrange my room quickly. I set up plates on the table for dinner and I got out some candles to be romantic.

31

It was 9:30. I heard a knock on the door. I went to open the door and it was her. She was wearing a tank top and real skimpy shorts. Her hair was done up and she had make up on. She looked very beautiful.

"Where's the party you were talking about. Where is everyone?" She said.

"Oh, right the party. That is next week." I said. Mental note to self: Throw party next week.

"Well come on in. Do you want to take the tour of my place?" I said.

"Sure. Show me around." She said.

"This is the living room. This is my large flat screen. My pride and joy. This is my very large and very comfortable couch. It feels so soft and warm." I said.

Nikki was smiling and looking around. "Why do you have so many duck things in your apartment? Are you a duck hunter or something?" She asked.

"What? You don't like the duck statues? No, I am not a duck hunter. Actually, my last name happens to be Ducksenhousser. Everyone just says Jack Ducks for short." I said.

She started grinning. "Your name is Jack Ducks?" She said laughingly. "What a horrible last name." She said. She was laughing so hard she started to cry.

"Yeah I guess. It is not that bad. It could be a lot worse. Sometimes they call me The Duck." I said smiling.

I started to walk down the hall. "This is my computer room. I have a very supped up computer. It is very fast. It has all the graphic and illustrator programs so I can do my graphic design work on it. I have a program where I can make movies. I also have 3 D programs which allow me to do 3 D work as well."

"That's pretty nerdy. You know that right Mr. Ducks." She said.

I motioned for her to come to the next room. "This is the torture chamber, I mean bedroom. This is where all the magic happens."

She slowly looked in. She stood holding onto the door frame as if she stepped in something bad would happen.

It was just a bed frame and mattress in that room. Nothing special. We turned around and went to the living room area.

"Well I am all dressed up and I am ready to go out. I know this bar close by that also serves food there." She said

"Cool. Let's go." I said and we were off. We walked to my car. I was sure to open the door for her.

"Thanks for opening the door for me. You are such a gentleman. "She said.

The bar was right around the corner. It was a little crowded but not too bad. It was your standard sports bar atmosphere. It had all the banners of the local sports teams hanging in there. The walls were brick. It had a modern feel. They had some big flat screen televisions hanging on the walls. I noticed a pool table in the corner. I played a lot when I was in college but I have not played in awhile. We went to the bar. She knew the bartender. She must come here often I thought. She told me the bartender also lives in the apartments. We saw an open table so we grabbed it quickly.

"What's good to eat here?" I said

"The nachos and hot wings are pretty good. That all depends on if you like hot things." She said in a sexy voice.

"Pfft. I am pretty sure I can handle it." I said. I ordered some beer and some wings and she got nachos and a margarita.

"How was your day or week? Did you do anything interesting? " She said.

"No. Not really. I went exploring around the property. I saw the doggie thunder dome. Two dogs enter, one dog leaves." I said jokingly.

"Huh, what are you talking about?" She said puzzled.

"Just kidding. I mean the dog park. It was completely nasty. It needed a giant breath mint. If I had a dog I would have to give it a bath every time it went in there."

"I agree. It is horrible in there. I took my dog in there and it got fleas. It had mud all over its feet and I had to wash her off with the hose before letting her into the apartment. She also smelled funny after that."She said.

"So did you do anything interesting at work this week?" She said.

"I am working on a logo for a skateboard company." I said.

"That's pretty cool. So you just sit at a cubicle and play on the computer all day. I want a job like that." She said.

"I don't just PLAY on the computer. I do serious work that affects many people." I said.

"You probably just stalk people or play that silly bird game all day." She said.

"No I don't. I have not looked you up on the internet. Actually, social sites are creepy to me because people put way to much info on there. If I was a burglar I would just have to go to your page to see when you are going on vacation and I could easily go to your house and steal all your things while you are gone. "I said.

"If you are going to be that way I will be sure not to friend request you then. Geez. Change of subject. Hey did anything happen with that Max guy? You didn't let him in your apartment did you? He is a monster." She said.

"Something weird did happen but I don't know if Max did it. I had a soda can that was half way full in my car and I put it on the ground before I left for work and when I got back it was dumped all over my door and the can was sitting on my door frame. I think he did it but I don't know. So that happened." I said.

"Yeah, that's weird. It sounds like something he would do though. Did you let him in anytime before?" She said.

I was starting to have panic sweats. "NO. Why would I let him in?" I said. In my mind I was thinking yes I let him in. He had to drop off my dryer.

"I don't know why you would let him in. He is clever and if he wanted in he would get in one way or another." She said.

"Just curious, why would that be bad? You make it seem like he is a vampire." I said jokingly.

Her face got completely serious. She looked me right in the eyes and leaned towards me. "Maybe he is."

She fell silent for a minute. I kept looking in to her eyes waiting for the joke to come. Waiting for her to say vampires are not real or I am just messing with you. Nothing came.

"I don't know what kind of monster he is. He just gives off an evil vibe. Trust me, as long as you didn't invite him in you have nothing to worry about." She said.

In my head I was thinking, why did I invite him in? He was just dropping off my appliances. He didn't seem hostile or a monster. "Well…foods here."I said. Maybe I should wait to tell her but only if it comes up again. The waitress came over carrying our food and drinks. My hot wings looked delicious. I was starving.

"Be careful those are the hot ones."The waitress said. I ignored her and eagerly bit in. Then I ate another. The heat hit me like a desert wind. It was slow at first then a fire was building in my mouth like never before. It was so hot my legs were starting to sweat. My nose started to run. The tears were coming to my eyes. I think I swallowed a piece of the sun. I am sure it was funny to watch.

"I didn't know they dipped this chicken in liquid hot magma. Water. Can I have your water?" I said in a weak voice. I swallowed my beer and the water. I ate the ice cubes whole. I was crying and snot was coming out my nose.

"Are you okay?" She said.

"I always cry and have snot shooting out of my nose when I eat hot things. I am used to way hotter. This is nothing. "   After the fire was put out I ordered some more drinks. Nikki finished eating her nachos.

"Do you like the Cardinals? I love baseball." She said.

36

I hate baseball. I kept that to myself. "Baseball is alright. I like football better though." In my head I thought, baseball is boring. There is not enough action to keep me interested. Most of the time you are watching two guys play catch. There is too much standing around. I always get nose bleed seats. The players are way over paid. The food at the stadium is way over priced. On my list of sports that I do not like to watch, baseball is only one spot under golf.

As if she was reading my mind. "Don't let the people at the bar hear you say that. They love baseball and we are at a sports bar. Baseball is Americas favorite past time. Here have another drink." She said.

I was a little tipsy after a few beers and some shots. I heard a song being played on the juke box and I started to sing with it softly. "Do you like music and dancing?" I said.

"I love music. I have over five thousand songs on my computer." The bar had a little dance area in the middle and some people were dancing.

"Do you want to dance? Just for one song." I said.

She shook her head.

"Come on, just one song. I won't do anything too crazy like spin on my head. I promise." I said.

"Let me do one more shot first." She said. We both did one more shot. I was feeling pretty good after that. My veins felt like they were on fire. I felt alive. I was a little tipsy but I was not to the point that I needed to hold the ground to keep from falling off the earth.

I took her hand and we walked to the dance floor. We started dancing. She was good. She definitely knew what she was doing. I usually step with the beat and swing my arms up in the air. She was moving far more gracefully. Her hips were moving to the beat. She swung her hair around and put her arms around me. We ended up dancing for the next few hours. Some of her friends showed up later. We all danced the night away. It was about one in the morning. "I have to go to work tomorrow so I need to get some sleep." She said. We left and drove back to the apartments. I walked her to the door.

"My parents hate it when I get home this late. I had a really great time. I hope we can do this again some time." She said.

"I also had a good time." I said as I looked into her eyes. It was dark in the breezeway. We put our arms around each other. Our bodies pressed tightly together. I slowly leaned in for a kiss. I felt her warm breath on my skin. I didn't know how this was going to go but I went for it. She leaned her head in. Her eyes were shut. She kissed me back. Her soft lips pressed against mine. Her lips were full and soft. We kissed for a few minutes. My heart was beating fast. It was magical.

"Have a good night Jack. I hope we can do it again." She said.

"Definitely, I had a great time." I said.

She opened her door and waved good bye. "Dream of me." She said. I waved good bye and I started to walk back to my apartment.

Chapter 3

The mind of Jack. June 8 Saturday.

I went to pass out in bed. I started to doze off.
My mind was starting to drift away. I was still a little
drunk. My eyes were beginning to feel heavy. I looked
over at the wall. For some reason I cannot explain, the
shadows in the corner looked darker than the rest in the
room. Just before my eyes completely closed, I think I
saw the shadows move. Maybe it was the alcohol in my
system messing with my head. In a minute my eyes
closed and I was out cold.

The next morning I slowly opened my eyes. I
vaguely remembered having some weird dreams but I
could not remember the details. What time is it? The
bright sun was casting its rays into my room. It was
blinding. I reached over at my alarm clock. 11:24. My
head felt great. It felt like my brain was trying to karate
kick its way out of my skull. I tried to make an attempt
to get out of bed. I knew if I moved to fast I might throw
up. My stomach was so queasy. I was sure of one thing.
I was either going to vomit or have to use the toilet. Here
we go. I put my feet on the floor one at a time and sat
up. The liquid in my stomach shifted. At least the room

was not spinning. I felt like shit. I went over and fully opened the blinds and the light poured in. My head screamed ahh. My hangover was in full affect. Luckily, it wasn't the worst one I have ever had. I made some eggs, bacon, and had a sports drink to refuel me. It was not a great food combination but it seemed to work every time. The breakfast fit for a champion.

I stepped outside and it was going to be really hot today. It was a good day for swimming. I really wanted to check out the pool scene. I have not been swimming in a long time. Today was a good day for it. I needed to work on my tan because I was pretty white. That is what happens when you work in an office. I wanted to see if Nikki could go but she said she had to work today. I text messaged my friends Dave and Steve to see if they wanted to hang out at the pool for a few hours. They messaged back that they will be over at 2:00 with some drinks. They wanted to see my place.

At two Dave, Steve, and his girlfriend Tara showed up. I opened the door. "Welcome to my sweet crib bitches." I let them in. I gave them the quick tour of chateau Jack. I put on my Florida swimming trunks which were black with red flames. We walked down to the pool area. There was a table not claimed yet so we moved all our stuff there. We brought a cooler with alcohol. There were a few white lounge chairs by the pool but most of them were taken. We set our towels on the table. I opened beer one and drank it in one gulp.

The deep end was about 9 feet. I took a few steps back and ran full speed. I dove into the pool. The water was a bit chilly despite the fact it was ninety degrees outside. My friends followed in after me. After I moved around it felt good to be in the water. My only complaint about the pool was the massive amount of dead ants floating on top of the water. I made a wave with my hands to push them away from my face.

"Want to race?" Dave said.

"Sure. Let's do this." I said.

We all went over to the wall at one side of the pool. We each put our feet on the wall ready to push off.

"On your mark, Get set, GO! Tara said.

I pushed off the wall as hard as I could. All three of us were neck to neck. I was starting to get ahead when somebody grabbed my foot and I fell behind. I sank fast and had to come up for air. Tara was laughing. I looked up and Steve won.

"Best two out of three. No cheating by your girlfriend this time." I said.

There were two different families in the pool. One larger man was in the pool playing catch with his kids. He was overweight and his head was shaved. He was giving us some dirty looks. Then he finally said "Do any of you live here?"

"Yes I live here and these are my friends. My name is Jack. I live at 6520 M. What are you security or something." I said.

"Oh. Sorry. I have never seen you before, that's why I asked. There have been tons of high school kids and adults that don't live here using our pool. They usually cause trouble. I live right over there and I can see the pool clearly. There is a group of high school kids that jump the fence and go swimming at night. Last night they threw all the chairs into the pool and broke some beer bottles. I had to call the police last night. The pool guy was here for awhile getting all the chairs out. Yes, I actually am security at the bank up the road." He said.

"That's cool. Do they let you carry a gun or anything?" I said.

"Actually no we do not get to carry guns, or mace, or tasers." He said.

"How do you stop criminals if someone tries to rob the bank?" Dave said laughingly.

"We don't. We just try to get the robber in and out without anyone getting hurt."He said.

"Let me get this right. So you just stand there all day. If someone tries to rob the bank you just tell everyone to be cool and you help the robber get in and out faster." I said.

"Yup. That's what I do." He said grinning.

"Wow. That's pretty crazy that you are not suppose to fight and you are the guard."

"Yes I know it doesn't make any sense. By the way my name is Craig." He said.

"Well Craig do you want a beer or anything." I said.

"Sure. Beer me." He said.

I threw him one. He opened it and took a drink. I jumped back into the water. My friends were getting out and they sat in the chairs to dry off.

"Throw me the ball." I said. So he threw it to me.

"How long have you lived here for." I asked as I threw.

"My family and I have lived here for a few years. It's alright. It has some good things and some bad things." Craig said.

"What is the weirdest thing you have seen here? Anything crazy happen." I said.

"Nothing to weird. Just some vandalism that goes on at night." He said.

"Do you know Nikki that lives over there? Brown, blonde hair, short, skinny." I said

"I know her. She hung out at the pool a lot last year. She was always with a guy who lived in that stairway over there. On the top floor." He said as he pointed at my stairway.

Wait a second. I think he means my apartment. I thought she said she was in my apartment before and her friend lived there. "Do you know what happened to that guy?" I said.

"That guy I think was dating this other blond girl who lived towards the front of the complex." Craig said.

"Where is that guy now?" I said.

"Well you are not going to want to hear this. I hate to break this news to you but I am pretty sure he is dead. I think he died a few months ago. The rumor going around is that he had some kind of drug overdose in his bedroom. It was sad because that guy was young and he had his whole life in front of him. I think his name was Ryan but I cannot remember for sure. " Craig said.

"WHAT? You are telling me some one died in my apartment. No way. So there could be a ghost in my apartment right now. "I said shocked. A chill went up my spine. My friends were silently listening.

"You know what is weird is that Nikki failed to mention that someone had died in my apartment and that it happened to be her boyfriend. That's a little odd that she had decided to omit that fact from me don't you think." I said.

I got out of the pool to get another beer and sit with my friends at the table. "Why do you think she didn't want to tell me?" I said confused.

"I don't know. Maybe she didn't want to worry you or scare you or maybe it was a bad memory she didn't want to bring back up. I am sure if your close friend dies you probably don't want to relive the pain again." Dave said.

"That makes sense I guess." I said.

I looked at Dave and he had a huge grin on his face. "Hey, since someone died in your apartment are you going to try out the ouija board? Are you going to do some ghost hunting?" Dave asked.

"You know those are a joke right. People just use those to scare the crap out of unsuspecting guests at parties. They sell those in toy stores because they are not really dangerous. If it was actually dangerous do you think they would let kids use them." I said.

"I don't know. I have known a few people that said weird things happened to them once they started using it. I do not think it was just coincidence."Dave said.

"It sounds like they just got deceived. Anyways, I don't think ghosts are real. End of conversation." I said.

"I have heard people say that they started to hear weird things at night. Their cabinets would open and close by themselves. They heard footsteps on the wood floor. When they went to sleep their blankets would move. They were scared and eventually burned their board to get rid of the evil spirits." Dave said.

"I hope you don't really believe that bullshit. I might use it but I have not decided. If I do are you going to help me? I think you have to have two or more people for some reason." I said.

"Hells yeah I want to find a ghost! I am in. I aint scairt of no ghost." He said excitedly.

"Let me talk to Nikki and see what she says about this guy first before we try anything. Maybe we can try next weekend. "

"So, when did you get a girlfriend? I knew something was wrong when you didn't seem to look at the ladies lying out. Usually you stare to long and its gets uncomfortable. I thought maybe you were going gay." Tara said laughingly.

"We only went out one time so I don't think that makes her my girlfriend. I did stare at those girls but I try to make it less obvious. Yeah I looked and I saw everything. You big jerk." I said in response.

"So when do we get to meet your non girlfriend friend? "Tara said.

"Her name is Nikki. Maybe after we hang out a few times and I get to know her better first."I said.

"Anyways so what have you been up too all week?" I said.

"Nothing I did some substitute teaching this week. These kids were being so bad. They were completely disobeying me. Two kids kept hitting a balloon back and forth. I told them to stop three times. Finally, I told them to come to the front of the class. You stand on this tile square and you stand on the other. Hit the balloon back and forth. Whoever misses I am sending to the principal's office. I said in my most authoritative tone. They hit that balloon for twenty minutes all the way to the end of class. I told them you want to spike it on the other guy. Don't be gentle. You want to send the other guy to detention. They were all

45

sweaty by the time class was over. The classroom was cheering. It was pretty funny." Tara said.

We were all laughing. We all spent the rest of the afternoon drinking, swimming, and lounging on the chairs by the pool. After it was about six we decided to pack everything up. My friends had other things they had to do so they left. I went back up to my apartment. I looked in the mirror I was definitely red as a lobster. I had to take a shower to wash the pool water and tanning lotion off of me. The water had a lot of bugs in it and after hearing about people having sex in the pool at night, I was urgent to take a shower. Note to self-check internet to see if pool water can give you a disease or a STD. I got in the shower. I slowly turned the water on. "Ow! Ow! Ow!" I was definitely sun burned. The warm water hurt when it hit my skin. I hurried through my shower and then I got dressed.

I kept thinking about what Craig said at the pool about Ryan the previous resident. If he did die in this apartment maybe I could try to communicate with him. I always wanted to try to talk to a spirit. If Nikki was friends with him I don't think he would be a pissed off angry ghost. I sure hope he doesn't want to hurt me. If he did, I am sure I would have seen or felt something by now. I come from a large family but no one in it has ever died. I have watched all the different ghost hunting shows. I found them to be very fascinating. It seems like I might actually have an opportunity to try to catch a ghost myself.

My curiosity got the better of me. So I decided I was going to try the ouija board. I had put it in a box of random junk I had. I had to dig through some boxes in my closet for awhile. Then I saw it. I took it out of the closet. It was still in the box. I looked for the ages that it was appropriate for. It said for kids age ten and up so how could it be dangerous? Guess we will find out. I know people say don't use it because it's a gateway for demons or angry spirits or some crazy shit like that. I guess if you really believe in that kind of thing. I set it on the bed. I had to find someone that wanted to use it with me. I think you needed at least two people it says. Maybe Nikki would be willing to help.

My stomach was growling. I was starting to get hungry so I went into the kitchen. I opened the food pantry. I wanted something quick and easy. Let's see. Nope. Nope. Spaghetti it is. I started to boil the water then I threw the pasta in. I heard a knock on the door.

Knock. Knock. Knock. "Jack." Knock. Knock. Knock. "Jack." Knock. Knock. Knock. "Jack."

I went over and looked out the peephole. It was Nikki. "Who is it?" I said being funny.

"You know who it is. Open up." She said.

"What's the password?" I said.

"Fist. I am going to punch you with it asshole." She said.

"Nope, not even close." I said laughingly.

She said "Fine I am leaving." I was still looking through the peephole as she walked off to the right.

"No don't go." I swung the door open quickly and stepped outside. I just happen to see a fist coming at me but it was too late. She punched me in the stomach. I had some of the wind knocked out of me. We were both laughing.

"Nice right hook you have there." I was hunched over grabbing my stomach.

"Come on in." I said smiling. She stepped inside. She always had a sweet smell to her.

"Did you just get off of work?" I said.

47

"Yes I did. It was a long and stupid day." She said.

"You are bright red. Did you go to the pool today? Sorry I punched you. It probably burned didn't it." She said.

"Yeah I was at the pool for a few hours. It sure doesn't take long to get burned." I said.

"Oh by the way are you hungry? I am making high class Italian cuisine. Do you want some? You better grab your head because this will totally blow your mind." I said.

"Sure I will have spaghetti. I did not know you could cook." She said.

"No I can't really cook. I can make the basics though. Let me set a place for you at the table. You are my first dinner guest. This is a special occasion. Let me get out my special dishes. Have a seat. What would you like to drink? I have everything."

"I will have a bottle of water please." She said.

I set a bottle of water in front of her. Then I strained the noodles and put them into a big bowl. I had sauce that I made and I put that into another big bowl. I set them both on the table. I then grabbed the parmesan cheese. "Bon appetito. Dinner is served." I said. We each took a few scoops of noodles and sauce.

"What did you do today?" She said.

"Well after my mini hangover went away I went to the pool with Dave, Steve, and Steve's girlfriend Tara. We swam and sat out in the chairs for a few hours. We met a guy named Craig. He seemed like an ok guy." I said.

"I know Craig. We hung out with him and his wife and kid at the pool a few times. They are alright people." She said.

I didn't know how she would take what I was going to say next but I had to test the waters. This was either going to go two ways either she was going to be pissed and leave or she will be okay. "Craig said that he knew the guy who lived here and that his name was Ryan." I paused for a second. Nikki continued eating. "He also said that he died here of a drug overdose or something drug related." I said.

Nikki stopped eating and looked at me. I knew I crossed some line. I was just hoping I didn't cross the line so far that I could never come back. She was either going to cry or jump across the table and stab me in the eye with a fork. I saw her eyes get a little teary. "Yeah, Ryan was my friend. I think that is what they said, that he overdosed on heroin. I don't like to talk about it. It makes me sad."

"I am sorry. I didn't mean to upset you." I said in a low voice.

"No I am not really upset about that. I was more upset when he told me he was dating this hooker who lived in the front section. She had blonde hair and was anorexic skinny." She said angrily as she cut her spaghetti. She moved her knife back and forth scraping the plate. She was moving her head back and forth. I could tell I had struck a nerve.

"Slow up there. Hey you are going to cut my plate in half." I said.

"Did Ryan work around here?" I said.

"Sorry. He just makes me so mad. Yes he worked at the new casino that opened up. He was a

49

dealer. I think he worked at the roulette and blackjack table." She said.

"How did he get involved with the drugs? I know there is a heroin epidemic going around. One of my friends is a cop. He said in South County it is becoming a problem. People are breaking into cars to get items to sell for drug money." I said.

"I think he started using it because his girl friend was. He just happened to use to much that time and it killed him." She said.

I kept eating my spaghetti. I was working up the courage to ask the question I really wanted to ask her. "I want to ask you something but I don't want you to get mad. It might be offensive to you."

"I can't guarantee that. You have to ask me now and I may or may not get offended. Grow some balls and just ask it."She said grinning.

"Ok. I know this sounds silly. This is a two part question. "I said as I looked her in the eyes.

"First, do you believe in ghost? Second, would you ever use an ouija board to try to contact a ghost? "I said. I could understand if she started to laugh in my face or if she slapped me and walked out. I did not know how this situation was going to go.

She started giggling. Well it looks like I am not going to get slapped so that's good. "No I do not believe in ghost. I think when you are dead, you are dead, there is nothing that goes on. Sure I will use an ouija board. That is just some toy kid's use on other kids to scare each other. I used one a few times when I was a kid at birthday parties and there is nothing evil about it. I always moved it to scare the crap out of girls I did not like at parties. You can buy those at any toy store so I don't think those are dangerous despite what they say.

So you want to try to contact Ryan's spirit is what you are saying." She said smiling.

"Basically. Are you in?" I said.

"Sure why not. I am going to need a strong drink first."

"Wonderful. Me too. I have some vodka. Let me get some shot glasses." She grabbed the bottle and took two big chugs.

"Let's do this." She said.

"Oh ok. Are you sure you want to do this tonight?"I said one last time.

"Yes get the board before I change my mind."

I took the vodka bottle and took a big chug. I went and got the board and set it up on the table in the living room. I turned off the lights and I light a few candles for ambience. It was starting to get dark outside. The shadows were starting to creep in as the sun was setting. This should be interesting. If it works it will be real interesting. I also set up my video camera on my counter facing the living room. I turned it on. I wanted to catch it on video if anything weird happens. No one will believe me without proof. They would just laugh and call me crazy.

"Ok we are ready to rock and roll. Do we say something first or do anything to get the ghost to come out? Do you know?" I said.

"I don't know that shit. Just sit here and put your hand on the planchette. We then start moving our hands in a circular pattern and ask questions. " She said.

"I am ready to talk to some ghost. Muahahaha." We both put our hands on the heart shaped planchette. We started moving it in a figure eight.

"Is there anyone here who would like to talk to us? I think it is working by itself. Look it is moving to the J." Then it seemed to move our hands to the U. Then to the M-P.

"Jump? Jump what?" Nikki said.

It moved to the J again. Then to the a-c-k.

"Jump Jack? What is it doing? What does that mean?" Nikki said looking confused.

Then it started to spell out B-o-n-e-s.

Nikki jumped up and punched me in the arm. I burst out laughing.

"God dammit! I am not going to play if you are going to joke around like that. If you do that again I am leaving. Just so you know Jack is not getting his bones jumped for a very long time." She said angrily as her face turned red.

"Ok I am sorry. For real this time. I swear no funny business." I said trying not to laugh. She shot me a look of hatred. "Come on. I am sorry. I won't do that again. I promise."

She sat back down by my side. "Sometimes I want to strangle you." She said. We both put our hands on the planchette and started to move it.

"Ok, if there is anyone here who wants to speak to us let us know. Ryan if you are here and want to answer our questions let us know." I said loudly to the empty air. We were silent. I was trying to hear anything moving, or a sound, or anything out of the ordinary. I heard kids playing in the next apartment over. Nothing happened as far as I could tell. I put my hands on the plastic planchette and so did Nikki. We started moving the heart shaped piece of plastic in a circular fashion. It made a scrapping sound as we slowly slid it across the board. I felt my heart beating excitedly.

"What should I ask?" I said silently as I looked at her.

"Does anyone here want to talk to us?" She said.

I watched the planchette move around the board a few times. It made that scrapping sound. Then it slowly moved to yes. I could not tell if Nikki was doing it to be funny.

"What is your name? " I said.

The heart moved slowly to the R then to the Y then to the A and then to the N. It spelled out Ryan. My blood ran cold. My stomach started to tighten.

"Ryan. " My heart was starting to race. I kind of thought that the planchette felt like it was getting colder. I had goose bumps up and down my back. I shot Nikki a glance to see if she was being funny. By the wide eyed look on her face I could tell she wasn't doing it. "Where did you work?" I said.

The planchette started to move slowly again. It slowly spelled out casino.

At this point I looked at Nikki who looked just as scared as I felt. She too was intently focused on the board. "Are you messing with me Nikki?"

"No I swear I am not doing it."

"Ask it something that only you and him would have known."I said quickly.

"Where did we first go out to eat at?" She said. Her voice was shaking. The planchette was definitely freezing now. My fingers felt like they were touching ice. The planchette started to move slowly to letters that didn't spell out anything I recognized. Hykalme is what it spelled. I looked at Nikki. "Does that mean anything to you?" I asked.

"No." She shook her head back and forth. She was looking scared now.

"How old are you?" Nikki asked.

The planchette moved slowly to a two and then hesitated. Then it went to the six.

Nikki looked at me and slowly shook her head. In a silent voice she said"That is wrong. He had a birthday a few months before he died. He is twenty three."

I was getting scared now. I was starting to doubt that we were talking to Ryan. "How did you die?" I asked.

The planchette stopped moving. I felt a change in the room. It felt like it was getting colder despite it being eighty outside. A feeling of intense dread was starting to overpower me. The hair on my neck stood up. I kept staring at the board. Then the planchette started to lazily move toward the M then slowly to the U. Then RDER. "Murder? What does the mean? You were murdered." I said. The planchette was moving slowly now. I felt that we were losing it. Maybe it was running out of power. I don't know the physics of spectral energy.

"Please, one last question. Who murdered you?" I said quickly as the magic was dissipating. There was a sudden breeze and the candles in the room went out. The planchette started to move fast. Really fast. I must have struck a nerve or really angered it. Nikki and I had our hands on the planchette but it started to move so fast we were no longer in control. We both took our hand off in surprise as it zipped around the board agitated. We watched horrified as it moved with a life of its own.

Back and forth it went forming a figure eight. As suddenly as it started, it stopped on N.

Nikki stood up frightened. "I DON'T WANT TO PLAY ANY MORE!" She yelled terrified. She grabbed the small table and flipped it. The planchette and board went flying and landed on the floor. "I am leaving. "She yelled. She got up and ran toward the door. After what I just saw, I was going to go with her. She stormed out of there like a bat out of hell. "Wait for me." I was right behind her. I grabbed my keys and shoes as I ran out the door. The door slammed behind us. We sprinted down three flights of stairs not looking back. We walked at high speed on the sidewalk all the way to the front section. There was a concrete table in the courtyard that we sat at.

"So what are you thinking?" I asked. She struggled to open her purse. She reached in and got out a cigarette. She was trembling uncontrollably. "What the fuck just happened?" She said with tears in her eyes. She looked like she was going into shock. She found her lighter and lit the cigarette.

"I do not know what that was. I honestly thought you were moving the marker until that last part." I said.

"I was moving it at first then I thought you were moving it. Shit." She yelled. We stared at each other for awhile. My heart was starting to go back to its' normal beating. My breathing was returning to normal. I glanced around to see if anything might have followed us. I didn't think ghost would do that but that is just what I have seen from movies. I realized how warm it felt outside compared to inside my apartment. I was going to give her a few minutes to absorb what just happened. She smoked her cigarette down quickly and went for another.

I finally broke the silence. "Do you think that was Ryan's ghost?"

"I have no clue. That could have been anything. I don't know what the fuck that was. I don't think it was Ryan though. When I asked it personal questions it always gave gibberish answers. "She said as she shook her head. "I don't think we should have been using the board."

"NOW you say that. I thought you said you were not afraid of ghost. Those ouija boards are fake and ghosts do not exist."

"I don't think it was Ryan's ghost. This was something entirely different. I think this was evil. I have used an Ouija board like six times at parties and it never did anything like that. I was always moving the piece that's why I thought it was fake."

Fear started to grip me as I realized I have to go back there. "Now you say that shit. I have to go back there and sleep with whatever is going to be back there waiting for me. What do you think I should do?" I said.

"I would get rid of the board. Burn it, give it away, or bury it." She said.

"I guess I will throw it away. When I go back you don't think it will attack me do you? Or that something else will attack me."

"No, I don't think it will attack you. But If I don't hear from you tomorrow I will think it got you. So call me or text me tomorrow after you wake up so I know you made it through the night." She said.

"Ok. I will call you. You know I have seen a lot of ghost hunting shows and no one ever got killed. Sometimes they get scratched or punched but I have not seen anyone get killed." I said

We sat there in silence for twenty minutes. "Are you ready to go back? I am getting eaten up by mosquitoes." She said.

"Sure. I can't wait to go into my haunted apartment where I will be locked in my bed room and holding a bat and crucifix all night with the covers pulled up to my eyes." I said

We slowly started walking back. I held her hand as we walked. "Don't worry I am sure if you get rid of the board you will be ok. Just try not to think about it. By the way crucifixes do not work on ghost."She said.

"True. Unless it happens to be a blood sucking demon from hell." I said trying to laugh.

We walked to her door. "Well here we are. You are lucky that you do not have to go with me back to that apartment." I said

"It will be ok. I promise." She said assuring. She put her arms around my neck for a hug. I put my arms around her waist. I held her close. We stayed like that for awhile. I didn't want to leave. I leaned over for a kiss and she kissed me back. Our lips locked in a passionate embrace. Everything fit together perfectly. I forgot about everything that happened for a moment. I was totally lost in her embrace. She knew how to get my blood pumping. We kissed for awhile.

"Get a room you two." I heard someone yell from the courtyard. We giggled and said our goodbyes to each other.

"Ok, I am going to go. Wish me luck." I said as I looked into her eyes. After kissing her I felt more like a man and that I would be able to handle whatever was up there. I felt stronger.

"You will be ok. Everything will be fine." She said.

I turned and waved as I started to walk to my place. I had to take a deep breath. I started walking away. When I got to the bottom of the stairs the warm feelings I had vanished. I started to slowly walk up the three flights of stairs. I walked as slow as I could. Each step was slow and steady. Thump. Thump. Thump. The door to my apartment seemed like it was a mile away. I was absolutely dreading going back in. I kept telling myself it will be ok. Nothing had happened before tonight so I don't think anything will happen now. I thought about sleeping at my parents tonight. I reconsidered because if I told them I was scared of a ghost they would laugh in my face and think that I have gone crazy. I decided if anything weird happens or I get attacked I can always get a hotel room or go to Dave's place.

I reached the top of the stairs and stared at my door. I looked like a gunslinger, from the wild west, who was getting ready to duel. I had my hands out to the side. I had my key in my hand I was ready to sprint in. I went through my plan in my head. The plan was to go in quickly grab the ouija board, put it in a bag, and throw it in the dumpster as quickly as I can. I wanted to set it on fire but there was no where here that I could do that. Adrenaline was pumping through my veins. It was highly probable that nothing was going to happen but you never know. I said that exact same thing about using the ouija board to talk to ghost.

I was ready. I moved closer to the door. I put my ear to the door to try to hear something. No weird sounds. I took a deep breath. I slid the key in the keyhole and turned it slowly. I twisted the door knob and pushed the door open. I only opened it wide enough to stick my head in. I don't know what I was expecting to happen. Nothing looked moved or changed. I ran in to the kitchen and grabbed a plastic bag. I went to the corner where Nikki had flipped over the table. The board was laying there. I grabbed it and the planchette and threw them in the bag.

"Ryan if your ghost is still here you have to leave please. You need to go and find your own place. You are uninvited here." My voice echoed in the darkness. Maybe I have gone crazy. I was having conversations with the air. I kept looking around expecting something to happen. As far as I could tell nothing happened. I turned around and shut the door.

I ran down the stairs as quickly as I could. I jumped down three steps at a time. I sprinted to the dumpster. The dumpsters smelled horribly like rotting meat that has been heated in the midday sun. I knew I was getting closer by the smell. It is just a few steps away. This should do it. All I have to do is to get rid of this board I thought. I was by the dumpsters now. I hurled it over the wall and into the trash. "Good bye and good riddance." I hope nothing like that happens again.

I started walking back to my apartment. Tonight, I am still sleeping with my bedroom door locked, a baseball bat, and a crucifix with me in the bedroom. I was still scared but a bit relieved. I doubt I would sleep well tonight anyways. I walked up the stairs. I really was starting to hate these stairs. By the time I got to the top I was sweaty and out of breath. I opened the door and went in. I closed the door and locked it behind me.

The apartment felt the same. I didn't feel any supernatural presence. I didn't feel like anything evil was lurking in the shadows waiting to get me. It was getting late. I went into the corner where the table was knocked over and picked it up. I examined the top of the table to see if it had scratches or marks on it. Nothing out of the usual.

I was getting tired. All the excitement wore me out. After I checked that I locked the door to the bedroom I jumped into bed.

"I am keeping the lights on tonight." I put my bat next to me. I don't know if I could hit a ghost with a bat but you never know till you try. I turned on the television. I usually watch shows about zombies but tonight I wanted to watch something funny to take my mind off of things. I was completely out after half an hour.

Chapter 4

The mind of Jack. Monday June 10.

    It was Monday. I hate Mondays. BEEP! BEEP! BEEP! I fumbled to turn off my alarm clock. It felt like I was having a mini heart attack. I got ready for work. I did the normal get ready for work routine. I grabbed a doughnut for breakfast. I looked at the clock. It read seven thirty. I better get going or I am going to be late. I was out the door five minutes later. I walked down the steps and to my car.

    When I got to my car I noticed the trash truck was here. It made a loud thundering sound that shook the ground when it moved. The truck was covered in muck and grime. It was hard to find a white patch of paint that wasn't coved in dirt. It was just starting to dump the dumpster that contained the ouija board. Farewell board. It will be gone in a moment. Once it was in the dumpster it would be gone for good. The truck had the dumpster in the lift. I stood silently as I watched the massive metal arms lift the dumpster effortlessly. It dumped its contents of trash bags and junk into a mouth of metal jaws. As far as I was concerned, the board was gone now forever. Good riddance I thought. Good thing I got rid of that before it caused more problems.

I started my car and drove to work. I got on highway 270. Morning traffic is horrible. After half an hour I arrived at work. I grabbed my stuff and went to my cubicle. I started to work on my weekly project. After a few hours Dave stopped by.

"What's new with you J-Dog?"He said.

We are calling each other street names today I guess. "Nothing. D-Money. I am just starting the new weekly project. Hey I have a story to tell you. After you left on Saturday Nikki came over."

"Oh yeah. So did you hook up with her? Was she DTF?" Dave said.

"No. This is serious. We used the ouija board. "I said.

"And what happened?" Dave said.

"Well we both had our hands on it. I thought she was playing a joke on me at first. We asked some questions and it was answering. This is when things went crazy. It started to move really, really, fast back and forth. "

"So she was moving it really fast back and forth." Dave said.

"No we both took our hands off of the planchette and it was moving by itself. We got scared and ran out of the apartment screaming."I said.

"OH shit. For real?" Dave said.

"Fuck yeah for real. I was afraid to go back and sleep there that night. I thought about calling to see if I could crash at your place." I said.

"Did you try to use the ouija board again after that? Did anything else happen?"

"No nothing that I noticed. I threw the board away that night. I didn't know what else to do." I said.

"Did you video tape anything?" Dave said.

"Actually I did. I watched it but it didn't show anything weird. When the planchette started moving by itself the screen went to static for a few seconds. Then the camera lost power after we ran out of there." I said.

"I really want to see that video. When you get home send it to me on the computer if you can. Or bring it to work tomorrow." Dave said.

"Sure. No problem. You are going to want to see this. This is some crazy shit."

"Awesome. I am really interested in seeing that video. Well I have to get back to work. Talk to you later." Dave said.

"Cool. Catch you later." I said.

At around 1:30 I heard my phone make a sound. Blurp, blurp. I got a text message from Nikki. I glanced at my phone and it said "Fuck you dick. That was a mean joke you played. I know you think you are funny but you are not." What?!? I squinted my eyes and shook my head side to side. What is she talking about? I could not text at my desk so I went on my lunch break. I went into the lunch room and texted her back. I typed "Hello darling. I have no idea what you are talking about." Then I hit send. I started to eat my sandwich. I didn't know if she was at work or school. It might be awhile till she is able to text me back. Blurp, blurp. I looked at my phone. "You know what you did. You put something at my door earlier today to be funny." Huh? I thought to myself. I stopped eating and texted back. "Still do not know what you are talking about." I continued eating. Blurp, blurp. "You didn't put the ouija board at my door earlier today?" I texted back "Uh, I threw that in a bag and tossed it into the dumpster Saturday night. I saw with my own eyes the dumpster get dumped this morning." Send. I started eating my chips. My phone beeped again. "Well if you are being serious then I am sorry for yelling at you. Sorry to bother you at work. I am working evening shift all week. We can hang out next weekend if you want." I texted back. "Apology accepted. Yeah we can hang out over the weekend. That's cool. Talk to you later. Bye. Bye." I hit send. Guess we are going to do something this weekend. That is pretty cool. As I went back to my desk I started thinking about how the board got to her door. I guess someone could have pulled it out of the dumpster but why would they put it at her door. Maybe a ghost really did put it there. No. Ghosts do not exist. At least I tried to not believe it even after what happened.

When I got home from work I went to my video camera. I watched the footage again to see if I would notice anything out of the ordinary. After analyzing it I could not see anything different. I played through it a few times but I didn't catch anything. I got on my home computer and downloaded the video. I sent it to Dave. I thought he had some video programs that allow him to check things more thoroughly. I was getting hungry so I made myself dinner. Frozen burrito. Mmm… It's not the best but it will do for now. I ate my burrito and watched television. I started to doze off.

When I woke up it was Tuesday. I must have dozed off. I got up as usual and went about my daily morning routine. Everything went as usual. I got in my car and drove to work. It was hot out and it was only 7:30 in the morning. I hate it when I get sweaty in my work clothes. My shirt starts to show sweat stains. Then I stink all day. Everyone looks at me like I have not taken a shower. I arrived at work only a little late. There was a big accident on 270. That happens about every day. I went to my desk. I was getting ready to start my exciting day. I turned on my computer and looked over. Dave came running up to my cubicle.

"Hey man, I looked at your video through some video editing software and I saw something." He said.

I took my eyes off my computer screen. Dave looked pale and scared. His eyes looked red and bloodshot like he had been up all night watching TV.

"You look like you have seen a ghost." I said.

"I think I did actually. I don't even believe in things like that."

"What did you see? I hope it was more than dust particles moving in front of the camera. What do they call those, spirit orbs or something?" I asked.

"No. These were not fucking spirit orbs. You are going to like this. Well I went frame by frame and in two different frames I saw an outline of a figure." He said.

"In another one of the frames is a close up of a face. Very clearly. It is not her face or your face either."

"Really you can see a face? Holy shit. Are you sure it is not just a weird blur with the camera?" I said

"Come over after work and I will show you." Dave said.

"I will be there. I have to see this."

"Cool. Guess I am going to find something to do to look busy till then." Dave said.

"See you later." I said as Dave walked away.

I will have to text Nikki at lunch time and tell her. Lunchtime came and I texted the info. "Hey you. My friend looked over the video from Saturday night. He says on a few different frames he saw a figure and a close up of a face. I am going over there after work to see the footage. What does Ryan look like? Does he still have a picture on the internet? What is his last name?" This should be quite interesting. I waited a few minutes and she texted me back.

"Ryan had a buzz cut. His face was shaved. He does still have a few photos on the internet. His last name is Delpont. I have to go back to work so I will not be able to text you again for awhile. CYA."

Cool, I quickly got onto the internet and typed in Ryan Delpont. His profile quickly came up. I slowly looked through the pictures. He did have short hair. His teeth were crooked. His nose looked like it might have been broken before. He had on a lot of camouflage on and it looked like he might have been in the military. My break was almost over so I exited out and went back to my desk.

I started thinking what if I do have a lost soul living in my apartment. It seems like most spirits that seem to linger are those that died before their time so I could see if this guy died from a drug overdose that his spirit would be lingering. In retrospect, I first thought it would be awesome to have a spirit living in my house. In those shows where they go looking for ghost to make contact with, they go to other people's places. Not their own house. I came to the realization that finding a ghost in someone else's house is pretty cool but finding one in your own house is not a good thing at all. When they tell the people at the end of the show that there is a high level of paranormal activity in their house and they think it is haunted the owners never seem to be too thrilled. The question they always ask next is do you think it is going to hurt me? I think it would eventually drive a person insane. If your things kept getting moved or you heard things moving all night long or unusually moaning sounds coming from the attic you would go crazy. Those kinds of things will drive a normal person mad. I am sure I could get transferred to a different apartment if I complained enough.

It was five in the afternoon. The best time is quitting time. I saved my work and shut down my computer. I grabbed my lunch bag and headed for the door while I waved good bye to my friends. I can't wait to see this. I hurried to my car. Dave's apartment was only fifteen minutes away, down Dorse Road. I drove quickly. I got there and jumped out of my car. I walked over to his apartment.

I knocked on his door. "Open up dawg." I said.

The door flung open. "Jack Ducks in the house." He said out loud.

"Come on in pull up a seat. You want anything to drink?"

"Sure give me a beer." I said as I looked for a chair. His computer was set up in his dining room.

"Ok, let's get down to business. I put the video you sent me on this movie editor. I went frame by frame through the whole thing. It was funny to watch you guys. So… you made it say jump Jacks bones. That was awesome. Even though it did not work I have to give you points for trying. I mean who does that? Anyways, at this frame when the pointer started moving by itself, there is a figure."

Dave pointed at the screen. I watched in disbelief. There was a black shadowy mass that seemed to stand on the other side of the table that Nikki and I were at. It was transparent. I could see what was on the other side of him. A chill went up my spine. Let's think this through. There had to be a logical explanation. I looked around the screen to try to see if there was anything else that could of cast a shadow right there. It was dark in the room and we did have a candle going. I thought maybe the candle flickering may have made the shadow appear and disappear maybe.

"Go a frame before." I told Dave.

I looked at it and I could not see a thing. The shadow was not there at all.

"Go a frame after the shadow frame" I told Dave.

Nothing. I did not see the shadow in that one either.

"Hmm. Interesting. I thought maybe it could be a shadow from the candle. Or perhaps it could be a shadow of something outside shining in? I don't know."

"Yeah I thought that at first too but I don't think it is. Here I can zoom in on it. It looks like a man to me." Dave said.

He zoomed in and I could see some of the features better. Dave pointed at the screen. "See this looks like the nose and mouth. At first I thought his chin came to a point but it looks like he has some hair on his chin. He has short hair."

"I see what you are talking about. I think you are right. Show me the other frame with the face." I said anxiously.

"You are going to love this. After you guys run out of there I guess the shadow walks right to the camera. It's like he is posing for the camera. Then the camera turns off. It was as if he turned it off. Watch this."

Dave scrolled through the film. He stopped at the end of the film. There was certainly a face this time. It appeared to have some white in it. I could see the features more accurately now.

68

In one glance I knew exactly whose face it was. "That's impossible." I yelled. It was easier to see the features. The eyes were black. The nose was pointy and it had hair on its' chin. He was smiling mockingly at the camera. There was no doubt in my mind whose face it was. "There is no way." I said.

"What's impossible? Do you know who this is? Is this Ryan?" Dave asked questioningly

"Well I pretty certain that it is not Ryan. I saw Ryan's picture on the internet and that is not him. I know this is crazy but the person who is showing up on the screen is not dead. He is alive and well."

"So what do you think is going on?" Dave said confused.

My mind started to form different theories and probabilities of how this could be possible.

"Maybe spirits can change appearances. Maybe it's not who I think it is. Maybe it's changing to different images in my mind. Maybe it's not a ghost at all. I can't even begin to form an answer. I have to give this some thought." I said as I rubbed my forehead.

"Well who do you think it is?" Dave said

"I am certain of one thing. The face on the screen belongs to …

Chapter 5

The mind of Max. Friday June 14.

It was eight in the morning. I started my day as usual. I walked into the break room. At eight I meet in the shop with the seven other maintenance workers. Our maintenance shop was once a two bedroom apartment. The inside of it had been gutted and now the walls are covered in shelves stacked with parts. The apartment across from the break room is the tool room. All the outdoor tools are in there.   The next apartment down is the boss's office. All the painting supplies are kept there in the back room.

My co-workers show up at eight. They don't actually go to work until our boss Stan shows up. Sometimes it's at eight thirty, sometimes its nine thirty. Even if you show up late you will not get in trouble because the boss doesn't like to make any decisions at all. I get along with the majority of people but every now and then they really get on my nerves, some of them more than others. I walk into the break room and try to find a seat that is clean. I almost put my hand on the table before noticing that there is soda spilled on the table. I guess this is karma paying me back for dumping soda on that guy's door. It did not look like anyone was planning on cleaning it up either. "Who spilled fucking soda on the table and did not clean it up. I am not going to clean up someone else's mess." I yelled. "Dirty pigs." Everyone started accusing each other. Finally someone said "I would have cleaned it up but there are no paper towels because Stan is hoarding the supplies again. Stan took all the paper towels to his apartment for his own personal use. The soda is going to stay there until someone finds me some paper towels to wipe it up with." He said.

The other grounds person is Jim. He is the boss of me, mainly because he has been there longer. I have no desire to deal with Stan, the boss, on a day to day basis so I let Jim carry the mantle of leadership, for now. "Hey buddy." I said. "What's the plan for today?"

"We are going to do a whole lot of nothing." Jim said.

"How is that different than any other day for you? You are going to do what I tell you to do." I said. Everyone in the room was chuckling.

"I am planning to work on a whole lot of projects. Don't try to steal my fun work either." I said.

"Do you want to hear a funny story? Last night I had the on call pager. The answering service had me call this woman who was locked out. So I called her and she was crying on the phone. She said she was locked out of her apartment. I asked her which one she lived at. She said 2530 L. I said that I would be there in a few minutes. So I drove there and opened the door for her. She said "Thank you, thank you." I left and drove home. Right when I pulled in the drive way I realized I let her into a vacant apartment. I called her back and she was sobbing worse than before. "My apartment has been robbed. All my furniture is gone. They took everything." I told her to stop crying, that she is in the wrong apartment. She went outside and looked around. "Oh, yeah you are right." She said. She then went over to the next breezeway and her key worked in her own lock."

I put my hand on my forehead and shook it. "Geez. What is wrong with these people?"

"Yeah I know. Hey did you see the news today about how an old lady ran her car through a school wall in Algraft? They must have some really bad drivers over there." Jim said mockingly. Everyone in the room was laughing.

I currently live in Algraft, Illinois which is right across the river from St. Louis. I grew up in St. Louis but only moved to Algraft 9 years ago. In the break room they love to make fun of Algraft anytime it comes up in the news. I think they do it to try to get under my skin but it doesn't really bother me because I grew up in St. Louis.

"I admit that the drivers in Algraft are worse than St. Louis. They don't seem to know which side of the street you are suppose to park on and they don't stop at red lights. But the only reason that they put stories like that on the news is to distract people from all the murders and drug activity that goes on in St. Louis." I said in my rebuttal.

"That's not true." Jim said.

"Have you been watching the news buddy? Every time there is some shooting or something about people getting raped they always throw something in the news about Algraft to try to change the subject. Just like last week the news said there was this shooting in downtown St. Louis, "BUT IN ALGRAFT." someone drew googly eyes on a hundred year old building as if that can even compare to the shooting." I said out loud.

"I guess that is kind of true. You don't hear about a lot of killings or drug deals going on in Algraft." He said.

"Yeah, no shit. The news doesn't say that the hundred year old building that got graffitied happened to be between two bars. It is also near the main strip which is nothing but bars. It was only a matter of time before some drunken asshole would think it was funny to scribble on the wall." I said as I smirked. I knew this was an argument I had won.

"Ok your right. Anyways, moving on, Stan said that his statue that was by his front door has gone missing. It's the white ceramic statue of Mother Mary holding a cross. You wouldn't happen to know where it went would you?" Jim said.

"I know where it went. You probably pawned it to buy meth." I said laughingly. "But honestly I did not take it. I know it sounds like something I would do though."

In truth, I was glad that the statue has gone missing. It was one of the religious items that blocked me from gaining access to his apartment. It had the same power as a crucifix to turn away evil things. As long as it stood a foot away from the front door I would be unable to cross the threshold. This was one of the few times I was happy that there were plenty of thieves around.

"Stan wants me and you to keep an eye out for it." He said.

"I have to say if I find it intact I am going to smash it to a million pieces." I said. I know Jim thought I was being funny but I really did not want it put back.

"I bet those bad high school kids took it and threw it into one of those pits on the side of the property." He said.

"They probably did." I said. I took a glance at the clock and it was time for me to go.

"I will keep an eye out for it. I will call you if I find anything." I said as I jumped up and hurried toward the door.

"Whoa. What's the hurry?" Jim said.

"I just love starting my day. I gots to go." I said as I ran out the door.

I usually don't like to stay in the shop long mainly because it's disgusting. The walls are yellow from the heavy smoking that goes on in there. Some of these guys regularly spit their chewing tobacco on the walls and on the ground. The walls are covered in brown spots. Sometimes they spit sunflower seeds all over the ground and don't clean it up. It's kind of pointless to tell the boss anything. Everyone does whatever they want most of the time, which is both good and bad. I can pretty much do whatever I want as well since there is no authoritative figure here.

I grabbed my trash bucket and grabber and started my day. As I headed off towards the front I noticed a resident coming down the stairs. Ah, here is one of my favorite people to torment. Resident 2830 H. At exactly eight thirty he brings his dog down so it can do its business every day. Sometimes he cleans it up, sometimes he doesn't. He also likes to just leave his trash outside his door until it piles up and starts to leak. The office sends him letters and then I usually have to take his trash to the dumpster because his neighbors start complaining. Today I decided I am going to have some fun.

I decided I was going to teach this guy a lesson. I don't like doing this but some people can't take a hint. What am I saying? I love to do this.

I got into my position about fifty yards away. It was close enough to see him but not close enough to really be noticed. As long as he was in my field of vision I could take control. I started to pry into his mind. I usually first appear as a voice on the winds. Just a slight voice that tells you what you should do. If that doesn't work I try to threaten him in his head. He kept walking. My voice in his head turned into a deep and booming sound. People don't usually respond to comfort but they sure seem to respond to discomfort. I know he heard me that time because he looked around every time I did it. I am sure it is like hearing a voice in your conscious that is not one of your own imagining. He started walking with his dog to the corner of the apartments. His dog squatted and went. He better pick it up I thought to myself. He just turned around and started to walk back.

That's IT! NOW I'AM MAD! I thought to myself. Then I just used the full power of my focus and I violently took control of him. My presence shot across the distance of land between us quickly. I looked directly at him. I felt the electrical charges surge in the back of my head. It made the skin on my face change. I felt different parts of my brain come alive as electricity radiated through my skull. My eyes felt like they were burning. My mind was focused. I could sense that his mind was terrified. He was scared now. Having another presence take control of your own must be frightening. After his dog relieved himself he took one step and froze. I knew I had control of him now. He was in a state of shock. I knocked him off the steering wheel and I was driving now. I made his left hand let go of the dog leash. I was feeling what he was feeling through his senses. Somewhere in his mind he was screaming to be set free.

"Release Me!" He yelled in his head.

"Ha, ha, ha. We are too late for that my friend. Just sit back and enjoy the ride." I said in a deep rumbling voice. I appeared in his mind as a black hooded human figure.

His screaming continued in his head. I made his body walk the length of a building. It was an unbalanced movement. One foot would shoot up fast and the other would drag slowly behind. The arms just swung lifelessly from side to side. It was not graceful. His head was turned sideways and drool was coming out of his mouth. I walked him to a dumpster. In my real body I followed him but kept my distance.

"See this is a dumpster. You pick your own trash bags up and put them in here." I said in a lecturing tone.

I could have freed him at that point but then I noticed there was a white trash bad sitting by the dumpster. I made him slowly pick it up and open it. His hands were difficult to control. He was trying to override me by forming a fist. I felt that he was becoming more difficult to control. At first, I was going to make him just throw the trash bag in the dumpster but then I changed my mind. He lifted the trash bag high above his head where it lingered for a second. In his head I laughed for a second. In one swift movement, he dumped it all over himself. Spaghetti, rotten salad, and other unknown things washed over him. His facial expression never changed as liquid nastiness poured down his face. Spaghetti sauce and jam oozed down his shirt.

He was starting to fight back now. In his head clouds were forming. He was trying to take back the steering wheel. I could sense he was getting ready to try something. There was a flicker in the purple clouds. White hot lightning shot forth from a cloud and struck

76

my hooded avatar that I had created in his mind. I was expecting this kind of an assault. It hit my invisible barrier and exploded in sparks. The barrier flashed blue for an instant but held up. The lightning traveled around the outline of my barrier. My eyes changed to blue glowing embers of anger surrounded by absolute darkness.

I turned to the blackening storm clouds. I knew he could hear me. *"Listen to me, I was going to release you but now I am really pissed and I am going to walk you to every dumpster here. Start walking. NOW."*

He made a grunting sound as he tried to yell in protest. His feet started to lurch forward. Another dog walker was walking toward him. He reached out and tried to grab her. His arm movements were slowed by me. The lady walking by had faster reflexes and she leaned away from him. I felt his lips move as he was trying to mouth the words help me to her.

"Hey buddy. Don't touch me. I am reporting you to the office." She walked by him and did a double take. She walked by my human body and said "Something is seriously wrong with that guy up there."

"No problem. I will keep an eye on him." I said smiling.

His body started to move. His feet were dragging now. It was like he forgot how to walk. His steps looked like he was limping as one foot dragged. I think he was trying to make his self sit so he would not have to walk. I heard his human body make a grunt whimpering sound.

"OBEY ME!" I thundered in his head. He started moving again.

I walked him to the front section. Jim, the other grounds guy, was walking down the sidewalk towards me on my left side. "Whoa. Hey come here? The office called me. They got a call that some guy was walking around here and they think he is really high. They said he was covered in trash and he smelled like a dumpster. They wanted us to check it out."

Dammit. I was losing control of my test subject. He was starting to wiggle free of my control. One of the limitations of mind control is that I could not have a lengthy conversation in my own body and keep my mind control over my person. He was also moving out of my line of sight. Oh well, maybe he has learned his lesson.

I laughed. "Really that is crazy. Yeah I saw that guy walk this way. It's that guy up there. I have been following him from the back section. I saw him walk over to a dumpster and then dump a bag of trash on himself. He seemed like he was pretty high or really drunk. He was also walking funny. It was kind of how I picture a zombie would walk. We need to keep an eye on him." I said in a serious tone as I was having my own personal laugh on the inside.

He was the standing in the front section. I could see he was coming out of it. He was rubbing his head and looking back and forth at the sky as if something might swoop down and attack him. I guess he realized he was covered in trash and spaghetti sauce. He quickly walked to the nearest tree and wiped it off. 2820 B was walking towards us back to his apartment. He was walking normally and fast now. He still seemed confused and scared.

He was approaching us. "Hey are you ok." Yelled Jim.

"Yeah I am ok. I don't know. Maybe. I know this sounds strange but I was walking my dog and then a voice took over in my head. I felt like I was no longer in control of my body. I really think God was trying to talk

78

to me. My head really hurts now." He said as he kept looking up at the sky.

"Sorry but I have to ask this. Are you high or drunk? The office got a call that someone was walking around and scaring other residents." Jim said.

I had to turn around to keep from bursting in to laughter. I had to bit my lip to hold it in.

"No, that wasn't me. No I am not high or drunk. I just took my dog for a walk and I am going back to my apartment." He said as he started to walk past us.

"Ok that's cool. Just making sure everything is ok. Are you going to be able to make it back to your own apartment?" Jim said.

"Yes I will be able to make it."He said as is offended. The guy walked past us and hurried back to his apartment. We started walking in the other direction.

"Wow that guy smelled like rotten fish. He didn't seem drunk. He just seemed a little confused, almost like when you first wake up." Jim said.

"I saw him pick up a trash bag and then dump it all over himself. What is going on with the people here?" I said.

"I don't know? He didn't smell like alcohol. The police say that the drug hair-ron is on the rise." Jim said.

"I think it must be something in the St. Louis water. People here are going nuts for some reason." I said as I laughed.

"I am going to go tell the office what happened. I will catch you later. Call me if you see that guy walking around again." Jim said.

"No problem." I said.

Jim walked off towards the front. That was fun I thought to myself. I am pretty sure that he will do things differently now since he thinks God was messing with him. I hope his dog went back to his apartment. I could not control his hand fast enough when I first entered his mind. I am sure it will turn up. I walked toward the left side of the property. I had to circle around the front still. I walk the same pattern every day so I am sure that I cover the whole property.

I made my way to the front. I picked up a few cups here and there. I guess there were no big parties last night. I walked past the office and I waved to the office people through the window. I could see Jim was still in there. It was hard to miss Jim. He was tall and sort of fat. I continued to make my rounds.

After an hour I finished cleaning up the grounds. The bushes around the property were getting tall so I decided I would work on trimming them today. I went over and started to cut the hedges. My arms usually get tired after awhile because I have to lift the hedger above my head in some areas. I try not to cut off too much because the office manager gets upset when I cut out large chunks.

Anyways, I kept cutting for a few hours. I try not to get too far ahead of myself because I have to go back and pick up all the trimmings. I also have to sweep off the patios where leafs have fallen or residents complain. My arm was feeling the burn after a few hours. I decided to stop and go pick up what I had already cut. I was wondering where Jim was at. His lazy ass needs to be out here helping. I got a trash can and rake. I went up front and started raking.

I felt that someone was watching me. I was focused on raking up the leaf clippings. "Whatcha doing today?" I turned around and Sidewinder was standing there. The maintenance workers who preceded me gave weird names to every resident here. They called her that because she is seventy and her head is hunched over in front of her body. When she goes around a corner her head goes around first like a snake. At least that is how they described it to me. She lives in the second section on the second floor. Her apartment overlooks the second pool. She is actually one of the residents I don't mind chatting with.

"Just cutting some bushes and chillin like a villain on penicillin." I said.

"What? Chilling like a villain." She chuckled. "That doesn't look fun. At least it is a nice day out. Not too hot, not to cold. Breezy. Did you hear what happened at the pool last weekend?"

"No I have not heard the gossip yet but if it happened at the pool I am sure it's good."

"Young people gone wild. These young punks now days are out of control. One person will invite ten friends to go to the pool at a time. I think you are only supposed to have 2 guests with you. Anyways, so a group of ten people show up. I think one of them lives in the apartment across the courtyard. Her and her friends are completely drunk and acting like clowns. They were standing on the tables and dancing. They looked like prostitutes. They were acting really trampy and this is in the middle of the day when there are children and families there."

"They were really sluttin' it up huh. I think I know which girl you are talking about." If I didn't I could find out really quick. I work around a bunch of guys. They know where every attractive girl lives here.

"So anyway, Bev, the large redneck blonde woman who lives down stairs, said something to them and they got rowdy. Bev said you want to fight and one of those girls ran up from behind and shoved her to the

81

ground and ran away. Bev would have beaten the crap out of that little girl. Bev said you better run you little bitch. Bev said she is calling the office and maybe the police. Most of the other girls in that group decided to leave after that. Anyway at night I guess they came to Bev's door and scratched Die Bitch on the door."

"I can't believe Bev and her husband didn't hear anything since they have two dogs. That's pretty brave since the next door down lives a retired police officer." I said.

"I guess she didn't hear a thing. So the next day after that, those girls set the dumpster on fire. It is the one that is closest to her apartment. There is no way to know for sure if they did it but I am pretty sure they did." She said.

"You know I thought it looked like it had something burning in it. There was a melted pink raft stuck to the side. I saw burnt paper and ashes on the ground around it. The wall was charred looking." I said.

"A fire truck had to come to put it out."

"Hey why are you talking to my worker?" Jim said jokingly.

"You are not the boss of this place. I can talk to whoever I dam well please." She said as she shook her head back and forth. She put her hands on her hips.

"Whoa looks like she told you." I said laughing.

"Oh no she didn't. So why were you lighting the dumpsters on fire and writing things on your neighbor's door? I heard there were police cars and fire trucks here all weekend." Jim said.

"It was those girls at the pool that probably did it. I am pretty sure it is that girl who lives on the top floor on the other side of the courtyard from me. She walks a brown dog every day. It's the girl I see you guys checking out all the time."

"Wait, wait, a second. We are gentleman. We don't check out anyone. We make sure everyone is safe and ok." Jim said. I was laughing.

"Is that why you follow her every day? I see you staring. I am seventy five. I know what you are looking at. Those girls have shorts on that barely cover their back sides." She said.

I took Sidewinders side. I stood by her and said. "Yeah you dirty pervert."

"That's not true I resent that. I am a gentleman and I support whatever these woman want to wear" Jim said.

"Oh, brother. Well Max, you need to give this guy a laxative because he is full of shit." She said.

I was laughing. I put my hand over my mouth. "That was a good one. She got you." I said.

"Well boys, I gots to run to the grocery store to get my drink on. Peace out. I'm mobile." She said as she walked away.

"Ha ha. She said you are full of shit. Where did she learn to talk like that anyways?" I said.

"I think she has been watching too much TV. Anyways, I need you to come with me." We started to walk towards the back section.

"We have two work order tickets to take care. First one is a ticket to replace a dryer. It's for Mr. Jack Ducks 6520 M. He says it's not drying. He is probably putting too much in at a time. Let me try to locate a dryer that is in descent condition. We will do that ticket later. The other ticket is to go check out an apartment.

By the way, have you seen a dead body before?" Jim said in a serious tone.

"Umm… no?" I said. But in my head I was thinking if you only knew. I have seen hundreds of dead bodies and usually I am the cause of it.

"Well you might get your chance to see one today." He said.

"Great." I said with enthusiasm. We kept walking to the back section.

"Do you know that old lady who lives at 5576 D?"

"No it doesn't ring a bell."I was flat out lying.

"Well she calls the office when she needs someone to come to her apartment to pick up the rent check and take it to the office. It is a few days past due now and she never called this time. She usually calls the last day of every month."

"So no call this time?" I said.

"No. She did not call." He gave me a serious look. "Hey listen to this. Here is where it gets a little shady. The office said if she is dead they still want me to find the rent check so they can cash it."

"What? You are kidding me right? They told you to STEAL from a dead person. That is kind of low." I said.

"Whoa. Steal is kind of a strong term. She is still in there and it is a new month. Even if she is dead she should still pay rent for this month." He said.

"That is kind of low but whatever. Her ghost is going to come after you." I said chuckling as we walked to the apartment. "Oh I know who this is now. She moved here to St. Louis to be close to her son so he could take care of her. I think the son got cancer and she had to take care of the son instead. Then he died and she was all alone." I said. That's not exactly what happened though. I played a role in the son's demise.

"That is her." Jim said. We arrived at the front door. "Are you ready for this?"

"I guess. Are you?" I said.

Jim stared at the door. He kept taking deep breaths. I could tell he was prepping for the worst. He stopped to talk to her whenever he had a chance. I am sure he didn't want to see the life less corpse of his friend. He put his hands on the door frame and stared at the door for a few minutes. "Alright. I don't know what we are going to see in there. What about you? You don't look agitated at all?" Jim said.

"Well at college I had to take a lot of biology classes. I had the pleasure of dissecting every kind of animal out there. You can't imagine how many hearts and organs I had to rip open and analyze. So if I see a dead body it is probably not going to really affect me." I said.

He shook his head. "That's pretty cold. Alright I am doing this." He started knocking on the door. I stood off to the side of the doorway.

I already knew what lie on the other side of the door, mainly because …I did it.

He knocked again. "Maintenance." He yelled. He knocked a few more times just to be sure. He gave me one last glance and then he said "I am going in." He aligned his key in the lock and slid it in. This is it. He put his hand on the doorknob and slowly pushed the door open.

It was dark and silent as death in there. Jim finally worked up the courage and stepped inside. The

85

over powering smell hit us. There she was, in her pajamas lying backwards on her kitchen table... right where I left her.

Jim ran over to the table. Her frail body was stiff and lifeless. "Mrs. Wheaton. Mrs. Wheaton." Jim said. He stood there and shook her arm to make sure she was dead. Her face was frozen in absolute terror. It looked like she was trying to scream. The part that was the eeriest was her opened unblinking eyes that endlessly stared at the nothingness on the ceiling.

Jim and I stood above her. "Mrs. Wheaton." Jim yelled as he went to check her pulse. I knew he would not find a heartbeat from this one. He put his hand by her mouth to try to feel her breath.

"She is as dead as dead can be." He said in a monotone voice.

Her bodily fluids leaked out across the table and onto the carpet. I had a stronger stomach then Jim but it was even making my stomach upset. Jim looked down for a second.

"I dunno how much of the smell I can take. I am starting to puke in my mouth." I said. As I glanced at Mrs. Wheaton I noticed she was laying on top of her bills and the rent check was sticking half way out from underneath her.

"Jim there is the check!" I said excitedly. The check was already filled out and signed.

"Dam I have to move the body over. I don't want to touch her." Jim said.

I didn't blame him. She had been dead for a few days. "I can't believe you are stealing the rent money from a dead person. Have they really sunk this low?" I said.

"Listen, the office still wants it. These are tough times. Now grab the shoulder to tilt her." He said.

"I am not going to grab anything." I said.

"Ok I will tilt her. You grab the check." He said as he moved her. Using my thumb and index finger I grabbed the part of the check that had not been under her and I quickly pulled it out.

"Here you go buddy. Here is your dead lady money." Jim put his hand out. I took the side that had some juice on it and I made sure it touched his hand.

"Why did you touch me with that? I can't believe you did that. I need to go outside I might…. Blaaa… He ran out the door.

It was quiet in the room now. I moved over to her head and looked into her soul less eyes for a minute. I put my face up to her ear and softly whispered. "You knew too much so I had to end you."

At the same second, I suddenly heard something move in the darkened corner. I quickly breathed in. I jumped back from the table. My heart felt like it skipped a beat. I stood up and backed away from the body. I could not see what was moving because of the trash on the floor. The creature darted under the couch. I walked over to the couch. I cautiously bent over and put my head on the floor to look under the couch. There it was looking right at me. I saw its green eyes gazing back at me and I realized it was just a black cat.

"Sorry cat. We will try to find you a new home little buddy." I said.

I stood up and decided to have a look around the room. I could tell she was a religious woman. There was a crucifix on every door. She was certainly trying to keep me out but she forgot to place one at my main point of entry, the window. That is where she made the mistake. I walked into her living room.

The living room was a mess. On the coffee table something caught my eye. It was a very ancient book. The pages were yellowed and cracked. This book had to be older than her and she was pushing ninety. I picked it up and looked at the page it was on. Vampiradow   vam-pir-a-dow. A living shadow that sustains its own life by draining souls from people while they are sleeping. It enjoys tormenting mortals by using its own heightened mental powers to control and deceive them. Rumors say it is the soul of a vampire that has refused to pass on.

"Hmm. Vampiradow. I think I like that term. It sure beats Incubus." I said out loud. I slammed the book shut. Jim could barely read so I knew he probably would not want to look at an old book.

"Vampiradow. That sounds Spanish or something." Jim was standing behind me. "What's that you are looking at? It looks really old. It could be worth something."

"Don't loot her stuff. I am sure she has grand kids or someone who might want her belongings." I said.

"I want her belongings. Ok I guess I won't take anything until we are told to clean out her apartment." He said.

I walked down the dark hall into her office. Hundreds of jars of ingredients and other things lined the wall. Some were labeled some were not. I stared at some of them and had no clue what was in them. I picked one up and looked at it for a minute. It looked like grass and vomit mixed together. I grabbed one and opened it. It smelled like curry and rotten meat so I closed it quickly. Whew. I had to open a window.

"That made the apartment smell even worse. I didn't think that was possible. I called the office and told them she was dead. The police are on the way to check on the body." Jim said.

Within minutes I heard the sirens outside. They pulled onto the property and turned their sirens off. The police were almost here. We walked outside to greet them. A cop car and an ambulance showed up. They quickly got out of their vehicles. Jim went outside to talk to them.

"She is in the apartment over here. She was in her nineties. I think she gave the office instructions on what to do with her body before she died. She kind of knew before hand she didn't have much time left." Jim said quickly.

"We have to take a look just to make sure there was no foul play involved." The officer said.

"Sure follow me." Jim said to the two police men. They walked in and went right over to her body. They started to check her vital signs just to be sure she was deceased. They examined Mrs. Wheaton's body for a few minutes.

"Well guys she is dead. By examining her decomposition it looks like she has been laying here for about six days which explains the horrible smell. If she lay her much longer her cat would have probably started to eat her since it is out of food."

"Oh nasty." I said.

"I have one question. Did anyone move the body at all?" The police man said.

I looked at Jim. His eyes got real big. He was horrible at keeping a poker face. I know he was thinking about how he lifted the body to get the check.

"I uhh… No we didn't move the body." Jim said unconvincingly.

"I was just wondering because most people don't suddenly die and fall backwards on the table. It is just an unusual place to find a body." He said.

"Oh. I see. No we didn't move her. She was like that when we came in." Jim said.

"I believe you because her fluids are all over the table. Judging by what I have seen I think she had a heart attack. She is quite elderly. Well did you say she already made arrangements with the office to call the funeral home to come and pick up her body?" He said.

"Yes, that is what I was told. I am not sure how that works though. She made all the arrangements with the funeral home and the office. I guess she just knew her time was about up and she made plans two months ago." Jim said.

"Well we will handle it from here. You might want to do something with the cat." The police officer said.

"We will see if the lady upstairs wants a new pet. I think she has pet sat for this cat a few times before. She might take it. She loves cats. Max grab the cat." Jim said.

I leaned over to pick up the cat and it arched its back and hissed at me. Our gazes met each other. It looked at me as if it knew that I was the one who killed its master. I remember seeing its green eyes watching me from the shadows that night. The elder woman tried to fight me off but then I grabbed her throat and slammed her backwards onto the table. She tried to scream as I drank what was left of her life force.

As the cat stared at me Jim reached down quickly and picked him up. "Easy buddy. Let's take you upstairs." Jim and I walked upstairs and knocked on the door. "Maintenance." Jim yelled.

A woman answered the door. "Hello. Hi there kitty. I heard you guys talking down stairs. So she finally died huh? I knew she wasn't doing well." She said.

"Yeah she passed away. We were wondering if you want her cat? If not, we were going to take it to the humane society." Jim said.

"Sure I will keep him. I have watched him before. If it doesn't work out I will take him to the society." She said.

"That's great. Alright here you go then. You are a life saver." Jim handed her the cat. It looked at me one last time and let out a loud hiss.

"Bye kitty." I said as the door shut. Good things animals cannot talk. If that cat could talk he would share the same fate as his master.

We started walking towards the office. "That wasn't so bad. So are you worried about her ghost coming after you?" I said.

"Pfft. No. I don't believe in ghost. Even if I had a genuine picture of a ghost I would still be skeptical. Anyways, I got the check so I have to go the office. I need you to locate a dryer that we can take to that Duck guy's apartment." Jim said.

"I can't believe you don't believe in ghost. Alright I will go look for one. I will call you when I am ready."

"Awesome." Jim said as he walked off towards the front.

Chapter 6

The mind of Jack. Friday June 14.

"They will be coming over today to take a look at the dryer. What do you think I should ask him if he shows up? What should I say that would not sound insane?" Jack said on the phone to Dave.

"I am not sure. Just strike up a conversation. Like, hey me and my lady friend thought it would be fun to try to talk to a disembodied spirit with the ouija board and something showed up and it looked like you for some reason. Say something like that and see what he says back." Dave said.

"Do you think I should show him the pictures from that night? What if he gets angry then what?"

"You can show him the pictures if you want. Well I don't think he is going to hurt you. It's probably just some weird coincidence that it looks like him on the video images. He will probably just think you are strange and that will be the end of it." Dave said.

"Ok we will see. I will keep questioning him. I will try to get some information out of him but he might not cooperate." I said.

"Well good luck with that. Call me later. Peace out." Dave hung up.

They will probably be here soon to change out my dryer. I had to come up with an excuse so they would show up. I called the office and said my dryer wasn't drying my clothes. It was probably normal for these dryers but I needed an excuse to talk to this guy.

I heard a pounding on the door. Bam. Bam. Bam. They are here. "Coming." I yelled. I looked through the peep hole. It was Jim and Max. They were whispering something back and forth to each other. I opened the door.

"We are here with your new dryer." Jim said.

I looked down at the dryer. "Why does it look so old and beat up if it is new?" I said jokingly.

"By new we meant new to you, not brand new out of the box. These older metal ones work great, much better than the new ones with plastic parts." He said with pride.

"That's what you said about the other one. The other one wasn't heating up at all. I would run my clothes through the cycle a few times and it would not dry. I even took your advice about putting a few things in at a time." I said.

"Sorry about that. I think the heating element inside of it might have gone out." Jim said.

"Come on in and check it out." I said.

They stepped inside of the apartment and Max followed Jim down the hall. I watched them closely especially Max. He had a grey hood on and sun glasses so it made it difficult to see his face without being two feet in front of him.

I guess now is a good time to try to make conversation. You can't catch a fish if you don't throw your hook into the water. "Are you guys into the paranormal or anything like that? Hey I know this is a weird question but have any of you used an ouija board before?" I said. Jim was lifting the dryer off the wall. He stopped and turned toward Max smiling. Max's face was serious looking as far as I could tell. It was half cloaked in shadow.

"That's funny that you said that. When we were standing outside Max said you might bring up something about an ouija board." Jim said.

"My girl friend Nikki and I were using it to try to talk to Ryan's spirit. He was the guy who lived here before me. " I said. I noticed when I said Nikki's name Max's top lip turned upward into a snarl. He clenched his teeth. It seemed to agitate him. "When we were using the board things started to get freaky."

"What happened?" Jim was curious. I got his attention. Max just stood brooding silently off to the side.

"Well the planchette started to move out of control. We took our hands of off it and it was moving in a circle all by itself. Then we ran out of the apartment screaming." I said.

"Really, I thought those things were a joke. I used one when I was a kid but nothing happened. Just like if you say Bloody Mary three times in a mirror she comes and gets you." Jim said.

"Here is the weird part. I had a video camera going and in two different parts it caught something. My friend looked over the footage frame by frame and he saw some things. In one frame there is a human figure and in the other there is a face. He sent me the pics of it and I printed them out, do you want to see?" I asked.

"Yeah I want to see them." Jim said excitedly.

I went to my room to get the pictures. I could hear them whispering to each other. I grabbed the pictures off my table. It looked like they were arguing when I started to walk down the hall. Jim was shrugging with his shoulders and Max was pointing.

"Here they are." I said. I handed the one to Jim. "See this darker opaque looking shadow here. It looks like the upper torso of a person. It looks like shoulders and a head and part of the face. On the other side of the table Nikki and I were kneeling there. This is when the planchette started to move by itself." Jim was very focused on the picture.

"That's pretty wild. So you actually got the ouija board to work. Do you think this is the dead guy who lived here?" Jim said. Jim handed the picture to Max.

"I don't think it is the guy who died here. I saw a few pictures of him and to me it doesn't look like him." I said.

Max took off his sun glasses and placed them on the counter of the bathroom. It was the first time I saw the upper part of Max's face. He was looking at the photo. He moved the photo a few inches from his face.

"That's interesting. This picture is blurry and out of focus. You know that could just be from a bug moving in front of the camera especially if it wasn't in the frame before or after." Max said as he handed back the picture. He was shaking his head as he dismissed it as nothing.

They didn't seem that impressed. This should blow their mind. "That first one is a little blurry. Ok here is the second picture. This was after Nikki and I flipped over the table and ran out of the room screaming. This one is clearer than the last one." I handed it to Jim. I know this will have to impress him. Hopefully he thinks it looks like Max without me saying it.

Jim took a long look at it. "Whoa this is definitely a face. It looks like someone I know."He said smiling. He held up the picture to the side of Max's face. "It does sort of look like you. The picture is a little blurry. The face is also too transparent to tell for sure. Here what do you think?"

He handed the picture to Max. Max studied it for awhile. "That looks nothing like me. It has a different mouth and nose then me. Any resemblances are purely coincidental. This mouth looks nothing like my mouth. Mine has a fuller upper lip. It all depends on where you think the blur ends and begins. If it starts here it looks like me. If it starts over here it looks nothing like me. Besides how do you think I would be able to appear in a picture and not physically be there? That's just silly to even think it is me in those pictures."

The more he talked about it the more doubt I started to have that it was actually him. I guess I was jumping to conclusions.

"Good point. You are right. I guess. But I can say that I did actually see a ghost." I said.

"Yes there is something there." Jim said. Jim had the dryer down and Max rolled it outside. They picked up the new one and walked it down the hallway.

"You should put those pics on the internet or send them to one of those ghost hunting shows." Jim said.

"Maybe I will. I have not seen anything like that before." I said.

"That is crazy that something actually showed up on camera." Jim said.

Jim and Max finished connecting the dryer. "Well you are all set. Sorry about the other dryer not working. I hope this one works better for you." Jim said as they walked out.

"Sure. Well take it easy." I said. I shut the door. Well, I guess it wasn't Max in the picture. How would he be able to do that anyways? I heard a knock on the door. I looked through the peep hole. It was Max. This might be bad. I was tensed up for a second. I opened the door.

"I forgot my glasses on your bathroom counter." I stood on the side of the door. He walked by me, down the dimly lit hallway. Max put on his glasses as he made his way past me toward the door. He lingered facing the door.

"Your friend Nikki is going to get what's coming to her." Max said in a low threatening voice. Max had his hand on the doorknob.

I was angry. "What's that supposed to mean? Are you threatening her?" I yelled.

Max tilted his head down and spun around. "Oh by the way," He said. I felt a cold pain stinging my head. It felt like I might black out. I felt frozen spikes lance my mind. Cold radiated out from the back of my head. It felt like icy daggers of pain stabbed at my eyes from the inside. I could not see for a minute. Then I heard the sound. A deep monstrous inhuman voice spoke in my head. I heard it quite clearly. *"Don't try to save her."* I grabbed my face with my hands and hunched over. My sight was coming and going. I wanted to scream but all I managed to get out was, "Why are you doing this to me?" I yelled. I looked up and saw Max stand there for a minute then walk out. I was curled up in the fetal position on the floor. I heard the voice again, just as evil, but fainter. "*It would be foolish for you to try.*" The icy words chilled me to the core. The threat that he sent to me was received.

I slowly got off the floor as quick as I could. I wanted to yell at Max before he ran off. I was holding my stomach as I hobbled to the door hunched over. I might vomit. I swallowed that thought down. "Wait!" I yelled as I tried to open the door. I went through the door and outside. I could see Jim and Max rolling the dryer down the sidewalk. They were quite far away.

I yelled at the top of my lungs. "SHE IS A GOOD PERSON. YOU DON'T HAVE TO HURT HER!" They were too far to hear. Jim did not hear me. Max was walking behind Jim. He must have heard me or sensed me. Max turned toward me. Watching his grinning face turn and look directly at me sent shivers up my spine. Oh no, I thought to myself. My body froze up. What is he going to do to me? He shook his head and put his index finger over his mouth in a shushing gesture. I was bracing for a mental assault. I flinched back with my arms up and I turned my head sideways as if I was going to get hit. Nothing happened. I looked over the court yard again and they were farther away now. I just stood there watching them round the corner.

I have to warn Nikki. I ran inside and went looking for my phone. Where is it? I fumbled through my belongings. "Here it is." I called her number and she did not pick up. She is probably at classes. I decided to text her. "Please, please, call me or come over after your work tonight. It's important." Send. Well at least I tried to contact her. There is nothing more I could do.

It was about ten at night. I was watching television on my couch. I was starting to get ready to go to bed when I heard a knock on my door. I opened the door and it was Nikki. She had her work uniform on. "Hey what's up? Come on in." I said as I smiled.

She stepped into my apartment and hugged me. She always smelled good even after working. She was smiling. I am glad she must be in a good mood. She won't be after I tell her everything that happened. "Would you like a beverage or something to eat or anything?" I said.

"No I am good. What's so important that you needed to talk to me?" Nikki said.

I really didn't want to be the bearer of bad news. My heart sunk. "Well first, do you want to see the pictures from when we used the ouija board?"

"Yeah I want to see them."She said excitedly.

I went down the hall and brought them in. I am sure she was going to reach the same conclusion as me. I handed her the pictures. "The first one is when the planchette started moving by itself." I didn't have to point anything out. She saw it clearly.

"You know it felt like something was standing there for some reason. I thought it looked darker there but since the candles were flickering I was not sure. It looks like there is a cloaked figure there. Show me the next one."

"Ok but here is where it gets really weird. Like it has not been weird already? Right?" I said.

I handed her the second picture. I could almost hear the gears in her mind clicking and forming the same opinion as me. She stood up and put her hand over her mouth while she still stared at the picture. I could sense the cheerfulness she had when she entered the apartment melting away like snow in the heat of the sun, leaving only a feeling of dread in its place. "Oh my god. This looks like Max. How is this possible? This is not Ryan."

"I have been thinking about it ever since I saw the picture and I cannot come up with a solid answer. I have looked up different theories on the internet as well but nothing seems to fit either. I have read some similar stories of experiences on the internet but nothing is like this." I said.

The next part is the part I had to tell her because it seemed extremely important. However, it was also what I least wanted to tell her. "I thought it would be a good idea to confront Max and ask him about the pictures."

"That was pretty brave of you. So how did that go?" She said.

"Well I said my dryer was broken to get Max and Jim up here to change it. I talked to them and showed then the pictures." I said in a serious tone.

"I am surprised he didn't hurt you for doing something like that. He probably just denied everything. Then what happened?" She said.

"Jim seemed to like the pictures. He thought it looked like Max too. Max convinced us that it wasn't him in the pictures. He said the pictures were blurry and the facial features looked nothing like him. The more he talked the more my opinion changed." I said

"I am sure he did say something like that. He denied everything huh. That's how he works, by creating doubt and confusion in people's minds." She said.

"I was actually starting to believe his bull shit. Right when he was leaving he then said that you were in big trouble and things were going to get real bad for you. I jumped up and yelled he better not and then he mind froze me like he did before. Then he left. I ran outside and said you were a good person. I hope things don't get worse for you because of what I did."

She got really quiet. I didn't know what her emotional response to all this was going to be. We were both sitting on the couch. She looked me in the eyes and said "That was a very brave thing you did. That is one of the nicest things anyone has done for me. I mean that." She started sobbing then crying. She put her hands up to her face and leaned forward. I put my arm around her. I started rubbing her back to try to calm her. Through the crying and the sniffling I heard her say. "I hope he didn't hurt you to bad. I know the mind attacks are painful."

"I am ok. It didn't hurt that bad. It feels like a really bad migraine. It just stuns me for a few minutes. I am usually fine after that."

"I know, I know. I really appreciate you trying to help me." She said. She looked into my brown eyes for a minute.

"I have to tell you something but swear to me you won't laugh or judge me because it sounds crazy."She said with tears in her eyes.

"Ok I swear. If it has to do with what's been going on, I will believe whatever you say." I said as I tried to reassure her that everything was ok.

"Things have been getting worse for me since Ryan died. Just like Max said they would. I have been having dreams. Really, really scary bad dreams. I usually wake up screaming. Then I cannot go back to sleep. When the lights go out and I start to dream it feels like there is a pressure on my chest. I can't breathe. I feel paralyzed and unable to move. Somehow, I know it sounds strange, but I believe Max is making it happen. It's like he is slowly torturing me. All my dreams start off good. Then they start to transform to my worst fears. I can be dreaming of my favorite day at the lake. Next thing I know I am being drowned or attacked by fish.

Sometimes I see someone try to save me and they end up pushing me further under the water or worse."

I held her hand and looked her in the eyes. "Hey after my brief encounters with Max I believe you. I believe everything you are saying. I think that guy is a demon."

"He is something." She said.

"We will take care of this. I promise. There has to be something we can do."

"I sure hope so." She said.

"If you want to sleep here tonight or anything that's cool. I promise I won't try anything sexual." I said.

"That sounds good. Just lay by me here on the couch for awhile." She said as she threw the back cushions on the floor so we both fit. I grabbed a blanket. She put her head on my shoulder. She put her small arm across my chest. She smelled good. She pressed her warm body against mine.

"Well, I hope you sleep better tonight. Sweet dreams." I kissed her forehead and slowly rubbed her back.

"I am sure I will." She was smiling. In a few minutes she was out. I could hear her slow breathing. She was snoring slightly. She felt nice and warm. That's all I remember. My eyes slowly closed as well. I was out.

Chapter 7

The mind of Jack. Saturday June 15.

It was Saturday. I felt the warm rays of the sun hit my face. I slowly opened my eyes. Where am I? Why am I in the living room? What am I doing on the couch? I looked over at my clock. It was about ten in the morning. It took me a minute to remember what happened. My back was certain feeling sore from sleeping on the couch. Oh yeah we fell asleep. I glanced around the room. I could not find Nikki. "Nikki?" I yelled. "Nikki are you here?" I walked down the hallway glancing into each bedroom on the way down. I looked into the bathroom. Hmm. Guess she left and didn't tell me. She sure was silent when she left. I must have been out cold. I didn't hear a thing.

I decided to get some breakfast. I opened the cabinet. Then I opened the fridge. Cereal sounded good today. I poured some cereal and sat down on the couch. I turned on the television. What do I want to do today I thought to myself. I guess I will call Nikki later. I will probably play some games, watch a movie, do my laundry, go to work out. I finished my cereal and the phone rang.

"Hello, go for Jack."I said.

"Hey sweet cheeks. What are you doing?" It was Nikki.

"Nothing right now I just woke up. When did you leave last night?"

"Right after your snoring became so loud I couldn't take it." She said chuckling.

"Ha-ha, you sure think you are funny." I said.

"No actually I left at midnight. I told my parents I wasn't going to stay out all night. Even though I am an adult they get worried if I don't come home and don't call. Anyways, I talked to some of my friends that live on the other side of the courtyard and they are going to barbecue this evening and we are invited to hang out with them. There is a large group of us that use to all hang out at the pool last summer. We usually eat, drink, and swim." She said.

"Sure that sounds like fun. Should I bring something? Chips or anything?"

"No I don't think so. You can offer to give him a few dollars if you want. Bring your own alcohol though. No one likes to share. I learned that the hard way. Be ready to go at five. I will meet you down there. Does that sound cool?" She said.

"That sounds fun. I can't wait. Can I wear my banana hammock?" I said laughing.

"Sure. We need something to laugh at. I am not the fashion police you can wear whatever you want." She said laughing.

"Well alright. I will see you there."

"Can't wait." She hung up the phone.

I need to go to the grocery store to get some food and some more beer. The grocery store was right around the corner. I walked in. I wanted to get some beer. Usually I go shopping on Sunday morning and then I realize I can't buy alcohol until after noon. They have the alcohol section carted off like it is so horrible to buy something on Sunday morning. As if God might strike me down if I bought alcohol on the lord's day. Luckily for me it was Saturday. I found what I wanted quickly. Perfect. I paid for my stuff and went back to my apartment. I was ready to get my party on.

It was five. I looked off my balcony to see if I could see Nikki at the pool. I can only see a portion of the pool area because there is a large tree blocking my view. I can't stare at the ladies at the pool all day from my apartment. I started the party a little earlier then I planned. I had a few tequila shots to loosen up. I grabbed my cooler of beer and a towel. There were a few different groups of people at the pool swimming. I recognized a few faces but I didn't know any names. I walked to the other side of the courtyard. I saw a few people with a grill out so I figured that's where I was going to meet Nikki. I heard someone yell my name. "Jack Ducks over here!"

"Helllllloooooo." I didn't even recognize Nikki. I saw Nikki's body shape for the first time and it was close to perfection. Every time I have seen her before she had on a baggy t-shirt or her work uniform. She had on a pink bikini top and short swim shorts. Really skin tight shorts. I saw every curve of her body and it was wonderful. I would say she had the body of a Greek sculpture but that would be insulting to her. Greek sculptures of women are pudgy and not so fit. She could of easily have been a model. Good thing I had sun glasses on so I could take glances without looking like a total pervert. My eyes slowly followed the curves of her body.

She was giving me a similar look. I had my shirt off. My six pack was showing. I had really great pectoral muscles. She looked me up and down and back up again. Her mouth was open. "Goddam. Hello Mr.Ducks. Sooo… Do you go to the gym often?" She said as she squeezed my arms.

"You have been holding out on me. You never said you had big muscles. Are those real?" She said as she pushed on my chest muscles.

"I would have to ask you the same question." I said as I looked at her tan chest.

"Geez, get a room you two." Said the lady standing by the grill.

"Sorry, this is my friend Trudy. This is her apartment. Her husband is over there playing washers. Those two boys over there are hers too." Nikki said.

"Nice to meet you and your family. Do you want me to go to my apartment to grab some chips or something? I feel bad showing up empty handed." I said.

"No you don't have to give me money. How about next party you bring the meat or cheese or something." Trudy said.

"That sounds fair. Ok I am ready to have some drinks." I opened my cooler and grabbed a beer. I already had my buzz going from earlier.

I noticed Nikki was drinking something in a red cup. "What do you have there?" I said.

"I don't know but it is really strong. Here have a drink." She said.

I took a sip and nearly spit it out. It burned as soon as it hit my throat. I coughed a little. "That's a good drink. So who are all these people here?" I said.

"They all live in this courtyard. That guy lives there with his girl friend. That girl lives over there. That guy lives there I think." She said.

"Wow you know most of these people huh?"

"We all hung out here last year." She said.

Nikki was starting to look tipsy. "Let's sit down." There were a few lawn chairs out and we sat in them. They were close to Trudy who was cooking at the grill.

"Trudy, can you teach me to barbecue? I have only seen it done I have never actually done it myself. I am not sure how to even light the charcoals. I tried one time. I doused the charcoals with lighter fluid. When I lit it the flames shot up five feet. I thought that is how you cook the meat." I said.

She chuckled. "You have never cooked before? What is a matter with you? You light the charcoals and you have to wait till the black burns off and they turn grey. The heat from the grey charcoals cooks the meat."

"Oh. That makes a lot more sense. Did you know that?" I asked Nikki.

"No I don't cook. My parents do the cooking. I have no idea how to barbeque." She said.

Trudy shook her head. The charcoals turned grey and she started throwing meat on the grill. She then sat down by the empty chair by us.

"So, Nikki tells me you tried to make contact with the other side." She said smiling.

"We didn't try. We succeeded. The marker you push around on the board started moving by itself. Then Nikki got scared and ran out." I was laughing.

"I see how it is now. It's funny that you said that because you were right behind me. You passed me running down the stairs." She said.

"What terrified me the most was thinking that I had to go back to the apartment and sleep there that night. Although, I have not felt or heard anything since then. I slept with a bat and crucifix that night. I kept the lights on and I huddled under the blankets. "

"That blows my mind that you had a ghost encounter." Trudy said.

"It was an encounter, with what is the part I am not sure of."

"I better flip the burgers. We have washers set out if you guys want to play." Trudy said.

One of the kids ran up and said they have wiffle ball too if you want to play.

I looked at Nikki. "Maybe we will check it out later. I am ready to eat."

Trudy's husband walked up. "So you are the guy living in Ryan's apartment?"

"Yes that's me." I said.

"Ryan was a good guy he just got involved with the wrong crowd. He started dealing and using drugs. There was a constant stream of people pulling up in front of his apartment and he would run down and sell them drugs. There was this one time that we were all at the pool and these thug looking guys came down to the pool and they asked if any of us knew where Ryan was but we didn't know. I think they were carrying guns. It doesn't really surprise me that he ended up dead. It's a shame that he died. When you get involved with the wrong people that is usually what happens. You wanna drink or anything?"

"No thank you. I am good. Sorry to hear about your friend dying." I said. I was not good with sympathy. I come from a big family but no one has passed away.

"COME and GET IT! First round of burgers are done." Trudy yelled.

"Smells great." Good I am hungry and a little drunk. Nikki and I started to make our burgers. I wanted to eat something to sober me up some. I put pepper jack cheese on mine and some barbeque sauce. Then I added lettuce, onion, and pickles. I bit down and it was delicious. I had not had a grilled burger in a long time and it hit the spot. The flavors were amazing. The juices ran down my hand, so much for cleanliness. Nikki must have thought the same thing. She had sauce all over her face. "This is a good burger." I said to Nikki. We ate for a few minutes. When we were done I asked her "Do you want to play washers?"

"Sure I will gladly beat you at washers." She said.

"We will see about that."

So we stood at the tossing distance. "Ladies first." I said.

"Look at you being a gentleman. No you go first I insist." She said.

"Stand aside then. You are going to learn today son." I said.

I tossed my first washer. It bounced and hit the side of the box. "Dangit." I said. I swung my arm back and tossed. It landed inside the box. "Yes one point." I swung my arm back again and tossed. It hit off the middle of the box but still stayed in the box. "Two points. You are up slim."

She held the washer out in front of her like she was aiming. She swung her arm back and tossed. It landed right in the center of the box. Those are two points each. "Someone is in trouble." She looked at me and winked. She threw the second one and it landed in the box. "Who is going to learn today?" She threw her final washer and it landed in the middle. Two points.

"Wow. Looks like you won. This is hard for me to take. I have never been beaten by a girl before." I said disappointed.

"Get used to it. We played a lot last summer. I am a pro." She said.

Trudy's husband walked by laughing. "We don't play her anymore because she usually wins."

"Thanks man for giving me the heads up. " I said smiling.

"No problem anytime." He said.

We played a few more games but I was unable to beat her despite my best efforts. I even took a few steps up and tossed and she still won.

More people kept showing up. Everyone was sitting in lawn chairs. There was a concrete table on the outside of every pool area on both sides of the pool. We all sat around and had drinks and had some laughs. I got asked what I do for a living and I said graphic designer and they had no clue what that was. Everyone was impressed that I have a career. I tell them that I do logos and ads, things like that. I do not do web pages but I do know how to do web pages. Then they always ask if I can draw really well for a tattoo for them. I always say yes if you give me money up front. They don't like it when I say they have to pay. I don't work for free.

I noticed the sun was starting to set and I still have not gotten into the pool yet. It was still warm out.

It was probably around eighty five degrees. I have been sweating the whole time I have been outside. "Nikki do you want to take a dip in the pool?"

"Yeah let's do it. I have been waiting for you to ask. I have been sweating since I have been out here." She said.

"We are going to jump in to the pool everyone. The burgers were great. " We announced it to the group.

We grabbed our towels and went into the pool gate. There was a few people sitting at the concrete table around the pool but no one was in the water. She had brought a few noodles to float on.

"I have never used the noodles before. Do those actually work?" I said.

"They keep my fat ass floating." She said.

I ran over to the deep end and took a running start. I took a big leap and tried to dive in funny which only resulted in a belly flop. The water was refreshing. After a few days of it being ninety five or hotter the water was perfect for me. It felt like bath water. I looked at Nikki. She was taking the slow way in. She was going step by step down the stairs and inching her way to the deep end. It is my least favorite way of entering the pool especially if the water is cold.

"The water feels great." I said. I swam a few laps back and forth. It felt good to stretch my legs out. "Do you want to race?" I said

"No not really I just want to float here." Nikki said.

She just floated on her noodles. I swam up and started to push her around the pool.

"Now I like this. I like it when you push me around the pool." She said. I grabbed her feet and pulled

111

her around for awhile. It was relaxing. We watched the sun slowly set from the pool. The clouds were a magnificent shade of orange and purple. Then finally it was gone. Nikki let go of her floaties and swam up to me. I was at the corner of the pool. She put her arms and legs around me. Her body was entwined with my own. She slowly kissed me. Her lips were nice and soft. I felt like I was floating both mentally and physically. My heart was feeling tingly and my body felt alive. We made out in the corner for awhile. I was caught up in the passion of the moment. I had lost track of time.

"Jack." She said as she slowly kissed my lips. I thought she was going to whisper something sexy in my ear.

"Yes baby." I said.

"There is someone standing behind you."

I tilted my head back. "Oh shit." There was someone standing behind me. It was a large man. His legs were standing across the corner of the pool.

"Hello Jack Ducks." He said in a friendly voice.

I moved forward and quickly spun around. "You startled me." It took me a minute to realize it was Jim the maintenance man. "For a larger man you are quite stealthy." I said. I didn't notice everyone leaving the pool because it was nine. Guess that is what happens when you are making out and a little tipsy.

"In case you didn't know the pool closes at nine. I came around to lock the gates. I am not the guy who usually does it. They just had me do it this week cause of the problems we have been having." He said.

"Yeah that's cool. No problemo." I watched Nikki swim over and get out of the pool on the shallow end.

"Hey can you throw me a towel." I yelled. She knew what she did to me. "If you don't throw me a towel I am going to need a few moments." She knew what I was getting at. She chuckled and tossed it to me. I gathered my shoes and shirt and went to the only gate that was unlocked. Jim followed us and locked the gate. Most of the courtyard group was still sitting in lawn chairs by the grill. I wanted to ask him a few questions and I thought now might be a good time since he was alone. "Hey you want a drink or anything." I said.

"No, I can't because I am working. I still have the front pool to close."

"Hey it is little Jimmy." One of the ladies in the lawn chair shouted. She was in her mid forties. She had blonde hair. Jim knew who she was.

"How are you doing Dorthy?" He said in a friendly voice.

"I am doing well. How's the family?"

"Everyone is doing ok. Well Tony is in jail, but he is used to it. He has been in and out of jail all his life."

"Sorry to hear about that. Hey, remember when we were high schoolers and we use to hang out here. We use to have big parties with bonfires toward the back of the property."

"Those were the good ole days." Jim said.

"I remember my brother telling me that you and he would take sewer lids and roll them down the hill at incoming traffic." She said.

"When I look back and think about all the crazy things we did we are lucky to be alive. But, yeah that was fun. We hit a few cars and ran off. Cars would

113

swerve when they saw the lid coming their way. I think we only caused one accident."

"Oh yeah. Just one accident. No big deal." She said jokingly.

"You know the last time I saw your brother I think we got picked up by the police for something like hitchhiking and we were waiting for a parent to come pick us up. I had a small bag of weed on me and I didn't want to get caught with it so I slowly tossed it under the bench we were sitting on. My parents came to pick us up. On the ride home your brother says hey when we were sitting on the bench I happened to find a bag of weed and I picked it up. After he said that I was cracking up." Everyone else was laughing.

"So what was it like growing up here?" I said after the chuckles died down.

"Well it was mostly farmland. There was only one main road. All the other roads here were gravel roads. There was only a grocery store and a few other little stores and that was it. There was no shopping mall or strip malls. This apartment complex was originally an apple orchard. I dated the girl whose parents owned this land. Their last name was Swiftfoot. Her parents sold this land about 30 years ago and then they built these apartments. That's why it is called Northfield Orchards."

Dorthy's little boy ran up. "I cut my finger. I need a band aid."

"Well looks like I have to go play doctor but it was nice seeing you."

"Well it was nice seeing you too. I have to go close the other pool. I will tell my wife you said hi." Jim said.

"Hey can I come with you." I said. I whispered to Nikki. "I am going to get him to talk about Max even

114

If I have to scrape the information out of his brain with a fork."

"That's fine. I need to take a shower and go to bed. I have to work in the morning. Tell me what happens tomorrow." She hugged me and kissed my lips. She put her cheek to my cheek. "Be careful." She whispered in my ear.

We started walking on the concrete pathway up to the front pool.

"You know all these people?" I said.

"Yeah I do. I grew up around here and I have been here all my life. I was the big cheese in these parts. I had six brothers and a sister. Everyone knew us. We were total bad asses. No one at high school messed with me because they would get their ass kicked by my older brothers."

"Hey so what did you think about those ghost pictures? It sure looked like Max in those pictures."I said.

"It did look like Max but that is just a coincidence. Just like Max said."

I am sure that is what he wanted us to think I thought to myself. "Max sure seems to know a lot of things huh." I said.

"He is just a really smart guy. Really, really perceptive. He went to college. He said he has a master's degree in some science field." Jim said.

"How long have you worked here for?" I asked.

"Let's see it has been about eight years. Eight years to long."

"How long has Max worked here?" I asked.

"He has been here for about six years." Jim said.

"What is Max's last name?"

"His full name is Maximus Rathengor and he lives in Algraft Illinois. We always give him shit for living in Illinois." Jim said.

"That's pretty funny. What did he do before he worked here?" I said.

"First, he said that if he told me someone would try to kill me. I always thought he was joking but after he told me all the science stuff I wasn't so sure. Well he says he was a brain scientist. A neuro or bio something or another. He said he was studying brain waves and how to increase the intensity. I think he said something about conscious projection. He went into a lot of technical jargon but the gist of it was he was trying to create a machine that would help humans mind control the minds of animals or insects. Things started to go bad. He thinks some government agency wanted to use his findings to control humans instead of animals. All his computers started to get hacked. His office got ransacked twice. Some people started following him and his assistant wound up dead. He said all that but he could be full of shit. Half of the workers here say crazy shit like that all the time."

"Wow so he had been a scientist. Who would of thought?" I said.

We were getting close to the front pool. I noticed there were two guys and a girl in the pool area. Jim turned and whispered to me. "Ahh. This guy is a douche bag, especially for being under thirty." I looked at him. He was tall and skinny with short black hair.

Jim opened the gate and walked into the fenced in area. "Hey you have to leave. It is closing time." Jim said.

116

"Hey it's Jimmy. So when are you guys going to fix the light in the pool?" He said.

"Honestly. Probably never. You have to keep calling the office but I don't think Stan will ever fix it. Besides, the pool closes when it gets dark so I don't think you really need it. The lights in the courtyard light it pretty well."

I could see this resident was getting agitated. "Whatever. I called last year every week about it but nothing was done. That fucker kept telling me the part was on order then the pool season was over. Anyways, I will call the office again and so will most of the people in this courtyard."

"Good I hope you do. You know I just do what I am told. I would fix it if we had the parts." Jim said.

I just stood there. The three people in the front courtyard got up and walked out the side gate. Jim went around and locked the rest of the gates. They didn't seem happy. I could hear them muttering a slew of cuss words under their breath. We started walking towards the back section.

I didn't know Jim that well but I thought I should tell him not to tell Max I talked to him. "Hey could you not tell Max that we talked tonight."

"Sure. No problem." Jim said. I thought to myself, Max probably already knows that I was asking about him.

"Max has no problem with you but he says that Nikki is evil and you should probably avoid her. She is not all peaches and cream you know." Jim said.

"Why would he say that?" I said.

"I don't know. I don't ask him questions." He said.

117

Jim was at his truck. "Well have a good one. Stay out of trouble." Jim said.

"Yeah you too. Take it easy." I said. I walked across the courtyard back to my apartment. I passed the back pool. Looks like everyone packed it up. Guess the party is over. I walked up the stairs to my apartment and thought about what I should do next.

Chapter 8

The mind of Jack. Sunday June 16.

It was Sunday. I was determined to do some researching today. By research I mean internet stalking. In the old days a person would have to go ask people a hundred questions to find out anything. Now days all you have to have is a computer and you can find out anything you ever wanted to know about a person with a click of the button. The internet is a stalkers best friend.

Let's see here. First I typed the name Max Rathengor. A whole slew of names showed up. All these different social media sites popped up. I clicked on a link. There were a few Max Rathengors but I couldn't go that far because of the privacy settings. I clicked some of the other ones and there was no information I could gather. They didn't have any friends or any personal information. They were blank pages with nothing but the person's name. This is a dead end. I went back to my internet search. I scrolled down a few pages but nothing interesting popped up. Nothing here was helpful. I tried Maximus Rathengor. The same kind of things popped up. Let me try Maximus

Rathengor scientist. A few new things popped up.   Here we go.

There was about ten links that looked to be science related. This looks promising. These were science experiments. They were full of technical details. I read though some of it but I did not know what half of the words even meant. It was getting technical. There were a few diagrams. It looked like one person had these electrodes hooked to his head to increase electrical activity in a region of the brain. I clicked on another link. This link had an experiment with some kind of machine that goes over the head and it looked like they wanted to increase brain waves. The purpose was to see if a person could transfer thoughts or commands to another human or animal.

There were about ten videos on the internet. I watched a few of them. All the experiments they did pretty much reached the same conclusion. That Max was quite a master in psychic abilities. There were too many abilities for to me to classify but if I separated it into categories that main ones would be reading minds, telepathy, astral projection, and partial mind control.

I heard my phone ring. I had to run down the hall to find it. It was Nikki. "Hello baby.   What's up?

"Nothin. What are you doing?" She said.

"I thought you had to work this morning. I am looking up information on Max Rathengor."

"I have to be at work in an hour. Can I come over?" She said.

"Hey girl, you never have to ask to come over. The door is always open for you. Get your lovely face over here."

"K, I will be there in a sec." She said.

Knock, knock, knock.

I opened the door. "Come on in. Wow that literally was a second later." I said.

"I was standing outside your door when I called you. I thought you would have heard me in the breezeway talking to you. I like this. You wearing no shirt today." She said as she entered. She wrapped her arms around me.

"Yeah it's no shirt Sunday. You are welcome to participate if you want. Shirts are optional today." I said

"Oh really I am welcome to participate huh. Well in that case." She started to untuck her shirt. She started to lift it up.

"No I am not going to take my shirt off. I have to go to work in forty five minutes." She said laughingly.

"Got ya. You should have seen your face though. You can close your mouth now it's not going to happen." She said.

"Why do you do that to me? You are so mean." I said.

"That is because you are too easy."She said

"Anyways, want to see what I found on the computer." I said

"Sure. Yeah I want to see it all."She said.

We went over to my computer. I pulled up another chair for her. "So yesterday when I was talking to Jim I got some information about Max. He said Max's full name is Max Rathengor. He lives in Algraft Illinois. He also was some kind of scientist. He videotaped some of his experiments and put them on the internet. You should watch these. Some of them are pretty interesting. At the end of them he does an

121

interview section which I think is very informative. In one of them he says how he is able to separate his mind from his body. Here I will show you one. Watch this with me."

I clicked on one of the video links. Video is more my style. It was Max. He was younger and clean shaven. He had a clean white lab coat on. "Hello my name is Max Rathengor and this is my assistant Wilson Hammerstein." "Write that name down. Wilson Hammerstein." Nikki said.

"We are testing out the idea of astral projection. That is when a person can send his conscious or soul outside his body to see his surroundings without using their eyesight. I am going to sit here and my assistant is going to go in the other room. He is going to flip over a card and I am going to write down what card he flips over. I am going to send my conscious out of my body to see what card is flipped. He put the helmet on his head. Wilson are you ready to commence? Ready." Wilson shuffled the cards. And pulled out a card and set it on top. Max sat in the chair for a minute with his eyes shut. After a few seconds he turned his head to the side. He wrote down ace of hearts. "The test is complete. What card do you have Wilson?" He came out with the ace of hearts.

"Hmm. That is interesting."

"They did the same experiment ten more times in the video and Max guessed right eight out of ten times. For the times he guessed wrong it was just the suit that was wrong." I said.

"Wow that is pretty good." Nikki said.

At the end of the video there was an interview with Max. "Results when I use the helmet are different then when Wilson uses the helmet. Wilson only guessed right two out of ten times where I am right about eight out of ten times. In the future we are going to try to get a few different people to try the helmet and see how well it works for them. "

Here is the next video in the series. It was made a few months later. Max is being interviewed. "We have come to the conclusion that the helmet is not effective. It has more to do with the individual then the helmet itself. Even without the helmet I scored much higher than anyone else. "

"How do you do it? What do you do in your mind to make your conscious leave your body?"

"How do I do it you say?" He rubbed his chin and hesitated for a minute. "I am not sure how to explain it. I don't think it is the same for everyone. I form a door in my mind. When I am in my body I feel like I am behind a steering wheel or in a control room. It is like letting go of the steering wheel and walking out a door. When I leave the door I am floating above my body and I am flying. I think to do this you have to really believe that your body is just like a car that you can get in and out of. It's not something you are bound to as much as a person might think. But, I can see my body and sense what is going on but I am not actually connected to it. I am usually drawn towards the lights. On a side note, I think electricity in lights can be affected by this for some reason. I have caused light bulbs to pop and go out on many occasions."

"Well that is how he says he does it." I said.

"There has to be more to it than that. So you are telling me all I have to do is picture myself letting go of a steering wheel and leaving my body through a door." She said.

"Yup that's the gist of it." I said.

"Hmm. Well dam it is about time for me to go to work. I will have to think about that while I am at work."

"I am going to keep looking up information and I will tell you if I find anything that might be useful to us." I said.

"Yeah that sounds like a good time. I am glad I am going to work because this seems like more work than me actually going to work."

"Thanks for the support." I said.

"Anytime. Hey look up that assistant guy's name. See what happened to him?" She said.

"I will do that next." I said.

She pushed back her chair and I walked her to the door. She hugged and kissed me. "Hey, just wanted you to know I had a fun time yesterday at the pool." She said.

"Yeah me to. Maybe we can do it again sometime." I said.

"That sounds like a good time. Well, see you later." She said. She was standing by the door and I was starting to go back down the hallway.

"Hey!" She yelled.

I turned around and she lifted her shirt all the way up.

I looked at her in amazement. My mouth dropped open.

"Well have fun on shirtless Sunday." She said as she walked out the door.

"You are so NAUGHTY!" I yelled down the hallway.

Guess I will go back to searching. I decided to look up the assistant's name. Let's see Wilson Hammerstein. I clicked enter. A lot of name search sites popped up. Not what I wanted. I tried Wilson Hammerstein Scientist. Some new things popped up. This looks promising I thought. These looked like news articles. I clicked on the top one.

This was dated from ten years ago April 2003. Wilson Hammerstein, 25, was found dead in his home in Hesterfeld. Police were baffled. It did appear to be a suicide. The gun that was used to shoot Wilson in his head was found in his hand. Police found it odd though that every window in the house was blown out. The light bulbs were all blown out. Black marks were found around the electrical wall sockets. All the electrical appliances seemed to be victims of a power surge. The neighbors were asked if they saw or heard anything and they said no and their electrical power was fine.

I clicked on the next article and it said about the same thing. In one of the articles one neighbor said that there was a black van at that house earlier that week and guys with suits got out of it. He was quoted as saying they looked like typical FBI agents you see on TV but he didn't see the name on their van or anything. They went in the house and an hour later then came out and Wilson came out and was yelling at them and arguing. He had papers in his hand like he was trying to explain something to them. A few days later he was found dead.

Hmm that is interesting. I typed in the name Max Rathengor Algraft IL. I clicked on one of the people finder sites. Max Rathengor lives on 5005 Birch Street. I wrote it down and book marked the page. That may be useful later I thought. I then went to the site where you could see his house from the sky view. This was one of the biggest invasions of privacy that the internet has to offer. It is way too easy to find out anything you ever wanted to know about a person. In a click I had exactly what his house looked like from the sky view. However, I could only see a portion of his house because there were three giant trees towering above it. I could only see the back side and it was a small white ranch style house, with a small back yard. It had a large privacy fence around back though. I could not see the front at all cause of the trees.

Enough of this. I was more interested in the experiments. I started clicking on some of the links. Here is an interesting one. It was titled Mind Control.

Chapter 9

The mind of Jack. Sunday June 16.

It was about eight at night. The sun was setting in the horizon. I heard a knock at the door. "Coming." I said. I looked out the peephole. It was Nikki.

I opened the door "So did you just get off of work. How was your day?" I said.

"Yes. It was long and stupid if you must know."

"That sounds awesome. Let me guess you are back for more shirtless Sunday?" I said

"Ha-ha. No. I wanted to see if you found any more information." She said.

"Yes. I found out a lot of information. Where do you want to begin?" I said.

"Well I need to go to the laundry room to wash some clothes for Monday and I was wondering if you wanted to sit in there with me for an hour." She said.

"Doesn't your apartment have a washer and dryer?" I said.

"Yes, but you can only wash a few items at a time. Since I live with two other people it is a slow process. I would rather pay three dollars and get it all done in an hour." She said.

"Come on your not doing anything. Put on some shoes and come with me. I want to hear everything you found out. Pretend like you are my boyfriend." She said.

"Ok I will go with you. Give me a minute." I said. She wants me to be her boy friend, I think. That sounds good to me. I could live with that.

I put on my shoes and grabbed my keys. We were out the door. I followed her down the stairs. We walked up the path to her apartment. I noticed the sun was setting. The sky was filled with fiery red oranges and little hints of purples. "Look at the sunset. Isn't it beautiful?" I said.

"It is really quite a sight to see tonight. It is so romantic." Nikki said. We looked at the sky for a few minutes before moving on. I put my arm across her back and held her against me for a few moments.

We walked to her apartment which was on the ground floor. "If you want to wait here for a sec while I grab my laundry basket." She said.

"Sure I see how it is. You don't want me to meet your parents." I said just jokingly.

"It's not like that I swear. My parents would like you a lot. I don't want you to see my room." She said.

"Ok if you say so." I said. So I waited in the breezeway. I sat down on the stairs. After a few minutes she came out carrying a basket and her detergent.

"Alright let's be on our way. " She said. So we walked to the next breezeway where the laundry room was.

"I have never actually been in here before. I walked by and looked inside."

"This is it. All your laundry needs can be taken care of right here. You have to have a key to get in and I have mine right here. Here. Can you use my key? My hands are full." She said.

I put the key in the hole and opened the door. So, this is the laundry room. It was fairly clean. We walked in and set her clothes on the counter that ran along the wall. I glanced around the room and noticed there was a bulletin board hanging on the wall. There were a few papers hanging on it. I looked closer at it. Scraped into the board was an eye shape with 666 in the middle. Different symbols were scratched around the outside of it. The devil sees all was etched into the bottom of the board. "That's awesome." I said.

"Probably one of the teenagers did that. You know how they are always tearing things up." Nikki said.

I noticed there was an old lady in here folding her clothes. Her face had deep wrinkles. Her hair was black at one time but now it had more grey in it. Her skin on her hands looked frail like tissue paper. She did have a friendly smile though. "Hello." I said. I was trying to break the silence.

"Hello. The washers are ready for you." She said as she smiled at us.

"All of them seem to be working today which hardly ever happens."

"Great. We only need to use two of them." Nikki said. She went over and put her dark clothes in one and her light clothes in the other. I know I shouldn't look but she had some really sexy underwear in there. She dumped soap in the washer. She put the coins in and hit the on switch. "All right now we just wait." We pulled up two chairs and sat at the corner.

I looked at the laundry detergent the old woman was using. It was like cut up pieces of soap in a clear container. "Are you looking at my home made soap? It's my own special recipe. Here smell it tell me what you think."

She opened her container and held it toward my face. Nikki and me both leaned over and smelled it. It was awful. I could not even think of what exactly that smell could even be compared to. I could tell Nikki was thinking the same thing I was. "That smells....interesting." That was the best adjective that was not offensive that I could come up with at the moment. I would not want my clothes smelling like that.

"Yeah it only costs twenty cents to do a load compared to fifty cents." She said.

"That is very thrifty of you. You have to save money these days every way you can." I said.

"That is how it was in the old days when I was a kid. No one had much except for a few pairs of clothes and that was it. Everyone just had the bare essentials."

"Did you grow up around here?" I said.

"Yes I lived about thirty minutes down the road a little ways. When I was about ten, none of this was here. It was just a gravel road. All this was farm land. I think this property here was an orchard."

"I think I heard someone else say that as well." I said.

"My family had some land and we had a horse and a few farm animals. I had a few brothers and sisters but my mother was insane." She said as she folded her clothes.

"Really? That's just what everybody says. I think my mom was insane." I said.

"No I mean really clinically insane. She set my legs on fire one time when I was ten. Another time she pulled a gun on my eight year old brother and she was getting ready to shoot him in the front yard. Someone called the cops and when they showed up she made my brother take the gun because she was shaking and then she told the cops that my brother was going to kill her."

"No way. Really? That is not good." Nikki said.

"Where was your father at during all this? Did he know your mom was crazy?" I said.

"He worked at a factory. He was at work all day while my mom stayed home and raised us. My mom I think slept around with a lot of different people. I think that some of my brothers are from a different dad. Once he dies I am going to get a DNA sample and test it against my youngest brother and sisters. They don't look anything like the rest of us."

"That's pretty crazy that your mom was like that since that was the sixties. I thought most of the people from that time were sweet and innocent." I said jokingly.

"Pfft. That is just something they show on the television. Everyone was far more crazy back then compared to now. There were fewer rules then. Why do you think there are tons of laws and more safety devices now? That's because people back then did all kinds of crazy shit."

"I guess that is true. When I was younger we didn't have to wear helmets to ride bikes but now you do if you are a kid. You know we used to make fun of kids that wore helmets on their bikes." I said.

"Exactly. So anyway, my dad followed my mom and caught her doing some inappropriate things with the dentist. So the next day he came home, packed all his stuff, said see ya. He moved out and left all of us. He didn't even want to have anything to do with any of my brothers and sisters. He then called the city inspector. The city inspector came to our house and condemned it. The house was in poor condition. There was a hole in the roof and water had been coming in when it rained."

"There was a hole in your roof. Why did you guys never get that fixed? How could you live with a hole in your roof?" I said in disbelief.

"Like I said it was a different times back then. That kind of thing was common in the sixties and fifties because no one had money back then. After the inspector came, we were evicted and the house was boarded up and plowed down."

"That sounds absolutely horrible. How could he abandon you guys like that? Where did you guys go and live after that." Nikki said as she moved her wet laundry to the dryer.

"Well we moved in with my grandparents since my mom didn't have any money. My mom was small but she got into fist fights with my dad, who was much bigger then her, and she would win. I think my dad got tired of dealing with her and thought that this was the way to get away from her. My dad refused to give my mom any money for child support so we went and picketed outside the factory. We all walked around the front with signs so everyone there knew what kind of person my father was. Eventually the bosses there told my dad he has to do something or he is going to get fired so he agreed to pay some child support."

"Well that's good that he was forced to give your mom some help with money." I said.

The old woman finished folding her clothes and put them into her clothes basket. "Yeah it was nice that he helped my mom out. Well I am all done kids. It has been fun chatting but I have to be going." She said as she picked up her laundry basket and walked toward the door.

"You need any assistance? Want me to carry that for you?"

"No I got it."

"So what happened when you lived at your grandparent's house?" Nikki said as the lady was getting ready to walk out the door.

She was really quiet for a second. She started to talk in a whisper. "Well honestly, the family life was better. We got fed better and we had better clothes for school. But, I have my suspicions that my grandpa might be a serial killer though. In his basement there were areas of the concrete floor that had been dug out with a jack hammer and then refilled with concrete. There were ten of them and they were all human sized. Right after he died we cleaned out the basement. We found these gruesome old photographs that showed bodies that had been mutilated. They were pictures of severed arms and legs with human sized bite marks on the skin. At first I thought it was some scary Halloween decorations but I looked at it more closely and they were real bodies cut up. Well young ones I got to run. Hope I didn't ruin any romantic thing you two might have going on later. Bye."

I just sat there with my mouth wide open in a state of awe. Nikki had a similar expression. I watched out the window as the woman put her basket in her white car and drove off to her apartment.

"That was quite a way to make an exit. Oh by the way my whole family is insane and my grandpa happened to murder a whole slew of people. Sometimes he eats them with a fork and knife." I said in an old lady voice.

133

Nikki leaned over from her white plastic chair and nudged me with her elbow. "You are so bad. That lady was telling you her life story. There is nothing wrong with that. She had a rough life. What was your life at home like?"

"Well my mom was a workaholic. She was a manager at her work. She left for work early in the morning. She would get home late. We would only see her for ten minutes at dinner then she would fall asleep on the couch. So I really didn't get to know her that well. It was like living with a stranger. I know very little about her actually. I don't know anything about her parents or relatives on that side. She always avoided it when it came up in a conversation. My dad was almost the same. Occasionally he would play sports with us but that is it. If I was having trouble with school or anything else there was no one I could seek help from. For the most part, I always felt alone."

Nikki was taking her clothes out of the drier and folding them. "Well that is sad that you never knew your parents. I know my parents pretty well. I feel like I could go to them for anything. I could not even imagine not being able to ask my parents for help. My mom is my best friend. I ask her all kinds of things. We talk girl stuff, and boys, and about my future. She gives me confidence and advice on how to handle tough situations. She is my rock."

"Well that is good for you. Are you about ready to go?" I said in a bitter voice.

"Okay. Yeah my stuff is folded and ready. Do you mind carrying this basket for me?" She said in a sweet voice.

"I guess I will carry it." I grabbed it and we walked out of the laundry room.

134

We walked to her apartment. "Do you usually meet strange people in the laundry room and listen to them tell stranger stories?" I asked.

"Sometimes but mostly I just sit there and read my magazine so I am glad you came with me." She said.

"It was no problem. Hey, I have been thinking a lot about the Max situation." I said.

"Oh yeah. What about?"

"After researching and watching all the mind experiment videos Max did I think if we work on building up our psychic abilities we can actually challenge Max. Maybe if we can show him that we can be a threat he might leave you alone." I said.

"That sounds great. I don't really have much of a choice. I am willing to try anything."

"Great we can start training tomorrow." I said.

"Ok I am in." She said.

She leaned in and kissed my lips. It was nice and sweet and way too short. I wanted more. "I will take my basket now. Thank you for being such a gentleman. We can talk more tomorrow about the Max situation. Bye Jack. I will see you in your dreams." She said as she walked inside.

I stood there for a minute thinking about what she said. Does that mean she knows how to visit me in my dreams because that seems to be possible now? Or was that just a figure of speech. Guess I will find out tonight I thought as I walked back to my apartment.

Chapter 10

The mind of Jack. Monday June 17.

It was about seven. The sun hung low in the horizon. I was just waiting for Nikki to come over. We had decided to start mental training so we could eventually challenge Max and hopefully defeat him. I didn't really know what Nikki had planned. She said she did some online research. There were some videos and books out there that talk about expanding your psychic abilities. I heard a knock on the door. She's here I thought to myself. "Hello baby" I said as I opened the door.

"Hello baby yourself." She arrived in workout clothes.

"Why are you are dressed like we are running a mile." I said.

"Well fist I thought we could do some yoga to help relax us." She said.

"Yoga? I hate yoga. That's what real athletes do before they do the real work out. It is just a fancy name for stretches." I said.

"It's not so much about the actually stretching it's about the meditation and making your body feel more relaxed. We will do that first then we will try some mental exercises."

"Ok I will try whatever you want."

She brought over a yoga DVD. "Put this in and I will move your coffee table over and we can begin. Wait a second. You can't do this in jeans goof. Go put on some workout clothes." She said. "We are going to do some yoga to bring some inner peace and relaxation." I went and changed to some workout shorts. I did not want to do yoga at all. I came out from the back room wearing my workout shorts. "Are you ready?"

"I was born ready bitch! Let's do this." I said with enthusiasm. She chuckled. She put in the yoga DVD.

"I like that attitude coming out of you. Alright let's begin." There was a lady on the screen ready to work out. She had a nice relaxing tone when she spoke. The music playing in the background was also very mellow. It was making me feel sleepy. She started off with her legs crossed and palms up. She had us breathe in and out slowly. We did that for a few minutes. Then we went into plank pose. I held it for a few minutes. This is cool. I got this. After awhile I started to get a little shaky but Nikki was holding straight as a board. When it was done my stomach muscles were tired. She said we were going to do warrior pose next. We both stood up. One foot was forward and the other was behind me. My arms came to a point above my head. Then it had us stand on one leg and extend the other straight out behind us with our arms extended forward. I held it for as long as I could but I started to lose my balance. The yoga instructor said now we are going to lie on our stomachs. Ok no problem I can do the laying on my stomach part I thought to myself. Now push yourself up in the front. I started to do it then I felt a pop in my back. "Oww" I yelled as I laid flat back on the ground. I had to stop and rub my back.

"Are you hurt?" Nikki said.

"Yes, I just did something to my back. I felt it pop. I am going to be ok but I am out of yoga time." I got up and moved to the couch. I rubbed my back and watched Nikki.

"I am going to finish the video. It is over in ten minutes." She was on her stomach and had to reach back and grab her feet. I saw her muscles strain as she tried to hold the pose. Beads of sweat formed on her skin. Even with my hurt back I wanted to press my sweaty body against hers. I have to say that I am not a fan of doing yoga. I do however like to watch Nikki bend and move her body in ways I never thought possible. All I could think about is dirty sex positions.

"Alright one more position and I am done."

"No take your time I am enjoying the view." She smiled and shook her head. The yoga instructor said put your hands on the floor. Then put your knees on your elbows. And you can balance on your head and hands or just your hands. Nikki must have done this regularly. She was balancing her body on her arms. I was amazed and really turned on. Her face was looking right at me.

"Are you getting a good view?" She said.

"I am getting a great view. This is definitely the best view in the house." I said. She started laughing. Her body started to shake a little.

"This is nothing you should see what I can do in the bedroom." She said laughing but still holding the position.

"Dirty! I know I can barely move now but I just want you to know that if we get to the point in our

138

relationship that we have sex I am going to expect you to give me some freaky gymnast sex. I have seen how flexible you can be."

"Well you are going to have to work on your flexibility. How are you going to be able to keep up with me if your back goes out? Maybe I am going to want YOU to bend in weird positions." She said.

"Fair enough. I will certainly work on it once my back feels normal again. That will probably be about a week. By the way is this the advanced yoga? I cannot see a bunch of beginners being able to do this."

"Well actually it is the intermediate. I thought the beginner would be a little easy for you and you would make fun of me. Maybe you do need the beginner level." She said.

"Yeah I guess I do. You know me well."

The yoga video came to an end. Nikki stayed on the floor stretching out. I stayed on the couch. Different parts of my body that I didn't know could feel pain now felt incredibly sore. I thought I might have pulled something in my back. My groin area was feeling sore as well. I am an athlete. I am still fit but my flexibility is not that great.

"How do you feel?" She asked.

"Honestly? My body is now sore as shit."

"See, even you Mr. Athlete can benefit from some yoga. It was harder then you thought it would be huh."

"Yeah, I guess. I need yoga like I need a twisted back and a pulled groin." I said.

"Stop being a baby. That was supposed to relax your body and mind. I am going to put on some classical music. Are you ready to try some mental exercises?"

"I will try anything to make me forget about the burning pain in my back."

"I saw this in one of Max's experiment videos. First, I want you to sit Indian style facing me."

"I will certainly try my best. If my legs were not in pain it would be a lot easier." I said as I moved in position.

"Stop being a pussy. And put your hands on your knees palms facing up." I did as she said. I didn't want her to make me do any more yoga as punishment.

"I want you to close your eyes. Now just breathe in and out taking deep breaths. Focus on the music. Keep breathing. Feel the music by using your other senses. Forget about the pain." I did as she said. I focused for a few minutes. I started to really feel the music. It engulfed me and filled me with new sensations.

"Are you feeling it? I mean really feeling it." She asked.

"Yes I think so." My heart was beating in sync to the beat of the song. I felt it all around me. In my head I pictured the different sounds forming different patterns in my mind.

"Now feel the music going up to your head. Once it is there form a door in your mind." I did as she told me. It was a front door similar to what is at the apartments. "Take all the energy and emotions. All the pain and happiness, everything that is you, and form it into an orb in front of the door." Something was happening. I felt electricity flow across my face and skin like I have never felt before. It radiated out from the back of my head and covered my face. Somehow, it felt like I was inside the orb that was inside my mind.

"Now, picture yourself moving through the door."

In my mind I did move forward. I did see something. I don't know if this was real or if I was just thinking it was real. It felt like I was able to see around the room but I wasn't relying on my eyes.

"I think it's working" I said.

"Here's the test. Can you see how many fingers I am holding up?"

"Hmm six." I said.

"That's right good guess. Are you sure you are not looking through your eyes." I shook my head no. Maybe it really is working and I am not imagining it. "Alright now how many this time?"

"Mmm. three."

"That's right. One more time."

"Eight."

"No. I had six that time." My confidence dropped. Now I wasn't sure if I was actually doing it or not. "Ok can you see anything else? If I turn around and put up my fingers can you see how many are up?" I moved forward in the room without moving my body.

"Yes there are four."

"Wow impressive. Are you moving around the room right now?"

"Yes, but I can only see what's in front of me. It's just like looking through my eyes. I can't see through walls yet. I am going to open my eyes now."

"No wait..." She said. It was too late. I opened my eyes and everything was a bright white light. I couldn't see anything. My mind felt like it was poked by a red hot branding iron. I grabbed my head in panic.

"What is going on with my eyes?" I said in a frightened tone.

"You disconnected to fast from your mental projection. You have to hover back to your head before you disconnect or you will get mind burned."

"Why did you not tell me that in the first place? It feels like my head is throbbing. I can feel the blood moving through my face. My body is shaking. Are you sure I am not having a stroke?"

"Don't worry, it will go away and you sight will return to normal in a few minutes."

I got up and stumbled to the kitchen sink. I dumped water over my head. It felt like I was burning. The cool water felt soothing to my skin. My vision was starting to return though. I stood there for a few minutes. I didn't know if I was going to throw up.

"Are you feeling better? I am sorry I didn't tell you about always trying to go back to your head before disconnecting." She said.

She walked over and put her arm around me and walked me to the couch. I brought a bottle of water with me. I plopped down on the couch. I was starting to feel normal again except I felt extremely tired and my body felt weak.

"I want to try now." She said. She took a seat on the floor and crossed her legs.

"Do you want me to talk you through it?"

"No. I know what is supposed to happen. I will tell you when I am ready for the finger test." She said.

I sat there on the couch watching her. She sat with her back straight up. She placed her hands on the legs with palms up. I could hear the classical music still playing. I watched her lungs move as she took deep breaths. I looked at her face. It looked like she was in a deep concentration. I saw beads of sweat form on her forehead. After ten minutes she said I am ready.

"Ok. How many fingers am I holding up?"I said.

"Five?"

"No." She was wrong. "Let's try again. How many am I holding up now?" I said.

Her face looked stressed. "Seven."

"No. Sorry. Let's try one more time. What about now?"

"Two."

I was starting to feel bad for her. "No that is wrong as well. Are sure you are doing it right? Maybe you just are not capable of doing it?"

I could tell by her facial expression that she was getting mad. Her eyebrows started to arch. She was tilting her forehead down at me. She started to raise her upper lip and show her teeth. Then she spoke.

"I AM DOING IT RIGHT!" She yelled in anger. As soon as she spoke, the light bulbs in the light fixture in the middle of the room all made a loud popping sound and burned out. It startled me. I jumped off the couch and moved to the kitchen. Nikki never moved as some sparks fell around her. "Now try. Put out your fingers." She said.

I put out six fingers. "Six." She said.

"That's right. Try again." I put out nine.

"Nine."

"Great one more time." I said.

"Two."

143

"Great you did well that time. I will turn around and you see how many fingers I have up." I put up four.

It took her a minute. She finally took a guess "four?"

"Yes. That's right. You are good at this. I want to try something. I am going to go out into the breezeway and I want you to take a guess. Give me ten seconds." I wanted to see if she could go through the wall or if she would be only allowed to stay in this room. I opened the door and went to the other end of the breezeway. I held out eight fingers.

I waited a few minutes outside. I kept facing my apartment. I looked at my door the whole time. Now I didn't actually see her come through the door but I think I felt her presence. It just felt like Nikki was standing right in front of me. I didn't know if my mind was playing a trick on me. I felt like she was standing in front of me then floated back into the apartment. I decided to go back inside.

"So how many fingers?" I said.

"Eight."

"That's right. Impressive. Now come back into your body. I want to ask you some things." I said.

She was silent for a few minutes. Then she slowly opened her eyes.

"Are you ok? Is your brain on fire? Do you have the worse headache ever? Can you see alright?" I said as I went to sit by her on the floor. I was prepped to run her to the sink.

"I can see normally. I feel mostly fine. I flew back through the door in my mind before opening my eyes. I do want a bottle of water though." She said.

"So that really works if you go back through the door you won't wake up screaming." I said.

"Yes. That appears to be true. Or it is true in my mind."

"So what was it like going through the door to the outside of the apartment?" I said curiously.

"Well, honestly it was like jumping into a pool of water. It just felt like I was moving through a different thicker kind of surface. It got dark for a few seconds as I passed through the metal. Then I emerged on the other side. I have to say the further I was away from my body the weaker my projection got. I was able to see less and it was becoming harder to control. I felt like I was going to dissipate if I stayed out there much longer. Then I came back through the door in my mind. I am starting to feel really tired now though." She said.

I grabbed a pillow and blanket off the couch and we both started to lie on the floor. I put my arm out and she put her head on my shoulder. "That was a good experimental test. I am glad that something happened and we didn't end up hurting ourselves except when I did the yoga." I said.

"Maybe when we do this again we won't be as tired. We can try again in a few days or something." She said

"That sounds great. I might be healed from the yoga by then."

"Ha ha. You are so funny. Now be quiet I am trying to fall asleep." She said.

"Yes ma'am." I was starting to fall asleep as well. That takes a lot out of a person. I was feeling completely drained. We both lie there in each other's arms. I don't remember what happened after that. I was out cold after ten minutes.

Chapter 11

The mind of Jack. Tuesday June 18.

     I awoke the next morning. Nikki was gone as usual. Dam she is good. I had a colossal head ache. My head felt as if bowling balls were dropped in it. There was a weird throbbing in the back of my skull. I tried to stand up. Whoa. I had to grip the side of the couch to keep from falling over. I was feeling dizzy. I had to get ready for work. I stumbled into the shower. I turned on the water and put my hands against the wall to hold myself up. The sound of the water coming out of the shower head and hitting the bottom of the tub was thunderous. "Ahhhhh." I had to cover my ears for a second. This felt ten times worse than the worst hangover I have ever had. I knew I had to pick up the pace if I wanted to be to work in time. In twenty minutes I was dressed and ready for work. I hobbled over to my car and I was off.

     I arrived at work a short time later. I went to sit at my desk. My mind felt much different today compared to yesterday. I could sense what was going on around me without even looking around the room. It was like something had been opened in my mind and now I could not shut it off. My mind was picking up two different views of the world around me. One was coming directly from my eyes the other was coming from what my second sight was seeing. I decided to take a tour around the room. As I flew stealthily around the room I saw people doing all kinds of things they are not suppose to be doing. One person was surfing the internet for something non work related. One lady was texting her boyfriend. I snuck into their private conversation and saw what they were texting back and forth. It was extremely dirty. She texted she just shaved her legs and her boyfriend was going to find out how silky smooth they were when she wraps them around him. I decided to move my sight to Dave's desk to see what he was working on. He was working on a logo for some new sports company. Logos for restaurants or sports companies are usually more enjoyable to work on then say logos for insurance companies. Dave was a good guy for the most part but I think he choose first and took the fun projects and left me with the more difficult ones. He stood up and had a stack of files with him. The file on top said Gillman. I returned back to my own mind.

Dave was walking up to my desk. He walked up quietly behind me trying to be sneaky.

"Hello Dave." I said without turning around. He seemed startled.

"How did you know it was me? Can you see me in your monitor?" He said.

"No, I could smell you stinky cologne from a mile away." I said to throw him off. "Do you have the Gillman file for me?"

"Yes I do actually. How did you know? I just got these new files less than thirty minutes ago." He said.

"Magic." I said being funny. "What file are you working on now? I bet it is a sports company."

"You are blowing my mind. How do you know all this? Are you becoming psychic? Hey everybody. Jack is psychic." Dave announced to the office. I heard a few chuckles.

"I think you mean psycho." I heard someone a few cubicles over yell back.

"Anyways so what have you been busy doing? Have you hooked up with that Nikki girl?"

"Well, we have been hanging out more and she has slept over but I have not sealed the deal if that is what you mean." I said.

"That's cool. Taking things slow I get it. It's probably better that way if you are in a serious relationship."

"I am nooooott... Well maybe I am in a serious relationship." I said. He got me thinking.

"So whatever happened to the ouija board thing?"

"Oh that. Nothing happened. I pitched the board that night. It was pretty creepy. You know what is weird though. Nikki said that she found the board sitting in front of her door the next day. Then she threw it away again."

"That is pretty unusual. That would creep me out too if it happened in my own house." He said. Somebody was calling his name by his cubicle. "Well I got to get back to work."

"See you later bro. Thanks for giving me these insurance companies." I said.

"No problemo buddy." Dave went back to his desk. I was kind of stunned after he brought up that I was in a serious relationship. I never thought of it that way but I guess he was right. I was in a serious relationship.

Chapter 12

The mind of Jack. Thursday June 20.

It was Thursday evening. Nikki said she would be over later after work. It was going on nine. I usually go to sleep at ten because I have to get up so early. She better show up soon or I am going to bed. I was lying on the couch watching TV. I heard a knock on the door if you could call it that. It was pretty faint. But it still sounded like a knock. Nikki is here I thought. I went over and looked out the peep hole and it was black.

"Very funny Nikki. Take your finger off the hole." I said as I opened the door. To my surprise there was no one out there. I looked down the hallway. I walked over and looked down the staircase. I didn't see or hear anything. It was eerily quiet. If someone knocked on my door and ran I would have seen them running down the stairs. I decided to walk down the stairs to see if I could see someone. Hmm. Nothing. There were some people in the courtyard but I don't think they could have knocked and ran that far in that short amount of time. The people in the courtyard were all overweight and a little drunk. I walked back up to my apartment and went inside. Maybe I didn't hear a knock on the door. Sometimes when the wind blows there is a little give in the door and it makes a sound. Then again, the knock I heard on the door was the signature knock that Nikki always makes.

I grabbed my phone to text Nikki. "Where are you? Are you coming over tonight?" Send. Then I heard it again. A faint knock, knock. I looked up from the phone to the white door. My heart was beating a little fast now. I decided to remain seated unless I heard it again. I hit mute on the television remote. Maybe it was the wind. I stared at the door. My stomach was starting to get tight. I could hear my heartbeat in my ears. I tried to listen more intently. I waited for a few intense minutes. Nothing happened. I undid the mute on my television. Then BAM! BAM! BAM! It was so loud. It sounded like someone kicked my door really hard. I jumped up from the couch. I was a little scared now. I heard laughter outside. "Whoever is out there you are going to get it! I am going to call the police!" I said as I flung the door open. No one was out there. I ran down the hallway and down the stairs. No one was out there. I walked around the corner of the building to see if maybe they ran and hid in the bushes. Nothing.

I walked slowly back up to my apartment. I had to think about this logically. Maybe the someone, who is knocking on my door, is living in one of these apartments in my breezeway. It is the only way a person could knock on my door and disappear in less than five seconds. This time I was going to wait and look out the peep hole. After I shut the door I decided to grab my bat from the closet then I walked back to my door. I am certainly going to catch them this time. I am ready for them now. I slowly moved my eye to the peep hole. I felt my hot breath bouncing off the door and heating my face. There was a hooded figure standing, to be more accurate I would have to say floating, eight feet from my door. Whatever it was, it was not a human. When the wind blew, the bottom of its fabric moved and it had no feet. I was scared now. I quickly gasped for air. My stomach dropped. It must have heard me or knew I was there because it brought up its right blackened hand and waved at me. I stopped looking through the hole and turned my back to the door. I started to slide down the door. I was terrified. I was sitting on the floor holding my bat tightly. If it opens the door I can try to hit it. I thought. I pulled out my phone and started to text Nikki. My fingers were trembling. I texted "Nikki where are you? There is something at my front door. Please hurry! It must be from Max. I don't think it is human."

I put my ear to the door and I still have not heard anything. I worked up my courage and decided I was going to look out the hole again. I slowly stood up. I put my eye to the hole. I was having a cold sweat. I could hear nothing except my heart beating. To my surprise nothing was out there. Then all of a sudden a giant orange eye flew up and looked through the hole back at me.

"Wuhhh." I jumped five feet from the door and fell on my ass. I crawled backwards to the far wall. I sat there clutching my bat. "GET AWAY FROM THE DOOR WHATEVER YOU ARE! I HAVE MY PHONE AND I WILL CALL THE POLICE!" I yelled. It was silent as the grave in my apartment. I sat there shivering. I thought I might be having a minor heart attack. Ten minutes went by then there was a loud "WHACK" on my door. "Go away from my door! I will call the police!" I said again.

"Let me in. It's me." Bam bam bam. I heard her knocking. I went over now with less fear and opened the door.

"Hey, whatcha doing?" She said.

"Nothing." I said as I looked out in the hallway. I grabbed her and pulled her to the side quickly. "Did you see anything out here? Or did you see anything at the bottom of the stairs?" I asked as I looked over the railings in both directions.

"No, I did not see anything. What is a matter? You are being so paranoid."

"Get in here! It is not safe out there!" I grabbed her arm and yanked her in. "There was something in black robes with orange eyes out here. It had no face. It banged on my door and waved at me." I said hysterically.

She put her arms around me. "Oh poor baby. It waved at you. Is that why you are so sweaty? Are you scared?"

"Fuck yeah. I am scared. That's why I have this bat." I said as I shook it in her face.

"Why don't we relax and put the bat down. Here I will get you a drink so you can calm down." She went to the kitchen and grabbed a shot glass. She poured me some tequila. "Here drink this. It will take the edge off." She said as she handed me the glass.

I accepted it and swallowed it in one gulp. I slammed the glass down on the counter. I had to cough for a few seconds until the burning in my mouth went away. "I wanted to show you something. I have been doing some practice on my own. I have changed a few things. Move your coffee table and I will show you."

I went over and slid the table over. She sat Indian style on the floor. She motioned for me to sit opposite of her. "I know before we used classical music but I started to use metal music. Or more accurately music that brings out more of an emotion. Alternative music with a hint of sadness mixed in works better as well." She plugged her mp3 player into my radio and turned up the volume. She sat back down. We both put our hands on our knees with our palms facing up. She closed her eyes. I kept mine open because I was just going to watch what she could do. She started to take deep breaths. I listened to the songs that were playing. They sang about vengeance and hatred. I had those on my playlist as well but I could tell if these songs were influencing us and giving us power then we were heading away from the light and moving towards a darker path.

I could tell she was starting to really focus in. Her skin was starting to change. I could see the goose bumps on her face. There was electricity flowing around her head. I could feel it in the air. The air in the apartment felt more charged. Her eyes were closed but I could see her eyelids moving slightly. Her mouth flew open. The lights in the room started to dim until it was dark. Then it was silent for a few minutes.

"Alright Jack look behind you." She said in a monotone voice. I turned around and the cloaked figure with the glowing orange eyes was on my balcony.

"Huhhh." I said as I jumped up and moved behind where she was sitting. Then I realized something. She was controlling it all along. It started to come through the glass door right for us. I decided to test something out myself as well. I took both my hands and stuck them right into her armpits to see if she was ticklish. As soon as I did that she lost her concentration. She started laughing and leaned forward. Her hands went up to my hands to pull them out of her armpits. The dark spirit dispersed instantly as if it was just a hologram.

"So you think that is funny? Scaring the shit out of me like that with one of your mental projections. You are lucky I don't do something to you. I don't know what but I am just saying."

"Did you like that? Pretty cool huh."

"Yes. That is pretty cool. Looks like you have been doing a lot of practice without me. So now I have some questions for you. First when you created your mental projection can you still see what is going on?"

"It is not like being able to see everything in the room like it is when I am in the orb form. I can only see what my mental projection sees."

"Ok I see. So how did you knock on the door? I thought when we are in those forms we can't affect the solid objects around us?"

"We can but it takes a high amount of concentration and energy. After I pounded the door I was not sure it you would even hear it. My mind felt exhausted from knocking on the door. I watched you come out your door but I didn't have enough energy to keep up the projection so it disappeared and all I had is the sight. I was able to see what was going on but I was kind of frozen in place from fatigue."

"Here is another serious question. Do you think this is going to FUCK UP our brains? I know that sounds funny but I have been having some weird experiences at work. I am sitting at my computer doing my work but I am still able to fly around the office and see what is going on at other people's cubicle. In my head it feels as if was getting input of my surrounding from two different sensors. Almost like I am watching two TVs at the same time. I have tried to turn it off but it is not going away. I usually just try to make my sight go under my desk and stay there otherwise I would go mentally insane. I don't know if that is because maybe I have not gone all the way back through the door that my mind created when I first projected out. Have you been experiencing problems or anything like that?"

"Problems! You are looking at this all wrong. This is a blessing. I like having the extra ability to see what is going on around me. It has been more helpful to me then a hindrance. But yes I am seeing things differently in my mind as well. You should not think of it as a bad thing. You should think of it as we are evolving to something more than normal humans. This is the next step in evolution but we should probably not let anyone else know. You know what happened to the last guy who had said that he was a higher power." She said.

"Yeah that is true. So what do you want to do now? If you are staying I want you to teach me how to astral project a mental image." I said excitedly.

"Ok. I can help you try. Alright are you ready or are you still recovering from me scaring the crap out of you?"

"No I am ready." I said with fierce determination.

"I have to have metal music playing though." She turned it on and sat on the floor. I took a seat facing her. She sat with her palms together in front of her like she was praying."

"Do I have to do that?" I said.

"No you can sit however you want? Whatever makes you comfortable?" We closed our eyes and started to focus like we did days before. I breathed slowly in and out. After a few minutes I was ready. My body was relaxed and my mind was prepared. I started to form an opened door in my mind.

"This time form a creature in your mind that you want to send out. I would start with something small like a bird, or frog, or squirrel. "I liked the bird idea. I always wanted to fly like an eagle.

"Take all your emotions and form them in the creature." As I listened to the music I was able to focus my anger and rage into the bird. My bird formed and it was a cardinal. I don't know why that happened because I really hate baseball and that was their mascot. Maybe seeing all the red and promotions for the cardinal's baseball team on everything has put subliminal messages into my mind. Dam you St. Louis. I curse you. Or maybe it was one of the things I hated with a passion so it was one of the first things that formed from my mind.

"Now. Pass it through the door you have formed in your mind." She said slowly.

I started to flap my wings. This is awesome. I flew through the mental door and into my living room. It was amazing. I sent my cardinal through the door. I flapped my wings vigorously. I took a few laps around the room. I could see our bodies still sitting in place where we left them. It was a weird feeling being something so small. "Nikki where are you?" I thought to myself. Then I saw her creation. She took the black shape of a crow. Big and midnight black it was. The eyes were piercing. They reflected the darkness within it. I saw my glowing cardinal reflecting back when I looked into its glossy eyes. We flapped our wings a few times.

"I have to say I am a little intimidated that you are larger than me in size." I said to her telepathically.

"Don't be afraid. It would take a lot of energy and focus for us to physically touch each other. I am not going to try to hurt you."

I landed next to her on the table. I put my wing out to try to touch her but it went right through her.

"See I told you. It is as if we are ghosts. Now let me try and when I do I will try to focus with all my emotions." She moved her wing and gently touched me

156

and I felt her soft black feathers very firmly and they pushed me back.

"Well I don't know what you did but that felt pretty solid to me."I said.

"That has drained me a little to do that." She said.

"Hey are you thinking what I am thinking? I want to go fly outside like a real bird."

"Sure let's go." She said.

"We can go through glass and walls right?"

"Yes as far as I know."

"Well, we are going to learn today." I started flying right at the sliding glass door. I started flapping my wings. Here I go. I started to fly towards the door. I hope she is right about going through the door or this is going to be very unpleasant. Please allow me to pass through. I put my legs out in front of me because it seemed more natural if I was going to hit the glass. I wouldn't want to hit it head first. I was fast approaching feet first. I closed my eyes and braced for the sudden stop. I felt the surface of the glass and I passed effortlessly through it to my relief. I started flapping my wings harder. I wanted to go high, high in the sky. Nikki was right behind me. We flew above the apartments. "This is amazing." I said.

We flew down the road to the highway. I saw a large rusty brown bridge on the distance. "I want to land on the bridge." I said to her. I spotted a nice spot at the very top and I landed up there. "It is beautiful up here."

"Yes it is pretty amazing from up here. The best thing about flying is there is no traffic." She said.

"You are right. Can other people see us?"

"I don't think so. I think we blink in and out of existence of normal sight so no one knows if they see us for sure."

"I had to stop from flying any further because my mind was getting tired. I think we are not skilled enough right now to go very far. So how far have you gone?" I said.

"This is as far as I have traveled. I don't know how far a safe distance is. I am not sure if there is a limit or if this will do something to our minds later."

"Awesome. We might have mental problems when we get back." I said.

"Who are we kidding? You have always had mental problems."

"You are not as funny as you think you are." I stared at the cars moving underneath us for a few minutes. It was pretty cool from up here. "Are you ready to fly back?" I said.

"Yeah wait a sec." As we looked over the highway we saw an ambulance coming at us. It had lights flashing and the sirens were blaring. Then I saw it. Something was crawling on the roof, something dark and shadowy. The thing on top of the ambulance looked like death himself. It had black angelic wings. Its body was skeleton like. If it had flesh it was all dried and turned rotten black. It had some long hair that was dirty and matted. It hung loosely around the creature's skinless face. It was missing a bottom jaw. An instant feeling of dread came over me. I was stunned by just being in its presence. "We need to hide." She said. We moved across the top of the bridge to not be seen. I don't know if it saw us but as it passed underneath the bridge it looked directly up at us. Its head whipped up right at us like it knew we were up here. As it passed underneath us time felt like it stood still for a few seconds. I got a good look at the eyeless skull. I felt like it was draining me. I suddenly felt a pulling sensation from my gut. As the ambulance went further past us the thing continued to look back at us. Then it stared back forward to whatever it was doing. I think it was feeding or waiting to collect a soul, maybe? I was not sure. I didn't know how it could see us since it had no eyes. Even as it passed and drove off into distance I felt like I was becoming weaker.

"Do you feel as if your soul just got drained or pulled?" I said.

"Yes. I think that thing did something to us. It sure seemed to want whatever was inside the ambulance." We watched the ambulance get further away from us.

"Alright let's jet. Looks like the coast is clear. I guess we are not the only things out here." I said. I did learn something today. Dark things really do exist. We started to fly back. "What happens if I just wake up my body without going back through the doorway in my mind?"

"You will severely regret it. Your mind will feel like it is burning. Take the worst head ache you have ever had and multiply it by twenty. Trust me you do not want to abort if you don't have to." We were flying above the apartments now.

"I want to try something. Have you seen what eagles do?" I said.

"What's that?"

"They hold each other's claws while they spiral downward toward the ground. Since we can't die I want to try it." I said.

"Ok. I always wanted to sky dive.

"Let's start really high and remember to let go."
I said excitedly. We flew straight up. "Ok I am ready."
We both started to dive downward headfirst. We were
moving fast just like meteors aimed to strike the earth.
The wind blew through my feathers. We both reached
out our talons and held onto the other. We started to
spin. It felt like dancing and plummeting to my death all
at the same time. I looked lovingly into her black eyes.
The ground was coming up quick.

"Alright let go! Let go!" I yelled. Instead of
letting go she tightened her grip. I looked into her jet
black eyes. All I saw was a reflection of my own panic.

"Don't be afraid, Jack. We cannot die."

"LET ME GO!" I screamed.

"NO JACK. WE CANNOT DIE!"

Be that as it may, I did not want to test that theory
out. I tried to let go but she was the stronger bird. The
ground was coming up fast. I saw my life flash before
my eyes. We smashed head first into the ground.
Everything went dark. I didn't feel any pain and I knew
I was not dead. The worst thing that could have
happened is that my mental projection was destroyed and
I was instantly awoken back in my own body. I started
to move in the direction that I thought was upwards
toward the night light. I saw grass as I came floating up
from the damp earth.

Nikki had already emerged and was hoping
around on the ground. I could hear her laughing in my
head. "You are right Jack that was fun."

"We are not supposed to hit the ground goof.
You are SUPPOSED to let me go jerk." I was a little
pissed off.

"I know. I know. I am sorry. I was just having fun. Let's go back to our bodies." She said as she took off towards my apartment.

"Great let's go." I spread my wings and everything seemed alright. Nothing was broken like it would have been if I was in a physical form. It was magical. I took off behind Nikki. We arrived at my apartment. I flew back through the sliding glass door. There my body was sitting on the floor. I flew at my head. I saw my mental door I had created and I moved through it before waking up in my human form. I felt ok for now. My head wasn't exploding so that was a good thing. I slowly opened my eyes. Nikki was coming right at me with her arms out. She pushed me over on my back. She wrapped her arms around my head and pressed her lips to mine. It was full of passion. Her lips were warm and soft. She slowly put her tongue in my mouth and started to make a circular motion. I was lost in the moment.

She stopped kissing my lips for a moment and whispered to me in a seductive tone. "I am so sorry Jack. I didn't mean to upset you. We were not going to die. I hope you can forgive me." She said a she slowly kissed my neck.

"I can forgive you I guess. This feels good though. Don't stop." She kissed my neck for awhile. We kissed for a bit longer. We were getting sweaty. Things were getting heated. I didn't know if I should ask this but I did anyways. "Do you want to go back to the bedroom?" Before she could answer her phone started ringing.

"That's my mom's ringtone. I have to pick it up." She went over and picked up her phone. "Sure I will be over in a minute." And she hung up her phone. "My mom is locked out of the apartment and I have to go and let her in."

"That's cool." No it wasn't cool but what else could I say. "I really wish you could stay. Really, really want you to stay." I said holding her hand to not leave.

"I bet you don't want me to go. Well maybe we can pick this up another time." She said as we kissed some more.

"I can't wait." I walked her to the door. "Hopefully next time you don't try to scare the shit out of me twice."

"Yes Jack, I will try to not scare you. Maybe you need to man up and stop being such a pussy."

"You are so funny. I like that about you." I gave her another kiss and a hug. "Bye bye."

"Bye sexy." She said as she walked down the stairs.

Chapter 13

The mind of Nikki. Sunday June23.

It was nighttime. I was getting ready for bed. I did my usual routine. Brushed me teeth, used the toilet, put on pajamas, fixed my bed and then I prayed that I would live through the night. These last few months had been filled with terror every time I closed my eyes.

Earlier today I went on a secret mission to see where Max lived. I know Jack would not have approved of this so I went without him. No one happened to be home so I decided to take a look inside. Max ended up coming home and as far as I know I escaped unnoticed through the basement door. But somehow, I am sure he knew that I was there snooping around in his house. I had a feeling tonight was going to be unimaginably horrible.

Before everything with Ryan happened I had to take medicine to fall asleep but now I would try to do anything I could to not fall asleep. I knew no matter how hard I fought to stay awake I would eventually have to go to sleep whether it was tonight or two days later it always catches up to you. Always. So I just accepted my fate and closed my eyes. In a few minutes I was sleeping like a baby.

I was having the dream again. The same dream over and over. It was like my mind was playing a rerun over and over. I was walking up to Ryan's apartment. I knock on the door and there is no answer. I knock again. I knew he was home so I go for the door knob. It opens and I enter the apartment. "Hello. Anyone home?" I yelled down the hall. The apartment is dark and all the lights are off. I hear a mumbled sound coming from the bedroom. I slowly walk down the dark hallway to the bedroom. There is Ryan sprawled out on the bed with a syringe stuck in his arm. This is where the nightmare becomes different every time. I could feel a dark presence in the corner of the room. When this happened in real life I always thought something was there in the darkness watching me. Maybe things would of played out differently if it had not been there whispering to me. Ryan complained for a month or two about a demon that tormented him every night. I listened to his stories but I thought he was just full of shit. I thought it was a side effect from the drugs he was using. I didn't really believe in demons or magic until recently. This time the demon was there on one side of the bed and I was standing on the other side. Ryan lay mumbling in the middle of the bed. All of a sudden syringes appeared all around Ryan. The demon smiled at me. My hand reached down and picked one up. I already figured what was going to happen. I tried to resist but the demon controlled my hand now. I brought it down in Ryan's chest. I pushed the plunger all the way down. His body jerked a little. I started to cry. "I am so sorry Ryan." The demon laughed at me mockingly. My hand reached down and grabbed another syringe. "Nooo... Please.." My hand jabbed the syringe down into Ryan's neck. "Oh my God.. I am so sorry.." I managed to say through my tears. I tried to close my eyes to not have to see what I was involuntarily doing. My hand continued to grab syringes and stick them into Ryan for the next few hours.

In real life after I saw Ryan I slowly walked out of his apartment. In this case I was running. The demon was after me now. I ran terrified screaming out the door. I was in the breezeway now. I ran as fast as I could down the stairs. The demon followed me. He was covered in black liquid that seemed crawl with a mind of its own. The black creature was crawling on its front two arms. I leaped three steps at a time. The demon moved like a black liquid wave. Every time it got near me it would form a claw or arm and try to grab me and pull me into the darkness. As I ran across the wooden floor the beams started to fall apart and fall to the ground below. I was almost to the ground. I jumped and landed on the stairs. I was on the ground now. I looked up and there was my car sitting in the parking lot. Great if I run into my car and start it, I can get out of here faster. I ran as fast as I could. My legs were moving as fast as they could go. I reached my car. The door was unlocked and the keys were in the ignition. Awesome. I slammed the door and locked it. I am getting the fuck out of here. As soon as I turned the key, the car started to fill up quickly with blood. "Help! Oh God help me!" I yelled. I went for the door handle and it would not open. I then went for the windows and they would not roll down. I made a fist and pounded on the windows as hard as I could. "BREAK! DAMMIT!" I leaned back and put my foot on the glass. I started to kick with my heel hoping to shatter the window. Nothing happened. The blood started to fill the car. I moved my face towards the top in hopes of being able to breathe. In a few seconds I was engulfed in blood. Just as the blood got to the top of the car I took a deep breath. It became very dark and I could not see anything. I flailed my arms and kicked my legs but all of a sudden it did not feel like I was in the car anymore. It felt more like I was floating in a sea of darkness. I started to see a light form in the distance. It shined its rays right onto my face. It felt warm. I heard the demon's voice say "Wakey wakey." Then I suddenly awoke.

I shot straight up. My heart was beating fast. It felt like I was having a heart attack, except statistically I was too young to be having one. I lowered my head back down. The sun light shined through my window right onto my face. That must have been what I had seen in my dream that woke me up. Wow I actually slept through most of the night. That was first for me in a long time. Most of the time, I awake screaming like I am being murdered. I sat there with my eyes open for a few minutes. I was letting my body slowly wake up and turn back on. My alarm was about to go off in fourteen minutes. I sat there in bed just thinking about my day. I sure do miss Jack. He is a pretty good guy I thought to myself. I wonder what he is planning to do today after work. Probably play video games or something. I wonder if he thinks about me. My alarm suddenly went off. Time for school I thought to myself.

I jumped into the shower. I got dressed then ate breakfast. It was about time for me to go. I grabbed my books and headed out the door. There was my car sitting in the parking lot. It was just like my dream. I got out to my car. I just had a really eerie feeling that gave me chills. I decided to have a look around my car. I slowly walked around it inspecting the tires, the paint job, and the windows. Everything looked alright. It was just a weird spooky dream I thought to myself. I unlocked the door and sat in the seat. Everything looked ok in here as well. I put my key in the ignition and turned it. Everything started up ok. I turned on the radio and the air conditioner. I looked down and something seemed to be coming out of the ac vents. A few drops of something came out. I put my finger in the liquid. I quickly realized it was blood. "Ohhh." I looked at my hands and they were already covered in blood from the steering wheel. In the instant it felt like something wet was on my back and bottom. "Ewww." I screamed. It was as if I sat in a puddle of water. The whole back of my shirt and legs were covered with blood now. I didn't know what was going on but I had to go take another shower. I jumped out of the car. My arms and back were covered in blood.

I ran into my apartment. I ran to the bathroom sink and turned on the water. I turned to see what the back of me looked like. Then I saw that there were words written on my back.

"Stay the fuck out of my house bitch." it said.

It was a message from Max no doubt. I turned around and started to wash my hands off and then I noticed that the blood on my hands was now gone. What is going on? I turned around and the blood that was on my back was gone as well. The back of my shirt and pants felt dry. The blood stains were gone. All the areas that were covered in blood before were now clean as can be. I stood staring at myself in the mirror for a few minutes. "There is only one explanation. I must have gone mad. Or Max is really good…but actually, I think it is a little of both."

Chapter 14

The mind of Jack. Wednesday June 26.

Nikki was house sitting a friend's house for the week. The family had gone to Florida for the week and she got to watch the dog. I was going to stay over tonight. It was only ten minutes away. She gave me directions. I always had the internet on my phone to look up directions if I got lost. I drove through the subdivision and these were very upscale houses. All the houses looked like they were built in the last five years. From looking at the outside I could tell they were quite large. They were mostly two story houses. They had a lot of very large glass windows. It was getting dark outside. I could see the glow from the magnificent chandeliers from the street. The mail boxes were made out of bricks. These houses were amazing but they had one big flaw. Although these houses were nice looking I hated the fact that they had tiny back yards that backed up to one another. Who would want a house where your neighbor was only twenty feet away? It is even worse if they have dogs. Nothing like going outside and the neighbor's dogs bark at you nonstop. For all the glitz and glam I would not want to live here.

I slowly drove down the street looking for the address. This is the one. I saw Nikki's car in the drive way. I got out of my car and walked to the door.

I rang the door bell. I hope this is not a prank Nikki is playing on me. I patiently waited a minute and the door opened. "Jack I missed you." She said as she hugged me. "Hello. How are you doing?" I said.

"I am doing great now that you are here. Come on in. Let me show you the tour. I have to warn you the dog may jump on you but you just have to push him off and say NO." She said.

"That's no problem. Wouldn't be the first time I had to push a dog away." I said.

She nudged me. "Sorry about my dog attacking you. So this is the walk in area. Over to the left is the dining room. Over here is the kitchen. This is the living room."

I walked into the living room and it had twenty foot high vaulted ceilings with a large chandelier hanging in the middle. I looked up in amazement. The floor was a dark hard wood. "Nice."

"Over here is the bathroom and the master bedroom."

The master bedroom was large but not as impressive as the bathroom. The bathroom had a large tub with multiple jets. It looked like you could fit six people in there comfortably. "Wow look at this tub. We could have a lot of fun in there."

"You are such a pervert. No we are not going to do anything in their tub. Now the shower maybe."

I looked at the shower. It had glass walls. It looked like it was made for two people to shower at the same time. It had jets on both sides of the shower. It also had other spray controls on the sides. "This is one futuristic looking shower. Show me the rest of the house."

We went up some stairs and three bedrooms were up stairs. One was turned into a computer office. The other two looked like children's rooms. One was baseball themed. It had a lot of baseball items in it. The other room looked like a girl's room. It was pink and princess looking.

"Let me show you the basement?" She said.

"After you."

We went into the basement and it was like my dream come true. I swear I heard a choir of angels singing. My eyes went back and forth trying to take everything in. This was the perfect place for me. It had a large couch with a giant large screen television on the wall. A pool table. Darts. Ping Pong. A kick ass stereo system. All the new video game systems. A fully stocked bar. There was an old stand up arcade game in the corner and a pin ball machine. "I love this place. I never want to leave."

"All right you can stop drooling. Let's go make something to eat and focus on our plan for tonight. Remember why we are here. I need you to be ready for tonight and not distracted. I don't know what can happen tonight."

My stomach was growling and dinner sounded good. "What do you want to eat for dinner?" She said.

"What are my options?"

"Well let's go have a look shall we." The freezer was completely stocked. She named off a few things. I saw a pizza that looked tasty. "Pizza sounds great. Does this place have a pizza oven?" I said jokingly. She shook her head no. We grabbed it and went upstairs.

She went to preheat the oven. We sat down at the dining table. It was made to easily fit six people.

The lights were dim. I sat quietly looking into Nikki's eyes. We both sat there looking at each other. It was eerily quiet. I decided to break the silence. "So we are really going to do this tonight?"

"Yes." She said

"We are really going to try to become ghost to catch a ghost?"

"Yes." She said. There was a pause then she said "That is basically the plan. When we do this we are not really ghost. Ghost are like earth bound disembodied spirits. They usually are bound to a house and they don't know that they died. What we are doing is a psychic ability. It is totally different."

"You know what I mean. If you want me to be more specific I can use the term mind projection. I prefer the term ghost but I can use MP for mind projection."

"Yes MP is fine. So the plan is for us to go unconscious. Then while we are separated from our bodies we are going to go near my apartment and wait to see if Max shows up. We will have to be far enough away that he won't feel our presence. After he sees that my body is not there he will leave and go somewhere. We will follow him. We will not want to get that close. "

"What do you think will happen if he catches us?" I asked.

"That's easy. We fight." She said.

"Really you want to fight. Have you gone mad? This guy is way more experienced than us. If we fight him and lose what do you think happens?"

"I don't know." Nikki said.

"One theory I have is that we might not be able to go back to our bodies. Or maybe we get back and have severe mental damage." I said.

"Listen to me. That is a risk I am willing to take. He invades my mind every night. He takes my worst fears and uses them against me. It seems so real that it feels like I am there. I wake up in my bed screaming. You can't even begin to imagine the horrors I had to endure. So yes I want to make it stop any way I can. I need to make it STOP!" I could see her eyes getting watery.

"Ok, I understand but I think we should focus more on running or hiding but definitely more on running away." I said.

"Fine. Tonight we run if things go bad. Just until we know more." She said.

"Sounds good." I said.

Beep. Beep. "Pizza's done." It smelled good. I opened the oven. The melted cheese and pepperoni looked tasty. We ate in silence. "You want to turn on the radio or television?" I said.

"No not really."

"Are you feeling nervous?" I said.

"I am feeling more excited than nervous." She said.

"We agreed no confrontation. We will just follow tonight got that."

"Yes."

"For real?"

"Yes for real. I will not try anything." She looked me in the eyes as she said it. We paused for a few seconds looking in each other's eyes. I still didn't believe her. I could feel a knot forming in the pit of my stomach.

"So when do you think we should start?" I said.

"We probably want to lay down by ten so we can get there before him and wait." She said.

"What do you want to do before then?" I said.

"I want you to hold me tight on the couch." She said.

"Sure baby. Anything you want."

A few hours had past. I looked at the clock. It was about ten. "Hey it's about ten." I said.

"Alright I am going to take my sleeping pill. Then I am going to set my alarm for 3:00 AM. So we only got till then. When the alarm goes off we will be drawn back here."

"Alright. Want to meet on the roof here after we fall asleep?"

"Sure that's cool." I said.

Nikki took her sleeping pill. "See you in a little bit." She leaned over and kissed me. In a few minutes she was asleep. I was having trouble falling asleep. I was feeling anxious and stressed about what could happen tonight. I rolled over and watched Nikki. I watched her breathing in and out. I think I am falling for this girl. I sure hope we make it out ok because this is the girl I think I want to spend the rest of my life with. I did not want to get into a fight tonight but for this girl I would be willing to do anything. I think that is what being in love is all about. My eyelids slowly closed and I was out.

In what seemed like a few minutes later I was floating above my body. I floated through the ceiling to the rooftop.

"Geez what took you so long? It has been over an hour." I felt Nikki say.

When I looked at Nikki, her silhouette of her body was there. It had a faint pink outline. In the middle there was a glowing orb of pink light. When she communicated the pink light in the middle flickered. When she talked I felt her words in my mind. When we were out of our bodies we became glowing orbs of conscious.

I was not sure what I looked like, but I am sure I was similar. I was a glowing ball of blue light that flickered. It was certainly an interesting feeling.

"Are you ready?" She said.

"Yeah let's go." I said.

We started to float above the rooftops. I let her lead the way. It felt like I was a bird. I felt the wind blowing through my soul. I always wondered if people that were awake would see two glowing orbs in the sky. I guess not. I think I would have noticed this before when I was in human form.

I looked down as we flew. Even though we could fly in a straight line to the apartments it gets confusing looking at trees and rooftops so we followed the road. I moved up and down in the winds. I saw the apartment building coming up. We flew to the rooftop that was adjacent to Nikki's apartment section. We moved to the back side of the roof where we would be able to see her apartment but he wouldn't be able to see us if he came up the walk way.

"So what now?" I said.

174

"We wait. When he shows up he will probably go through the window or the front door." She said.

"That's kind of funny since we can go straight through walls." I said chuckling.

"Yeah but old habits die hard." She said.

"Want me to be the look out on the front side and you stay on the backside?"

"Sure just be sure to come get me." She said.

So we waited. I watched cars drive up and down the street. After an hour I floated back to check on Nikki.

"Still nothing." She said.

"Wait a second. I spoke to soon." We carefully watched as a dark creature suddenly materialized and floated up the walkway.

Its head was bent forward and it slowly crept down the sidewalk. I could barely sense it. This was nothing I have seen or felt before. This had to be what we were looking for. It was certainly a mental projection like us. I noticed it had a faint blue glow around its head and eyes. It appeared as a hooded robed figure. The hood it wore was torn and frayed. Its robe was ancient and black as charcoal. When the breeze blew, strips of fabric would flap in the wind. Even at our vantage point we could tell it clearly had large skeletal looking hands. The fingers were unusually long and ended in long sharp fingernails. It looked like death himself. This thing was hard to spot because it radiated darkness. When it crossed a shadow it became one with it and it would seem to fade out of existence. I could only see the eyes which had a slight blue glow to them.

We watched as it slowly floated toward Nikki's room. It looked around. The head turned back and forth.

It glanced towards us. It stared in our direction for a minute. We both moved back a little. We are spotted I thought. Then it slowly turned its head back and continued moving. There were lights in the courtyards and in the breezeways. This thing seemed like it did not want to go into the direct light. It crept along the building where the shadows were darkest. When direct light crossed its path it would follow the border until it came to a dark area.

It was now by Nikki's window. "Good thing I left my window curtains open so we can see what is going on in there." I felt her say. I watched the creature put its blackened hand on the top of window frame and step right through the window. We watched as one hand gripped the top of her comforter and yanked it down. It flung the blankets off her bed. It took her pillow and threw it on the ground. Its face turned quickly back and forth. It started to move quickly around the room. I guess it was looking for Nikki's body. It peeked into the closet and looked under the bed. Its hands clutched the sheets. It must be agitated I thought. Its head shot up quickly. Then it went through her door and down the hall.

"So help me God it better not hurt my parents." Nikki said as her light flickered a darker red.

"Wait a few minutes and we will go see what is going on if he doesn't come out. Don't dart out there yet." I said to try to calm her.

After a few minutes the creature came crawling out the window. It was moving fast now. It darted off to the left. Before it seemed to have a humanoid form but now it looked less solid then before. Lines of shadowy clouds were moving around its blackened core. The aura around it was pulsating more now. It appeared to be agitated.

It moved down the walkway and stopped at the next section which happened to be where my apartment was. It started to climb upwards. It reached its long bony arms up and jumped.

"Oh shit. I bet you it is going to my apartment." I said quietly.

It half floated half climbed up three floors to the balcony of my apartment.

"If it is Max he should not be able to get in since you never invited him into your apartment." Nikki said.

The creature stood on the balcony then it walked through the glass and into my apartment.

"Umm about that. I let Max in to drop off my dryer when I first moved in. I was sure to say that he is not invited to come in when he was leaving. So maybe this is not Max or maybe that is just for vampires and Max is not a vampire or maybe that is just an old legend." I said.

"Yes, you are probably right. He probably can just go wherever he wants." She said.

I lived on the top floor so I never closed my curtains because no one can see in. We watched as the creature moved down the hallway. It went into my room. The creature pulled down the blankets on my bed and shook its head. It tossed my pillows around. It then walked down the hallway and out onto the balcony. I watched his skeletal hands grip the arm rail of the balcony. He looked up at the sky and I heard a deep loud howl that shook me to my core. Then he shot into the sky like a bullet flying quickly towards the North.

"He is getting away. Are we going to foll..o..w?" I said.

177

I turned to look at Nikki and she was gone just as quickly. All I saw was a flash of glimmering pink light. Guess we are going to follow him. "Dammit wait up!"

I started to go after her. I just followed her pink glowing streak. We were flying fast. Faster than I have ever moved before. The landscape was moving so fast underneath us. The trees were starting to look different. We ended up flying by the river. The river was black as the night. I was fascinated be the light of the moon reflecting off the water. She started to slow up.

The creature was starting to slow up as he approached what happened to be a mansion that sat on top of the rocky bluffs that overlooked the river. There was a large beautiful house that overlooked the river. Nikki stopped. The creature flew over the amazing pool and then went through the back glass door.

I finally caught up. "Hey speedy what's the plan now? Do you want to follow him in?"

"We might as well. We have come this far." She said.

"Really you want to go in? What if he sees us?"

"I am not letting him get away." She said.

"You want to go into the lair of the beast. Listen to me. I think this is a really bad idea." I said.

"Stop being such a coward." She said.

"Ok. Fine, let's go in from the window on the second floor. If things go bad lets run ok."

"Ok we will run."She said.

We floated up to the second floor window and entered. The room we entered was a bedroom. The bed was empty. The walls were covered in tan pattern wall paper. The room had large wooden furniture in it. We looked out the hallway. The coast was clear. The hallway had rows and rows of family pictures on the wall. There were a lot of grade school pictures of two kids. We went farther down the hallway and there were some paintings hanging in the hallway. They just looked like abstract flowers.

We moved on down the hall. Nikki glanced down the stairs. Looks clear. We went down the stairs. It opened into the large living room area. The floor was wooden. This room had vaulted ceilings. There was a large flat screen television and a very large leather couch in this room. I also noticed there was a door open by the kitchen that probably led into the basement.

All of a sudden I heard a television or music coming from the basement. "Do you hear that?" I whispered.

"It is coming from the basement. Do you want to check it out?" She said.

If I was physically here I think my stomach would have been so stressed out I would have thrown up by now. "Fuck no I don't want to go in the basement. If that creature is in this house that's where it probably went."

"Let's just go have a peek and then we will jet." She said.

"Geez. I really don't ...wa....nt.." She was already crossing the floor. "Wait! Come back!" I tried to say without yelling loudly. I am really going to have to talk to her about charging ahead like that.

She was at the top of the stairs. I was right behind her. We slowly descended the stairs. It was dark down there. I saw the flickering of light against the wall so I assumed a television was on. The stair way ended in a wall and you had to go left or right. The light flickering was mostly coming from the right side. The floor down here was carpeted as far as I could tell. This was probably another family area or work out area. She grabbed my arm. "Be ready to run for it. I am going to look around the corner." She whispered as quiet as she could. I shook my head. God dammit. I moved toward the left side so I could look around the corner as well. I looked at Nikki as she slowly edged her face around the right side. I slowly moved my head far enough out so I could see.

About twenty feet away there was an elderly woman in pajamas sleeping on a couch and the creature was standing right by her. His back was facing us. He raised his hands and traced intricate patterns in the air. What is he doing I thought to myself. He reached down and placed a hand on her cheek. It was a gentle caress. I saw the aura of her life force go from a shimmering ocean blue to almost nothing. I don't think she woke up but her face contorted in pain. Her mouth opened. Instantly I thought more wrinkles appeared on her face. Her eyes looked like they sunk in. She appeared ten years older in a matter of seconds. It was one of the most horrifying things I had ever seen. I watched in awe as he was draining her soul.

Whatever he was doing it was having an effect on me. It felt like part of me was being pulled in as well. I felt my aura starting to be drawn toward the creature's mouth. I was getting ready to run for it before this thing ate my soul. Then I saw Nikki dash forward. The creature looked to be in some kind of a trance and it was too busy to see her coming. She wrapped her left arm around the creature's neck. "Sweet dreams evil prince." She said. Her right arm she bent back like a spear and with all her might she jammed it through the creature's torso where its heart would have been. Pink sparks exploded from the center of its chest. The creature wailed in pain. It looked like it was on fire as pink lightning danced across his body. I felt its screams reverberate within my soul. The illusion of the dark creature dissipated. The thing had taken too much damage to keep up its outer shell of the illusion. In its place was a glowing black orb that was radiating darkness. The creature was bleeding black smoke. It moved unnaturally around the room. It was like black liquid water floating in the air and it was blinking in and out of existence. The room started to fill with smoke to the point we could not see.

"Did I kill it?" Nikki said.

"Come on let's get out of here. NOW!" I yelled.

I grabbed her arm and we started up the stairs. The smoke was so thick I could not see what was going on. It happened so fast. Out of the smoke a giant mouth of pure darkness engulfed Nikki. Nikki's outer illusion of her human form collapsed. The pink orb that was her was surrounded by watery darkness. There was nothing I could do to save her.

Chapter 15

The mind of Nikki. Wednesday June 26.

Where am I? Am I even alive? I was lying on a sandy beach. I sat up and looked around. "Hello anyone here?" I yelled. Nothing. The sky was grey like a storm was going on in the distance. I was definitely on an island because I could see both sides. There was a small boat on the shore. This had to be some sort of trick. I sat down in the middle of the island and tried to remember how I got here. All I could recall was stabbing the monster in the back and then we started to go towards the stairs and then everything went black. I tried to separate from my mental projection and return to my human body that was sleeping safely back at the house. As much as I tried I could not release. "This isn't good." I sat on the beach and contemplated my situation. After what seemed to be an hour I decided to get in the boat. I started to push it into the water and I jumped aboard. It had a paddle so I paddled away from the little island. I know this sounded funny but I could swear I hear a soft music playing in the distance. Maybe it was just the sound of the wind playing tricks on me. I decided to paddle in the direction of the sound. After a few strokes I floated so far out I could not even see the island. I could not see anything else except water and sky. The music was sounding a bit louder now. "I don't know what this is but I DEMAND TO BE FREED!" I yelled to the grey clouds in the sky. All of a sudden I heard thunder in the distance. Well at least that's some kind of response. I sat there just floating. Everything went silent.

I watched the water as it started to turn black. "That's not good." I grabbed my paddle tightly and held it high. I was ready to hit something. Everything got really quiet. There were no waves on the water. It was just like I was floating on a smooth obsidian glass surface. "WHAT NOW? WHAT ARE YOU GOING TO DO TO ME?" I yelled.

I held the oar tight like a baseball player up at bat. I swung hard at the watery darkness. Thick black tendrils wrapped around the oar and yanked it out of my hand. Instantly the dark water shot up around the boat in all directions. On all sides the water was about twenty feet above the boat. The water was flowing upwards and formed a dome around me. "Oh no." Like a giant fist it came crashing down on the boat. The boat shattered instantly. I was drowning in the black water. Tendrils of shadows encircled me pulling me down. I frantically flailed my hands around. This is it I thought. I could no longer see the sky. The darkness was closing in on me. "Jack Please Help Me!" I screamed as loud as I could. I reached my arm out as far as I could. I was swallowed. I was starting to black out. In a moment of overwhelming terror I was drowned by shadow.

Chapter 16

The mind of Jack. Wednesday June 26.

I stood there and watched as Nikki was engulfed.
I still saw her pink orb still glimmering in the darkness.
Maybe she is not done for yet. I ran toward the darkness
and plunged my hand in. It felt quite cold and chilled me
to my core. I grabbed what I thought was her arm and
pulled as hard as I could. Her body came free. I held
onto what I thought was her. I grew concerned because
her once bright aura was only a small shimmer of light.
We flew up the stairs and out the door as fast as I could
go.

I held Nikki's limp body as I flew as fast as I
could away from the house. I followed the river. I
looked back and saw smoke engulfing the house. I don't
think it was real. It was all just part of the creature's
mental illusion.

I flew us down the river as fast as I could go. I had to put
some distance between us and the house on the bluff.

"Come on Nikki wake up! Wake up! Nikki, are
you still there? Nikki, please wake up. Please wake up."
I was frantic now. There was no response at first but
then her aura started to glow brighter again. I looked

184

back in the distance. At the house there was something large crawling to the top of the house. It was made out of complete darkness except for the teeth that were the color of the moon. I started flying faster. Hopefully it won't follow.

"What? What happened to me?" She said as she started to come back to life.

"I watched you get engulfed and then I went back and saved you. We can talk later. Right now we really need to connect back to our bodies. Are you ok enough to fly back to the house?" I said.

"Yeah I think so. Just follow me." She said as she took the lead.

"I want to get out of here before the guy at the house follows us."

"Let's jet." She said.

We went back to the house. It was a quick flight. I flew through the window and saw my body laying there unharmed. I entered my body and took the steering wheel once again. Home sweet home I thought. I woke up instantly. My first thought was that it was all just a weird dream but I knew better. Nikki did the same. She woke up instantly.

"Are you ok? I saw you get swallowed."I said. She ran over to me. Her eyes were starting to tear up. I put my arms around her. She started crying. Tears were running down her face. She put her arms around me. She placed her head against my chest. I held her tight as she sobbed. I rubbed her back and tried to comfort her. After a few minutes she seemed to be calmer.

"It's just that everything happened so fast. I thought I was going to die. I was hoping if I died at least you would make it out. I thought that you probably died and it was my fault for making you go with me into that house."

We pressed our bodies together. I held her tight. "Hey girl, everything is ok. It all worked out fine. I am alive and well and so are you." She stopped crying.

"I am just glad you are ok." She said.

"You have a pretty good sense of direction. All those tree tops and buildings look the same to me from an aerial view." I said.

"Thanks." She said.

She seemed really out of it. Maybe it was the sleeping pill. "So how do you feel?" I said.

"I feel really weak. I think he damaged my energy aura. He did something to me. It feels like he drained part of my soul. I think he tried to do to me what he did to that lady."

"So what happened when you were engulfed? I couldn't see what happened. You were standing by me then next thing I know you were swallowed by a wall of shadow." I said.

"This is where it gets really weird. When all that happened I woke up on an island in the middle of the day. I know it sounds funny. I was on a small island surrounded by water and there was a small canoe. I tried to wake up and return to my body but I couldn't. It felt like I was there for a few hours. The water started to rise so I jumped into this canoe. I started to paddle until I no longer saw the island. Then I was surrounded by dark water and it engulfed me. I don't know what happened after that. Next thing I know you are carrying me and we are flying away from that house."

"Wow. Hmmm. So do you think you were imprisoned in his mind?" I said.

"Maybe. I am not sure. It's possible I guess. What drives me crazy is that I could not wake up. All my powers were gone. It felt like I was a real person and not a projection. I could not fly. There was no escape."

"After you were swallowed I could partially see your pink glow coming from the center of that thing. I went back and shoved my arm into the center of the black mass. It felt chillingly cold. I grabbed your arm and pulled you out." I said.

"Thanks for coming back for me. I don't know what would have happened to my human body if you didn't. "

"Hey it's no problem. I am sure you would have done the same." I said.

"So do you think he is going to come after us tonight?" She said.

I was out of the bed staring out the window at the sky. I wondered if he followed us. "No. I highly doubt it. He doesn't know where we are at. So we can sleep well tonight. When we have to sleep back in our own apartment is when we might be in trouble." I said.

"All of this has actually worn me out. I know we were technically asleep but our minds were still working and now I feel exhausted. Come back to bed and hold me."

I turned off the alarm clock that I had set earlier for three. I went back to the bed and lay down. She put her head on my chest. I listened to her breathe for awhile. "Thanks. I am glad I can trust you." She said. I rubbed her back as she laid there. I could hear her starting to snore. She was out.

"Sweet dreams." I said as I fell into a deep sleep too. I had some weird dreams that night. I was being

187

chased by a large black dog and I had to fly like the wind to escape.

Chapter 17

The mind of Nikki. Thursday June 27.

I heard my alarm go off. I had to get ready for work. I was exhausted from staying up late the last few nights. Oh who am I kidding, I have been staying up late for the last six months. It felt like it was starting to take a toll on my body. I had to literally roll out of bed or I was not going to get out of it. I walked to the bathroom and looked in to the mirror. I had deep black circles under my eyes. My eyes look like they were blood shot. My hair was wild looking like I just got out of a wind tunnel. I used to get compliments on my hair all the time. I use to take better care of my hair when I had the energy. Now I am just exhausted. I turned on the shower. I slowly stepped in. The warm water woke me up a little. I picked up my shampoo to wash my hair. The bottle felt like it was a hundred pounds. I squirted some shampoo into my hand and washed my hair. I finished my showering routine and got dressed. This was another area in my life that I was no longer excelling at. Now I pretty much just throw on a sweatshirt with a team logo on it. I put on my ugly jeans and I put my hair in a pony tail and I leave.

I grabbed some breakfast and I was out the door. I walked over to my car and threw my books in. I started my car and drove off. I wondered if Jack ever gets mad about me leaving him in the middle of the night? I usually stay until about two in the morning. It seems like if I fall asleep in my bed, the nightmares are horrible and I cannot awake from them. If I sleep somewhere else until at least two in the morning and then I come home and fall asleep in my own bed I don't have nightmares that night for some reason. Or If I sleep somewhere else that night I usually sleep pretty well. Anyways, Jack starts snoring about that time really loudly. I am sure his neighbors can hear him from down the hall. It is loud. It sounds like he is choking sometimes and I am not sure if I should wake him up or not. I try to shove him but he usually does not wake up. That is usually my cue to leave. I usually slowly lift his arm off me. I try not to laugh but it always makes me giggle. Then I grab my shoes and slowly walk out the door. Jack, I have to say, is pretty patient and understanding with me. Most guys would be trying to seduce me or take my clothes off if I slept over this many times. Maybe I will let go a little. If this was baseball, maybe I would let him get to second base. Well, he did save my life. Maybe I will let him hit a home run.

I was about half way to work now. I started to think about everything that happened last night. I replayed the battle over and over in my head. It all happened so fast. We followed Max. I stabbed him. We fought. He tried to eat me. That was the weirdest part. I don't know if I was placed somewhere in his mind or if I was trapped somewhere in my own mind. Then I was swallowed by black water. I don't know how he did that. I contemplated about it for awhile. I could not reach a conclusion. Maybe Jack would let me practice on him later. He can be my guinea pig.

I then started to think about how Max was probably going to come after us. In my case he would probably kill me. I always had a feeling that he is the one causing my bad dreams every night. When I started to think about it, the feeling I get when I see Max during the day is exactly the same feeling I have at night. When I go further back, it is the same feeling I felt when I was in Ryan's room the night he died. I just feel so frightened every time. Before everything happened a few months ago it was never like that when I was asleep. I might have a scary dream every now and then but that was it. They were far apart. Now, after I make it through the night and I wake up, I have to grab my comforter and go crawl in the corner. I usually sit in the corner and rock back and forth telling myself it was only a bad dream.

Then I had an idea. A light bulb went off in my head. Well it might not be the greatest idea. Jack might be willing to help me though. Since I knew where Max lived now. I think it is time for us to launch an attack against him. I want him to be afraid of the dark for once. I thought about it more. Jack and I could wait till he fell asleep then enter his mind and challenge him there. I knew it was somewhat dangerous to try this. Maybe we would be able to change things in his head so that he would not want to bother me anymore. The choice to do nothing did not sound appealing to me. Jack and I were able to challenge him last night on common ground. I actually thought we might win until he did things that I have never seen before. I didn't know you can trap people. That was not on any training video or book I have ever read.

Yes, I was going to ask Jack to help me. I decided that we are no longer going to be victims. We are going to hunt Max. I was hoping he would still be wounded and not fully recovered from last night's events. I know I was slightly weakened. But, I am assuming that Max had to be hurting as well.   People don't get skewered and walk away like they are fine the next day.

Chapter 18

The mind of Max. Thursday June 27.

I was weakened from the battle. They are getting quite powerful I thought to myself. Too powerful for me to keep them under control. I have to be extremely cautious now since they saw that I can be harmed. I am going to have to attack them before they decide to attack me. I am going to have to kill Nikki. I read her thoughts and she wants what all people want, to become all powerful. I have to stop her before she hurts herself or others. But most importantly, I have to remain in control. I wish she didn't bring Jack into this. I think he is being dragged down the path she has set out for them whether he knows it or not. He probably believes that he is in love. He wouldn't be if he knew the truth.

I needed to feed. I was still in pain after the battle. She snuck up on me while I was feeding and psychic mind lanced me. Who stabs someone in the back when they are trying to feed anyways? I know she just attacked my projection but I still felt it in my mortal body. My head felt like holes were drilled into my mind. As far as I know, I was not physically hurt but I was experiencing painful sensation in my chest area where she hit me. My vision felt disrupted as well. I was seeing multiple halos of color. I urgently need to find someone to feed off of tonight or sooner I thought to myself as I hobbled down the street.

Then I felt it. A new presence has made its' way onto the property. I have not felt this one in awhile but I knew who it was as soon as they pulled in. She has dark thoughts that I recognized as soon as I sensed them. Her head was full of deceit and treachery which is something that I highly favored when choosing who I want to eat. There was nothing I liked better. I had no qualms about hurting people that I felt deserved it.

She was getting closer to me I could feel it. My mouth was starting to water. It could be none other than the one and only Courtney Farkill, the property manager. I knew she was pulling up behind me in her red sports car. I fake smiled and waved as she drove by. Fucking bitch I thought to myself. This lady was only about helping herself. She made it perfectly clear she did not care about any of us. She was as fake as her fake nails and the fake extensions in her fake bleached blonde hair.

I had reported to her months ago about the drug problem here. Stan, the boss, was growing a forest of marijuana in a vacant apartment. His step brother was smoking crack in the break room and nothing was done about it. The other maintenance guy, Bradon, would go into apartments and take pictures of ladies underwear and sex toys and post them online. I told Courtney all this but she didn't want to do anything about it.

With a little luck and trickery I was able to "intervene" and get Bradon fired. I had to help Bradon in an apartment and when he wasn't looking I turned on the computer webcam. I knew he was going to do something questionable. I hoped that the resident would see what was recorded and turn him in. Sure enough he went into her dresser and pulled out the largest thongs I have ever seen and then he started taking pictures of them on the bed. When the resident came home she was furious. She called the head office and they finally fired Bradon. One down, two more to go.

All this bitterness I was feeling was fueling my rage. I was starting to feel the rage and hate again. The darkness was starting to take control of me. My rational side was fading. I was also starting to get really hungry. It was not the kind of hunger that required food as nourishment. I needed to feed off of someone. Must feed! As much as I didn't want to admit it I knew that I was becoming some kind of monster. My body was starting to crave something in humans that no amount of food can ever equal. Life energy or souls, whatever you wanted to call it, is exactly what I needed. Real food was starting to make me nauseous whenever I ate anything. No matter what I ate it tasted like ashes in my mouth. Courtney was becoming increasingly tastier to me by the second. I knew she was at the front office right now. I tried to fight the urge to go up there but it was calling me. Her dark thoughts were calling me. I must drain her. There can be no other way. I can't let her escape me. I walked like a zombie strolling forward to the office. "She will feed me. It will make me feel better. If I drain her the pain will go away." I kept telling myself.

I lumbered down the street to the office. Stealthily, I walked up on the side so they could not see me from the office windows. There was Courtney's red car. I knew the other two office people were in there as well because their cars were parked outside. One woman in there was a leasing agent, who I didn't really know that well. She was new and I think I have only attempted to talk to her maybe four times. The other person was the office manager Janice. I have taken control of her mind so many times she was practically my puppet. I think too many late night parties, booze, and drugs have weakened her. It didn't take much to take control of her.

I knew they were probably in her office with the door shut. I walked to the back corner of the building where Janice's office was located. Some large bushes blocked off the side of the building. There were overgrown plants back here and leaves so if anyone saw me back here I would just say I was cleaning up leaves. I put my ear to the wall to try to hear what was being said inside. The walls are pretty thin and they talk loud especially when Courtney is screaming at Janice at the top of her lungs. I listened quietly. They were just talking about budget and things like that. That's a change no screaming? I started to use the sight to see in the office. Courtney was sitting in Janice's chair looking at the computer. Janice was sitting on the other side of the desk looking at the computer screen. This was as close as I could get to Courtney without her knowing. She was right on the other side of this wall. I was not sure how well this was going to work. I have only done this by touching the victim. She was about three feet away from me. I was ever so thirsty now. My heart beat rapidly with excited anticipation. I just wanted the pain to go away. My fangs started to extend. "I am going to drain you dry you fucking false leader." I put my hand on the wall and started to pull life from Courtney's immortal soul.

It was later in the day. I was trimming some weeds and I saw Jim walking down the street with a dryer. "Hey tons of fun." I said.

"Hey turd bucket. I need your help to switch out a dryer. You can leave your stuff here." He said.

"Sure." I dropped my tools and followed him.

"Hey did you hear what happened in the office?" Jim said.

"No. What?" I said. Pretending to not know. But, I knew exactly what happened.

"I talked to Janice and she said Courtney was in the office sitting in Janice's chair and all of a sudden she could not breathe. Her eyes started to blink like crazy and her skin started to turn a grey color. She started to tremble like crazy. Janice thought that Courtney was having a stroke so she called an ambulance. She moved Courtney to the floor so when she was jerking around she didn't crash into things and further hurt herself. The ambulance showed up after five minutes. When they walked in Courtney sat up and said she was fine. She had no clue that any of that even happened. All she remembered was going over some computer stuff with Janice and then waking up on the floor. You know what is weird is that she did say that she had an odd feeling that you were in the office standing right by them. Janice told her that no one else was in the office except the new girl."

"Really? That is pretty crazy. So Courtney had a stroke huh?"

"That's what they are thinking. They said right when they could hear the ambulance pulling into the property she sat up like nothing had happened. She was totally her normal self after that. She wanted to go back to working on their computer project. Janice insisted that she goes to the hospital to get a scan or something. She kept telling her what happened and that she needs to go get checked out. So she gave in and got into the ambulance. Janice went with her. I guess she is getting her brain scanned right now." Jim said.

"They won't find anything in her head." We started laughing.

"That is horrible if she had a stroke. Well looks like she won't be coming to the apartments to check on us for awhile." Jim said.

"So where is this going?" I said while pointing at the dryer.

"5032 H." He said.

"I can't remember who lives there but we are going to find out." I said.

Jim and I were walking down the street. Trent was walking quickly in our direction. He is one of the maintenance prep workers. He fixes up the apartments before the residents move in. Sometimes he is ok to talk to, other times he is a dick. His white shirt was covered with blood. Deep red fluid was dripping from his hand forming small puddles on the ground.

"Hey you bastards. Do you know where the first aid kit is or some duct tape? It is kind of urgent." He said.

"Bastards huh. That's not nice to say to people that you need help from. Try again." I said.

"Sorry I am freaking out. I really need some assistance. I am bleeding to death."

"Ok. There is a first aid kit in the shop but it is probably mostly empty since it never has been restocked. Duct tape is on the self by the sign in sheet."

"Hey buddy what happened? It looks like you butchered a cow." Jim said.

"Or a human." I said under my breath.

"No, I was using a utility knife and sliced my finger open." He lifted his left hand towards us. He showed us his finger, as he did blood spurted out from the wound.

"Oh my god! That's your bone." I said. Jim and I examined it more closely and it did appear to be his finger bone.

"Man you better go to the doctor or a med stop. That is a deep cut." Jim said

"I can't go to the doctor because they will drug test me and I will not pass unless you can find me some drug free urine." He said. They both shot me a glance. I just shook my head no.

I could have offered to help him but we have had too many conflicts in the past for me to care what happens to him. "Maybe you shouldn't smoke so much weed. You are probably high right now." I said in a condescending tone as I shook my head.

"So what if I am. Maybe you should shut your mouth or I can do that for you." Trent said in an angry tone.

"What do you have to offer me if I help you? Do you have any money or anything of …worth?" I said.

He pulled out his wallet and looked inside. He had a five dollar bill. "I have five dollars for you if you help me." He said.

"Pfft. Five dollars. Surely you can do better than that." I said. Thick blood was still pouring out from his finger. His situation was getting worse by the second.

"Alright. Alright what do you want?" He said more desperately.

"You can keep you money but I want… your SOUL." I said in an evil voice.

He laughed. "My soul? Fine. Whatever. You can have that. I am already going to hell. Right now, I really need to keep my job and my finger."

"Great. So we have a deal. Your soul for a cup of urine." I said.

"Yes, go now and pee in a cup for me. I am feeling a bit light headed." He said.

We walked towards our shop bathroom. Trading a cup of urine for an immortal soul is an all time first for me. That is about 2,138 souls I have attained either by force or deal making. It sure is getting easier and easier. I don't even have to try hard anymore. I thank God for the steady decline of human morals.

"Good luck with that." Jim yelled.

"I will catch up with you in a few minutes. Be right back." I said as I walked toward the shop.

Five minutes later I caught up with Jim. After walking down the street a ways we came to the breezeway. Then we had to lug the dryer up a flight of stairs to the second floor. "Ok here we are." I started to knock on the door. Bam. Bam. Bam.

"Hold on I am coming." I heard a woman yell from inside. We waited patiently for the door to open. "Should we knock again?" I said to Jim as the door flung open to our surprise. There was a woman standing there. She had just got out of the shower. She had long wet black hair that hung down. All she had on was a towel that she kept adjusting over her wet body. I was trying to be a gentleman but every time she moved to readjust her towel I saw her lady parts. I looked away but I noticed Jim was looking right at her.

"Hi. You guys are here to drop off my dryer? I just got out of the shower. Give me a minute to put on some clothes."

"Sure take your time." Jim said mesmerized. I nudged Jim with my elbow right after the door shut. "Every time I come over this lady is always getting out of the shower. What is up with that? Hey did you see her towel move. I saw everything below her waistline. I think this lady is married to a trucker and he is always gone. So she is probably extremely horny all the time." Said Jim.

"I know you saw. At least I made an attempt to look away. You just kept making direct eye contact with her vagina. For some reason, I think her face looks familiar but I can't remember where I have seen it before?" I said. Maybe I have seen her before walking around the property or something.

The woman came back with clothes on this time. I could tell that she did not have on a bra though. "Come on in. I am ready for you strong men to come and take it from me." She put her hand on Jims arm as we walked in. I looked at Jim and he shot me a weird look. I could tell this lady liked Jim. We walked down the hallway to the utility closet. Jim grabbed the dryer and heaved it effortlessly off the wall. I grabbed the other side and we walked it down the hallway and out the door. The woman grabbed the door for us. We set it down and grabbed the newer dryer and carried it down the hall. Jim started to put the dryer in place then I heard the front door slam. I turned around and it was one of the teenagers that constantly followed me around the property.

I can't lie. I drained her friend till she rotted away. This girl had stalked me around the property trying to find a way to avenge her buddy. Ah now I know why the older woman looked familiar to me. I looked down the hallway at the younger girl and I could tell by her puzzled expression she knew who I was and wanted to know why we were in her apartment. As soon as she made eye contact with me she dropped her things and jumped backwards toward the door.

Her mom was sitting on the couch now. "It's ok Carrie. They are here to switch out our dryer. Come sit by me."

I noticed there were a few crucifixes on the walls when we walked down the hall. The girl walked over and pulled one off the wall by the door and held it close to her chest while she slowly faced me and walked over to her mom on the couch. It was pretty obvious now what she thought I was. I half chuckled when she held the crucifix out in front of her hoping that the worthless piece of wood would actually keep me at bay if I decided to "attack".

Jim and I were a few feet away installing their dryer. We could hear the mother and daughter talking down the hall. "Why did you let those guys in? Did you invite them in?" She said with a hint of panic in her voice.

"Yes I invited them in. How else were they going to install our dryer? What are you doing with that crucifix?" The mom said.

"Oh I uhh. I just wanted to look at. I have never actually looked at it before." She got up and went into the kitchen. I heard the fridge open. The girl walked back to the couch and sat down.

Jim and I were back in the hallway hanging the dryer. The mother moved from the couch and stood in the hallway behind me.

"So is this one going to work right this time? The other one was making a really high pitched squeaking sound." She said.

"Yes this one should run better. We tried it out in the shop and it ran fine." Jim said. All of a sudden I caught a whiff of some strong spices. I guess Jim noticed it as well. "Are you cooking pasta? It smells like real strong garlic?" Jim said.

"No I am not cooking anything but I smell it too and it is strong." The mother said. I turned around and

Carrie stood behind her mother in the hallway. She must have garlic cloves on her somewhere. Her right hand was holding onto the crucifix and the other was reaching out for her mother. She grabbed her mother and started to pull her back.

"What are you doing?" The mother said to Carrie. "Are you playing vampire hunters again? Vampires don't exist. I told you that for the last time."

"I know what you are!" Carrie yelled directly at me.

Her mom looked at me. "I am so sorry. She thinks you are a vampire. She has been reading these silly books and now she just thinks everyone is evil. No honey he isn't a vampire." She said.

"He did something to my friend." Carrie yelled.

"Your friend happened to catch a weird virus. He did nothing to her." The mother said. She still held the crucifix up and was pulling her mom towards the front door.

I looked at Jim, who was just as dumbfounded as me. We both looked at each other and shrugged. "Well, look if I let you touch me with the cross will you believe I am not a vampire? Here." I held my hand out. She moved forward her arms were trembling. She eyes darted from my eyes to my arm and back to my eyes again. I stretched my arm out and nodded my head at it. Slowly she held the cross above me and hesitated for a moment. Then in one swift motion she pressed it against me quite hard. She touched the cross to my skin. It actually felt quite cool and soothing compared to the heat I faced outside. I quickly grabbed my arm and turned around. I started to yell in pain. I doubled over. "I am melting! Ahhhh." I looked at the girls face. I could tell she was surprised because her mouth was wide open. She had that look of shock. I looked at Jim and he had that same look on his face as well. My acting skills were not that great. As hard as I tried, I could not keep a straight face. I felt the giggles coming up from my stomach. I started laughing.

I could tell all three of them felt like they had been fooled. "Look. Seriously, look there is nothing on my arm. See. I am not a vampire." I said as I turned my arm back and forth. "I hope you are satisfied."

"I know you are a monster. You did something to my friend. She used to be healthy and happy. She has dreams every night that you are sitting on top of her in her bed and then you gently grab her arm and you bring it up to your mouth. Then the feeding begins. It has been the same dream every night since she has started to get sick. She said it felt so real."

"Look. That's not me. Your friend is just having some crazy dreams. How could I be in the sun all day if I was a vampire?" I said.

Her mom was standing there looking at me. "I am terribly sorry. She has been acting up lately and not taking her medication."

Jim found all this amusing. "Hey I can honestly tell you Max is not a vampire but he certainly does suck." I chuckled and then I elbowed Jim in his gut.

"Why did you say that?" I shook my head.

"Well you are all set. We just need to get the lint catcher bucket off your old dryer." Jim said.

The girl jumped forward. "I know why the crucifix and garlic didn't work. It is because my mom invited you in and that makes us powerless against your powers." She said so sure of herself.

"Good one, but no. Once again, not a vampire."
I stepped outside and Jim handed me the bucket I shot
him a glance.

"Just go in there and hook this bucket up. It will
only take ten seconds." Jim said.

"Thanks buddy. I am glad you think this is
funny. I need you to go with me to watch my back. I
hope that girl doesn't try to stake me in the chest while I
bend over."

"Ha ha. I think you will be ok." He shoved the
bucket at me.

"Awesome bro. If you hear yelling you know
what happened." I said as I went back inside. He
started to dolly the old dryer down the stairs.

I had to go back and hook up the vent bucket. I
walked back down the hallway and started to hook up the
bucket. When I turned around the girl was right behind
me. "I know what you just did. You were trying to
make me seem childish and stupid in front of my mom. I
know what you are. I know you did something to my
friend. She says she had dreams every night that you
came into her room and drank her soul and I believe her.
I truly believe her in my heart of hearts. I watched as her
hair turned grey and her skin started to shrivel. What a
coincidence that after her family moved out of here she
started to instantly improve. You are some kind of
monster and if I see that start to happen to me or my
mom I will get my dad's shotgun and shoot you in the
face in broad day light."

I just smiled at her with a wicked grin. I leaned
in close to her and spoke in a whisper. "I don't know
what you are talking about. Your friend probably just
had some unusually disease. She probably just dreamed
of me because she sees me walking around on the
property all the time. I wouldn't say your story to

anyone else. They will probably think that would sound pretty crazy." I said.

I could tell she was experiencing mixed emotions. Tears were coming out of her eyes. She was shaking her head and looking down at the ground. I could tell she was both furious and hurt that what she had thought was true, may not be so now. I turned and started to walk down the hall. As I walked out the door I turned and said bye to the mother. I stopped for a second and shot a glance down the hall at Carrie.

I could have just let it go but the evil side in me could not get past that a mortal girl just threatened me. Me. A higher power. I know she is just a stupid child but maybe I should just threaten her a little. I just wanted to put a little fear into her. I looked into her eyes and sent her a mental threat that only she would hear.

"Just so you know though, you are on my land and you are subject to any kind of torment that I see fit to dish out. Yes, I did drink your friend dry and she was one of the tastiest things I have ever tried. By the way, don't fuck with me or I will end your mother in one swift motion."

I shut the door and Jim and I started to walk down the stairs. This girl was full of anger now. I could sense it. It was the kind that took a person past the line of reason into that dark irrational place where anything can happen. It was as if I just shook the bee hive and the bees are going to be on my ass soon. I wasn't sure how she was going to respond but I knew I needed to start to put some distance between her apartment and us.

"I think we need to pick it up Jim." I said as I started to move past him.

"Who lit the fire under your ass? I have never seen you in such a hurry." He said in surprise as he was pushing the old dryer out of the breezeway.

206

I heard the door above us fling open. I knew something was going to happen but I could not tell what. I was starting to turn the corner and I glanced back. Carrie was outside now with a shotgun. Oh crap! I thought to myself. I could try to control her mind but that takes concentration and time. Two things I did not really have at this moment.

"I am going to kill you. You are not going to touch my mom!" I heard her yell as I bolted around the corner. I heard another woman's voice say something but I didn't want to stick around to find out.

I turned the corner just as I heard a shot fired. Jim was right behind me. I had hoped he was not shot. From the angle she was at it would have been hard for her to hit us. We started to run down the street to our work shop. "Are you ok? Call the police." I yelled to Jim. He didn't look like he was hit. He already had his phone out and was dialing. We reached the shop and locked the doors and closed the blinds. I had hoped she didn't know where our shop was.

"Yes 911. This is Northfield Grove apartments in St. Louis. We are hiding in 6155 C. A resident here pulled out a shotgun and fired it at us. Send someone over quickly please." Jim said.

"Well the police should be on their way. So what happened when you went to put the bucket on the dryer? "Jim said.

"She was accusing me of doing something to her friend that I clearly did not do. Then I just told her I did not do anything to her friend. I said bye to her mother and I shut the door and next thing I knew we were getting fired at." I said.

"Hmm. That is pretty weird behavior. Well, when we were in there she clearly thought you were a vampire. Who goes around pointing a crucifix at a person? Everyone knows vampires don't exist. I mean you are out in the sun all day. Wouldn't the sun kill you if you were a vampire?"

"Yeah I know right. I don't know why she said that. She told me that her friend was really sick and she was having dreams that I was there night after night torturing her friend. I told her that she probably just dreamed of me because I am out walking around the property all day. They see me all the time." I said.

We could hear the siren of the police cars pulling onto the property. We opened the door and looked around to see if the girl with the shot gun was still around. I didn't see her so we hurried out into the street and waved over the three police cars. They pulled up and jumped out of their cars.

Jim and I hurried over to meet them. "There was a girl shooting a shotgun at us around the corner. She lives at 5032 H. We work here and we went into her apartment to install a dryer. We were leaving and next thing we know she started firing at us." Jim said.

"Ok we will go check it out." More and more police cars started to show up. A few cops started to walk over to the apartment. We followed the police around the corner of the building and there was Carrie standing in the street. By the blank look on her face she looked like she was in shock. She was mumbling something but we were too far away to hear. I was confused when I saw her because she was covered in blood. "How did that happen?" I thought to myself. In her right hand she was still holding the shot gun. The police did not waste any time as they surrounded her quickly.

"Drop your weapon!" The first cop yelled as he drew his gun from his holster. Eight cops surrounded her. All of them had their guns out and pointed directly at her. It was intense. I could not believe this was happening. This was just like something you would see on TV. Carrie just stood there and did not respond. She mumbled something but none of us knew what she was saying.

"Drop you weapon or we will shoot!" They said again. All eyes were focused on her. She just stood there like she was in a trance. I wasn't even mind controlling her. Whatever was going on inside her head she was doing this to herself. "We are going to count to three. Please put your weapon down or we will shoot." Everything was so silent you could hear a pin drop. I could see some douche bags on their balconies videotaping this on their phones. Maybe I should have a cop aim a little high. "One…" The police man yelled. She just stood there like she had no clue what was even going on. These guys were for real. They were not playing any games. They were going to shoot her. "Two…" The police were starting to move forward. I guess they thought maybe they could knock her down or taser her. There were a few cops that were sneaking around the back of her that had on body armor and tasers. I didn't want her to get shot. I was a little bit off to the side. I decided to jump in. "Carrie, just drop your gun dammit!" I yelled. She looked right at me. At the exact second she must have had had a moment of recognition. As soon as she saw my face her face twisted in hate. She brought the shotgun up fast. At that same instant the police had no choice. They all opened fired on her. I watched as bullets tore giant holes through her in a grisly display of crimson blood bursts. She never lost eye contact with me even as blood poured out from her mouth. The shotgun slowly slipped from her fingertips and made a metallic sound as it hit the concrete. She just stood there staring at me. Finally, I watched in slow motion as her lifeless body fell backwards to the ground. She was killed almost instantly. The ground was covered in dark crimson blood. The police ran forward to get the gun away from her even though she was already dead and they knew it.

Jim was talking to a police officer. "Hey, her apartment is over here. Do you want me to unlock the door?" Jim said.

"What apartment did she live in?" The officer asked.

"It was 5032 H. I can let you in. I have a key." Jim said.

"That would be great." I followed them to the door. I saw a puddle of blood that had formed on the ground when I walked into the breezeway. That's odd I thought to myself. The officers had their guns out. We walked up the stairs and there was her mom's lifeless corpse laying on the wooden walkway. The officers ran over and started to check her vital signs. I could hear one officer radioing in that they need a paramedic up here stat. I was pretty sure if you could see a person's organs on the outside they are probably not going to make it. The big hole in her midsection was clearly from a shotgun blast. I told the police officer that I think the girl ran outside with a shotgun and I guess the mom jumped in the way and the gun went off. They asked me to leave the area they were going to take care of it from here. I went down to where Jim was. He was telling a police officer everything that happened. I told them my story was the same. I was with him the whole time. I told them the mom said that the girl wasn't on her meds and she was acting insane. "She kept saying I was a vampire and held a crucifix at me to keep me away." I said. After we talked for fifteen minutes Jim and I were free to go. Everyone, who was home, was outside now standing around the crime scene. I saw a few news vans show up and I wanted to get out of there as soon as possible.

Chapter 19

The mind of Max. Friday June 28.

It was Friday. I arrived at work a little early. I walked into the break room.

Gerard was talking. "Hey listen to this. Stan said that last night he had to go into the laundry room to kick out ten teenagers who were just hanging out in there. He said that they cornered him in the back area. He thought they were going to hurt him. He got on his knees and begged them not to hurt him…"

Kitchen jumped in. "I bet. When he was on his knees he said that he is going to have to suck his way out and told all those guys to drop their pants." Everyone started laughing. At that moment Stan walked in.

"Hey guys." He said. We all started laughing harder. Time for me to get to work'n. As I passed by Stan I said "You got something on your face." Everyone started to chuckle. I walked over to the grounds room across the hall. I quickly grabbed my bucket and grabber and went straight to doing the grounds. I had some unfinished business to take care of. I didn't say hi to anyone. I went straight to her apartment. I was in pain yesterday. I fed well and today I was feeling better than ever. Where is that fucking little bitch? My heart was pumping liquid fury. I could barely hold back the rage I was feeling. I was going to walk by her apartment to see if her car was there.

I have to say that was clever of them to hide their bodies and then to follow me. I will give them that. That bitch is going to pay for stabbing me. "Come out; come out wherever you are…" My mind had not fully recovered from being skewered. I still had a throbbing headache. I would of swallowed that girl whole if Jack had not come back to save her. She would probably be in a comatose state right now. So very lucky she was. So very, very, lucky.

I walked right to her apartment and looked into the window. I didn't care if her parents saw me. It was still ransacked. Guess she did not come home last night. I walked around to the front door. They had a welcome decoration hanging up. I was so mad I walked to the parking lot to look for her car. It was gone. I decided to go to the next section. Jack's car was gone as well but he goes to work before me so I didn't think it would be there.

I walked around the property for awhile to cool off. You can hide from me for awhile Nikki but you are eventually going to end up back here. I will always be waiting in the shadows to drag you down to hell with me.

Part Two:

The First Real Date

Chapter 20

The mind of Jack. Saturday June 29.

We were actually going to go on a real date today. I convinced Nikki that maybe we should take a break from our training and go out and have some fun. I was so excited. I think this is the first time we actually are going out together some place.   I know it is just a day date but that is still a real date. I woke up and jumped into the shower. I woke up in a good mood which does not happen often. I even put on cologne which is something that I never do. It is a little too strong to be in a small cubicle with other people nearby. I have had other people do that and if you don't like the smell it can be torture for your nostrils.

I was looking at myself in the mirror. I started to practice making weird faces in the mirror. I don't know if other people do that or not but it's just something that I do every time I look at myself in the mirror. After I had my fill I put on my serious face.

I started to get dressed. I had to decide what I wanted to wear. Getting dressed to go on a date was so different from getting dressed to go to work. For work I just throw on one of the five identical pairs of khakis and a dress shirt. It just something I wear to get past the dress code but it' is not something I actually am thrilled to wear. I knew we were going to be outside and doing a lot of walking so I didn't want to wear jeans. I was going to put on my nice grey and black polo shirt. And my dark grey shorts. Despite what anyone else said this was my favorite outfit.

It was about ten in the morning and I was getting ready to go on our date. I had to look in the mirror one last time. I ran through my mental check list in my mind. Alright, everything looks good and I am ready for takeoff. I grabbed my keys and my phone and I was out the door. Oh wait. Wallet. I kind of need that. I reopened the door and grabbed it. I was running down the stairs. I got to the bottom. I happen to notice the flowers growing in the landscaping. Aha, flowers good idea. Nikki would probably like that I thought. I hoped no one would have noticed me taking a few. Nah no one would probably care. I grabbed some. "These look nice."

I turned around and a lady walking her dog was standing behind me. She had an unfriendly look on her face. "What are you doing with my flowers?" She said in an accusing tone.

"Oh I am so sorry I thought these were planted here from the apartments. I didn't know you planted these I am so sorry. Here you can have them back."

"I don't want the top of those flowers back. They are no good now that you ripped off the roots. Don't let me catch you taking my flowers again."

"I won't. I am so sorry." I said.

215

"I hope whoever you pick those for likes them." She said.

"I am sure she will." I said as I walked away quickly.

I walked to the next stairway over and knocked on the door. Nikki answered. "Hello. You look nice today." She said.

"So do you." She had short white shorts on a nice tank top. She had some really nice sandals on as well.

"I brought these flowers for you." I said as I handed them to her.

"For me you shouldn't have. You didn't have to buy me flowers." She said as she put them close to her face and she smelled them.

"Don't worry he didn't pay for those flowers. He took them from my garden." The old lady yelled from the sidewalk. The lady was walking her dog up the sidewalk.

"I thought these flowers looked familiar." She said laughing.

I was laughing as well. "Hey girl, I honestly thought those were planted by the apartment workers. I was walking by and saw those flowers and thought of you."

"Well that was very nice of you." She went and put them in her apartment. "Alright let's go." She said.

We walked over to my car and I opened her door for her. "Where do you want to go? Is there any place in particular?" I asked.

"No I don't have anywhere in particular I want to go. You choose. I will go anywhere you want." She said.

"Great." I said as I gave the car some gas. "How about some music." I said as I turned on my favorite alternative radio station. There are really only three good radio stations in St. Louis. One is alternative. One is Hip hop party music. The other one is what I call old man rock but it seems to have fewer commercials then the other two.

After about forty five minutes we ended up downtown. "I thought we could do the whole downtown tour and maybe eat at my favorite Chinese restaurant." I said.

"Sure that sounds great. Where are we going first?" She said.

"You like animals? I sure hope so or you are not going to like this."

"I like animals. I am here with you am I not." She said.

"What's your favorite animal?" I asked.

"I really like big snakes. They really turn me on."

"You are so dirty!" I said. I found a place to park at the art museum. It was a little farther to walk but I didn't have to pay for parking which was good.

"I am ready to see some animals." I said.

We got out of the car. We held hands as we walked down the grassy path to the zoo entrance. I really liked the holding hands. It made me feel warm and secure on the inside. We entered through the more modern side. It had a few rooms where you could do some interactive learning.

"Do you want to go in there? I think there is a game in there where you get to be a bat and you are trying to catch a moth." We walked in and it was being played by a large group of kids so we kept walking. I looked at the different insects and small ocean animals that were in there.

We eventually made our way outside. We started walking to the right. We walked by the bears. They were always outside and moving around. There were a few different kinds of bears. The grizzly bears seemed to be more active, they were up and moving. The others were just lounging around. I always had to stop by the polar bears. They always seemed to be the most active. "We have to stop in front of the polar bears." They were always fun to watch. They would jump into the water and swim around for awhile then run and jump in again. It was pretty neat to see them swim. They seemed happy. "Does it remind you of one of those commercials for cola soda?" Nikki said.

"Yes it does. It's kind of depressing reading these information panels. It says these animals will be extinct in the wild in about fifty years because the polar caps are melting. That's one of the better ones. Most of these animals don't even have that long."

"That is a little depressing." Nikki looked sad.

"Hey let's have a good happy day." I said. I leaned forward and pressed my lips against hers. I could taste her chap stick on my lips. She put her arms around my neck and pulled me closer. We kissed for a few minutes against the guard rail. My eyes were closed.

When I opened them, there was a group of people standing around us. Instead of looking at the bears they were now looking at us. We started giggling. I grabbed her hand and we walked off quickly.

We walked up to an older concrete looking building. I wasn't sure what was in there until I entered and the smell hit me. She must have figured it out to the same time I did.

"Honey, are we visiting your relatives?" Nikki said.

"How did you know?" I said in a tone of surprise. "Yes, I am related to the bubble gum butt monkeys. They are right over here and they are waiting to meet you. There is cousin Joey, cousin Ronny, and cousin Jonny." I said laughing. They were weird to watch. Whatever was going on with their rear ends was tough to look at. It was like a train wreck. I wanted to look away but could not. One was peeing on the glass. "Eww. They are really ugly but they remind me of some people I used to know." I put my hands over Nikki's eyes. "Let's move on." I said.

We started to walk around the glass cages. The spider monkeys were pretty cool to watch. They swung around in their cages. They were black with some white on them. Their arms were extremely long and skinny. They also had tails that were equally as good at gripping and holding onto things. They moved like black agile blurs or fur.

There were other smaller monkeys hoping around. They came in every shape and size. Some were furry and some had no fur at all. Some had the oddest color for eyes. One had bright orange eyes that seemed to look right through you. Then we came to the gorillas, orangutans, and chimpanzees. It was weird looking at them because they looked almost like humans. There was a hairless one that looked very similar to a human. It was holding a little baby. "Aw, this one has a baby with it." Nikki said.

"Do you want kids someday?" I asked as I put my arms around her.

"Yes, I want 10."

"TEN! Holy Crap! That sure is a lot of mouths to feed." I said.

"But I would be ok with two or three. It has to be with the right person though." She said as she smiled at me.

"I would be happy with two or three but I really wanted twenty five so I can have my own reality show. I need a woman with a super amazing vagina to crank out all my babies." I said laughing.

"Well. That certainly IS a lot of mouths to feed." She said. I was pretty sure I just blew her mind.

We went to the snake house next. The snakes were cool but the least interesting to watch. They usually don't move at all. It could be a fake snake in there and we would never know. I did like to see the two giant snakes that are in there even if they didn't move at all. We walked to the lower area where the turtles and gators are. The large turtles are neat. They were like something left over from the age of the dinosaurs. Their giant armored shells, scaly skin, and long necks were interesting to look at. "Hey I know where we should go next. You are really going to like it." I said.

We walked to this area that had a double set of doors. "Close your eyes. Don't ruin the surprise." I covered her eyes.

The air was fragrant and filled with sweet smelling aromas. This room was filled with beautiful flowers full of pollen. We walked to the center of the pathway. "Ok you can open them." I said.

Butterflies were flying everywhere. They were every shape size and color. One landed on my hand. I raised my arm and showed her as it walked up my arm and flew off. Nikki's face told me she was in awe. One very pretty orange one landed in the palm of her hand. She stared at it mesmerized. She had a smile on her face. It walked across her fingers. Then it took off. "This is amazing. Wow this is so incredible." She said.

"I know. It makes me hope that if there is a heaven, I hope that it is like this." I said.

We stood there for a few more minutes in amazement. There were more people coming in so we had to start walking. I walked out the double doors. "Do I have any on me?" I asked.

"Yeah hold on." She grabbed a blue one that was crawling on my back. She picked him off me and put him back in the room. "Good bye little guy. Go back to your family." She said.

"That was so neat. I have never been in there before. How did you know I like butterflies?"

"I didn't. I just thought since you are a girl you might like that."

"I have something to show you." She pulled me off to the side where no one could really see us. She started to pull her shorts down a bit in the front. I hope she doesn't take her pants off at the zoo. Then again that would be hot if she took her pants off at the zoo. Is this really going to happen right here at the zoo. I looked down her pants and she had a two inch butterfly tattoo. It was right under her panty line.

"That is pretty cool. Where did you get that done at?" I said.

"I have had it for awhile. One of my old friends does tattoo's and he gave me a good deal."

"I always wondered if you had any tattoos." I said.

"That's the only one that I have that no one usually sees." She said.

"Nikki I have to show you my tattoo now." I started to pretend to undo my pants. She laughed and then she started to try to undo my belt. She got a hold of it and tried to unbuckle it. I was laughing as well. My pants were starting to fall down.

"Hell yeah I want to see your tattoo. I bet you have a smiley face down there." She said as she held the ends of my belt.

People were walking by and giving us weird looks. We were starting to attract some attention.

"WAIT! How dare you. I AM a gentleman. I can't do this."

"You are just so romantic. We better get moving before the security shows up." She said.

We continued walking around and looking at the different animals.

We walked towards the middle of the zoo area. "Do you see that building up there?" I said.

"Yes I see it." She said.

"You know when I was in sixth grade my class came here on five field trips, I think. Did your school do anything like that?" I said.

"No I think we came here one time in fourth grade or something." She said.

"Well we always met at the building towards the back up there. Then we would spend the day at a different animal house. Then this one time, my friend told me this joke. My class was watching a zookeeper do a presentation. It was really quiet and dark. Everyone was taking notes and being serious. A picture of a cow was on the screen. It was called a Vietnamese cow or something. The zoo keeper said that they are nearly extinct because of the Vietnam War. My friend whispered to me. "Hey.""

"Hey what?" I said.

"You know why those animals are going extinct?" He said.

"Why?" I said.

"I am going to tell you the answer in one word. Rambo." He said.

"I dunno why his joke was so funny to me but I burst out in laughter. I started to laugh so hard I fell out of my chair. I thought that was the funniest thing. Everyone in the room was looking at me. I was laughing so hard I was crying. The teacher came over and she said "What is a matter with you? I am going to have to separate you two if you don't behave. Ah, those were the good ol' days."

"Yeah it sounds like it. Did you guys actually learn anything on those field trips?" She said.

"Yes. I learned a few things that I am not suppose to tell anyone about. The first thing I learned is that if you interrupt a zookeeper doing a presentation more than three times they completely flip out." I said.

"That sounds like it has happened to you before." She said laughingly.

"Yes it has. Do you want to see the elephant area?"

"Yes. I love the elephants." She said.

We walked over in that direction. This area looked new. Or at least it was new to me. It was a newer area where there was a bigger outside area for the elephants to play. The path we walked down was well landscaped. There were large trees and bushes that you would find in a jungle. It made you feel like you were seeing the elephants in their natural environment which was kind of neat. We leaned against the railing and watched an elephant take water in its long trunk and blow it on its back to cool off. There were a few elephants in there. We watched them for awhile.

We walked inside the elephant building. There were hippos and rhinos in there too. It was dark and a little smelly in here. We leaned against the rail and watched the hippos for awhile. There was a five foot distance between the hand railing and the cage.

"They are sure amazing to watch. It's weird how none are living in the wild on this continent. They are all living overseas." She said.

One came over and looked at us for awhile. It would shake its head a few times. We saw it open its mouth. "What big teeth you have. You are so pretty." Nikki said. Nikki walked to the other side of the cage and it followed her. "Look it likes me." She said.

"Are you ready to go to get something to eat?" I said.

"Yeah I am hungry after all this walking in this heat. Feed me. You know I hate to walk outside especially when it is hot out. Gosh."

"Great there is a Chinese place close by that has really good food." I said.

"Cool beans. Let's go."

A few minutes later we got out of my car and walked in. We were greeted by the hostess. "We will have a booth please." I said.

"Sure right this way." The hostess said.

We walked over and sat down. "Can we start you off with anything special to drink?"

"Sure I will have a grand strawberry margarita." Nikki said.

"I didn't know we were drinking but I am all in. I think I will have the classic lime margarita." I said.

"Great I will be back in a moment with your drinks." The waitress said.

"Sure that sounds good." She said.

I looked admiringly into her eyes. "So did you like the zoo?"

"Yeah it was fun. The butterfly house was pretty cool."

"I was impressed the first time I was there too. That is how I picture heaven to be."

"Pfft. That's funny. You picture heaven to be a jungle room full of butterflies." She said.

"Ok maybe not heaven. I think I meant the Garden of Eden."

"Drinks are here."

The waitress placed our drinks down in front of us. "Are you guys ready to order?"

"Yes we will have Mongolian beef, some egg rolls, a few crab ragoon, fried rice, sweet and sour chicken and some ribs."

"Great do you want any appetizers? We have good wings as well."

"No thank you. We will pass for now." I said.

"Great your food will be up shortly." The waitress said.

I took a big drink of my margarita and it was strong. I had to do a little cough. I watched Nikki take a big drink of hers. "So... What do you want to do after this?" I said.

"I dunno. It is pretty hot outside. Do you want to go swimming?"

"I think I want to take my clothes off in the ac and eat ice cream." I said. She chuckled. I had drunk half my drink and was feeling a little tipsy. "So what's you plan after college?" I said.

"I really want to be a school teacher for third to sixth grade. That is the age group I would like to work with. I like that age group because the kids still think that the teacher is in control and they are a little afraid. I ultimately would like to get a teaching job around here. I like this neighborhood. You know how that goes though you have to go wherever you are lucky enough to get a gig. Then I would like to buy a house, have three dogs, twenty five kids, and be on my own reality show, you know the American dream. I already have the names picked out for the dogs."

"Really that is kind of odd. You have the dogs names picked out but not the names for the twenty five kids you plan to have." I said

"Yes I plan to name the kids as they come but I can go out right now and buy three dogs." She said.

"Ah, because that makes complete sense." I said as I shook my head and made a face.

"Hey I know I am not supposed to talk about training on our day date but I wanted to ask you something."I said. Half her drink was gone so I knew she had to be a little buzzed. I drunk most of mine and I was feeling pretty good.

"I guess you can ask me a question." She moved her finger over the rim of the glass to get some salt. "Why do you think you have an easier time separating from your body then me?" I looked directly at her. She met my stare.

"I have read some stories and articles and all seem to say that a person who has died, or has been close to death, or has had a tragic experience, will have an easier time separating their mind from their body. I have not had any kind of loss like that in my normal life but maybe you have. I have never had a death defying experience or a really close call. I have a large family and no one in it has ever died either. I fell headfirst into a rock pit one time but I was alright. A little blood on my face, but alright just the same. What about you? Did anything happen to you that may have caused you to "See the Light?" I said.

She was quiet for a minute. Her eyes were half closed. I knew she had to be a little drunk. Maybe the alcohol would make her more open to chatting. "I don't really want to talk about it."

"Please tell me so that I can understand better. You know so I can figure out what I am doing wrong. So I can have a reason why you can do these things better than me."

She looked down for a minute. She leaned forward and started talking in a whisper. "Ok. I will tell you. It was a frigidly cold day in February. I was only five years old. I was with my cousins and we were playing in the snow at this park. There was this giant hill that we were sledding down. I had my new shiny plastic red sled. My older cousins would push us part way down the hill to give us a giant boost in speed. It was my turn. My cousin pushed me and I went flying like a bat out of hell. I hit a bump and I went completely off course. My new trajectory aimed me right at the pond that was off to the right of this giant hill. I flew off the embankment and I stopped about ten feet out from the shore. My cousin who pushed me saw what happened."

"Oh god! Don't move!"" They yelled to me.

"I remember looking over and seeing the panic looks on their faces. The ice was cracking underneath me. I saw the white cracks spiral out from under me. I was scared. I remember casting one last look over at my family who were standing helplessly at the water's edge."

"Mommy! Help me! Help me!" I yelled.

"Then it happened. The ice gave way. I fell into the murky green darkness. I remember looking up and seeing the hole that I came through. I tried to swim but having snow gear on only weighed me down. Snow boots are definitely not for swimming. I sank deeper and deeper. The frigid waters were too much for my frail body. It started to shut down. All the warmth inside of me was sucked out. The last breath left my lungs. I watched in terror as the air bubbles floated away from me and I knew this was it. I really thought I was going to die. All I could see was a narrow ray of blue light coming from the opening. I started to black out. Next thing I saw was a tunnel of light all around me. I heard a voice say everything will be all right and I should not worry. Next thing I know I woke up in the hospital. Apparently my dad and uncle went onto the ice to get me. They swam down and pulled me out. Foods here." She said smiling as the waitress came over.

I wanted to ask her more questions after hearing that story. I wasn't sure what to say after her telling me she drowned and was brought back to life. That explains a lot though. I knew there had to be a reason why she was effortlessly able to separate her mind from her body every time. I guess it is easier to do once you have had the near death experience. Personally I don't think that is something I want to ever have to go through.

229

I kept opening my mouth to ask her more but then thought maybe I should wait. We both grabbed a few pieces of food. I took a few bites.

"Mmm. This is good." She said.

"It is good." I said. "You probably want to ask me more questions don't you?" She said.

"Yes. You can't tell me something like that and then expect me not to ask you more." I said. She giggled a little.

"I tell you what. Tomorrow you can ask me all the questions you want. I can't guarantee I will have an answer though." She said.

We finished eating. I paid the waitress. "Where to now? We can go back to the apartments and go swimming if you want. But first did you save room for dessert?"She said.

"Yeah I did." I said with an evil smile. I was thinking she meant something naughty and not the actually dessert you eat.

"Great I want to show you this new place I found. I will tell you how to get there. It just opened up down the road." She said.

"Cool let's go. I said. I was silent for the rest of the trip. I couldn't wait for tomorrow. I had a thousand of questions I wanted to ask her.

Chapter 21

The mind of Max. Monday July 1.

It was Monday. I started my morning as usual. I grabbed my bucket and grabber. I was walking along the road. I was feeling ok but this day was about to get a lot better. I could just feel it. Then I saw what I was looking for. It was Nikki's car. "Hmph. Just the person I wanted to talk too." I was still bitter about being stabbed. She had eluded me for a week but I knew that little bitch would eventually have to come home. I was going to hang out along this street. I wanted to be far enough away to not be seen but close enough to see her when she comes out to her car. She usually left for school around this time because I have seen her leave carrying books. I just pretended to pick up cigarette butts as I waited. I walked a little further down the street and I noticed that Jack's car was gone as usual.

I waited like a tiger stalking his prey. "Come on. Come on." I whispered. A few seconds later I saw her. Jackpot. I came up from my hiding spot on the other side of the street. *"Hello Nikki. I know you can hear me."* I whispered in her mind. She turned at me and started to pick up the pace. She must have gotten home late last night because all the close parking spots were taken and she had to walk farther to get to her car.

"*You can't run from me forever. You know that right.*" She was looking terrified now. She was starting to run. I could hear her mind crying out. "*Leave me alone. Please just leave me alone.*" I kept walking at a slow pace.

"*You know I am going to severely hurt you. You should have just let me eat you in the house. Now I am going to show you levels of pain and suffering that you never dreamt possible. Things that your little human brain cannot even begin to fathom.*"

I could feel her thoughts in her head. "*You are welcome to try but my friend and I are going to kill you.*" She said in her mind. She was fumbling with her keys and trying to unlock her car. I was about twenty feet away now.

"*You mean Jack. I really hope you don't bring him into this. He seems like a descent person. I bet that you didn't tell him what really happened to your last boyfriend. Maybe I should enlighten him.*" I grew tired of this. I sent out a psychic attack that would have brought the mightiest of my foes to their knees. I stood there smiling as my mental attack smashed into the core of her mind.

"*If you are so powerful then why are you running away?*" I said.

She unlocked her car and jumped behind the steering wheel. She started her car. I could tell she was in pain. Half of her face was tightened. Her right eye was closed tight. She reached one hand up to cover her

232

eye. The other hand was holding the steering wheel. I could tell her mind defensive powers were getting stronger. That usually causes the normal person to pass out. As she drove by I read her mind. She said. *"You better be afraid. Jack and I are training to become more powerful then you and it will be you who will be kneeling before us."*

She backed up fast. I was standing in a bad spot. The back end of the car almost hit me if I had not moved in between the other cars that were parked next to her. She put the pedal to the metal and peeled out. She sped off like a bat out of hell.

"You better run and hide." I said quietly. Wait till night fall. We will see who will rule who. I was certainly going to come after her later.

Jim came walking up the street. "Hey I got a call from the office that there is a disturbance at the pool. We have to go check it out." Said Jim.

"What's a matter up front? Are you too scared to check it out yourself?" I said mockingly.

"Nah I am not scairt. I thought you would want a reason to go check out the ladies at the pool." Jim said.

"Hells yeah I want to see some half naked ladies. So what's going on up there?" I asked.

"All the ladies decided to have a wet t-shirt contest and they said they want Max to come and be the judge."

"Ha ha. That's awesome. Although the women that generally hang out at the front pool are not the ones I would want to see topless." I said.

We started to walk up the sidewalk. "So what is really going on?" I asked.

"They said there is a blonde kid up there causing trouble and he doesn't live here. I think it's that one blonde chubby kid whose mom got evicted a few months ago. I think his name is Matt. He is about fourteen. He thinks he is a bad ass." Jim said.

"Hmmm. No I don't recall." I said.

"He lived in the corner apartment up front on the left side."

"I still don't remember." I said.

We kept walking. I was racking my brain to try to think who it is he was talking about. We got closer to the pool. I saw the kid who they must have been talking about but I still couldn't think who he was. He was a chubby blonde hair kid. He had a small raft in his hands. He was running through the courtyard holding a raft in front of him and then he would leap on it and try to surf across the pool.

When we were walking up I could hear the adults there saying "Busted. Pool patrol is here." We got to the gate and leaned on it. "What's up fags?" Matt yelled to Jim and me. I remembered who that kid was now quite clearly.

I first met Matt about nine months ago. I caught him in the act of vandalizing the property. A month later, Matt and his mother were evicted from the apartments. His mom got laid off from her job and could no longer pay the bills. I remember seeing a tow truck pull up and tow away his mother's car. I guess she could not afford to rent a moving truck to move all of her stuff. They just up and left all their belongings behind.

It is not the first time, I have seen that happen, and it wasn't the last. I think they only took their clothes but everything else was there.

We got the lucky task to clean out their apartment. There were certainly not the cleanest people. You could tell they hadn't vacuumed the whole time they were here. The carpet looked dingy and had stains on it. Their furniture looked like it had seen better days. They had a dog and it used the couch as a chew toy.

As we were throwing Matt's belonging down from the second story he happened to be walking up the street. Matt came over and called us a few unpleasant names for throwing out his things. At that point Jim was furious and started to ruthlessly smash anything that might have been valuable out of spite. He told Matt that he can get the pieces of his belongings out of the dumpster if he still wants them. Matt grew furious and walked off.

Anyways, back to my main point. Matt really, really fucking hates us. We stood looking at him from the other side of the fence.

"Matt are you causing trouble up here?" I said.

"You can't kick me out of here I am with my friends." Matt said.

"We CAN kick you out of the pool if you are being a disturbance. The sign over there says no horseplay." I said.

"Ok, I will be good. There's no problem." Matt said.

"Great make sure it stays that way." Jim said and we walked off.

Problem resolved. We started to walk off and got about twenty feet away and we heard him yelling at us. "Get out of here fags. They don't have the balls to throw me out." I know he was just showing off for his friends. We turned around and he was running and jumping on his raft again. I looked at Jim. "Are we ready to throw this asshole out?"

"Yup." We walked back over to the fence. I flung that gate open and we went inside the pool area. "Alright we gave you a chance and now you have to go." I said.

"No way. I am not going anywhere." He jumped off his raft and swam to the middle of the pool.   I guess he thought he was safe swimming in the water because he thought we would not jump in after him.

I had enough of this kid. In my book, this kid went from tolerable to annoying. I am going to have to take care of this situation.

We stood at the side of the pool. "Come on Matt just get out of the pool or we will have to call the cops and they will drag you out." Jim said.

"No way.   You call the cops." Matt said in true defiance as he tread water.

I grew tired of his games. I sent my presence out to dominate his mind. He had no clue what happened. I was in the control room of his mind. The steering wheel that controlled his every function was at my disposal. He did not really even fight it. I easily knocked his presence aside. He was treading water before I took over but not anymore. I made his legs and arms stop moving. He looked like a lifeless corpse. I saw his face look quickly back and forth at his nonfunctioning limbs. I saw the panic in his eyes. He lifted his head forward to scream for help just as his mouth sank in the water. Nothing but a gurgle sound came out. He was sinking fast now to the bottom of the pool. His little presence in his head was fighting back hard now. I felt air bubbles leave his mouth as his oxygen supply was running out. His head tilted back to look at us. A scream for help was frozen on his lips.

I stood at the edge of the pool and watched as Matt's body sunk to the bottom. Everyone watching thought it was just a joke Matt was playing on us by swimming to the bottom so we would not be able to reach him. After thirty seconds, they started to think he might actually be drowning or he could hold his breath for a really long time. I felt the pressure in his lungs. I felt air bubbles escape his lips and float to the surface. He was going to pass out if I didn't free him soon. I was going to give it another ten seconds. This was the best part. I got on my knees and put my hand in to the water for him to grab it.

"Is he messing with us or do you think he is really drowning?" Jim said.

"I cannot tell." I said. Jim was getting ready to dive right in. The other people at the pool started to grow concerned and started to circle the deep end of the pool.

After a minute I released him of the mind control. He was like a frightened little bunny. He came paddling up as fast as he could. As soon as he reached the surface he let out a big gasp for air. His arms were flailing everywhere. I had my arm in the water to help him out. He swam over to my hand. I grabbed one side and Jim grabbed the other and we pulled him out of the water.

"Back up!" I yelled to the crowd. He was hunched over and coughing up water. Water came shooting out of his lungs. We tried to help him but he pushed our hands away. He shook his head and kept coughing. I am glad I let him go before we had to do mouth to mouth resuscitation. If no one was around, I would have let him drown.

After choking for a few minutes he started to come through. He no longer had the scared look in his eyes. His face was starting to look angry. He would not turn his back to me. He put his hands up in front of him like don't hurt me. While he started putting his shoes on he grabbed his towel and walked backwards towards the gate.

"I know what you did." He yelled.

"What might that be?" I said with a smirk on my face.

"You tried to drown me!" He yelled as he pointed his finger at me. He was still walking backwards to the gate.

Jim and I gave each other puzzled looks. "What? Are you sure you are not high? I put my hand in the water. I was trying to save you." I said.

"Max had his hand in the water. He was trying to pull you up. He was not even close enough to you to drown you." Jim said.

"He did something to my head and I could not move my body!" He yelled.

"Really I froze your mind and you could not swim." I said in a condescending tone.

238

He was opening the gate and walking through it. He never turned his back to us like we were going to attack him or something. "Yes that is exactly what happened." Matt said.

I whispered into his mind. *"You can yell all you want but no one is going to believe you. You should probably just go"*

"There you just did it again!" He yelled.

"Did what? What are you talking about?" I said. Everyone in the pool was starting to laugh.

"Listen it's time for you to go and don't come back. You probably want to lay off the meth." Jim said.

Matt started to walk away. He would turn around occasionally and look back. I am sure he was shook up and really confused.

"Wow these kids these days are a little off. He was probably still bitter about you ripping his bunny apart when we tossed him out." I said laughing.

"Oh yeah. That was fun." Jim was quiet for a second then he said. "Why are there so many crazies living here?" Jim said.

"There sure are a lot. I think it is something in the water that causes everyone here to go nuts. If you drank the water you are probably next." I said. We started to laugh.

Chapter 22

The mind of Jack. Monday July 1.

So I arrived at work. I have been really tired lately. Nikki has been keeping me up with training all night. I keep having these weird dreams with Nikki in them. I am not sure if she is invading my mind when I am asleep or it is just naturally occurring. I got situated and started to get to work. I didn't even notice Dave standing behind me. He must try to sneak up on me on purpose.

"What is up slim shady?" He said.

"Nothing panic attack." I said.

"Haha. That's a good one. So what's going on? How are things going with you and Nikki?"

"They are going alright I guess."

"You have been seeing her a lot. Are you guys getting married?"

"I dunno maybe down the road."

"Are you and her going to go out tonight? I dunno maybe to do something illegal?" He asked.

"You sure are asking a lot of questions." I said grinning.

"Alright I will cut the bull shit and cut to the chase. Are you and Nikki planning to kill someone? You guys keep posting back and forth and my phone keeps getting posts and notifications. Then I read the stuff you posted and I am thinking you guys are about to commit a murder."

I looked right at him and said "No we are not going to commit a murder."

"If you were don't let me know any details because the cops would question me. But, if you need anything from me I would probably help. If you felt like the guy deserved it or he was a rapist or something I would help hide the body. I don't know what I am saying. If you guys need someone to talk you out of it. I am here for you man. I am your best friend and if you do murder someone and you need help hiding or a place to hide the body I may or may not be able to help. I don't want to see my best friend rot away in jail. I would help you out if I could. Are you guys going to rob a bank or something? If you have a fool proof plan and then are going to go to South America or something I might be interested. Shit I know someone who would even help."

"Listen to me we are not robbing banks or killing anyone." I said laughingly.

"Ok sure, sure." He winked at me. "If you say so. Well I am just saying. I am just putting all the cards on the table." He said.

"Anyways so what is new with you Dave? Are you and your girl friend getting along?" I said trying to change the subject.

"I know you are trying to change the subject but she is great. We went to a bar this weekend and that was fun. There were some really drunk people there who got rowdy. They were being loud and they tried to break shit. The bouncers had to jump in. The cops came and arrested them. It was fun to watch."

"That does sound fun." I said as I worked on my project.

"Well killer, I guess I will go back to work. My dad is starting to give me a few dirty looks. I just had to make sure you not going to do anything crazy. Peace out." Dave said as he walked back to his cubicle. I am going to have to be more careful about what I type on the internet that everyone can see. Technically no, we were not planning to kill someone. We are planning to change Max's mind by any force necessary.

Chapter 23

The mind of Max. Monday July 1.

I knew they would come for me eventually. They were extremely angry. The girl had that burning desire for vengeance in her eyes. Her heart was full of rage. I knew they would probably train for awhile and then try to attack me. Something told me they would be coming soon.

I waited and waited. I knew it would probably be after eleven when they showed up. I decided to wait in the basement. I watched television until about eleven and then I turned out the lights. I just sat there and started to doze off. It was boring and quiet waiting alone in the dark. I was hoping that I would be able to sense them when they entered my house. I was sure I would probably be able too but then again they might have figured out something beyond my own understanding. Maybe a new way to cloak or to sneak up on me undetected. When they got me at that house I had no idea I was even being followed.

When I was at the apartments I thought I felt their presences but there were so many in that tiny area it was hard to pin point their location. I thought I sensed them there but their mental presences were not in their bodies. When I went into their bedrooms and didn't see their bodies I just thought I must be wrong.

I should be able to feel them. Since I was in my own body I would be much more powerful than them. Their powers weaken over distance. Since I am in my body and that is the power source from which my energy flows I should be able to take them.

I waited in the quiet house. I had my two dogs with me in the basement. Animals always have better senses then humans. So maybe they will be able to help me hear them when they enter. They certainly have heard odd sounds in the house before and woke me up countless times in the earliest hours of night.

I kept thinking about the first time I met Jack and he said the thing about me being a vampire. How vampires are not suppose to enter a house without being invited in. I really tried to keep that legend alive but I think after they saw me go into their apartments and that ladies house they probably realized that is all just an illusion. It is something that people told each other in the old days to make themselves feel safe after dark when the real evil things come out to play. Just like that whole crucifix idea. The legend about using a crucifix to ward off vampires. If vampires are quick and strong they would snap your arm off like a twig before you could even get close enough to touch a vampire with it.

It was getting close to midnight and I was dozing off. I thought I heard a sound that was out of the ordinary. The house I live in is old and it makes unusual

244

sounds pretty often. Sometimes it sounds like the metal in the vent is adjusting to the heating and cooling. I hear a few pang sounds occasionally. But this, this was different. More like hushed whispering. Just so slight I am not sure I heard it as all.

I was listening in the darkness more intently then I ever had before. My eyes were open but it was almost pitch black down here. I was squatting on the ground behind the couch. The only source of light was coming from the night light upstairs and it was coming through the bottom of the basement door. My dogs both sat up. They turned their heads back and forth. They didn't bark which I thought was strange because these two bark at everything. They seemed to know something was askew as well. They went over and stopped at the sliver of light that flowed from the bottom of the door. One dog made a whimper sound and then they kept looking up the stairs. They kept walking back and forth at the bottom of the stairs and they looked like they were tense and ready to spring.

I heard a sound. It sounded a bit like static and a bit like a human voice. My senses were picking something up. I could not tell if it was the neighbors or an animal outside. There are some woods behind my house so it could just as easily be a deer. Or maybe even a Piasa Bird. It's an old Indian legend around these parts. I kept trying to determine where it was coming from. It seemed like it was coming from the outer wall or the far corner of the basement. I slowly stayed close to the ground as I crept over to the wall. My hand was shaking a little. I stood up by the small window that was in the corner. I slowly moved the curtain just far enough to look outside. It was pretty dark outside. I could only see at ground level all the way to my fence and that was only because the moon was mostly full tonight. I didn't see anything out of the ordinary. I closed the curtain. I ducked down and crawled back to the couch.

I waited alone in the dark. I pulled me dogs close to me. I was trying to hear the sound again. It was hard to hear over the pounding in my chest. Bom. Bom. Bom. I was trying hard to concentrate. I heard the sound again. It was definitely a man's voice and it was coming from right outside. This time it was louder and much closer. It came from right outside the window. I started to back away from the window. That window was on the back of the house. I pulled the dogs with me so they didn't bark. "Please don't bark." I whispered to them.

I slowly walked to the top of the stairs. I was lucky that the steps didn't creak like they usually do coming down. I stood behind the door leading to the basement. I had my ear close to the door. I was trying to listen for anything. Sweat was starting to form on my forehead.

"Click." I am pretty sure that was the dead bolt to the back door being unlocked. I have locked and unlocked it so many times before I knew exactly what the sound was. I thought that was odd. If Jack and Nikki were going to attack me why would they physically go through the back door instead of just floating through the walls? It also takes a large amount of energy to turn that bolt then it does to just go right through the wall. I heard the door knob turn. It made the squeaky sound it always does. Erreere. I knew the door had been open. The air around the door that I was standing at felt instantly colder.

I could sense that there were two presences standing close to me right on the other side of the door. They couldn't sense me or they would have popped through this door and attacked me. That's a good sign then that their powers are not that strong yet. I could tell they were walking through the kitchen to the dining room. I felt their pounding footsteps in my head. When they passed in front of the basement door there was a slight shadow cast. They are moving to the bed room I thought.

I waited till I thought they would be in the dining room. Here we go I thought to myself. I slowly opened the old white basement door. My heart was certainly pounding fast now. I leaned my head out around the door. Coast was clear. I didn't notice anything unusually. I was silently moving across the kitchen floor. I carefully put one foot down in front of the other to not make the slightest sound. Now was the time to use my power. I focused my energy into my hand making a sword of psychic energy. In human form you could not see it. Sometimes you can see a faint aura but for the most part it was invisible. To a mental projection it would appear to be a completely solid beam of pure energy. I felt my hand vibrate with the power. I slowly looked around the dining room. I did not see anything. They must be going toward the bedroom. I moved as silent as a shadow across the wall. There is no going back now. I heard the door knob on the bedroom turning. They must be in there. I moved quickly now. I was very close to them.

I ran in to the room with my hand blazing like the heart of the sun. I did not know exactly where they were standing. I watched the blankets being moved as if someone was pulling then down. I swung with all my might in that direction. My sword of fire cut through something. The invisible barrier around my attacker glowed red for a second and shattered inward. The human shape glitched a few times then sparks flew to the ground. I knew that was a direct hit. It hung for a second then slid in half exactly where I cut it. Whoever that was is going to have a major headache tomorrow. That projection was destroyed.

The blue energy that dispersed from the fallen arched out into the room and it gave away where the other one was hiding. The electricity flowed over his hidden form. I was able to clearly see his silhouette. This all happened so fast I don't think it knew what was happening. It was cowering in the corner with its hand over its face. Time to die. I swung at its head in a downward sweeping motion. Direct hit. I cut that thing in half. It split open and electrical energy spilled out everywhere. I don't think they will be bothering me again for awhile. I laughed in my head. I watched the last of their energy arch out into the universe.

"Whatcha doing honey?" My wife said as she rolled over in the bed. "I am cold and my blankets keep getting pulled down."

"Nothing honey I was getting ready to come to bed as well. I love you."

Chapter 24

The mind of Jack. Monday July 1.

We were inside the bedroom. It was a small room. There wasn't much room on either side of the king size bed. We were finally getting ready to get this guy back for all the pain he has caused others. He looks so helpless all wrapped up in the blankets just laying there asleep. We watched his lungs inhale and exhale. He was snoring quite loudly I thought. Nikki stood at the front of the bed and I stood on the side. "Poor little guy you must be all tuckered out." Nikki said. We looked at each other and laughed.

"We got you now sucker. Wakey... Wakey..." Nikki said.

She started to pull the covers down.

"What trickery is this?"Nikki said. It was a woman laying there. We were both confused for a second. We looked at each other for a second. Instantly I thought, "Are we in the wrong house?"

All it took was that one second pause, and Max was on top of us. With a blazing sword he cut through Nikki first, she barely had time to react. She stuck her arms out but he cut her clear in half. I tried to form a weapon of any kind but before I could, I was broken into pieces.

"You have come a long way to get me. So please stay. Stay and die. Hahaha." It was Max's voice. All I heard was dark laughter before my form was shattered into a million pieces.

My conscious was instantly painfully separated from my mental projection. I awoke back in my human form.

I woke up screaming. "AARGH! MY MIND IS ON FIRE!" I said as I gripped my head. All my senses were so overloaded I could not take it. Parts of my brain that I have never known that they were capable of feeling were suddenly alive. I felt a great burning inside my head. It was like he made parts of my head able to suddenly feel and then he set those parts on fire. I lay on the floor shaking. I was burning and freezing at the same time. I lost control of my functions. I grabbed a trash can nearby and puked out my dinner.

Nikki wasn't faring any better. I looked over at her and her body was convulsing on the floor. I thought she might be going into shock. She then was scratching and clawing at her face and head. "Argg. Help me. I am burning. My skin is burning." She ran over and put her head under cold water. It looked like her eyes were bulging out of her skull. She started to grab her face again. She got a bag of ice and put it on her head. Her nose started to bleed. "Hey your nose is bleeding." I yelled from the floor. She grabbed a rag and put it over her nose. She then came over and lay down by me.

"What did he do to us?" I said.

"I dunno. There is no telling. He cut me in half with a psychic energy sword. I tried to form a shield but it sliced through it like a hot knife through butter."

"What makes me mad is that when we looked up where he lived and found out all the information about him on the internet it failed to mention that he had a wife." I said.

"Well maybe that is his girlfriend. Or maybe they are married but she never changed her last name. There a hundred reasons why it might not of showed up." Nikki said.

"Also how did he see us? I thought we were supposed to be invisible or nearly invisible." I said.

"I think he is just that good. He has done this so many times before and he knows all the secrets. I think his senses in general are just more fully developed then ours."

We both lay together on the floor. I looked over at her. I reached my hand out to hold her hand. She put her small delicate hand in my hand. She looked at me with those dreamy eyes as we slowly passed out together.

Chapter 25

The mind of Jack. Wednesday July 3.

It was Wednesday. The only good thing about Wednesday is it wasn't Tuesday. It seems like everything bad happens to me on Tuesdays. My alarm went off. I was too tired to jump up and turn it off. This must be like how it is when you have young kids. You are so exhausted and tired but you have to take care of that little bundle of joy. I slowly dragged my body out of bed and sluggishly got into the shower. Nikki has been making me train with her every night which is starting to take a toll on me. When I fall asleep my mind wonders around on its own now and I feel like I never really fall asleep. I am going to have to start taking sleeping pills. I finished showering, got dressed and went to work.

I went to my cubicle and plopped down in my chair. I was so tired I was getting ready to use tape to keep my eye lids open. If I get through the first two hours I will be ok I kept telling myself. I started to look at my files for the week.

"Hey buddy you look like shit today." Dave said.

"I must be tired I didn't even hear you sneak up behind me." I had my arm holding my head up to stay awake.

"Have been staying up late?"

"Yes, Nikki has been keeping me up late."

"Ohhhhhh shit. You dog! You have been hittin it hard haven't you? She looks like she would be good in bed. She probably broke your dick off didn't she?"

"No she was... uhhh...teaching me a few things."

"Uh huh. I bet she was riding your bologna pony all night." Dave said pretty loudly. I looked at him with the look that said not so loud dude. "It's ok my dad owns this place. I can talk as loud as I want." He said practically yelling.

"So anyways, yeah we have been hanging out a lot. She comes over at night and she teaches me things."

"So it is getting pretty serious huh?"

"I can see asking her out to be my girlfriend. She has a lot of qualities that I want in the woman I want to marry. We both are just seeing each other and no one else."

"So are you going to make it official and ask her out?"

"Yes I think I am. I want to make it really romantic though. I might need your help. I will think of something totally awesome."

"Cool. I am totally in. Under one condition."

"What's that?" I said hoping that it was not an unreasonable request.

"I want to be the best man at your wedding if you two decide to get married later down the road."

"Haha." I chuckled. "I am not ready for marriage yet. But alright. If I decide to get married down the road you can be the best man."

"Great that is totally awesome. I won't let you down I swear. I already have a kick ass idea for a bachelor's party." He said full of excitement.

"I believe you."

"Alright. I guess I will get back to work. I see some people giving me dirty looks. Well peace out brotha." He said as he started to walk back to his desk.

Chapter 26

The mind of Nikki. Thursday July 4.

It was Fourth of July. I hope there is not a lot of walking. I have on my highest heels. As I walked into the breezeway I noticed a chalk line on the ground but I didn't think that much of it. Kids draw on the concrete all the time. I slowly walked up the steps. With heels on it takes a bit of effort to walk. One time my heel went in between the space between these boards and it broke. It was my favorite pair of heels so now I am more careful. My dress was tight but still respectable. It was short but it was the length that said I like to party but I am not a whore. I dressed to go out somewhere nice like he said. I made my way up to the top of the stairs and I noticed a note taped to the door. He better not of canceled on me or he is a dead man. I knocked anyways then I grabbed the note. I was kind of mad for walking up three flights of stairs and he is not here. "My dearest Nikki, I have a very special night planned for us. I need you to look down." I looked down. On the ground it said, "See this chalk line I need you to follow it." Great, he better not have me go on a cross country scavenger hunt all over

255

the property. I am all dressed up. I started to walk back down the stairs. My five inch high heels are not really meant to be walking shoes. The arrows went to the right so I went in that direction. "So help me God if he is not here I am going to be so pissed off." I said under my breath. It was about ninety five out and I was starting to get sweaty. I started to follow the chalk arrows on the concrete.

My friends at the pool saw me. They started to whistle and call my name. I waved. I was looking good today so I couldn't blame them for noticing. "Hey Nikki you must have a hot date tonight." My friend yelled.

"Yes I do actually." I heard a few people whistling at me. I stood there and did the Miss America wave. I started walking again. I followed the line to the street. I was between two buildings and I could see down the sidewalk but I didn't see Jack anywhere. The words on the ground said "Stand right here." "Ok. I am standing here." I started to look around. Is this some kind of joke? I think I am getting punked. I didn't see Jack anywhere. Then I started to see a pink limo coming down the street from the left side. Jacks head popped out of the top.

"Oh no. What did you do?" I was so surprised. I brought my hands up to my mouth. "This is crazy. You rented this for me?"

"Yeah girl. I did it all for you baby." Jack stuck his head in and ran out and opened the door before the chauffeur could come around and do it. I got in and he handed me some roses. "Here I bought these for you." He said.

"Aw for me. You are so sweet. You didn't have to do that." I said. "Wow this is so spectacular. I have only been in a limo one time in my life and that was for prom." I said.

"Me too. Except it was such a weird group of people in the limo with me that it was no fun. My high school was different. Home coming was always the bigger party and it totally rocked. There was barely anyone at my prom and it was in a hall that was in the middle of nowhere. Whoever was in charge of the decorating did a horrible job. The food sucked. It was not fun at all."

"Aw poor baby. Well I am sorry to hear that. My prom was awesome. It was like something you would see in the movies. It was at a big hotel ball room and it was decked out with everything. I had a blast."

"You were pretty lucky then." He said.

"This limo is much cooler though." I said. It was pretty neat. It had lights on the ceiling that looked like stars when we went through a tunnel. It also had special light on the doors. "So where are we going on our hot date?"

"It's a surprise. You had to know I was going to say that."

"You know I hate surprises." I said.

"Well you are going to love this one." He said smiling.

I was pretty impressed. "So can we drink in here or what?" I said.

"I don't know? Can we?" He said as he pulled out a bottle of wine and two giant glasses. "I wanted to save these for tonight's festivities but I brought another bottle for later if we finish this one." He said.

"You are so prepared." I said. This guy is good, too good. He thought of everything. He poured the wine out into our glasses. It was a sweet white wine which is my favorite. The red kind always seemed to bitter to me. It tasted like drinking antifreeze. "Fill up my cup. I am getting fucked up since I don't have to drive."

"Awesome." He said. I drank the first glass quickly. "Wow you better pace yourself." He filled me up for round two.

"Hey have you stood outside the sun roof yet?"

"Yes when we pulled up."

"I want to do it. That's on my bucket list. I always wanted to stand outside the sun roof. I didn't get to at prom."

"Uhh. Don't do it now. We are on the highway."

"Good point. I will wait to get on a slower road." I said. I looked out the window. It looked like we were going down town. I knew it would probably be packed since it was the fourth and everyone was down there. There are some things I like about downtown and other things I didn't like. You definitely don't want to be down there alone at night. There are some really bad areas. The tourist attractions are ok but I would not stray too far from them at night. We were driving towards the arch. Then I realized where he was probably taking me. After a few minutes I saw the brick wall to my favorite restaurant.

"We are here." He said. The chauffer got out and opened our doors. I was so excited.

"I have not been here in a few years. I can't believe you remember that I said I really liked this restaurant. The food is expensive but it is so good. So so good. You will like it trust me."

"I hope you enjoy it. You can get whatever you want. My wallet hopes you get the soup though." He said laughing. "No really you can get what you want. I remember you saying you really liked this place so I made reservations."

"Ok wow that is so nice of you. They have great sea food here. I hope you like sea food."

"Yes I like shrimp and lobster. But my absolute favorite thing is fish sticks. They are so good."

"Are you trying to be funny? They don't serve fish sticks here jack ass. It would be funny if you did ask the waiter though." I said as I gave him a slight elbow nudge. Guys like it when you slap them around a bit. So we walked in. I could smell the spicy aroma coming out of here from down the street. I looked at Jack. "I think it smells great in here don't you?" I said.

"Well, if you like the smell of dead fish then if smells amazing." I gave him an evil look. "I am sorry. I am just joking. I like fish too." We were quickly seated. Good thing. I was a little tipsy from the wine. I looked down the menu. I saw the fish I had been craving. It was covered in cheese and it was a little spicy. Just the way I like it. Jack ordered the lobster tail.

"Wow you are going for it huh. That is the most expensive thing on the menu." I said.

"Well, I am splurging today so I am going for it. It is Fourth of July. You are lucky I am not eating crab legs. So are you having a good time so far?" He said.

"Yes it is amazing. Just like something out of a fairy tale."

"So, we are at my favorite restaurant. What is your favorite restaurant?" I said.

I had to think for a minute before speaking. "Well it makes me really sad to talk about it because it is closed down now. It was just another one of the casualties from this incredible shitty economy. In my heart it was a special place to me. I ate there with my family. I ate there for homecoming. I ate there for my twenty first birthday. So to me it was special. It was Casa Gabrielardo. It was the best restaurant."

"I have eaten at one. I liked it." I said.

"Every time I went I always got a grande margarita and the fantastico sampler platter. The platter was perfect. It had quesadillas, which were delicious, a few chicken drummies, some tequitos and some potato skins. I know that is a weird grouping but it hit the spot every time. It was perfect for me. Then I got deep fried ice cream or the sopapilla with ice cream which was also amazing. I know I can buy those things at the grocery store or at other restaurants but it does not taste the same. I looked online to see if I could find the recipe that the restaurant used but I could not find anything. Now I get this horrible craving that can never be satisfied."

"Whoa you need to simmer down. Wow you sure are bitter about this babe. You better calm down. I see that blood vessel popping out of your head." I said.

"Ok. Ok. I will try to not be so bitter or depressing. It is just that all my favorite things growing up are no longer there now. Like Northwest Plaza, Famous Barr, Venture, Service Merchandise, all the

Hostess products, my three favorite movie theatres. I just don't get it. How could something that is in every store and in most vending machines go out of business? It just blows my mind. Ok I got it all out of my system. I am probably depressing you so I am moving on. So what do you usually do for the fourth?" He asked.

"Well I usually go with my family out to my uncle's house in the country. They shoot off fireworks there. It is still legal. Last year since it was super dry. We almost caught his yard on fire."

"I bet. It was a hundred degrees for two months with no rain."

"So what do you usually do?" I asked.

"Well I would go with my family and we would park along the highway and watch the show from there. I know that sounds cheesy. One time I went down to the arch to watch the firework show and there was a big fight that broke out right in front of us. So we stopped going down there. One group of African Americans walked by another group and then fist started swinging. The security jumped in pretty quickly and broke it up though. For the last few years my friends and I would go to this park late at night and shoot fireworks off at each other. We would take bottle rockets and shoot them right out of our hands. One time I took one of those things with thirty shots and I turned it sideways at someone. It was pretty funny to watch. He had to jump behind a port o potty while those little missiles zoomed by."

"Oh my God, that is so dangerous. Did you guys ever get hurt?"

"Well one time this new guy came and a bottle rocket actually hit him but he was ok. The worst thing that happened to me was I was throwing a smoke bomb, that wasn't supposed to blow up, but it did and my hand was engulfed in blue flames. I have scars from it." He reached his hand out to show me. The scar was shaped like a lightning bolt pattern on his fingers.

"Hey you are like that wizard guy. Ha ha." I kept rubbing my fingers against his hand as I looked into his eyes.

"I had to run a mile through the woods in pitch darkness to find my way back to my car. It was pretty amazing that I did not get lost." I looked over.

"Hey foods here." I was starving.

"This looks delicious. It does smell good. Can I have a nibble of yours." he said. "I just want a sample I promise."

"Sure I will cut you a piece." I said. We ate. I kept having flash backs of when I use to come here with my family. Jack was tearing into his lobster like a barbarian. I took a little piece and dipped it in the special butter they had and it melted in my mouth. "I might get that next time." I said.

"I know I am."

"Are you going to save room for dessert?" I said.

"Maybe I have to see what they have. I think I saved just enough room to share a dessert."

"The proportion size here is monstrous. We can share. Just don't cross the border into my side of the brownie."

"Alright, I want the ultimate brownie sundae." I said to the waiter.

"Coming right up." He said.

"I know you probably didn't want to share but this is a huge sundae. It is literally the size of your head."

"Ok I believe you." In a few minutes the biggest brownie I have ever seen was placed at our table. Jack said "Whoa you are right. That is the biggest brownie. This is a whole brownie pan." He said in disbelief.

"I think this usually feeds four people so don't be a hero and try to eat it all." I said.

"Gotcha." He said. I took a bite. I got a bit of ice cream and brownie. It was the most decadent brownie I have ever eaten. It was moist and chocolaty. The ice cream had caramel and whip cream on top. I took another bite. I was getting lost in the chocolate kisses.

Jack said "This is good."

"You bet. It is like a party in my mouth." I said.

"I want to party in your mouth." Jack said. "You know how I know you like it. You are humming while you are eating it."

"I can't help it. It is so good. You are not a girl. You don't have a vagina so you don't understand."

"That's true. I don't have a vagina." After ten minutes we both put out forks down and looked at each other.

"I am so stuffed." I said. I looked at Jack who had chocolate and ice cream on his face.

"Me too. Are you ready to go?"

"Let's split." We left the restaurant. "Hey if you really want to make this romantic you will carry me to the car. He squatted down.

"Hop on."

"Oh, piggy back style. I was thinking you would carry me in your arms, not have me jump on your back. My skirt is too short for that. My hoo ha will be hanging out." He then leaned over and put me on his shoulder. "Ahhhh this is what cavemen do. This is not keeping it classy."

"Do you like this better?"

"No. I just ate a ton of food." He carried me to the limo and that was so romantic.

We hoped in. "That was good food." He said. "Are you ready to go cruising down town?"

"Sure show me around. I want to be near downtown to watch the fireworks. Maybe we can have our own fireworks later." I said in a sexy voice.

"Hey girl, that's sounds good to me."

As we sat there in the limo he grabbed my hand and looked me in the eyes. I don't know what he is doing but I hope he doesn't propose to me, although I would probably say yes. I don't really want to get married till I am twenty five and have my first child at twenty six. I know it's very by the book. Better then getting pregnant at eighteen and ruin my life. He took my hand and looked into my eyes.

"Nikki, you know we have done a lot of things together. Some of it so weird I can't tell anyone else about it. You have many qualities that I truly admire. I know we have gone on a few dates together and I had a great time. I want to ask you a question. I want you to know I want to just date you and no one else. I think you have a good time with me as well. Do you want to make it official? I want to call you my girlfriend."

"That sounds wonderful." I said to him. "Yes I want to date only you. Exclusively." I said.

"That's wonderful. You are not just saying that because we are in a limo together and we just had a great meal together and if you said no it would be really awkward now?" He said.

"No, it's not because you rented the limo." We both leaned our full bodies over and hugged and kissed with incredible passion. He started to kiss my neck. "That feels good. So we are a couple now?" I said.

"Yes. Cool, so I want five kids and I already have the names picked out. Cecil, Lemon, Zeus."

"Whoaaa there. We have all the time in the world. Besides, I didn't say anything about kids or marriage. Those are some unusual names. Do I get a say in it?"

"Yeah like twenty five percent."

"All those names I veto. Well let's not be too hasty we can think about it." He said.

"Sure. So I am going to move in with you now."

"Wait a second. We are going too fast. Anyways you live there practically already except you sneak out when I wake up.

"I always feel bad about that. You know that right?"

"Sure sure. You do it every time. What is the reason why you leave?"

"When I fall asleep at your place I don't have the realistic nightmares."

"Well I hope one day you stay the whole night and I don't end up waking up alone. It worries me when I wake up and you are not there that's' all." He said.

"Well maybe we can make that start to happen." I said as we embraced each other. We kissed each other for the next twenty minutes. I didn't want anything else except to be near Jack.

I lost total track of time. It was starting to get dark out. We watched the sun set and it was beautiful. The sky was filled with purple and orange clouds. The fireworks were starting soon. I could not wait. I have never watched fireworks from the sun roof of a limo before. We had an excellent view as well. We found a close spot to park at. It was about nine and the grand show was about to begin. We both stood up and watched as the first boom signaled the start of the show. "This should be fun." I said. We stood in the limo looking into the sky. It was a cloudless sky filled with stars, a perfect night for this. The show suddenly began as the first rocket burst forth. One rocket shot off into the sky and exploded. The sky lit up in shimmering blue. Oh pretty. More and more fireworks started to burst forth. I liked the red ones best. Sometimes when they exploded they looked like they formed shapes. I know that is coincidental but I liked to believe it was done on purpose. We watched as the sky was lit up in beautiful colors. It was mesmerizing. Then I thought of an idea.

"Hey I thought of something." I said.

"What's that?"

"Come into the limo with me." I could tell by his facial expression he thought I meant something sexual. "No not sex. But maybe we will do that later." I said in a naughty tone. "I am going to fly into the sky where the fireworks are going off."

"What? Really? Well I am trying to decide if that is a good idea. Well since we can't get hurt that might be fucking awesome actually. Cool let's do it." He said. We both sat next to each other. In a minute I was hovering outside my body. Jack separated a minute later. "Alright let's go." We shot up to the sky. "Are you sure no one can see us." He said.

"Yes. I think to them we blink in and out so they are not sure what they are seeing. Unless you are trying to be seen they can't see you. When I look at you I just see your glowing silhouette. Where your chest is, there is a glowing light."

"Ok I trust you. I just don't want to be photographed and my face end up on the cover of a magazine." He said.

I chuckled. "You are so funny." We flew across the crowd of spectators and then above the river. The fireworks were shot from a barge in the river. We floated right above the barge now. "This is going to be fun." I said. I heard the boom and saw three streaks fly toward us. It was weird knowing that you could not get hurt. It went against my natural instincts to flee. Here it comes. Boom. Boom. Boom. They exploded all around us. The sky was on fire all around me. It was amazing. I could see the explosions through Jack. He was transparent. Colorful sparks flew all over. "It looked like you were walking on glowing flowers." What people saw from the ground was nothing compared to what I was seeing from this view. The sky was on fire. Sparks rained down and went through us. Jack had his arms out like a kid who was standing out in the rain.

"This was a great idea." He said.

"I want to try something. I am going to hold onto the rocket as soon as it launches."

"Cool let's try it." We flew downward. We would have to be quick. I flew near the barge. I was looking for a light. Then I saw it. I saw sparks shoot out the bottom then it launched. I was right there with it. I did not know for sure how fast I could fly but this had to be testing the limit. I stayed right by the rocket. I had my arms out to my side as I circled it as we moved toward the heavens. I orbited around my rocket as the sparks shot out of the bottom of it. Higher and higher I went. The wind went through me. I knew it was going to explode soon. I wrapped my arms around it hugging it and then it exploded in a shimmer of bright light. All I saw was green light all around me. I felt the sparks move through me that time. It didn't hurt but I felt the sensation of them burning through my phase of existence. I looked down as the last of my green fireball burned out. I looked over and I saw Jack flying up holding onto two rockets as he spun wildly into the black sky. He must be using the focus to control the rockets. He zoomed past me. I watched as he went higher and higher. Then boom. Both exploded at the same time. These two had multiple color changes. As it fell around me it changed from blue, to green then to red. "That was cool." I said.

"Thank you. In case you didn't know I do all my own stunts." He said.

"Here comes another one. Watch this. You are going to learn something today son." I saw a fireball speeding my way. I started to focus on forming a solid barrier around myself. And I moved under the rocket as it zipped by me and exploded. A shower of red sparks rained down and cleverly followed the outline of my barrier. I saw some flashes coming from the crowd that was watching.

"Wow. Did you make that look like a heart on purpose? That was amazing. I am sure the spectators were wowed. They probably didn't know fireworks can do that. I saw some flashes in the crowd you will probably be in the news tomorrow." He said.

"No, fireworks cannot do that. Not without help anyways. It is your turn to try something. Impress me." I said.

"You better hold onto your head because you are about to have your mind blown." He said. A few rockets shot up at once. He moved towards them at lightning speed. I watched as he raised his arms. I was not sure what he was going to do but I could tell he was really focusing. The rockets flew upwards then they started to curve downward forming an oval shape. All four seemed to follow a circular path. Each rocket had a path that was slightly smaller than the other. It formed four glowing circles one within the other. They started to rotate in opposite directions. Then it exploded in colorful sparks. I heard a few sounds of amazement coming from the crowd.

"The crowd liked that one. We are so going to be on the news." I said. "My turn." I saw a flash of light as one came flying by me. I was going to really amp up this explosion. I saw the rocket reach its height. I held my hands out in front of me. This is going to be an explosion to remember. It started to explode. I focused on the sparks as they began to spread. I made the sparks go faster and farther. This one was a red burst and it lit up the whole sky. It looked like it was daytime out for a few seconds. The sky was an unnatural red hue. It was if the sun itself exploded. I watched as the sparks rained down into the water.

I flew over to Jack. "That's was a good one. We are probably freaking out the crowd. They are probably thinking this show is amazing compared to the shows before." He said.

"Hey I think the finale is coming up. Do you want to try anything special?" I said as I heard the thunder of multiple rockets being shot.

"Yes, I do actually." He put his arms around my waist and pulled me towards his hot body. I put my arms around his shoulders. We started to slowly spin together. I closed my eyes. We both tilted our heads and moved in closer to kiss each other. He moved his mouth in to kiss me. When our lips pressed against each other the world around us exploded in colors. It was so amazing watching stars explode around us. I felt the passion from his lips as sparks rained on us from every direction. This was the kiss that made all other kisses seem like little unemotional pecks. I felt the thunder of the explosions going off. We were engulfed in flames as we pressed our bodies tightly together. It felt like we were becoming one. I looked into his eyes as he gazed into mine. I was focusing on him and he was using the focus on me. Our thoughts and bodies were merging together. I felt all hot and warm inside. "I want you so bad." He said. "I want you too." I said. I didn't know what was happening. I was fading into him. It felt like my soul was being pulled away from me and into Jack. I was having a sensory overload that was so intense I was screaming inside my head. Our thoughts were merging. I was smiling and happy but sad and crying at the same time. "I have to…stoooppp. Musstt…goooo back too…my...boddddyy" I tried to say as my energy was leaving me. I felt like I was becoming water. It was too much for me to handle. My concentration was lost. I had to get away. I left Jack and tried to get back to my mortal body before my projection faded. I didn't make it.

"Nikki, wake up! Please wake up! Oh god! Please don't be dead or in a coma. Wake up." He said. I was starting to come through. I was lying on the seat with my head on Jack's lap. I was feeling weak and I had a really bad headache. "What happened?" I said.

"Well we were in the sky kissing and you said you had to go back to your body but as you started to leave me you faded before getting back to your human body. I came back here and I tried to wake you for ten minutes and you were not responding. I was getting ready to take you to the emergency room."

I was starting to come through. "Yeah I kind of remember now. I don't know what you felt, but when we pressed together it was as if I was merging with you. I felt like my soul was being drained. I had to separate from you and go back to my body." I said.

"For me it felt like I wanted to be with you and I was surrounding you. I am sorry if things got out of hand. I didn't mean to hurt you. I am still trying to understand our powers and I really didn't know what was happening."

"No I didn't hurt." I was quiet for a minute. "The best way to explain what happened would be to say it was as if I had a thousand orgasms all at one time. It was just so intense that I didn't know if I could take

271

anymore. It felt like we were becoming one person." I said.

"I think your right. That would be the best way to describe it." We were quiet for a few minutes as the limo drove us back to the apartments. "So, I was that good huh. It felt like a thousand orgasms." He said.

"Yeah you were." I said chuckling. "So out of all that happened that is the first thing you say." I said.

"Ok. Ok. I am sorry. I was that good that you passed out and had to leave the party." He said.

"Oh my God." I said as I punched his arm. "Listen I don't know what was happening. That is just the best way for me to describe what happened. Stop being such a cocky bastard." I said.

"Ok. I will stop bragging. I just know that this is stuff I can't tell anyone else. They will think I am freaking loco. That's why I say this stuff to just you. I am usually not like this." He said.

"Please. You are the cockiest athletic guy I know." I said.

We sat quietly in the limo together. I was a little tired so I laid my head in Jacks lap as we rode back to the apartments. I kept looking at his face and he kept staring down at me. I was really starting to fall in love with him. I was resting up for the rest of the crazy night I was planning to have with Jack. He doesn't even know that tonight is the night I am going to rock his world. He probably just thinks I am tired and ready to go to sleep. After twenty minutes we arrived back at the apartments.

"Hey I want to stand out of the sun roof one last time." I said.

"After you." We both stood up and put our heads out the roof. I saw a few people that I knew standing on their balconies and I waved at them. I watched as we pulled up in front of Jacks apartment.

"Oh no our fun time is over." I said.

"I know but we had fun though right." He said.

"It was a blast. I loved it."

We both got out. Jack went over and said thank you to the limo driver. I waited patiently. Jim came back over and I gave him a big hug. "I had a great time tonight." He said. We kissed for awhile. I didn't want to let go. "Well I will walk you home." He said.

"I don't want to go home I want to go to your place."

"Ok we can hang out there." He said.

"No I don't think you understand. I want to stay over the WHOLE night." His eyes got real big.

"Ohhhh... Ok."

"You catch my drift."

"Yes. I want to make this special."

"You already have made everything special up to this point. That was the most fun that I have had in a while." We both walked up the stairs holding hands. We got to the front door. I think we both didn't know what to expect. I like Jack a lot and he is a special guy. I think he is the type of guy you marry and settle down with so I was willing to have sex. He treated me way better than the other losers I had done things with in the past.

We got to the top of the stairs and Jack put the keys in the door. He looked at me. "We don't have to do anything if you are not ready or want to wait." I looked him in the eyes.

"I am for sure ready. Are you?" At the point I pushed him through the door and threw my arms around him. We embraced each other. We kissed each other passionately. I think all of our pent up sexual feelings and urges were coming out all at once. I knew when I first saw him we would probably end up having sex. I am pretty sure he felt the same way. When he saw me at the pool I could tell he wanted me. We kissed and walked to the bedroom. We were trying to take off each other's clothes as we walked. We entered the bedroom and I grabbed his belt and his pants fell down. He started to undo his shirt. I pushed him onto the bed with just his boxers on. I stood at the foot of the bed and I slowly took my dress off. I still had my underwear and bra on. I jumped on top of him in the bed. We kissed for a few minutes. Our bodies were pressed closely together. Then he rolled over and was on top of me.

"So what do you want to do?" He said. I was getting ready to say something then I heard a loud buzzing coming from outside. "What's that? Get off of me." I yelled. The sound was really loud and ear piercing. Jack stood up and I sat up.

"I think it's the fire alarm." He said. "Hey it is probably just some kids playing a prank. Let's get back to business." He said.

"I don't think that is a prank. I really smell smoke. I am really sorry. I know you are ready to get it on but we need to get out of here. Besides that sound is annoying. I cannot be horny with that alarm sound blasting in my ears. Find your clothes we have to go." I said as I quickly jumped out of bed and started to put my dress back on. I grabbed my shoes.

I could tell Jack was extremely disappointed. He grabbed some shorts and a shirt and we walked to the door. I opened the door and the alarm was going off. We walked to the bottom of the breezeway. A fire truck, police car, and ambulance had pulled up. We walked over to the front side of the apartments and on the second floor there was smoke coming from the balcony. It was thick and black. We walked over to the other residents that were standing outside and asked them what happened. They said someone was shooting fireworks off and something landed on the balcony. The balcony started to burn. Firemen were getting ready to hose it down.

"Well. Let me walk you to your door." Jack said.

"I don't mind waiting out here with you."I said.

"No it is ok. It will probably take them two hours to make sure everything is out and no longer smoking. You have school tomorrow and I have work in the morning. I will probably just go sleep at my parent's house." He said.

We both held hands as we started to walk to my apartment. "You know when the alarm first went off I thought maybe Max did it but I guess this time it probably was just a firework that happened to land on the balcony. Anyways, well I had a really nice time tonight. I am so sorry we didn't get to have sex. I know you have been really patient. You are a really great guy. We can try again some other time. I promise." I said.

"It is alright. I am going to be ok. I know we will have other chances. Don't worry about it. I had a great time with you tonight as well."

I hugged him and gave him a big kiss. I whispered in to his ear. "Hey if you are feeling fearless you can try to sneak into my window and have your way with me."

"Uhh. Well, see if we got caught your dad could easily rip my arms out of their sockets so I am going to pass right now. But I do appreciate the offer." He said smiling.

"Alright well I will miss you." I said.

"I will miss you too. Bye Bye."

"Bye." I said as I slowly shut the door. Maybe I will keep the window slightly open in case he changes his mind.

Chapter 27

The mind of Jack. Saturday July 6.

I was waiting for Nikki. We were going to do some training tonight. She said tonight is going to be different. We are not going to try to travel or anything like that. Too bad. I was starting to get the hang of flying. I could move as fast as lightning. I could fly at least as good as a bird if not better.   Tonight we are going to practice fighting. I like to fight so I am cool with that. From our previous training together I knew that to have an actual influence over a physical object you had to really focus. If I wanted to make something move a few feet I had to really push it as if I wanted it to move a mile. While I waited for her to show up I practiced for a bit. I projected out of my body and I would create different weapons. I did really like carrying an ax. Axes have weight to them that swords usually don't have. An ax was my weapon of choice. I was good with swords as well. Swords just don't have power to cut things in half.

I set out a board across two chairs to see if I could break it in half with the ax. Alright I am ready to show this wood who is the boss. I sat two feet away from the wood. I sent my projection out. I stood by the board now. My creation was fully armored. I raised my mighty ax high. I waited a second. I wanted the wood to splinter and then shatter into a thousand pieces. "Just brake!" I yelled. I brought the axe down in an arc. When my blade was right at the wood their surfaces touched and the ax went right through it as if I was a ghost. Dangit. I brought it back up and took another swing. I passed right through it again. I don't know what I could do differently to influence a physical object. In real life I could break boards with my fist and the side of my hand. I had taken a few karate lessons and I knew how it was done.

I heard a knock on the door. "Who is it I yelled?" No one responded. I knew it had to be Nikki. She was probably playing a prank on me like the last few times. This time I was ready. I sent my projection right against the door. I could sense see had her projection right on the other side of the door waiting to spook me when I look through the peep hole. Not this time I thought to myself. This should be funny. My mental avatar stuck his hands through the door and bear hugged her image. I could sense her struggling. She knew she was caught. I backed up and pulled her threw the door. "You were going to try to scare me again huh." I said smiling.

She was laughing. I could not actually see her face but I heard the sound. She was a thing with a black cloak on and it had one orange eye and tentacles where its mouth would be. She knew she had been caught. "I am on my way over. I thought you were going to fall for my tricks again Jack. You are getting better." She said as her tentacles moved around creepily with a mind of their own.

"Hells yeah I am. I can almost cut this board in half."

"Haha. Almost what does that mean? It is still in one piece." She said.

"I am working on it. I still have not completely figured it out yet." I said.

Her image vanished. I guess she was almost here. I walked over to open the door. "Welcome baaabyyy!" I said. She was standing outside my door looking beautiful as ever.

"Hello. What is going on? You are not a one orange eyed, tentacle monster this time. But this form is your scariest creation yet. I was really frightened when I opened the door."

"Haha. You think you are so funny. You totally ruined my fun. I was only going to make you pee your pants." She said as she hugged me as she walked in.

"Great you are to kind." I said as I kissed her cheek. "So what is your plan for tonight?" I said.

"We are going to learn how to fight." She said as she fake punched me in the stomach. "Are you ready for this? I have been practicing in real life. I am getting pretty good at the speed bag."

"Oh yeah so you are getting good." I walked over to the board I had set up to brake. "Can you do this? HIYAAA!" I brought my hand down with full force. I struck the board with the side of my hand. I was out of practice but I still knew how to do it. To my surprise it did not break. I have to say if the board shatters, like it is suppose to, your hand does not hurt. If your hand doesn't go through it, it feels like your hand may be broken. "Owww. Shit." I said as I grabbed my hand and turned around. I bent over as I tried to get the feeling back into my hand. Nikki was laughing hysterically.

"Really Jack. Hiya. That was awesome. But, seriously is your hand ok?" She said.

"Yes I don't think I broke it if that is what you mean. I swear I could do it. I use to do that all the time when I was younger. I know I have not tried in awhile but if I know anything it is how to chop boards in half with these killing machines." I said as I raised my hands up.

"Ok killer. Come over here and sit by me. I will get some ice for your hand and then we can begin."

"Ok." I went over to sit by her on the floor. She put some ice in a bag and came back over and sat by me.

"Alright, here you go." I placed the ice under my hand. "Alright are you ready to begin."

"Yes let's do this. At least my projection won't have a damaged hand. " I said smiling. I think my ego hurt more than my actual hand. We both closed our eyes and started to focus. I didn't know what she wanted to fight with. I didn't know if she wanted to go with swords or bare knuckled fist fighting. I imagined myself wearing a black kimono with a dragon on it. She appeared next to me in a red kimono. We faced each other in the middle of the floor.

"Ok so we are going to just try to fight each other for fun and training so don't go crazy. You can try to hit me as hard as you can. Don't hold back. It is only a mental fight so no matter how much you hit me it won't physically hurt my human body."

"Ok just some friendly sparring. Remember that. I am more worried about you hurting me then me hurting you actually."

"You mean like this." She thrust her right fist right at my chest. I thought it would go right through me but she certainly knew what she was doing. It hit me square in the chest and I flew back a few feet. She charged at me again and I went to block this time. My block was ineffective as I soon found out. Her right hand smacked me in the face and I hit the wall. As I spun around from the hit I brought my right hand up to back hand her and my hand went right through her. Her foot came up quick and kicked me in the stomach. That hurt bad. I almost lost my concentration. I fell to the ground. I made the time out sign with me hands.

"Wait a second. How are you hitting me and I cannot hit or block you? This seems a bit unfair wouldn't you say." I said.

"When I hit you, I put my full concentrated energy into my hands or whatever I am going to use to make contact with you. Instead of trying to use energy and focus to keep my whole projection seen I just try to concentrate on my hands. Stand up I will show you." She stood by me. She reached her hand out with a finger extended. I watched as her finger came closer to me. She moved it right through me. "See that is what normally happens. Now this is what happens when I focus. "She reached out her finger again and this time when it got near me it felt different. It felt like it was pushing me away without even touching me. Sort of like two magnets that had the same charged ends being pushed together. She moved it closer to my outline and this time she touched me. I saw a few bolts of static electricity jump from her finger to me. She easily pushed me back a foot with just her finger.

"Let me try it on you now." I said as I brought my finger closer to her skin. I started to move my energy into my finger. I brought my finger to her skin. I pushed it forward and it hit solid skin this time. She moved back a little.

"That's good. Now throw a punch at me."

"Are you sure?"

"I will give you a free one. First one is on the house."

"If you say so." I raised my hand and punched forward and it hit solid flesh. Nikki moved back but for the most part she didn't budge.

"You have to really want to hurt me if you want to be able to move me or it doesn't work. You have to want it." Try again.

"I really don't want to hurt you."

"Yes hit me. I give you my permission. We are training and I want you to try to hurt me."

"Ok, here we go." I said. I took a step back and got in a boxers stance. I brought both my arms up in front of my face. I swung my right hand forward. I really meant it this time. I hope she knows what she is doing. Nikki didn't move or try to block this time. I hit her hard in the chest. Her feet flew up into the air. She flew back and landed on her back. That would have knocked the air out of a normal human body. I know. I have had it done to me before. Usually you end up gasping for air for a few seconds. I watched as Nikki just smiled and sat up. It was very unnatural.

She stood up and moved over to me. "That was a good one. Alright you seem to know what you are doing so let's fight." She said with a left fist that came flying at me. I moved to the right barely able to jump out of the way. I brought out the old knee and hit her in the stomach she went flying back a little. She quickly came at me again with a series of quick punches. I decided to just try and deflect them. I was able to stop most of them. One got through though and smashed me in the face. My head went back. When I opened my eyes again I saw a foot coming right at my nose. I ducked and grabbed her leg. I spun around and threw her at the wall. Normally a person would just smash into the wall but she went through it. I stood there by the door waiting for her to jump through the wall at me.

"I know you are waiting for me. Come on. Come on. Where are you hiding? I am waiting." I said facing the wall I just threw her out of. I looked around the room. Maybe she was going to attack me from behind. I however did not plan for an attack through the ceiling. She dropped through the ceiling and her foot hit me right on my shoulder. I dropped to the floor. That really hurt. I almost lost my concentration with that hit. She was standing in a karate stance a few feet away by the screen door. "RAARRRRRR!" I yelled as I charged at her. She tried to throw a punch but I caught her arm. I grabbed her by the waist and we floated through the glass door and through the railing. I watched in what seemed like slow motion as we hurled towards the ground. It came up quick. We fell three flights and smacked into the ground. We didn't have anything to fear since we could not die. She was up before me and her foot came down right on the back of my head. I grabbed her by the leg and shoved her down. I got behind her and punched

283

her hard in the back. I knew that had to hurt. I started to repeatedly punch her in the back of her head. She started to fade out. I guess it was too much for her. I hope I didn't kill her. I felt regretful for a few moments. "I am sorry. I didn't mean to hurt you. Where ever you are?" I said.

Then I heard a whistle. "Hey up here handsome." I looked up and Nikki was on the roof. I was guessing it was her. It was a giant suit of armor and it was carrying double weapons. I flew up there. "Think of a weapon and we will fight." I pictured myself with a sword and shield. "Great let's dance." She started to swing her swords at me and I blocked with my sword. She swung her right arm and I blocked with my sword. Then she thrust forward at me with her left and I barely blocked it with my shield. We circled each other trying to find a weakness in the others defense. I swung in with my sword and she blocked and counterstriked with her other sword. It struck me on my side. I was in some pain. I knew we were not supposed to feel pain but this actually hurt. I quickly swung forward at her legs and I clipped her right above the knee. "Arhhhh." I heard her yell. She was getting angry I could sense her feelings. She put both arms out and spun towards me. I blocked with my shield. Sparks flew out. I don't know if it was more than my little training could handle but my shield was starting to fade and become transparent. I swung at her and she ducked then when I came back around I swung down and hit her across the chest. She was certainly in some pain now. She grabbed her side. "Do you yield?" I said to her.

She stood up straight and got into an attack stance. "I will NEVER yield to you Jack." She yelled. She swung with all her might and I stuck my sword out to stop her and it shattered in a blue brilliance. She then spun around and swung high. I brought my shield up to block but it was to no avail. Her emotional anger focused into her swords was too much for my defenses. It broke through my shield and stuck me in the chest. My body trembled. I knew she had gotten the better of me today. "That was a goo...d on...n...eee." I managed to say as my projection was destroyed. I was no longer able to focus. I tried to go back to my human body before I was awoken. I traveled back at incredible speed. After a moment of entering my own mind I awoke. Nikki's body was still there in the trance form. I guess she was on her way back. I woke up and moved around. After a few minutes she came through.

"That was a good work out training session huh?" She said.

"That was fun. Sorry about pounding your face in a few times." I said smiling.

"Oh, yeah. No problem. Sorry about slicing you in half with my sword." She said.

"I need to do some more practicing." I said.

"Yes you do. How are we supposed to beat Max? We need to have fight practice all the time." She said.

"I totally agree. I am so tired. I don't know what happens to me when we do this whole out of body experience but it makes me exhausted." I said.

"I am tired as well." She said.

I was lying on the carpeted floor. She moved over and put her head on my shoulder. This is nice I thought. It was comforting. I grabbed a blanket nearby and covered us up. In a few minutes I fell asleep.

Chapter 28

The mind of Jack. Sunday July 7.

It was about five in the afternoon. I was getting ready to officially meet Nikki's parents for the first time. I was somewhat nervous. I know how these things usually go. They end up asking you a series of questions about your likes and dislikes. It is very similar to a job interview or some sort of demented game show to see if you're a good match for their daughter. I tried to dress up a little since this was serious. I did really want a relationship with their daughter. I put on a dress shirt and tie like I would wear to work. Someone once told me if you want the job you have to dress for it. Dress to impress. I wanted her parents to think I was serious about their daughter.   I will look way better than the other losers she would date. I threw on some cologne. I knew it was strong but you have to smell good now days. I was about done. I took a long look in the mirror. Dam I look good. I would date me. I did my final check before I left the mirror. Nothing in my teeth. Check. Zipper up. Check. Nose all clean. Check. All my hair in place. Check. Great I am ready to rock and roll.

Nikki said she never takes her boyfriends over to meet her parents. I hope it not because her parents are psychos. She seemed to avoid answering the question when I asked why. I hope this meal is not going to be super awkward.

I went in to my living room. I grabbed the flowers and wine I bought earlier. I hope her mom likes the wine. Nikki told me that she did. Well alright I am ready to make a great first impression. I walked out of my apartment. I was optimistic about meeting them. I walked down the stairs and up the sidewalk.

I arrived at their door. It was really weird not driving to a girl's house. I better not mess this up because I live in the next breezeway over. I would probably run into her family at the pool and around the property. Here we go.

I started knocking on the door. The door flung open. A short beautiful woman with dark hair opened the door. "Hello, you must be Jack." She said in a very nasally voice.

"Yes that's me." I stuck my hand out for a hand shake. She went in for a hug. "Oh, ok. You are a hugger." I saw where Nikki got her looks from. Her mom was still attractive for being in her late forties. I have to say that she has the biggest fake breasts I have ever seen. They seemed to defy gravity. Judging by the shirt she was wearing she wasn't ashamed of them. I followed the rule of the sun. I kept telling myself don't stare directly at them. This is going to be an interesting night.

"Come on in. It is finally nice to meet you. Nikki has told us so much about you."

"I brought you a gift. Nikki says you like wine."

"Aww think you. You didn't have to do that." She said.

"No it's no problem."

"Nikki your handsome young gentleman is here." She yelled. I thought it was funny because these apartments are not that big. She came down the hall. She was truly stunning. Her hair was done up and she had make up on. She had a shiny dress on as well.

"Wow you look amazing. Did you get your hair done?" I said.

"Yes I got it cut and highlighted. I even put make up on just for you."

"Thanks I totally appreciate it. I wore a tie."

"Boys have it so easy. You wear a tie everyday you go to work though."

"That's true." I said. It was silent for a second.

"Oh this is your first time here. Do you want me to give you the tour? Remember when you gave me the tour of your place. You were such an arrogant asshole" She said. I didn't think I was being an asshole. She grabbed my hand. "I am only kidding."

"Follow me. This is the living room." It had a black leather couch and matching recliner. They had a very expensive looking entertainment center. There was a large sixty inch flat screen TV in the middle of it. "This is the dining room where I do all my schoolwork on. It is usually covered with books and papers. This way to the bedroom. This is where the magic happens." She laughed at her own joke.

"There better not be any magic happening in there young lady." I heard her mom yell down the hall.

"Isn't that what you told me when you showed me your place? Actually there is no magic happening here with my parents in the next room over." Her room was pretty basic. There wasn't a lot of stuff in it.

"Wow you are pretty clean for a girl. Most girls have piles of clothes all over and shoes scattered all over." I said.

"My mom comes in here and cleans. It is usually like that." She opened her closet door and there was the girl mess I was talking about. "You mean this mess." She said smiling.

" Jackpot. Yes that mess. Nikki I have to tell you this. It would appear that you are a real girl." I said.

"I just want you to know you look really beautiful. I usually only seen you in your work clothes. You look really nice all done up."

"No you don't have to flatter me but can you stop steering at my boobs."

"No actually I was looking at the necklace you have on. It just happened to fall right between your cleavage. Where did you get that necklace it looks silver?"

"I got it from my grandma after I slid into the lake and practically died. It is my favorite piece of jewelry. It's also my only real piece. The other stuff I have is fake or plastic. There are a few pieces in there I really like."

"Well I really like the silver snow flake you have on right now. It reminds me of a cold snowy day in January. It looks fancy."

"Well you look fancy too with your dress shirt and tie."

"I wear this to work all the time you just never see me before or after I leave work." I said

I heard the front door close. "Dinners ready." Her mom yelled down the hall.

We walked down the hall. I saw some brown bags and little white containers with dragons on them. "Hope you like Chinese." Nikki said.

"It is one of my favorites. I thought your mom was cooking steak or something."

"Pfft. Yeah right. My mom doesn't cook shit. She comes home tired at night so we usually pick something up or I cook. Sometimes my dad cooks."

"Smells great. Where do you want me to sit?"

"Right here by me." She said. We started to dish out the food. I grabbed a little of everything. There were a few different cups of the different sauces lying on the table. I took a little of each.

"Jack do you want anything to drink?" Nikki's dad said.

"Sure I will take a beer."

We all sat down and started eating. "So… Jack, Nikki says you just got out of college. What is your major?"

"I have a bachelor's degree in graphic design." I said.

"What does that mean? Do you do web pages?" Ralph asked.

"No we were not taught that. Web design is a different program. I do logo design, posters, brochures, business cards, ads things like that. Basically any printed material." I said as I tore into my mongolian beef.

"That is pretty cool. Did you have to take art classes for that or was it all on the computer?" Jenna asked.

"Half of the classes I took were art classes. In my opinion they didn't teach me enough about the programs on the computer though. I had to basically learn two programs on my own. Most of the time we spent drawing and redrawing designs, the other half of the time I spent waiting for the teacher to help me in the computer lab because the computers kept breaking down. I didn't even get to use the two other programs that are usually required to be a graphic designer. I was extremely disappointed in how much I spent to go to college compared to what I got out of it. I feel like college is a form of modern day robbery. Most of the classes you take don't have anything to do with your major. The other half of the classes the teacher is reading straight from a book and I am pretty sure I can do that myself." I said. The parents laughed a little.

"Nikki has said similar things. So are you good at drawing?" Ralph asked.

"I am pretty good."

"If I give you an idea for a tattoo will you draw it for me?"

"Sure I have done that for other people. This one guy wanted this epic battle between angels and demons while aliens watched on in the background. I have a picture of it on my phone. Here let me show you."

"That is pretty wicked. Hey look at this" He showed Jenna. Then Nikki looked at it.

"So when you took your art classes did you have to draw naked people?" Jenna asked.

"Yes. It is not like what they show on TV though. The people we are drawing are not super models. Most of the ones I drew were large unattractive woman. It was funny because the teacher would tell her to do different poses so she would pose as if she was playing naked tennis or naked golf. Those people did get paid twenty dollars per hour though, which isn't bad for just standing around or sitting." I said.

"What about guys? Did you have to draw any man parts?" Jenna asked.

"Well in the drawing classes I set off to the side so I didn't get the whole full on frontal view. Now in sculpture class the model would turn around and the teacher made sure everyone added genitalia. It was funny the first time the model came in and disrobed. All the guys were like ewww. Half the girls, I don't think have ever seen a penis before. I could tell that everyone was trying to not look at it. It was extremely awkward for everyone involved. I don't know why they don't just let them wear boxers or something. It's not like anyone is trying to be a master of drawing people's genitals but I am sure there is someone out there doing that."

"So you got a job right out of college. That's pretty amazing."Jenna said.

"My friend's dad hired me. Without their help I think I would have had an extremely difficult time. I have not even seen a job ad for a new college graduate. Most say need five years experience. Besides knowing the three main Adobe programs you usually have to know how to do web pages and a few extra programs. I am not entirely sure what my college training was for. They only taught me at beginner level in one program. I had to spend my own time and money trying to learn the other things."

"I sure hope Nikki is able to find employment. She only has a year left of classes." Jenna said.

"I think she will be ok. There always seem to be jobs for teachers, nurses, and over the road truckers." We all laughed except Nikki.

"I am a manager of three bars that my family owns. Ralph is a union electrician. Right now construction is down across the country though. There are not a lot of construction jobs going on around here. He is just sitting in the union hall. Sometimes a small job comes up but he doesn't want to take it because he will lose his place in the line. If he decides to take the job and it is over quickly he will be sent to the back of the line. It's weird how that works. A few years ago he was doing great and he was getting a lot of big jobs. So we bought a very large house. Then things got tough and we could no longer afford to live there." Jenna said.

"I am sorry to hear that. My parents just retired from the post office. It sounds like the post office is getting ready to go under." I said while eating an egg roll.

"I heard they are getting ready to stop delivering on Saturday." Ralph said.

"I think the Internet is taking away their jobs since you can now pay all your bills online and you can email people. I think we are not too far off from having robots do everything for us."I said.

Nikki was getting bored. She had not said anything all dinner. She finished eating before us. I could feel her hand crawling up my leg. I just gave her a look that said "What are you doing?" So I started talking again. Then she did it. She moved her hand to my crotch and squeezed it. Hard. Now if we were not sitting and eating dinner with her parents it would have been great. It took me by surprise. I freaked out and I spit water from my mouth. I quickly expelled it in a forward stream of spit and rice. Her mom was hit in the face with chewed sweet and sour chicken and rice. Nikki lost it. She was busting up laughing. She fell out of her chair laughing. I just kept looking at her. I was shaking my head and laughing too.

"I am so sorry. I can give you money for the food if you want I insist. I am really sorry for that outburst." I said to Ralph and Jenna. Ralph looked pissed and confused. I wasn't afraid of him for being Nikki's dad. I was afraid because he was built like a tattooed gorilla. He was six foot five and three fifty of muscle. I didn't want to agitate him.

"Are you ok?" Ralph stood up. "At first I thought you were choking, I was getting ready to give you the Heimlich maneuver." Nikki was laughing. "It's not funny. He spit water and rice all over my food."

"Look dad you were done anyways your plate was mostly empty."

"Yeah but I was saving that last crab ragoon for the end of my meal and now it has been spit on."

294

"Here there is one left in the bag and you can have it." Nikki said. In my head I was thinking please don't kill me. Your daughter made that happen.

"Ok that's fine." He said. Jenna was using a napkin to wipe off her chest area and Ralph was noticing.

"I am going to have to take a shower and I might need someone to help me later." She said to Ralph seductively.

"Dinner's over. Get a room you two geez. I have a guest over. I will clean up in here. You two go to your room." Nikki said.

"Wow. Yes ma'am. It's that teacher side of her that is taking over. She is learning to be the boss and take control. Ok we will leave you two alone." Ralph said.

"Well it was nice meeting you guys. I am really sorry once again about the food." I said as they walked down the hall.

"Sure Jack. Sure you are sorry. I think you did that so you can have all the leftover food. If you wanted to take it with you, you could have just said so." Jenna said jokingly.

"Hey since you might have just helped me get some sex tonight you are ok in my book and you can come back anytime." Ralph shouted down the hall.

Nikki started to wrap up some of the leftovers that I might have spit water on and put them in a bag for me. It was only two things but lucky for me I love left over Chinese food. We stepped outside and started walking back to my apartment. Nikki held my hand. "So... What do you think about my parents?" Nikki said.

"They seem great. They seem like two people that really care for each other." I said with a smile.

"Every guy I have brought home has fallen crazy in love with my mom. They end up liking her more than me and then when we break up it's hard for me. They still want to be friends with my mom. I have had people unfriend me on the internet and still want to be friends with my mom. They even write her every day."

"I don't think that will happen with us. I have an online account but I don't check it often. By the way thank you for totally embarrassing me. Looks like that is probably the last meal we will be eating together with your family." I said.

"Don't worry I will tell them later what I did. I am sure they will think it is funny. They like you I can tell. Most of my boyfriends before were unemployed or had dead end jobs or were covered in tattoos. You are the most normal guy I have ever brought over. You are fine. That actually went really well."

"Really? You think so? After I spit water and some rice all over your mom, you consider that going well?"

"Don't worry about it." We walked over to my breezeway. She seemed like she was in a good mood.

"Do you want to come up?" I thought I would ask.

"I do but I have to go clean up the mess you made. You are a dirty boy." She put her arms out for a hug. Our faces were close together. I turned my head slightly to kiss her and she pressed her lips against mine with such incredible passion that it took me by surprise. My heart felt like it was on fire with lust. She was forceful but I liked it. She pressed her body against mine. Our tongues moved against each other in a circular dance. She lifted one leg up and wrapped it around me. I started to kiss her neck. She ran her hand through the back of my hair. I was almost ready to go. This kiss made the previous ones seem meaningless. I think she might reconsider going up to my room.

"Hey we can see you!" We heard people yelling and laughing from the pool. "Get a room!"

Nikki started to pull back. Nooo... I didn't want this to stop. We were getting ready to have some adult fun.

"Well I think dinner went well." She said with her arms around my neck.

"Sure, hey you know what? This is the first time we kissed good bye at the end of a date. You usually leave before I wake up. I usually end up screaming down the hall and looking into the rooms to see if you are still there." I said.

"I guess that is true and I am sorry about having to split sometimes. Well, I have to be going Jack but we will have fun again don't worry."

"I won't baby." She started walking away. I had to take a deep breath. My body ached to be with her. I watched as she walked away. I saw the curve of her hips. She turned and waved good bye. It was like I was watching it mesmerized in slow motion. Her hair perfectly blew in the slight breeze. The orange glow from the sunset perfectly radiated her face. I stood there for a few seconds after she left. I really think she is the one. I started walking up the stairs. I have had girl friends before but none have made me feel this way before. Is

this what real love feels like? In my book there is
nothing she could do wrong.

Chapter 29

The mind of Max. Wednesday July 10.

I arrived at work as usual. I knew something different was going to happen today because Stan's truck was already at our workshop. That fat pig gets here late and then goes to the front office for forty minutes to chill out and pick up the work order tickets. Everyone else just sits in the shop till he shows up. This should be interesting I thought. So I suited up and walked to our shop. I slowly walked in to make an appearance just to say hey I am here. I usually just step in for five minutes. If I didn't come into the shop our paths would not cross the entire day which is one of the things I actually like about this job. I came from a job before where the boss was breathing down my neck constantly.

I walked in and took a seat at the table. The other workers were showing each other gross things on the internet. "Whatever you do, don't look up red pancake or blue muffin on the internet. You will see some of the most disturbing images you have ever seen in your entire life." I heard someone say. Jim looked at me. "Hey buddy I have some bad news for you." He said.

Oh shit here we go I thought to myself. I was already having a rough day from lack of sleep. "What might that be?" I said not really wanting to know.

"Durron from the other property is coming down with the pole saw to cut trees with you guys today." Stan said.

"Great." On the inside I was thinking oh hells no. "Really do you think that is necessary? Last time he came down he butchered the trees in the front by the office and they all died." I said. Jim and I both laughed. "You know we have been cutting the trees for a long time now. I am pretty sure we can handle it without him." I said.

"That may be true but he is already on the way here." Stan said. We heard a truck door slam. "Sounds like he is already here. Just make sure you don't bend over in front of him." Stan said laughing.

Today really wasn't the day that Stan should be fucking with me. I was already tired and my mind was in some pain from the events that have been playing out over the last few night. Stan just got put on the top of my shit list today. If I saw an opportunity to hurt him a little I was going to make it happen. He better be watching out.

Jim started to do his best impersonation of Durron. He put his hands to the top of his chest to pretend that he had suspenders. "I got my rainbow suspenders on and they pull my short shorts up so tight you can see the outline of my package." Jim said. Everyone started to laugh.

A minute later Durron came through the door. Jim and I looked at each other. I said "Dammit." under my breath. Durron was the step brother of Stan or some shit. I was not sure of their relationship. It was weird because Durron was African American and Stan was white. Everyone who worked for this company was related to each other one way or another. The thing is, the family members were not good workers at all. They were often getting high or drunk on the job. It was only a matter of time before these idiots ran this company into the ground.

"Where are my two handsome assistants? Heavy on the ass. Where are my two big strong men?" He said. Jim and I just shuddered. The other thing about Durron, he was extremely gay and he wanted the world to know. You know when you meet someone and you think they might be gay but you don't know for sure. There was no doubt in anyone's mind here. He had a company coat that had a giant rainbow on the back of it. He usually wore short cut off jean shorts and rainbow suspenders. Even without him talking, if you saw him walking down the street you would know.

"I am going to get my saw and start cutting and you guys can pick up behind me." He said. He left the room and went back to his truck to get the saw.

"Great. We certainly don't want to pick up things in front of you." Jim said out loud. Everyone in the room started laughing.

"This is going to be a long day. It's probably harder for you guys since you have to watch what you say with him here." They all just nodded in agreement.

Jim and I slowly walked out of the room with a look of defeat. Jim said. "You go first." These guys were grown men and they were not afraid of most things.

Nothing really scared them but if you put a loud gay person in the room they start acting like school girls.

Jim and I trailed behind and picked up braches for the next few hours. We tried to go slowly so we would be far behind him. Jim was afraid that Durron would be checking him out the whole time.

"This must be hard for you since you can't say the N word or the F word around him. That is a double whammy." I said laughingly.

Jim looked around to make sure Durron was out of earshot. "That is true. But since I am trying to make sure I don't accidentally say those two things I am actually saying them over and over in my mind. Nonstop. "

"Ha Ha." I laughed out loud. He was getting quite far ahead of us. "You would think he would stop cutting for a bit and help us pick up. It is kind of far to drag some of these limbs to the dumpsters."

"No kidding." Jim said.

I walked up to the next set of branches. Then I heard a voice. "Hey come here." It took me by surprise. I looked up and there was an elderly gentleman waving me over to his patio. He was old and his hair was white as snow. I had seen him before. He always had on a white t shirt and white shorts. Ok I didn't want to go over because most people need to call the office to get an actual maintenance person to fix the problem and I am a grounds person. I usually can fix what they need help with but since I am not getting that higher pay to do that I tell them call the office. "Hello sir what can I do for you?" I said.

302

"Well I have a small problem." Uh oh here we go. I thought. "Well it's kind of personal."

"You probably need to call the office." I said.

"I don't want to scare the ladies at the office. I need a special kind if toilet." I was hesitant to ask why because I didn't know where he was going with this but it sounded like it was going to be gross. But curiosity got the better of me.

"Really why? What is a matter with your toilet?" I said.

"Well I need one with a thicker seat." Oh no here we go straight to crazy town. "Well it's personal. Well I didn't want to say this but my testicles hang low and I don't mean slightly low I mean that they go into the water when I sit on a normal toilet." I started laughing. That was one of the funniest things I have ever heard.

"Ok let me run this by you one more time so I can make sure I understand you correctly. You are saying your balls are hanging in the water when you have to crap." I said.

"Yes that is correct." He said in a straight face. I thought he might be fucking with me but he was completely serious.

"Well why don't you just sling them over your leg?" I said.

"That is so uncomfortable. It hurts when I do that."

Jim came walking up. "Hey this guy wants a thicker toilet seat so his testicles don't hit the water." I said.

"I talked to Jim about it already." He said.

"We are looking into it. Well if you are serious, we can take two phone books and cut out the middle of them and secure them to the top of the toilet if you want. That will give you about eight inches. Surely that would have to be enough distance or your nuts would be hanging on the ground right now. If that is true then you best call the record books because that has to be a record. Anyways, so what's new?" Jim said.

"Well my bushes are getting kind of high. I want them cut real low so I can see over them. Like this high. About two foot high." He motioned with his hand.

"Ok I will do that next time I cut bushes. You are not looking at those cute girls at the pool are you?" I said just giving him a hard time.

He smiled. "Well I am not looking at the men." Ha ha. We all had a good laugh.

"Well alright take it easy. We will see about the toilet and your bushes." Jim and I walked off.

Once we got out of distance. "So you got to talk to ball dipper today?" Jim said.

"Yeah he pulled me over. That guy must have a serious problem. So how far are your nuts from the water?" I said laughing.

"Well I have never measured but I am going to say about three to four inches." He said. We both chuckled and went back to picking up the branches.

We made our way around the property. We saw Stan's truck parked in front of an apartment. I thought he was going to work on a balcony today. I knew he needed a permit for that but this company does whatever it wants. Permit or not. We got closer. I noticed he had a four by four sitting on top of a tiny hand jack. It looked really unsafe. I am sure there was actually a special tool to do this. When do they ever do things the safe proper way here? I thought to myself. He was going to use that to prop up the sagging end of the balcony then screw the balcony to the wall. Stan was getting ready to start cranking. Jim went up to talk to him. I tried to keep a safe distance in case the whole balcony fell and crushed them. "So how are things going with Durron?" Stan asked Jim.

"Ok I guess. He is cutting everything and we are picking things up. He butchered some trees. They look like Halloween trees now and will probably die. At least when I do the cutting I don't cut the trees down to stubs." Jim said.

"I think you do a better job. My boss sent him down here. I didn't get a say in it." Stan said.

"I bet he likes working with you Max. He probably likes to watch you bend over." Stan said.

I was already having a bad day. I think that was the straw that broke the camel's back. "Whatever you say. I am sure your wife likes to watch me too." I said.

"What was that?" Stan said.

I went back to picking up branches. I watched as Stan started to turn the crank. I was pissed and offended that he said such things to me. I felt my anger rising. I focused on the jack. Stan slowly turned the lever. It was getting harder to turn the higher the balcony went. When he turned it his face got closer to the board. I focused on the lever. Stan turned the lever one last time. As his face was toward the bottom of the crank the four by four slipped off. I watched in glee as it sprung off the jack and hit Stan right in the mouth. Stan fell onto the concrete. The other end fell into the sliding glass door and it exploded into a million little glass pieces that rained down onto Stan.

I watched as a puddle of dark blood started to spread across the ground underneath Stan. Stan wasn't moving at all. Wow I really outdid myself this time. Jim was standing a few feet away. I think he was in shock. I stood frozen for a second as well. I think I might have actually killed him this time. If he was dead I wouldn't feel bad. I wouldn't feel bad one bit. He was a piece of shit leader. His fate should be a lot worse. The only thing I would have regretted is that I didn't make his suffering last long enough. What was the point of killing him quickly if I was not able to really enjoy it?

Jim was starting to come out of the shock that Stan might be dead. Jim for the most part was a nice guy but even he paused. Maybe we should just let Stan die and not try to help him. I could see the turmoil on his face. Jim decided to help. The good side always won out. He rolled Stan over. Around his mouth there was blood pouring out like a fountain. Jim found a dirty rag nearby and shoved it into Stan mouth to stop the bleeding. I walked up. I could see that his whole upper set of teeth had been knocked out. That has to hurt a bit. He also had cuts on his face and arms from the glass. "Maybe he will learn to keep his fat mouth shut after this. Serves him right. That is karma coming back around." I said. Karma and my pissed off rage.

"I know what you mean." Jim said. He hated Stan almost as much as me. The woman in the bottom apartment called an ambulance after she saw all the blood.

"Is he alive? I called the ambulance. Not a big deal right now but I am going to need a glass door put in before tonight. If that is possible? Please." She said.

"We will get that fixed as soon as we can." I said. Stan was starting to come through just as the ambulance showed up.

"Whaaa...tt Hap…en...ed? He tried to say. His mouth was all tore up.

"You got hit in the face by a four by four. Now you are going to the hospital to get stitched up. I will go with you." Jim said.

Stan slowly got up and wiped the glass of his shirt and arm and stepped into the ambulance. Jim looked at me as he got into the ambulance. As the paramedic was shutting the door Jim shouted "Have fun with Durron. Better start picking up those branches." He said mockingly just as the back doors to the ambulance shut.

"You lazy bastard." I said quietly to myself as the ambulance pulled away. I went back to picking up branches. Maybe Jim is more intelligent then I give him credit for. Wait a second I thought for a second. I walked around the property looking for Durron. Eureka I found him.

I walked up and told him to stop the pole saw for a second. "Hey buddy. Your step brother got hit in the mouth with a 4x4 and an ambulance had to take him to the hospital."

"Really how did that happen?" He said.

307

"He had his face down by where he was cranking the jack and the board slid off and hit him in the mouth. He wanted you to meet him at the hospital since you are the closest one around that is related to him."

"Ok, I will head up there." He stopped cutting and walked to his truck. I went back to picking up the branches. He waved at me as he drove off. Looks like you are going to have a buddy there with you Jim and I am almost done picking up these branches. Who is the master now, bitch? I thought to myself. I went to get a broom to clean up the glass that broke. I made my way over to the door. I started to sweep up the glass. I swept it all into a pile. Then I saw what I was looking for. It was Stan's two front teeth. I picked them up and put them in my pocket. I know it was gross. I know they say a lot of serial killers like to keep trophies from their kills. I don't believe in that because it can always be tracked. If you do something bad you need to lock that away in the vault in your head and never tell anyone. This was different though. I was going to put those teeth in a jar and look at them and think "Stan you fucking dumb ass." Then I will laugh my ass off for the next five minutes.

I shoved the teeth in my pocket and started to focus on the task ahead of me. "Now, how am I going to clean up all this blood?"

Chapter 30

The mind of Jack. Saturday July 13

It was Saturday. My phone rang and it was Nikki.

"Hey girl."

"Hey to you." She said. What does Mr. Jack have going on today?"

"Nothing really. So you want to hang out?" I said.

"With you? I guess I can. Sure why not. It's going to be hot out do you want to go to the pool or something?" She said.

"Sure let's do it. Come and get me." I said.

"Yeah right. I am not walking up all those stairs. It is a hundred degrees out there. How about you come and get me."

"Ok I will meet you there at noon. Don't be late."

"Cool. Bye bye darling." That gave me an hour. I definitely needed to take a shower. I cleaned myself up and I ate something. I had a few drink as well just to loosen me up. It doesn't feel right to be at the pool and not drinking. It was about twelve so I grabbed my towel and went down there. As soon as I opened the door the wall of heat hit me in the face. I am getting in the water today even if it is a little chilly. As I walked I could feel the coldness, from the ac, on my shirt dissipating as the heat was quickly taking over. I went to Nikki's place first. I knocked a few times and her mom answered.

"Why, hello. Can Nikki come out and play?" I said

"I guess so. Nikki it's your boy friend." She yelled. "She is just putting lotion on. She will be out in a second."

"So what have you been up to? Anything good?" I said.

"Well not really. I have been staying up late to take care of the bars. Usually I am not up this early. Oh here she comes. You two have fun. I might be down a little later. I have to work on my tan."

"But mom you are already tan." Nikki said.

"That is spray tan that doesn't count. I will eat some breakfast and then I will be down."She said.

"Sure take your time. Ok I love you." Nikki said.

"I love you too." Her mom said.

"Make sure you have on sun tan lotion Jack. You don't want to burn." Nikki said.

310

"I put some on before I left. I have not done my back though." I said.

"Sure I can help you when we get to the pool." We started to walk towards the pool. Nikki looked back then started to whisper to me. "I hope my mom doesn't come down without my dad. All these drunken young guys will be hitting on her like crazy. She comes down wearing the smallest bikini and all these guys say the rudest things to her. I usually want to slap some of these assholes. If she does come down you will probably have to say you are her husband or she will be get harassed."

"That sucks. You know how guys are. This is day time so I can't see that much of inappropriate behavior going on." I said.

"Believe me it happens all the time." She said. I opened the gate to the pool.

"Sweet we are able to get a chair." We ran over and grabbed two lounge chairs.

"Max must have cleaned the pool this morning." She said.

"Why do you say that?"

"He is the only one who sets up the chairs at an angle like that. The other guys just leave the chairs wherever they were left from the night before."

"I see." I said. We sat down and got comfortable.

"I like to get hot and sweaty first then jump into the water." She said.

"Sure that sounds great. Can you rub lotion on my back?" I said.

311

"Sure."

"Put your hands out." I said. She did. Then I squirted a large amount in her hands to be funny.

"I am going to wipe this all in your back. It doesn't matter to me if your back is covered in big globs of white shit." She said.

"Ok. I am sorry." She wiped it on me then we sat down. We started to sun bathe. There were two families at the pool with kids. I closed my eyes and I heard kids playing in the pool. Someone brought a radio and I could hear music playing as I dozed off. I always put my shirt over my face. Even with sun glasses on and my eyes closed the sun is still too bright. So I have to cover my face. I started to fall asleep. It felt good to be in the sun. I was in an office all day and it is cool and dark in there. I never get to be outside in the sun. I was totally white and I didn't want to burn which reminded me that I need to turn over. I was starting to feel really relaxed and I did something that I never do at a public pool. I fell asleep.

I felt someone shaking me. At first, I thought I was in my bed at my apartment. I suddenly woke up and pulled my shirt off my face. "I woke you up. You were snoring."

"Oh sorry." Everyone at the pool was giggling. "I must have dozed off."

"That's what I figured. Hey you are looking a little red. Do you want to jump into the water?"

"Sure." We both stood up and walked to the deep end of the pool. She stuck her toes in to see the temperature. I just walked up and pushed her in. I saw my chance so I took it. When she came up she was mad.

312

"You are going to get it." She said.

"Why are you going to hurt me? You fell for the oldest trick in the book." I said.

"I am going to do a lot more then hurt you." She said. She swam up to the side and splashed at me. It missed.

"Is that the best you can do you? That was pretty weak even for a girl." I took a few steps back then came running forward. I did a flip then hit the water making another big splash in Nikki's direction. The water felt good. It was like bath water. That is just how I like it. As soon as I came up I swam over to Nikki. Nikki didn't take long to get her revenge. She jumped on top of me trying to dunk me. I went under to be funny. I swam over to the wall. "Alright you win." I said. She swam over and wrapped her legs around me. She clung to my back. "That's pretty nice. Do you want me to carry you around the pool a few times?"

"Sure let's go." She said. She rode me around the pool like I was her horse. We went around a few times. The pool was starting to get crowded. There were a lot of kids at the pool. I had to swim and maneuver around them.

"Alright I am done." She wouldn't let go so I swam straight down and she finally let's go of me. I like to swim a few laps when I am at the pool. I started to go back and forth. She just floated on the noodles. After we swam in the pool for awhile we got out and went to our chairs. There were more people showing up. Then Nikki noticed two blond girls. Her upper lip curled up. I could tell by her facial expression she knew who those girls were and she was not happy.

"What's a matter?" I said.

"That girl with the blonde hair and the bangs is Jess." From the way her voice sounded she obviously did not like Jess. The two girls opened the gate and entered the pool. There were a few chairs by us so I knew they would probably end up over here. Sure enough they walked over.

"Hey Nikki what is going on?" Jess said.

"Hello Jess. What are you doing here?"

"My friend lives here and I am visiting."

"I see. So how does coming back here make you feel?" Nikki said.

"It brings back memories of the good times that me and Ryan had together. It also brings a few bad memories as well."

"I bet. That memory of you killing Ryan is probably eating you up inside." Nikki said. I shot her a look. I have never seen this mean jealous side of her before.

"Yes it does bother me. I wish I could have been there to help him. Every day I think about it. So, is this your new boyfriend?" Jess said.

"Yes. My name is Ja…."

Nikki jumped cut me off. "You don't have to know who he is. I actually prefer you not to know."

"What's a matter? Are you scared I might steal him away?" Jess said.

Nikki just gave her the meanest look I have ever seen. "There are some things I always wanted to say to you. I wasn't going to but I think I will actually. Listen bitch, I feel that you killed Ryan."

"I wasn't even there." Jess said.

"But he said he was getting the drugs from you. So if you didn't give him anything he would not be dead."

"Listen you can't blame that on me. He took them on his own free will."

"Well you coaxed him into it with sex. He said that you only like to have sex when you and him are super high so he started to get high all the time."

"Still I didn't hold a gun to his head." Jess said. They were standing right by each other now. There were both close enough to pop each other in the face. The claws were starting to come out. I was standing nearby. I didn't want to get involved but I was ready to pull someone away if thinks got crazy.

Nikki was fuming mad and up in Jess's face. "Listen bitch if you want to go we can go right now." Nikki looked down and shook her head. The other girl said "That's what I thought." She turned her back and was getting ready to sit down. Nikki bear hugged her from behind then pushed her into the pool.

"That's what you get bitch for killing my friend. Come on Jack let's go." We grabbed our stuff and started to haul ass through the gate. The girl was swimming for the edge of the pool. I didn't know if she really wanted to fight or not. We were not sticking round to find out. Nikki was walking fast and she was pissed. We got a little way from the pool.

"Hey Nikki!" It was Jess screaming from the pool. "Hey where are going bitch? You are just fucking jealous that I was Ryan's girlfriend and not you. He would have probably gone out with you but you were to chicken shit to ask him out. You just kept stringing him along as friends. You should have known he was going to want to be more then friends eventually." Jess yelled.

"No you are wrong. You are wrong about everything." Nikki screamed. She started to run back to her apartment. She was crying. Her mom happened to be walking out ready to go to the pool. Nikki ran past her. Her mom had the "what just happened" expression.

"Nikki and Jess were at the pool arguing." I said.

"Oh I see. Was it about Ryan?" She said.

"Yes." I said.

"Her and Jess were friends a year ago."

"Should I go talk to Nikki?" I said concerned.

"No she usually just shuts her door and won't speak to anyone for a few hours. Well I am going to the middle pool then. Ralph I am going to the middle pool." She yelled towards her apartment.

"Ok, dear I will be there in a minute." Ralph yelled from the breezeway.

"Walk with me to the second pool. So what happened down there?"

"Jesse started talking about that Ryan guy. Nikki pushed her into the water and then we left." I said.

"Good thing they didn't start punching each other. When Ryan died Nikki took it pretty hard. She was really depressed all the time. She didn't want to come out of her room. She said she had to lay low for awhile. Sometimes I had to hold her while she sobbed like crazy. She would say that she killed Ryan and I had to keep telling her Ryan died of a drug overdose you did not kill him. It was really rough six months ago."

"I am sorry to hear that." I said.

"So, I have a question to ask you and I don't want you to get upset. I just want to ask you if you are on drugs? I am not trying to offend you. I just don't want Nikki to be hurt again and I don't want anyone to overdose. I knew Ryan and I felt that I should of asked him to get help because I kind of thought that he might be a dealer. There were an awful lot of people going up to his apartment at all hours of the night. I feel somewhat responsible for not intervening. It is just the mother side of me that's all. You will know when you have kids." She said.

"Oh. Well I can honestly say that I am not a drug dealer and I do not do drugs except for the over the counter ones." I said.

"That's great. Ralph and I both like you, even after you spit food at us. Ralph usually doesn't like anyone. We just want to make sure that you don't use drugs. That is all. If you do use drugs and need someone to try to help get you off of it we are here for you."

"Thanks for the support. I will keep that in mind."I said.

"You seem like you have a good head on your shoulders." She said.

"Thanks I try to be a good person. Well here we are." I said. We were at the gates to the middle pool.

"I like this pool because there is more privacy. The fence around this pool is six feet tall and the bushes around it are higher. At the back pool there is this old guy who watches me every time I go down there. He gets out his binoculars. I am pretty sure I have seen him pee in his bushes. Well alright take care. Here comes Ralph. I would try to call Nikki later after she cools off." She said.

"You two have fun. Be sure to wear sunscreen. I will try to call her later." I smiled and waved good bye. I started to walk back to my apartment.

Part Three:

The Final Confrontation

Chapter 31

The mind of Nikki.   Friday July 19.

Sorry my sweet Jack. From the loud snoring I knew he was out. We had been training hard all week. I slowly moved his arm off me and got up. I grabbed a nearby blanket and covered him up. I leaned over and kissed his cheek good bye. Before I left I did what was becoming my usual routine. Turning off the TV, turning off the lights, and quietly shutting the door. I hope he doesn't get mad when I do this I thought to myself as I walked down the stairs. I quickly walked back to my apartment. Some people had jumped the pool fence and were swimming at night illegally. I opened the door to my apartment and went quietly to my room trying not to wake my parents. Falling asleep quickly is what I wanted. I had a covert operation planned for tonight. I made a promise to Jack that I would not go out without him. I know he would not approve of what I had planned and I did not want him to know what it was about either. I was starting to doze off. Operation memory extraction was about to begin.

I drifted off to sleep. After an hour I separated from my body and floated to the sky. It was about one in the morning now. I flew to the river and followed it towards the north. It took me straight to were Max would be. I knew his sleep patterns. I had watched his house for a few weeks now. On Thursday he usually stayed up super late. I am not even sure if he goes to sleep. If he does it is around three or four in the morning. Then on Friday night he usually konks out around nine. Staying up late always catches up with you eventually.

It was amazing being up here on the sky watching the lights of cars and buildings fly by. The night was warm and there was a nice breeze. I was almost there. I saw his house coming up ahead. It was easy to find because it had two very large trees in the front yard that were the tallest in the whole area. If they ever fell one way or the other they will certainly take out his house or the neighbors. Hopefully they fall on Max. That would be great as well. Jack and I have been inside Max's house before and that did not go so well. He knew we were there and he attacked us before we had a chance to do anything.

I know his bedroom is in the back corner. I was going to float through the roof this time and enter his mind quickly. I will probably only have about twenty minutes maybe less, to get inside and find what I want. I was hovering above his roof. Jack I am sorry I am breaking our promise I hope you can forgive me. I should have brought Jack along. I hope I can find my way through his mind without being noticed. I flew right through the roof and into the bedroom. He appeared to be sleeping. It must be my lucky day. He looked so defenseless laying there. I should come here with a gun at night and just shoot him. I headed right toward his head. Within seconds I was entering his mind.

In his mind I took the shape of a bird since it could move quicker than me walking. There was a flash of light and I was flying through a dark tunnel. It was cloudy and I could only see a dim ray of light. Almost like flying through a cave. I exited the tunnel and I saw some land up ahead. When I exited I looked back to make sure I could find this exit quickly if I have to make a hasty escape. It looked like I came out of a sewer drain. As soon as I got to the other side I saw something that amazed me. It was an exact replica of the apartments. I flew to the rooftop and perched myself on the gutter. There were all kinds of people here. They were engaged in their normal activities. I guess these were all memories in Max's mind. I saw people that I recognized. They looked exactly like they do in real life. The only thing is that they all had slightly blue glowing eyes. Some people were washing their cars. Others were walking their dogs. Some were swimming in the pool. I was curious to see what my apartment would look like. I flew by my window and it looked exactly how it does now. I wanted to see what I looked like. Where was I? Pool maybe. I flew to the pool and there I was talking to a group of people. I turned around and I was mortified. My form had its throat torn out and my body looked like that of a long dead corpse. My stomach area was all shrunk in and my mouth was permanently stuck looking as though it was trying to scream. My skin looked like it had been in the sun and it dried to my bone. What does this mean? Does this mean that he wants to kill me? Or that he wants me dead. It gave me the chills. I had to refocus and try to get past the grisly image.

I saw some kids playing in the courtyard. There was a boy standing off to the side that did not look like the others. He looked like an eight year old boy. He had blonde hair and his skin was a pale grey color. His eyes were not blue like everyone else's. His were black and he was staring at me. He was also wearing black heavy armor which I thought was weird for a child. As I looked closer at the child's facial features I realized this was Max when he was a kid. I decided to go talk to him.

"Hello there. Can you help me?" I said as I landed by him.

The boy's eyes got real big as I started to talk to him. I was not sure if it was because I was a talking bird or something else. He was certainly startled. He looked like he was going to run.

"Wait! I am not here to hurt you. I just need some assistance in finding an object." I said.

He looked like he was calmer now. "You need my help? Really?" He said. His voice was a little shaky.

"Yes. I need to find a memory that happened in one of these apartments."

"I am not supposed to help anyone. The master says that we are all supposed to be on guard against anything out of the ordinary. We are supposed to summon HIM if anything unusually happens. See I am here all day and night and everything plays out like a recording over and over. Now, I have never had a talking bird land and ask me where a memory is. I find that quite unusual." The child said.

"Yes that is unusual. I see your point." I had to think quickly. "The master has sent me to get a memory

323

from you and take it to a safer place so no one can get to it. He says he wants to go over it more thoroughly." I said. Please don't call the guards I thought to myself.

He hesitated for a moment. "Ok that makes sense to me. Walk me to the apartment you want the memory from." He said.

"Sure it is this way. It is in the corner back here. On the top floor at apartment M." I said as we moved to the door of Jack's apartment.

"Alright this is the one." I said. This was easier than I thought.

"In each apartment there have been different families of people living there. You just have to tell me which year and which month." The child said.

"I want to see this year 2013 February. The hour before Ryan died." I said.

I walked to the back room of the apartment where everything happened. I got a little teary watching it. I watched what Max saw through his sight on that night. Max floated in through the shadows. He watched Ryan shoot up on heroin and then collapse on the bed. Max came out of the shadows and was about to feed off of Ryan then he heard a knock on the door. A woman's voice yelled down the hall. I recognized the voice as my own. The memory of myself entered the apartment.

"Stop! Please make it stop! I can't watch anymore!" I said.

"Is this what you are looking for?" The child said.

"Yes this is perfect. Ok, how do I take it with me?"

"Give me a minute and I will shrink it down so you can take it with you."

"Great." I waited patiently. I knew I would have to get out of here real quickly. I am sure he knows I am here by now. I could hear what sounded like thunder in the distance. I could see out the door and it was starting to get dark outside. The sky was turning dark grey unnaturally quick.

"Alright here you go." He turned the memory into a small glowing object the size of a quarter. "Wow that thunder is getting loud outside. Be careful. Just so you know usually when it gets dark like this the things beyond the gates start to become more...active." He said.

"I will be careful. Thank you. You have been so kind." I put it in my beak. I was still in bird form. I flew out the door and towards the front entrance. The sky was getting quite dark like it was getting ready to thunderstorm. I landed on the top of the front wall. It started to downpour. The way the water was coming down was going to make flying difficult. It was coming down so hard it was pushing me downward. Everything was turning to mud.

A thick fog started to blanket the ground. To my horror, I watched as giant skeletons started to shamble out of the shadows. I could hear them start to talk. Their voices made a gravely unearthly sound. "Intruder we know you are in there. Give us back what you took you fucking thief. We will trap you here forever. Give us back what you took!" They all yelled in unison.

I started to fly back the way I came. I didn't think they could see me because I was so small. They also didn't have eyes in their eye sockets. As soon as I flew over them they looked up. "There goes the thief! Get her!" They yelled. They grabbed whatever was on the ground and started to hurl it at me. I easily dodged the giant boulders and dirt. One giant boulder flew right at me and I had to quickly swoop to the right. I decided to just fly higher where it is safe. I thought I was home free until giant trees started to fall out of the sky. This was obviously Max's doing. He was trying to knock me to the ground. I swooped low to avoid being hit by branches. One branch knocked the memory out of my mouth. "Nooo." I said. I slowly watched it fall. I did a downward spiral after it. I lunged forward and managed to catch it just before it hit the ground. I was close to the ground now. The skeletons were waiting for me on the ground. They swatted at me with claws as I flew by dodging their blows. I darted through the giants legs to avoid being swatted. I flew as fast as the wind and headed up to the sky once again.

Then I heard a loud thundering voice that caused the air in the sky to vibrate. "I know you are here Nikki and I know you have taken something of MINE!" The clouds were coming alive. I watched as they started to thicken and form a face. It was Max's face. I could no longer see the ground. The ground seemed to disappear. "Give me back what you took or I will keep you here forever." The voice came from Max's face. Lightning cracked and thunder erupted every time he spoke. I flew faster to where I knew the exit to be. I decided to fly lower to get away from the evil clouds. The entrance had to be close by. I glanced back and saw the clouds were following me. A giant mouth was right behind me. I didn't know if it bit me I would be hurt but I did not want to find out. My wings flapped as fast as I could move them. I saw the hole where I came through. I tried to fly faster as the clouds were closing in. It felt like the forest itself was trying to stop me as well. It was becoming thicker. Branches were starting to grow and sprout. I felt the branches touch me as I jetted through small holes in the overgrowth. I am going to make it. The clouds were following me through the forest. He knew I was trying to get to the exit. The hole I came through was getting smaller. Hurry! I flew faster and faster. In a second it was going to be closed. I need to make it! I jetted through the hole as it closed right behind me. The clouds that followed me hit the wall and shot out in all directions.

There was a flash of light and I was in Max's house. I was floating above Max's head. He woke up the same time I did. His arm shot up super fast. It moved unnaturally quicker than me. I think I was a little stunned from separating from Max's head. I didn't think he could hit me in this form. His hand swatted me like a fly. I flew towards a wall and passed right through it. That really hurt. I almost lost my concentration. I still had the memory in my hand. Out in the real world it was just a small glowing orb the size of a pebble. I saw from the front of the house the light clicked on and Max came running out of the house in his pajamas. He knew he had swatted me to the ground. I didn't know he could see me or physically hurt me but he was coming right at me. He made a dive as I shot up to the sky and started to fly towards the river. My heart was beating fast. I knew I would probably sleep alright tonight. I better find a hidden place to sleep far away from Max's reach. I am sure he will be too angry to sleep tonight. Tomorrow, he probably will come seeking revenge or maybe the day after that.

Chapter 32

The mind of Max. Saturday July 20.

It was early Saturday morning. I was really furious. I rocked back and forth trying to control my rage. Nikki had entered my mind when I was sleeping last night. She ran off with the memory of what happened the night her boyfriend had died. She did not do any real damage to my mind. My own dark deeds were still hidden and known only to me. That vault of dark knowledge was locked and hidden deep. Very deep. I had to really focus my will to get her out of my mind before any real damage could have been done. She was eventually overwhelmed by my defenses and had to quick exit because I was getting ready to decapitate her. She better hope we don't physically run into each other. I don't know if I would have the control right now to play along like nothing happen. My first instinct would be to grab the nearest blunt object and beat her over the head with it until the screaming stops.

It was my turn to go in early this weekend to clean the pools out. I drove by where Nikki's car usually is but it wasn't there. I guess she was at work or something. I will wait till we meet again.

I started at the front pool and worked my way to the back. I always throw the hoses in first starting at the back going forward so that the pools can fill with water if they are low. I made my way to the front. The front pool is close to the office so it usually is not that bad compared to the other two back pools. People are less likely to vandalize the front pool. I have done this so many times I was pretty quick at it. I first emptied the skimmer baskets. They were filled with leafs and other nasty things that I did not know what it was but it looked like snot. Then I hooked up the vacuum hose. I started to vacuum up the dirt and leaves. It actually is pretty relaxing to me for some reason. My anger was starting to subside. I finished in twenty minutes and then I got out the pole with the net and skimmed any floaters off the top. I then went around and opened the gates. I straightened the white lounge chairs to make it look like a hotel resort pool. I wasn't required to do that but I usually did it anyways. This pool is ready to rock and roll.

I left and went to the second pool. The second pool was newer and had six foot tall gates. Apparently one winter before I worked here the water drained out of it. A few days later there was heavy rainfall and it caused the pool to pop out of the ground. I got closer to the gate and looked in. The water was turning green. "Goddammit. I was gone for one day and they didn't put the chemicals in." When the summer is super hot all it takes is one day for the green algae to start to form. There was a thick green spot forming in the corner of the deep end. To get rid of it you need four days with high chemical levels. I went to the pump house and got out the close signs and started to tape them to the gates. I started dumping chlorine, soda ash, and clarifier into the water. "I am just glad I don't work in the office. The complaints are going to pour in today. They better not blame this on me." I closed the pump house and went to the third pool.

I made my way to the third pool. Hopefully Jim checked the chemical level yesterday. So I arrived at the back pool. The first thing I noticed was some lawn chairs were missing. I looked into the pool and there they were. At the very bottom they sat. The rope the separated the shallow end from the deep end was wrapped around the chairs and then knotted and wrapped around the ladder to get out of the pool. I went to get the sheperd's hook to pull it up from the bottom and it was missing.

"Dammit!" The poles had been thrown into the pool as well. They were all floating on the bottom under the chairs. Whoever did this was good. They knew what they were doing. They are probably watching me from their apartment and laughing right now. The rope was tied to the ladder in a hundred knots. I started to try to untie them.

"Double Mudder." I said in frustration. Sometimes there are not enough curse words in the English language. I only have a certain amount of time to get the pools done and when things like this happen it throws off my schedule. I must have been very focused on the rope because I didn't see a person standing at the pool gate. I just had the feeling like I was being watched.

"Hey why are you attacking me."

I looked up and Jack was standing there. I was sitting down but I moved into a more defensive position in case he attacked me. "Well well if it isn't Mr. Jack. If I was attacking you, you would be laying on the floor in the fetal position." I said in a threatening tone. I curled my lips and showed my teeth. I met his gaze with my own.

He had an angry look on his face. He stared at me for moment before speaking. "I heard yelling in my mind. I tried to block it out but it didn't work. I just followed it to the source and it led me here to you."

"Fair enough. Did you go out with your girlfriend last night?" I said.

"No she slept at her parents. I don't know what she did last night." He said. I believed him. He didn't seem like he was lying. I didn't see him with her either last night.

"She broke into my mind last night and stole something of mine." I said in a deep voice.

"How do you know it was her? She promised me she wouldn't try anything without me. What did she take?" He shook his head in disbelief.

I was standing now with my arms out. "COME ON MAN! Are you for real? Who else could it of been? I almost got your girl friend but she was quick. She barely escaped. Anyways, she slithered off with the memory of what happened on the night her old boyfriend died. I was there in the shadows and I saw what went down."

"How do you know that was what was taken? " He said.

I looked him in the eyes. I was creating an illusion in his mind. I made the pool water look like it was turning to blood. "That's the funny part. Even though the memory is gone I still know everything else associated with it. It is like cutting a hole out of a sheet. There is a small hole but everything around the hole is still there. I cannot remember the details of what exactly happened. All I remember is I wanted you to see it and she didn't. It is the one piece of crucial evidence that she did not want you to see. It will show you what kind of monster she really is."

Jack was shaking his head in disbelief. "First of all, Nikki would not have lied to me. She promised me she was not going to do any adventuring without me. Second, she is not a bad person she wouldn't do any of those things that you are saying." He said defensively.

I shook my head and laughed. "Well you certainly have no clue about the person you have aligned yourself with. You have been absolutely... DECEIVED. Your feelings for this stupid girl have blinded you. She is covering her tracks. Go ahead. ASK HER! ASK HER if she went out last night. ASK HER if she stole my memory. ASK HER what happened that night her boyfriend died." I yelled at him at the top of my lungs.

He was mad now. He was pointing his finger at me. "Fuck you. You are a liar. She would never do anything behind my back. She would never lie to me. She is not like that. It is you who should not be trusted." He yelled at me.

"I have never lied to you Jack."

"God dammit! Why can't you just let her go? What does it matter if she has done bad things in her past?" He screamed.

332

"I wish it was that simple but it is not in my nature to just let it go." I said in a growling voice.

"Fine. I see you cannot be reasoned with. When we meet again in the dream world, you better watch your back." He was red. He turned around and started to walk away.

"Hey Jack." He turned around to face me.

"Tell your girlfriend she has till tomorrow to return what is mine or I will strangle her in her sleep." He shook his head and started to walk back to his apartment.

I stood watching as Jack walked away. "Goodbye Jack. We will meet on the battlefield but it is you who will fall." I said in a hushed voice. I was certain I had just planted the seeds of doubt within him. Even though he said he wasn't going to ask Nikki, I knew he would. There is just something in human nature that makes people want to search for answers. I went back to untying knots. I better be on my guard tonight. The lions are onto me.

Chapter 33

The mind of Jack. Saturday July 20.

I couldn't stop thinking about what Max had said About Nikki. I know Max is an evil bastard but he seems to believe that Nikki is just as evil. I didn't want to have to question Nikki about what he said but maybe I should. I know that would be like admitting Max was right. If she is innocent then it shouldn't offend her if I just ask her a few questions. She might have a hissy fit and leave or maybe she will be cool about it. I will wait and see.

I looked for my phone. I seem to never remember where I placed it. They should make an app that allows you to find your phone easier. All you would have to do is yell "Where are you phone?" and the phone responds. Now that would be something I would invest in. I looked around for awhile. Aha it's on the counter. I pulled up the text screen. "I have to talk to you tonight it is urgent. It is about Max and he is pissed off. Want to come over later after you get off of work?" I typed. I waited for a few minutes then she responded.

"Sure I will be over at 8. Can't wait to see you sexy."

"Yeah you too." I typed.

Awesome. I started to clean up the place a bit. It wasn't horribly dirty but I still like to keep the appearance of neat. Having my dirty socks strewn all over the floor in the living room doesn't convey a clean environment. I picked up all my clothes and threw them in the hamper. My pile of dirty dishes was quite large as well. I let them pile up till the weekend and then I do them. They had all kinds of dried up gunk stuck to them. I scraped them and threw them into the dish washer.

There was nothing to do so I turned on the TV and I slowly started to doze off. Shows now days just don't really hold my interest. Everything is a reality show now. It was cool ten years ago. Now it just seems like I am only watching a repeat of something slightly different over and over again. I flipped for awhile until I fell asleep.

I was awoken by a knocking at the door. I ran over to open it. Nikki is here. "Helllllloooo sexy." I said as I opened the door. She walked in and gave me a big hug. I leaned in for a kiss and she pressed her lips against mine. We stood with our arms around each other for awhile.

"Thanks for the hug. Work was rough today." She said.

"Hello yourself. I like it when we kiss and hug at the beginning of the date. You always seem to disappear at the end and I don't get to properly kiss you goodbye ever." I said.

"You need to stop being so needy. I don't sneak off. I have to be somewhere and I don't want to wake you up when you are sleeping like a baby. Your incredible loud snoring wakes me up and I leave."

"So I am really needy and I snore loudly now huh. I am learning new things about myself today."

"So anyways, what fun stuff did you do today?" She said.

"All kinds of fun stuff. Well not really. Hey did you eat dinner already? If you want I can make you some pancakes."

"I am not a big fan of pancakes but I am starving. I will take four if they are smaller. If they are the bajumbo size I want two."

"Coming right up. Chef Jack is in the house. Today I did some grocery shopping so I am all stocked up. I have got everything your heart desires. Chocolate, ice cream, cookies. The remote for the TV is on the table if you want to change the channel." I was going to wait till we were done eating to ask her about what Max said. I got the batter out of the fridge and fired up the griddle. I started to pour out the batter in perfect circles. In a few minutes they were done. I brought them over to the table and I got out the syrup, strawberry syrup, and powdered sugar. "Dinner is served. So how was work today?"

She sat with me at the dinner table. "Work was slow. I hate working there but it is the only job I could find close by and it fit into my schedule. The register was having problems and everyone was yelling at me. I hate it."

"That's too bad. Well I hope these pancakes will cheer you up. Is there anything here that you want and I don't have?" I said.

"No, it looks great. Some silverware would be nice though."

"Coming right up. What? You are not going to eat them with your hands?" I went into the kitchen and brought back some silverware.

"No I am not a monkey. Well these smell delicious." She said. I handed her some silverware and she started eating. "Mmm. These are good. I have been starving."

I thought now might be a good time to start asking her some questions while she is in a good mood. "So … what did you do last night?"

"Nothing, I stayed at home. I did some computer stuff." She said.

"No you know what I mean. Did you do any out of body adventuring without me by any chance?"

"No why would I do that." She said.

"Are you sure? So this morning I ran into Max. He seems to think you broke into his mind and stole something."

"Really that's weird. What is he doing here on Saturday?" She said.

"Well he was here to clean the pools. It was early in the morning and I heard someone screaming a slew of cuss words in my head. There was a horrible pounding in my head so I followed it to the source. It was coming from Max who was at the pool. He was surprised to see me. He said that you broke into his mind last night and stole a memory. To be more specific, he said that you stole the memory of what happened the night your friend died. I told him that it must have been someone else because you PROMISED ME you would not try anything alone."

She looked down at her plate and stopped eating. Her eyes were pointed down at the table. "Ok I will be honest. I did break the promise I made and I am truly sorry. I am sorry I lied. I didn't want you to find out. Please don't be mad at me. I did go out and try to attack Max." She said in a silent tone. I could see the tears starting to form in her eyes and she was almost crying.

"What about the memory he claims is missing? What is that all about?" I said questioningly.

"I don't know what he is talking about. How would I steal a memory? I did enter his mind and I tried to destroy everything I could. His mind is filled with nightmarish things. I don't know for sure what I destroyed. The memory he is thinking of may have been one of the files I destroyed. I dunno. But I didn't steal it. Besides how would he even know if a specific memory is missing? Maybe he just forgot what happened?"

"I said the same thing but he explained it like it was a hole in a blanket. Even though the memory itself is gone all the other thought traces that were linked to it are still there. All the threads that are near the hole know that something is missing."

"Interesting explanation." We sat there in silence for a few minutes. "I am sorry that I went out without you. I shouldn't have gone alone. I know it is dangerous out there. I won't do it again." She said.

"It's all right. You are free to do what you want. If you end up dead or in a coma I know what happened." I said.

She finished eating and we moved over to the couch. I hope there is something good on, a comedy perhaps. Nikki was quiet and didn't seem like herself. She sat at one end of the couch and me on the other. I was hoping this negative vibe in between us would go away.

"Let's watch something funny. Hopefully there is a stand up special on." We watched TV and laughed for a few hours. I was starting to get closer to her. We were holding hands and talking so that was a good thing.

We started to get comfortable. I was holding her in my arms. We were pretty comfortable. I was slowly rubbing her back. "Hey I have something to ask you." I said

"Yeah go for it. You are free to ask me anything." She said as she was half smiling.

"Hey, Max said that I should ask you to show me your memory of what happened the night your friend Ryan died." She was quiet for a minute. I knew I probably hit a sensitive spot. I would rather her get mad and yell but please don't start crying I thought to myself. I hate the crying.

"I am kind of insulted that you are actually listening to that maniac. I don't like the fact that you are listening to what Max is saying. Max is the enemy. He is the bad guy here. I saw some things in his mind that he has done over the years. Trust me, he is more demon now than human. If it will satisfy your curiosity then I will show you what I can remember. When we fall

339

asleep you can look into my mind and I will show you what happened. I hope you will learn to trust me more than Max."

"I do trust you more than Max. It's just that... whenever I bring it up you change the subject or try to avoid answering the question. Max seemed pretty sure that there was things there you did not want me to see. He said that he saw what happened. He was lurking in the shadows there that night."

"He probably did something to kill Ryan. All I did was walk in. I saw Ryan was high or he was sleeping so I left. That is all that happened. I will show you later when we fall asleep."

"Ok. I can't wait to see what it is like in your head. Oh you are going to see alright. It is like paradise in here." She said laughing.

"Great. See you then." I said smiling. I turned off the TV and it was quiet in the room. I could hear her slowly breathing. I kept rubbing her back until I fell asleep. Whenever I rubbed her it made me tired. After half an hour I was out.

Within an hour I was floating above my body. I saw Nikki standing above her body.

"Are you ready?" She said.

"Ninja please. I was born ready." I said.

"Alright follow me." I watched her spectral form hover over the head of her body and then it disappeared. I floated over to her head region. "Now what?" I thought to myself. I moved my mind over the area where her brain would be. I felt something happening. It felt like I was water going down a drain. There was a tunnel of flashing lights for a second. I was starting to get panicky. Then I felt myself enter her subconscious.

After the flashing lights I awoke. There was a white fog all around me. Here we go. There is no going back now. I was seeing what Nikki saw that night through her eyes. She was walking up the stairs to Ryan's apartment. She knocked on the door a few times but no one answered. She waited patiently for him to come to the door and answer but he did not come. She tried the door knob and it was unlocked so she went inside. "Hello anyone home?" She yelled down the hall. No response. The lights were on in the living room. She looked around the living room. His keys were still here and so was his wallet. She didn't think he would leave without those things at least. She slowly walked down the hall. There were no lights on in the hallway or bedroom. "Ryan? You here?" She looked into the bedroom and there he was on the bed. It was pretty dark in the room. I could barely see what is going on. On the ground, there was a small baggy with some white substance probably drugs. On the bed by him there were a few syringes two were full and one was empty. She ran over and sat on the bed "Ryan. Ryan, are you alive?" She said as she shook him hoping to wake him up. "Uhhh. Jess is that you. I am so high right now I can barely move. There is a monster in the closet." He said. "No, it's me Nikki. There is no monster here you are really high." She said. "Nikki? You should go. You don't want to see me like this." He moaned.

I was watching this and all of a sudden the movie seemed to have a glitch. It seemed to skip ahead a few seconds. I could not see what happened because it was really dark in the room. Then Nikki said "Ok I will go." She got up and left the apartment. She was crying as she left. Her hands covered her eyes and she was wiping her nose a lot. End of movie.

I stood up and Nikki was standing there. "Are you satisfied now? I have showed you what you wanted to see. I don't know what Max is talking about. Did you see me do anything wrong? She said.

"Well no I guess not. Yes I am satisfied with what I saw." I said.   Except for the one part when there seemed to be a glitch over a few seconds but I didn't say anything to her. If I brought it up I wondered how she would respond. Since I am in her mind I wonder if I would be instantly kicked out or would I be stuck here. If I tried to stay would I be able to? How very interesting I thought to myself.

"Great let's get out of here. It's not you but everyone's mind and memories are extremely personnel so I would kindly like you to get out of here if you don't mind."

"Yeah that is fine I understand." I said.

"I am not sure what to say. I have never been in someone's mind before. Well, I guess I will see you outside your mind. Sweet dreams. See you in the real world." I said as I shrugged.

"Yes that is fine. Go back to your own mind kid. Get out of here scat." She said trying to be funny.

"Well alright." I said. I kept walking into mist until it got darker and darker. I started to feel something happening but I wasn't sure what exactly. Next thing I know I was floating outside Nikki's head. I made it out ok so that was cool. I let my projected form dissipate. I went back into my body and slept for the rest of the night.

Chapter 34

The mind of Jack. Sunday July 21.

I must be having a nightmare. I was strapped to a wooden chair. I could hear my name being called.

Jack...

There was a man in a suit with a black mask over his face. He had black leather gloves on. There was a table nearby with nails and a hammer sitting on it.

Jack...

The man picked up a nail and hammer. He showed them to me making sure I saw the nail.

Jack wake up...

The man placed the nail over my hand and raised the hammer high. I started to scream. "NO DON'T DO IT! PLEASE DON'T!" He brought the hammer down hard on the nail.

Jack wake up NOW!!!

I was feeling a little tingling pain in the back of my head. I sat up quickly. I was gasping for air. It was just a dream. Just a really bad dream. I moved my hand to my face to examine it. I looked at my hand just to be sure there wasn't a nail in it. I must have fallen asleep on the couch again. "Nikki." I yelled as I walked down the hall. "Dam."

Jack.... Come to the Pool.

That was Max. I didn't want to go but if I tell him what I saw maybe he would call off his quest to ruin Nikki. I looked out my balcony. Max was down there waiting for me of course. I put on my socks and shoes.

Come down here...NOW!!!

My head was tingling more than before. I opened the door and headed to the pool. I couldn't figure out why if he could talk to me telepathically then why can't he just read my mind about what happened instead of torturing me. I was walking across the grass to the pool. I tried to be as stealthy as possible. Max's back was turned to me as he was vacuuming the pool. It looked like he was a witch stirring a giant cauldron.

"Hello Jack. I have been expecting you." He said in an even toned voice.

He didn't even turn around. He just knew I was there.

"So what resulted from your conversation with Nikki?"

"Well she first said it wasn't her. Then she admitted that she did try to attack you but she doesn't know what she destroyed." I said.

He turned to face me now. He had sun glasses on but his face was distorted in rage. "What a fucking LIAR!" He yelled shaking his head back and forth. I saw some spittle leave his mouth. "So did she show you HER version of what happened to Ryan?"

"She took me into her mind and played it back for me. I saw what she saw through her eyes that night. It was really dark in the room though so I couldn't see exactly what was going on. She walked into the apartment. He was lying in the bedroom on the bed. I saw that there were a few needles on the ground. She asked him if he was ok. He said that she should go and she left sobbing. That was the end." I said.

"SHE HAS LIED TO YOU. Is there anything that you found unusual with what she showed you? Perhaps something she may have omitted. Or maybe parts seemed distorted somehow." Max said.

I was debating on telling him about the glitch. "What makes you think that she distorted the memory?" I said.

He took his glasses off and looked me right in the eyes. I could feel his gaze upon me. He waited a minute before speaking. "Well what you said was the same parts that I have in my mind. The part that I am missing is whatever happened in the room. That is where the hole in my memory seems to be. I know that is where something really bad happened but I am not sure what. I think you are not being totally honest with me because in your mind right now you are debating on something. Your thoughts are filled with confusion. Are you sure that nothing unusually happened? Maybe it got blurry or seemed to jump forward a few minutes?"

I knew he would drill deeper into the core of my mind until he finds the answer he seeks. I was going to just tell him what I saw or thought I saw happened. "Ok fine. When she was showing me what happened there did seem to be a glitch for a few seconds. I mean that could be anything. The glitch happened in the part when she was in the room. The guy told her to go and then something happened but it was too dark to see what was going on and next thing she was walking out of the apartment. It was like it fast forwarded through a minute." I said.

"Hmm. I knew it. She is hiding the truth." Max said. Max turned around for a minute. He brought his hand up to his chin. He was thinking. "Ok I have a message for you to give to her. Tell her to meet me in dream form down the river at midnight tonight. Follow the river south for ten minutes. There is an old abandoned hospital with a clock tower on the right. You can't miss it. Tell her to bring my memory back. That's the message I want you to give to her." Max said.

"Alright. I will make sure she gets the information." I started to walk away.

"Hey Jack. If she is not there by midnight I will be coming to her apartment to end her. Make sure she is there." Max said.

I hurriedly walked back to my apartment. I feel like I just got dragged into a shitty situation just for knowing Nikki even though I don't know what this fight is all about. Why can't she just give back what she took? My heartbeat felt irregular. It was beating fast and out of control. I might actually pass out. I feel like I can't really trust Nikki and definitely not Max. My stomach was tightening up. I felt like I was going to throw up.

346

Phone. Phone. I have to find my phone. It was sitting on the coffee table. I pulled up the text message screen. I started typing my fingers were a little shaky. Nikki, Max made me talk to him today. He wants you to meet him at this abandoned hospital down the river by midnight. He said it has a large clock tower on it. He wants his memory back. He said if you don't show up he will come to your apartment to destroy you tonight. Sorry I couldn't sugar coat all that but it seemed urgent and important. I didn't want the severity of what he said to be lost. He really means it this time. I finished typing. I think she may be at work right now since it was Sunday. I didn't know if she had her phone on her. I wouldn't want to get that message till after work. Maybe I will drive to the quick shop to check on her.

I heard my phone buzz. She texted me back a few minutes later. I was surprised she text me back. I raised the phone to see what her reply was. I am sure it wasn't going to be good. "I will come over later. You better prep yourself for tonight. We are going to battle."

Chapter 35

The mind of Jack. Sunday July 21.

It was about nine pm. I waited anxiously and then I heard a knock at the door. That must be her. I went over and opened the door. Nikki was standing there. She had all black on. She certainly wasn't the same girl I had met a few months ago. "Come on in." I said.

We sat on the couch. "Do you want a drink or anything?" I said.

"No. Thanks. I see you have helped yourself by all the empty cans on the counter. I need you to be focused and SOBER." She said in an accusatory tone.

I held her hands and looked her in the eyes. "Well I needed something to help me forget about the situation. I have some things to tell you and I don't want you to shut me up. Yes, I am a little drunk but I wanted you to know how I feel. Honestly, I think he is going to kill you. I am starting to really fall for you and I don't want you to die. I have real feelings for you. I beg you to just give him back what you took. Please tell him you are sorry. Let's try to work something out with him. If worse comes to worse we can move somewhere else and he probably won't be able to find you." I said.

"Wow that is a lot of different things to take in all at once. I have feelings for you too. No one has ever been as kind to me as you. I do want to have a future with you. You are smart, funny, charming, and ever so brave. You have great hair and a sweet ass. I want to be with you too. Here is the thing though. I don't think if I give him back the memory he is going to quit. Not now. Not ever. He wants to hurt me, severely. He won't stop. Even if we moved he will eventually find us. He will track me to the ends of the earth. I need you to sober up. If you want me to be alright I will need your help. WE, as in you and me, have to kill HIM." She said.

I sat there silently for a minute. "What exactly do you mean kill him? If you want to fight him and beat him in the dream, I am ok with that. Whatever your problem is with Max is between you and him. I don't know what exactly will happen if he is defeated. Maybe he will leave us alone after that. Maybe he won't. Now, if you mean physically go to his house and shoot him I am not down with that plan and there is the door."

She started to cry. "So you are not going to fight alongside me? I need your help! He is going to kill ME! Please Help ME!" She said.

I looked at her crying. My gut feeling told me to not get involved. It wasn't my fight. In my head I kept telling myself to just kick her out of my apartment and tell her to not come back until this problem is resolved. My heart was telling me you love her and can't bear to see her in pain. You have to help her.

"Please Help Me!..."

I knew I would regret this.

"Please... "

"Alright. Alright I will help." It was the first time I saw absolute terror in her eyes. She was scared. Trying to fight him is like trying to stop an avalanche by standing there with your arms out. It is stupid to try to fight I thought to myself.

"So now what do you think we should do?" I said.

"I think we need to meditate for an hour before we fall asleep. I think you need to drink some water to sober up. I need your mind in a good place if we are planning to fight." She went to the fridge and threw me a water bottle. She started to scope out a place on the floor where she could stretch and work on her focusing.

"Come here. I cleared out a place on the floor for you over there. Just do what I do." I sat by her on the floor. She had her feet touching each other and her hands were pressed together in front of her. She was breathing and trying to be more relaxed. I did the same. I don't really believe in yoga as an exercise but I did feel like it is good for stretching and bringing peace to the mind. As long as I stay away from the moves that could possible hurt my back I would be fine. I did start to feel more relaxed from the breathing. She went into another pose. This one was a standing pose this time. She had her arms out to the side and one leg in front of the other. I did what she did. We continued to do yoga for an hour. I was feeling more relaxed and focused.

It was getting late. I was ready as I was ever going to be for this. She was done meditating. "Are you about ready to fall asleep?" I said.

"Yes. I want you to take this sleeping pill. We have to be there in less than an hour and we still have to fall asleep. It takes you a long time to go to fall asleep. " She reached into her purse and got out a pill.

"For the record I am not cool with this. I trust you that what you are giving me is a sleeping pill." I said as I looked her in the eye. I put the pill in my mouth and drank the rest of my water. I really hope I am ok and she didn't just poison me.

"My God, I am not going to poison you. I really need your help. It was just a sleeping pill. We have to fall asleep so let's go to bed." She said.

We made our way to the bed room. If this was a normal relationship we would be going back to the bedroom to have sex. Why did I not meet a normal girl? Why did I get involved with her? I thought she was a nice good natured normal person. That is what happened. I was somewhat fooled or I fooled myself. I guess I am still here because love makes you do crazy things. I lay in the bed and got comfortable. She got comfortable on the other side. She put her arm around me. She took my hand as I was starting to feel the pill kick in.

"I hope we make it out of this alive. I just want you to know that... I love you." I said.

"I know. I love you too." She said.

In a few minutes I was out.

Chapter 36

The mind of Jack. Sunday July 21.

In what seemed a few minutes later we were both hovering above our bodies. "Come on baby let's fly." I said. I took her hand and we flew through the roof toward the stars. I felt the winds carry me to the heavens. I did enjoy the flying. Nothing makes me feel more alive. There was a half moon out tonight. I didn't know if it was in the waxing or waning phase. The moon looked like it could not decide which side was going to win. Would the white side triumph or would the dark sides grip spread and hide the moon from our view for the next few days. The stars were glistening. I have never really looked at the stars before now. To me they shined more brightly tonight then I have ever seen in my life. It was a wonderful night to be out. I felt more alive now then I have in a long time.

We started to follow the river. It was pitch black against the night sky. The reflection of the moon flickered off the water. I looked at Nikki. She had already armed herself with weapons and armor. I was still in the glowing orb form. She looked like a futuristic valkyrie to me. She had two shiny swords that had a faint pinkish red glow.   She had white armor on that looked like something from the past mixed with the future.   It looked like it could withstand hits but it was still flexible and built for speed. It was sleek and impressive.

"I guess you are expecting to be attacked as soon as we get there." I said as we flew.

"You can never be too careful. I expect him to ambush us before we get there. He is a monster. No I don't expect him to play by the rules." She said.

We were flying over the bridge right now. I looked down and saw some cars on their way to wherever. It looked really pretty from the view up here. It lit up the sky. He said it was on the right a few minutes past the bridge. "I think we need to fly lower and closer to the shoreline to find it." She shook her head and she started to descend. We started to fly lower closer to the shore line to get a better view. I sure hope this is easy to find.

After about ten minutes I thought I saw it. There was a clearing in the woods. I saw a tower looking structure sticking out of the woods.   It looked like an obelisk pointing to the sky. "This must be it. We have to get closer to the tower to check it out." I said to her. As we got closer I could see the ruins. There were walls that looked like they have fallen over. Bricks and chunks of concrete were scattered across the landscape. I could see that the roof had partially collapsed in. Most of the windows were broken. Off to the side, I wasn't sure, but I thought the area looked like it was probably a cemetery. A broken metal fence surrounded the area. The stones there were square and laid out in a pattern on the ground.

We landed near the tower. "Be ready Jack to end this evil bastard's reign forever."

We looked around. This is certainly an eerie looking place. We were at the bottom of the clock tower standing in its shadow. The tower itself was only about four stories high. It had been ravaged by time. It looked like it could fall at any minute. We were standing on concrete. This must have been a courtyard fifty years ago. Now, the weeds and grass were growing up through the cracks. Nature was trying to reclaim its land. I knew he was here somewhere. I cannot detect anyone else but I could usually sense his presence. To be more precise, part of my mind started to tingle whenever he was nearby. I could feel something happening in the back of my head.

"Come out, come out, wherever you are." Nikki shouted.

I kept turning and looking around in every direction. I heard a crackling sound in the distance. Something started to happen. I watched as parts of living shadows started to move from every corner across the floor. They had a thick blackness to them. They slithered across the ground, past where we were standing. It started to coalesce into a larger black mass.

"This is him. Be on guard for anything." Nikki said as she raised her swords. She stood in an attack stance.

The shadows formed a man if you could call him that. What stepped out of the shadows walked on two legs that were more wolf-like than human. He was charcoal grey and stood eight feet tall. The body looked like that of a blackened corpse. The fleshy muscles hung loosely to exposed bone. The stomach area on the torso was sunken in. Dried skin hung in tatters in a few areas. There was a grey smoky aura that followed it when it moved. The face was lighter in color. I looked more closely and I noticed it was clearly Max's face. His eyes were solid black orbs with a faint blue glow. In his right hand I saw our doom, a giant black two handed sword. I saw how sharp it looked when the light from the moon reflected off of it. It looked heavy and slow to swing but I am sure he would have no problem wielding it.

Max's eyes were glowing a faint blue now. "Have you brought my memory back with you?" Max said in an unnatural deep booming voice.

"No. We will never let you have it. Your memory is ours now forever." Nikki yelled as she raised her swords preparing to attack.

Max's eyes started to glow brighter. "I see. What a shame. You will have to suffer now. Is that your final decision?" Max said. He started to put both hands on his sword. The smoke around him seemed to get agitated.

"Yes." Nikki yelled at Max.

"Nikki do you want my help?" I asked quickly.

"No this one is MINE!" She yelled.

I stood off to the right. This is not good. My stomach started to feel nauseated. I was trying to move to the back of Max. I raised my futuristic looking battle axe. I knew he was going to attack. My heart felt like it had stopped beating. Everything got quiet.

"So be it. Then your fates are sealed." He yelled as he let loose his attack. I saw his sword of darkness flash for a second. He moved toward Nikki with lightning speed. He swung his sword and Nikki dodged sideways to avoid being cut in half. He spun around in the same swing and came around again. Nikki had two smaller swords and was much quicker. She saw her chance. She thrust forward and hit his arm. Blue light glowed from the cut she made. Liquid shadows spewed forth like blood. The blood seemed to gravitate together forming something in the liquid puddle. Max let out a growl. "RRRAAAARRR." He was furious now. I could sense his rage building up. Nikki attacked again and he blocked. Their swords clashed a few times. I heard the sound of metal hitting metal. Sparks flew all over. Their swords flashed again and again like lightning.

I was watching the battle progress. I was getting ready to jump in but I wasn't sure if Nikki wanted me to steal her kill. I just happened to see something move out of the corner of the eye. I turned in the nick of time to see a four legged shadowy beast lurch at me. From the puddle of his shadowy blood this creature took shape. This thing was skeletal like Max was. The creature's eyes had the same blue glow. Fur stuck out of it in patches. Its stomach area was all shrunk in like it had not eaten. It looked at me and its lips curled up as it growled. I raised my axe ready to attack. I was having flash backs of when I just moved in to the apartments and a dog cornered me in the back of the moving truck. This time things are going to be different. I held my ground. The beast charged forward. I held my axe tightly. I waited for just the right time. The creature jumped high in the air. Its menacing mouth was wide open ready to tear me apart. I swung at the right time. I swung sideways and my axe cut deep into the head region of the creature. Since it was a shadow solidified the axe went all the way through the creature. The creature howled in pain and seemed to get smaller in size every time I sliced part of the shadow off of it. It was like fighting water. I knew I was winning. I had scored multiple hits again and again. The thing was getting smaller and smaller. This time it faced me. It started to walk up close. I was ready to swing and then out of nowhere black tendrils shot forward and encircled my arm and my torso. I tightened my grip on my weapon. The torso of the creature turned into a giant gaping black mouth. Fear was starting to grip me as it was pulling me towards it large teeth. Another tendril shot out and grabbed my feet. I fell to the floor and my axe slipped from my grip. "Oh Shit." It pulled me in quick now. Massive amounts of tendrils shot out and wrapped around me. I put my arms out on the upper and lower jaws of the beast. I could smell its rotten breath in my face. "NIKKI HELP ME!" I managed to scream.

Nikki was winning the fight. She had a few cuts but seemed ok for the most part. She looked over at me. Max took advantage of the glance and struck downward. His massive swing missed and stuck into the ground. Nikki saw her chance. She had the upper hand. She formed an x shape with her swords. She moved over his sword. In what seemed like a split second she cut Max's sword hand off. "NOOOO." He yelled. I watched as his hand fell to the ground. Nikki spun around and roundhouse kicked Max's body. He went flying onto the concrete. She ran over to me. She leaped high into the air blocking out the moon. Her swords and armor glistened in the moonlight making her look like a deadly angel. She came down behind the creature. Both swords hit their target, entering the head of the creature. It let out a deathly shriek as it as it shuddered once and then turned to black liquid. I was lying on the floor covered in the black ooze.

"Where is Max?" I said as I was wiping black sludge off myself. I glanced around for my weapon.

At that moment Max appeared out of the fog behind them and swiped at Nikki's leg. He got a hit. Nikki screamed in pain. She was limping. Max swung with all his fury. Nikki brought up a sword to block and it shattered into pink glowing pieces.   Nikki was on the ground with one sword.

"Your focus has improved. I would have killed you with one hit before. Too bad I have to destroy you." He smiled as he raised his sword above his head. "Jack!" Nikki yelled. I grabbed my weapon and took a mighty leap into the sky. I came down with my axe in front of me. It went straight through the shadowy core of Max. He didn't scream. It seemed like time froze for a second. His face looked startled then he laughed maniacally. I ran to Nikki's side. There was blue light and black smoke coming from the wound I had inflicted. Max walked back. He brought his arms up. The shadows and darkness all moved towards him. There was a large glowing light coming from Max. Different beams of light were shooting from his wound.

"What is going on? I said.

"I dunno. I think we should move NOW." Nikki and I started to move away from the light.

"This is not good." I said.

The flashing lights stopped. We kept on moving away. I looked back. Then I saw it.

"What is worse than a twenty foot great white shark?" I asked Nikki.

"I don't know. What?"

"I don't know what you would call it but it is right behind us." I said

From the core of the fog and smoke was a creature. It was big and long. Its mouth was large enough to swallow a bus. It had charcoal grey skin. It had a large tail and fins more suited to water than land or air. I guess if it is something from Max's head it did not have to follow the rules of nature. To me it looked like a one hundred foot long flying demon shark with rows and rows of serrated teeth.

"We have to go NOW!" I screamed. Nikki half limped and half ran.

It saw us and swan through the air at us. We jumped to the side. It passed us and circled around and was coming back. "Let's go into the building." I said as I ran that way. We made our way into the broken entrance. "You know it is a mental projection like us right, and it is going to be able to go through the walls like us." Nikki said as we moved down the hallway. Through the doorway I saw it coming right at us. "But it can't see us. So we can still move around in the building while it sticks its head in. Follow me." We flew through to the upper floor. The shark came flying at the building with its gaping maw of sharp teeth. It stuck his head in. We were on the roof looking down at the monsters body. I saw my chance. I always wanted to slay a dragon. I jumped from the building and I landed on top of the demon shark. I started hacking away at its back. It started to shake and dart around. It shot forward through the building. I grabbed a hold of the top fin to keep from being launched off the beast. The shark darted into the sky. It started to spin around and throw me but I held on tight to the monster. It started to fly down the river towards the bridge. I hacked with one arm and held on with the other. Smoke was spewing from the wounds I inflicted. I looked over and Nikki was flying behind us. "What now?" I yelled.

"Aim at its brain, if it even has one." She yelled. As soon as she said that the creature jerked its tail and it hit Nikki. She was falling straight down towards the water. The beast saw that it had wounded her. It turned its head changing direction and was headed towards Nikki. It made a loud bellowing sound. Its mouth was wide open. It planned to swallow her whole.

"NO!" I yelled. I started to make my way to the front of the head. I saw what was going to happen. I stood at the area that I thought was where its brain would be and started to hack like a mad man. Sparks flew and more and more light started to pour through the crack I had made. "YOU WILL NOT HARM HER!" I raised my axe high with both hands and swung down with all my might. "JUST DIE!" I yelled. I broke the entire upper part of the head. Huge cracks formed and broke off like glass. Smoke and light started pouring out. The beast started to spin around trying to throw me off but I held on tight. I was on my stomach holding on to the gaping hole I had made. It stopped spinning. I saw my chance. I lifted my arm like a knife and thrust it into its head. I started to tear out black fluid and shadows. This thing had no brain or organs as far as I could tell. It felt like that was doing something. Its body jerked a few times back and forth. The shark's body went limp and was no longer aiming at Nikki. The eyes that were blue glowing orbs before went dark. I jumped off as it did a nose dive at the water. I watched as it hit the water. I flew over to see what was happening. I saw flashes of blue light and bubbles coming from where the shark hit. I flew over to Nikki who was floating above the water.

"Nikki, are you ok?" I said. She looked a little beat up and bruised but no major wounds.

"I think so." She put her arms around me. "Thanks for saving me again."

"What is that, like ten times now? Who is really keeping count?" I said. She pulled me in for a kiss. Her eyes were closed. We pressed our soft lips together for a long time. We kissed for awhile as we danced above the water. I forgot where I was for a second. "We should get out of here. I think it is this way back to the apartments."

"My directions are all off now. No let's go this way." She started to fly the opposite direction from me towards the shore. "The bridge is over there which means we have to go this way." She said.

It all happened so quickly I didn't even have time to yell. The demon shark exploded out of the water and swallowed Nikki whole. One of the gigantic fins hit me and I went flying towards the beach. I hit the sand and rolled a few times. I think I was almost unconscious. It took me a minute to recover. "NOO! BRING HER BACK YOU BASTARD!" I shouted at the sky. I lifted my head and saw the shark flying quickly back the way we came towards the clock tower. I felt my heart sink. For me to challenge Max alone would be quite difficult. It would take me and a small army to do it.

My head started to feel tingly. I heard Max's voice in my head. *"If you want her back come back to the tower. I don't want to fight you. I still need your help."*

"Dammit" I yelled. She better be still alive or I swear I will find Max's human body and shoot him down. I started to fly back the way I came. This could be a trap I thought. Why would he need my help? That is odd. I flew slowly down the river. I saw the tower. I landed cautiously looking back and forth. I was waiting for the demon shark to attack me but it was gone. There stood Max in a black suit. He was clean cut and well groomed. Nikki was to the left in a sphere shaped glass cage. She appeared alive and unharmed as far as I could tell. When I showed up she banged her hands on the walls and was shouting things but I could not hear what she was saying through the walls.

"Hello Jack, glad you could make it." He said in an even tone.

"Hello. You seem real chipper for someone who just tried to kill us a few minutes ago." I said in a growl. "Nikki, are you ok? I will kill you if you harmed her in any way!" I pointed at him as I held my other hand tightly around my axe.

"No, she should be fine. I only captured her and brought her here. I will skip all the bullshit and cut to the chase. I need you to retrieve the memory she took from me. She has hidden it far from me. It is probably in her apartment somewhere. She has put an enchantment on it that makes it impossible for me to find. I don't think that it would stop you from finding it though. Go search her apartment first. If it is not in her apartment think about any special places she has talked about or places that were significant in her life. She might have hidden it

362

there. Bring it back to me and I will release your girlfriend in return."

"First off how do I know you will keep your promise?" I yelled.

"You have my unbreakable word as a demon that I will release you girlfriend unharmed." Max said.

"Secondly, how do I even know what I am looking for? What does a memory look like?"

"In the form you are in now you should be able to sense it. It will have a faint glow that none of the objects around it will have. You will be drawn to it." Max said.

"Alright I will go check her apartment." I turned to fly away.

"Jack if you are not back by sunrise her mind is going to be stuck here and her human body will not wake up ever again so hurry back if you really care for her."

I gave him a look of utter despise and flew off. I flew like the wind this time. I was like a horizontal lightning bolt blazing a trail of light behind me. The bridge was coming up. The cars and trucks wouldn't see me as I flew through the cables. They might have thought they saw something but they would just dismiss it or risk being laughed at by friends. The apartments were coming up quickly.

It was about three in the morning I am sure her parents were asleep. I noticed there were trespassers in the pool area again. They were drinking and carrying on. I am surprised no one has called the cops on them yet. The pool closed at nine. I was hoping everything would be quiet so I could sneak in and out.

I landed and went through Nikki's window. Let's see where would someone hide a memory? Nikki's bedroom door was closed so that was fortunate. I first looked under the bed. There was nothing but clothes and books under there. I lifted up the mattress and looked between the bedsprings and didn't see anything. Maybe it's in a junk drawer. Everyone has a drawer they keep random crap in. I opened her computer drawer. It was filled with junk alright. There were markers, pens, toys, paper notebooks, drawings, and cds in it. Nothing was really giving me a vibe. Underwear drawer maybe? I opened her dresser. There were some really nice panties in there. Nikki has never showed me any of these. She was clearly holding out on me. I went through her drawer. She had some personal things in it but nothing I was looking for. I found something that looked like a diary. Maybe she hid it in here I thought. I flipped through the pages. Nothing. I felt under each drawer to see if she taped it to the bottom of the drawer or something. Well there is not much left for me to search. I glanced around the room one more time and then something caught my eye. Her jewelry box. I opened it up. There was a variety of different rings and earrings. Most of them were fake and plastic. My hand felt drawn to one piece in particular. There was a necklace in the box that was silver. Nikki showed me this necklace before. It was the necklace that Nikki said her grandma gave her after she almost drowned. It had a blue stone in the center with a snowflake made of silver around it. I could hear it whispering to me. It had an unnatural faint glow that none of the items in this room had. It felt remarkably cold in my hand despite being ninety outside. When I picked it up, I was suddenly filled with sadness. It felt like it was trying to communicate with me. I need to get flying. This has to be it.

I carried the necklace through the window. I shot into the sky like a bullet. I started to fly back down the river. As I flew I could feel the memory in the necklace communicating with me. Images of what happened started to flood my mind. *"Let me show you. Let me show you what happened on this night."* It said to me. I was debating on letting it show me and then it took over my mind. I was suddenly in an apartment. It took me a second and I realized it was my apartment. The furniture was different though. Ryan was lying on the bed. There were three hypodermic needles lying by him on the bed. He picked one up with his right hand and injected the substance into his left arm. Some time went by and a girl entered the room. It's Nikki.

"Ryan, are you alive?" she said.

"Jess is that you?" Ryan said.

"No it's me Nikki." She said as she sat on the bed by him.

"I am so high right now. Nikki, I don't want you to see me like this you should go." Ryan said.

This is the part of what happened that was different then what Nikki showed me. Nikki was sitting on the bed. She slowly picked up the needle. "I am so sorry Ryan. I love you so much. Just relax I am going to take care of you." She grabbed his left arm and injected the drugs into his vein. I couldn't believe I was seeing this. She then set the needle perfectly back into place. She then picked up the other needle and without hesitation, plunged it deep into his vein. "No Nikki." I heard Ryan say as he tried to lift his arm but was too weak to push her away. She put the needle back into place. "I am so sorry Ryan. I wish we could have spent our lives together." She started sobbing like crazy as she

365

walked out of the apartment. I watched as Ryan started to foam at the mouth. White stuff oozed at the corners of his mouth. Blood came out of his nose and that was the end, the memory was over.

My mind returned to itself. I couldn't believe it. I didn't want to believe it. No, that didn't happen. That had to be made up. There is no way that Nikki killed that guy. How could she do that? What trickery is this? He must have changed the memory in order to confuse me.

I headed back to the tower. The wind whipped through my hair as I flew back as fast as I could. "Max where are you? I have found your memory." I yelled. From out of the blackest shadows he stepped. Nikki was still floating in her glass prison nearby. She banged her hands on the glass when she saw me.

"Excellent. You have found it?" He asked questioningly.

"Yes I believe so."

"Let me see it then." He said.

We walked toward each other. I still did not trust him. I had one hand on the necklace and the other on my weapon. He reached out with his hand and took the necklace. I stepped back a few steps.

"Yes this is it." He separated the memory from the necklace and tossed the necklace aside like it was trash. The memory was a small glowing orb of blue light. He lifted it to the sky with both hands. He slowly moved it down on to his forehead and then it vanished into his head. He kept his hands on the sides of his head for a short time. In his eyes I saw the change. His face shook slightly as everything realigned. His body trembled. The memory went back into its place and filled the hole in the fabric of his mind. What was once gone has returned to fill the void. "I can feel it. So that is what happened. I remember quite well now." He then turned his gaze towards me.

"You have your memory back monster, now release Nikki. By your code I demand you fulfill your part of the deal." I yelled as defiantly as possible.

"Jack. Jack did you see the memory? Did you see what your sweet little princess did? I can honestly say I did not do anything to corrupt that memory. That is exactly what happened." He said smiling. "Your friend is a killer." He said with glee.

"You are a liar and deceiver. I don't believe what I saw." I said. We started to circle each other.

"Believe it buddy. I know it probably hurts. Think about it. What she showed you, skipped over that part didn't it. The part where she injects that poor guy with enough heroin to drop a horse was gone from what she showed you wasn't it? I have no reason to lie to you."

"That may be true but you promised to release her. You made an oath so fulfill it." I yelled.

His face twisted in anger. "As you wish. I will fulfill our agreement." He said. He walked over to the orb and put his hands on it. He said a few words that were unknown to me. The sphere glowed for a few seconds then it shattered into a thousand glowing pieces. Nikki fell to the ground unharmed.

"Nikki, are you alright?" I yelled as I ran over. She seemed startled but unhurt. I helped her off the ground.

"So did you see the memory?" She asked.

"I saw the whole thing. It's alright. Let's focus on getting out of here for now." I said. I held her hand as we started to walk away from the tower.

"Hey kiddies where do you think you are going?" Max said in an ominous tone.

"Then Jack I am truly sorry." She said as she looked into my eyes.

"What?" I said. Nikki suddenly vanished. "Nikki. Nikki where are you?" She seemed to fade out of existence. I watched her body dissolve. I ran over to where she was standing and stuck my hand through the empty air.

"Where is your girlfriend now Jack." Max said mockingly.

"What did you do to her?" I yelled.

"I did not do anything to her. She left on her own free will."

"Where did shhhhh….." My body was filled with a burning pain. I gripped the side of my stomach. I fell over in agony as white frothy foam poured from my mouth. I reached up to Max in hopes he would aid me. "Help Meee pleaseee!" Was all I was barely able to get out. I curled up in the fetal position on the floor.

Chapter 37

The mind of Max. Sunday July 21.

I stood there watching as Jack keeled over. His eyes were glossed and filled with horror. Foam spilled from his mouth.

"I dunno what is happening to you Jack. I think Nikki poisoned your human body." I went over and kneeled by him. He reached up his hand to me. I grabbed his head with both hands and stared into his eyes. "I told you Nikki was an evil bitch."

"Help me!" Jack managed to gasp. His eyes were opening and closing rapidly.

"She probably wants to kill you because now you know what happened. She is trying to cover her tracks now." Jack's body was starting to convulse. "Well Jack, I have seen into your mind and I think you are ultimately a good person. Even though I totally despise human beings and it is not in my nature to save people, I am going to give it a try. Hang in there Jack." I raised my hands and in a cloud of smoke I let my mental projection dissolve and I returned to my physical body.

I woke up in my human body. It was about 4:00 am. I hurried to my phone. I was debating on calling the 911 or the fire department. Second thought I decided to call the emergency pager for the apartment. I knew Jim was on the pager and he lived close by. He would be there the fastest. I live over an hour away. I don't think Jack will last that long. "Hurry pick up." I thought.

"Hello this is the emergency maintenance hotline. What seems to be your problem?"

"Hello I see a lot of water coming from the utility closet of my apartment. The carpet is soaking wet and it is spreading to the other rooms. The address above my apartment is 6520 M. Can you send someone to check it out?"

"I will send someone over quickly."

"Great. Thanks. Bye."

"Well someone should be there shortly. If not, well it was nice knowing you Jack. I hope Jim finds you before it is too late. That is all I can do."

Chapter 38

The mind of Jim. Monday July 22.

It was 4:10 in the morning. I heard the phone ring a few times. I didn't want to answer it. I didn't have to guess who it was. It could be no one else except the emergency pager service. This was the third call tonight. "Hello." I said as I fumbled with the phone.

"Yes this is the messaging service there may be a possible water leak at the apartment 6520 M. The people below them said there was a lot of water coming from the wall in the utility closet. We really need you to check that out please."

"Ok fine I am on my way." I jumped out of bed and started to get dressed. "Dammit." I have to go check out the problem. How did I get stuck with the pager in the first place? I am not even a maintenance person I am a grounds person. "Dam it is 4:00 AM. Why can't this shit happen in the middle of the day while I am already at work?" I thought it was weird that they had a leak coming from their closet. That sometimes happens when the washer has a malfunction but who washes their clothes at four in the morning? I was kind of mad as I jumped in my beat up truck and drove to the apartments. It only took me about three minutes to get there.

I jumped out of my car and walked to apartment 6520 M. I realized this is that Jack Duck guy's apartment. "Why is it always on the top floor when I get a call?" I got to the door. This is going to be fun. I started knocking. Everyone in the breezeway is going to be pissed. Bam! Bam! Bam! "Maintenance." I yelled at the door. Ok no response. I tried it two more times and nothing. I am going in. I really wished someone would have answered because this is how people get shot. People do not like it when a strange person is walking in their apartment in the middle of the night. I put my key in the key hole and turned. It felt like the door was already unlocked. I turned the doorknob and I slowly pushed open the door.

"Jack its maintenance." I yelled down the hall. So help me god I do not get paid enough for this shit. "Maintenance." Good thing he does not have a dog. I walked to a light switch and turned it on. Now I can see at least. It was very quiet in the apartment. I was waiting for something to pop out at me. "Maintenance." I made my way down the hall to the washer and dryer closet. The bedroom doors were open. I looked into the bedroom and Jack was lying on the floor.

"Jack wake up! Maintenance." I walked into the room. "Jack we are here to check your washer for a water leak. Jack?" I knew something was wrong. He started to convulse on the floor. He had white foam coming out of his mouth. I went over and shook him. "Jack buddy wake up!" I looked at his arm and noticed a needle sticking out of it. "Oh Dammit. Double Mudder!

372

I have to call an ambulance. I frantically got my phone out and called 911.

"911 what is your emergency?"

"I need an ambulance at 6520 M Northfield Grove apartments. Looks like this guy has overdosed on something. He has a needle in his arm."

"We will send an ambulance over quickly."

"Should I move him or take the needle out of his arm or anything?"

"No I would leave that there so they can see what kind of drug he might have used. The paramedics will be there shortly."

I sat and waited with Jack for the ambulance to show up. "Well at least your washer machine isn't leaking." I put my hand on his throat to see if his heart was still beating. I took me a second to find it. It was beating but barely. I slapped him gently on the face. Nothing. "Where is the adrenaline shot when you need one?" I saw someone recover, from a drug overdose, that way in a movie once. I lifted up his eyelids and his pupils were extremely dilated. "Please don't die on me." I opened the front door and waited at the front of the breezeway. I heard the ambulance coming from down the street. They always turn their sirens off when they get in the apartment complex. Thank God they are here. I saw them pull in and park in the front.

"Hey up here." I yelled. They grabbed their gear and ran upstairs. "He's in the backroom. I think he overdosed on something."

"We will take it from here." They went in and gave him a shot of something. They put him on a stretcher and carried him downstairs. "How did you find him?" They asked.

"I am a maintenance person here. Someone called the emergency service hotline and said there was a water leak coming from this apartment and I came to check it out."

"Well good thing you did. He would have probably died."

"Well we have to get him to the hospital."

"Cool. Thanks for showing up so quick." I waved goodbye as they drove off. I guess I need to check the apartments underneath to see who called about the water leak. This sure is going to be fun. Good times definitely.

Chapter 39

The mind of Jack. Monday July 22.

I was starting to come through. Where am I? I thought to myself. I was lying on a bed. There were medical things all around me. I had an IV bag hooked to my arm. I guess I am in a hospital. I glanced around. I hit the button for a nurse. In a few seconds a nurse walked in.

"How are you feeling right now? Is everything all right?" She said.

"My stomach hurts. I don't feel well. Where am I? What am I doing here?" I was confused.

"You are in the hospital. You injected something in to your arm and it caused you to overdose. What do you remember exactly?"

I thought deep and hard for a minute. "All I remember is falling asleep in the bed with Nikki and waking up here." That was not entirely true. I remember talking to Max and then kneeling over in pain. I thought Max had double crossed me. "Is Nikki here?" I asked

"No there is no one here with you. Well you apparently overdosed on something. They found you with a needle in your arm."

"What! I don't do drugs." I said angrily.

"Well that's what happened as far as I know."

I was remembering my confrontation with Max. As much as it pains me to say this, he was right. Nikki was trying to cover her tracks and I guess after I saw the memory she knew she would have to kill me. Nikki was the evil one all along, maybe not as evil as Max but still evil. I did think that Max was lying to me. No way Nikki would do that to me, would she? I thought our love was real. Somewhere inside of me I felt my heart break into a thousand pieces. Deep down I had to face the fact that the girl I was falling in love with tried to murder me. It was a bitter pill to swallow.

"Nurse is there a police officer on duty? I would like to file a report on what happened."

"Sure I can find one for you."

"Great." I said as she left the room. My eyes got watery as I felt a single tear run down my cheek. Sorry Nikki my love. I had high hopes that you were the one. How could you betray me so? I felt my heart breaking. My hopes and dreams of spending a lifetime with her were all ruined.

A uniformed officer walked into the room with a clip board.

"Hello. Are you feeling better? Are you feeling well enough to talk?"

"Yeah. Pull up a seat and I will tell you everything…

Chapter 40

The mind of Max. Monday July 22.

It was Monday morning and I had just arrived at work. I went straight into the break room. I took a seat at the dirty old table. Jim was looking tired. He was talking to everyone about last night.

"Last night was a busy night for calls. So last night I get a call at four in the morning from the pager service about water leaking into an apartment. It was that Ducks guy who lives at 6520M. I go over there and keep knocking and no one comes to the door so I go in. I go down the hallway and he is sprawled out on the floor with a needle in his arm. He was overdosing on something. He was stroking out and drool was coming out of his mouth. I started freaking out. I had to call an ambulance to come and take him away. He was getting ready to die. Here is the weird part. I went to every apartment under his in the stairway to see who had the water leak and no one had water leaking in their apartment. Everyone was pissed that I woke them up. It was a pretty crazy night." Jim said.

"So is that Jack guy alive now? Do you know which hospital they took him to?" I said.

"I think they got him in time. They probably took him to the hospital that is down the road on the right side. It is Saint Anthony's or Saint Mercy. I can't remember for sure."

"Wow so you had a busy night. It is probably good that you showed up. Sounds like he would have probably died. So you are like a hero or something. Jim the hero." I said laughingly.

"Yeah I am a fucking hero so you assholes should buy me lunch today. How many people have you guys saved today? Or this month? What's that? None. That's what I thought."

"Well it sounds like you did a good deed and I am sure you will be rewarded somehow." I said.

It was time for me to start the grounds. I wanted to see if Nikki's car was here. I hurried and grabbed my bucket and grabber. I walked outside and quickly walked toward her apartment. As I got closer I could see her car was here. She must be at home hiding. I walked by her apartment. All the blinds were closed so I could not see inside. I wanted her to come outside so I could confront her. I stood twenty feet from her window. I started to use the focus.

I know you can hear me, you back stabbing bitch. I can't believe you would do that to your own boyfriend. I could tell he loved you. He stood up for you even against all the evidence I showed him about you. I am pretty sure Jack is still alive and he is going to report you. They are going to come and take you away for a long time. You are going to rot away your life in a jail.

Then I felt something I have not felt before. I heard her words in my mind.

Really? Really Max? Max I have no plans to go to jail. Max you are the monster here. I saw some of the things that you have done. My list of evil deeds pales in comparison to yours. How many lives have you twisted and ruined? The fate that you have contemplated for me is not going to happen. At first I thought I would have to kill you and Jack but now that I have thought things through I don't think I have to do anything. The only evidence you have is Jack waking up with a syringe in his arm and for Ryan you just have what you saw from the shadow form. That is not going to stand up in any court. Looks like I am going to go free little buddy. I might still try to kill you. You can count on that.

At that moment I heard the sirens of a police car coming down the road to the apartments. I heard them turn the sirens off so I guess they are turning into here. I wonder if Jack woke up and told them Nikki tried to kill him.

Ha Ha Ha. A police car is coming this way. I can hear their sirens in the distance. Told you they will be coming to get you. I hope you run I do enjoy a good chase. Please resist them. I want to watch them shoot you in the back. I am going to be waiting out here for them to drag you out in cuffs.

I heard a response from her that did not even seem like it was human. It was a deep thunderous growl that was so loud I had to reach for my head. She is getting good at these mental games I thought. I think from being around me, it has made Jack and her more powerful.

I walked down the sidewalk toward the side of the building. I was going to circle around to the front. I made my way around the corner. I never like to be too close to these situations. I like to be far enough away to not be involved but close enough that I can see what is happening. Two cop cars pulled up to the front of her apartment. Two brown uniformed officers stepped out of their cars. They slowly walked into Nikki's breezeway.

They probably just want to take her in for questioning. What Nikki said was right. Whatever we said would probably not stand up in court. With Jack it is his word against hers. She could say he is a raging drug addict. Or that he wanted to try something for the first time and he took too much and now he is trying to say she injected him. The whole Ryan thing wouldn't hold up in court either. You can't tell people you can astral project without getting laughed at and ridiculed. I was getting discouraged. She was going to get away. My heart was starting to sink. Unless… I intervene.

The police walked out of the breezeway. Nikki wasn't in handcuffs. They were just escorting her. I am sure they just wanted to ask her a few questions. Now, I could have just let it go. She said she was going to try to kill me later. That seemed like a big problem that had to be dealt with as soon as possible. I decided I have no choice but to intervene. I had to act quickly. I was standing about fifty feet away. I started to use the focus. I felt electricity surge through every crevice of my being. I knew Nikki had more mind protection now then she did a few months ago. It was probably going to be a struggle to maintain control once I was in. I was going to have to use everything I had. The back of my head was trembling as I mentally invaded her mind. Her mind was a little bit off since she was distracted by what she was going to have to tell the police.

As soon as I started she knew instantly what was happening. She stopped walking suddenly and turned to face me. She started to raise her arms but stopped. She opened her mouth to scream just as I took control of the steering wheel in her mind. She started to shake. She tried to make a sound but only a whimper came out. I could tell by the look of fear in her eyes that she knew I had the control. She was instantly under my spell. The officers behind her knew something was up as well. They probably thought she was going to run.

"Ma'am, are you ok?"

I was doing my best to make her talk against her will. I could hear her screaming in her mind. She was desperately fighting me. I tried to make her mouth form words. She was trying to make it sound like gibberish.

"I.. I…I wa…ant to c.c..con..fess that I did inject Jack with the in..intent to k…k..kill him. I did the s..s…same to Ryan Delpont who d…died here earlier this year."

The two officers started to surround Nikki. One moved to the front of her. "What did you just say? So you are confessing that you killed Ryan Delpont and you said you tried to kill Jack." I could tell by the look in her eyes she was furious. Her facial features kept twisting and changing. I tried to keep her smiling. She wanted to show anger.

I kept telling myself to hold on to her mind just a little bit longer. It was like trying to hold onto a mountain that was trying to shake me off. With all my might, I managed to make her say just four more words.

Her mouth slowly began to move. I felt the vibrations in her vocal chords. Just four more words...

"Yes that is correct."

I felt a thunderous sound in her head. I let myself be expelled. I was violently thrown out of her mind with extreme force.

The officers surrounded Nikki. They started to get out the handcuffs.

"Please put your hands on the car where we can see them. You have the right to remain silent. Anything you say can and will be used against you in the court of law..."

"NOOO!" She yelled as they started to handcuff her. "This isn't happening to me! " She was hysterical by now. Tears were flowing down her face. She looked at me and yelled. "He did this to me. He made me do it. Max I hope you burn forever in HELL! FUCK YOU MAX! I swear I will kill you! I will find a force darker then you and I will come after you."

The police man opened the back door and guided her head into the car. He turned and looked at me and I just shrugged. "I have no idea what she is talking about." They got in their cars and started to drive off to the police station. Nikki turned her head in the back of the police car and continued to stare at me as they drove off. I just stood there with a big smile on my face and I waved. Bye Nikki it sure was fun. Thanks for playing. You did make things interesting , for awhile.

I turned around and Jim was standing there. He saw everything that went down.

"What was that all about? Why was she so mad at you?" He said.

"Man I have no clue why she was yelling at me like that. I don't know what she means when she said I made her do it." I said.

"I mean she looked like she wanted to kill you. She looked like if she had a gun or knife within her reach she would have tried to kill you. So she just confessed to injecting Jack, who I saved last night, with something. Have you even talked to her before? Did you two get it on?"

"No and No. We might have said hello once or twice but that was it. I knew she used to hang around that drug dealer guy who died in the back but no we didn't talk. So it sounds like she injected Jack and then left the apartment to make it look like he overdosed on something." I said.

Jim and I watched as the police car drove off into the distance. It was silent for a minute until Jim spoke. "This place is getting crazier and crazier. I am starting to think it is something in the water. How come so many people here are going crazy? I still don't understand why she was so mad at you. That is really weird."

"Tell me about it." I said smiling as I went about my day.

Chapter 41

The mind of Max. Monday July 22.

It was Monday night. I knew I would have to attack Nikki tonight. She had that fire in her eyes. She wanted me dead for sure. She wasn't going to give up. I respect that in an opponent. I would do the same thing so I can't really criticize her for that. I have to make sure I get into her mind as soon as she falls asleep or she will be coming for me. My guess is that she would probably still be held in the jailhouse where the police took her. I had to fall asleep early and head there and wait for her to fall asleep.

It was about nine at night so I decided it was time. I went to bed early. I got comfortable under the blankets. I hope this goes smoothly. I pray for a swift kill. If I can't stop her, this could go on for days, months, or even years. We will both go insane eventually. I mean, if she is in prison she will have nothing to do except attack me every night. That will be her sole purpose of existing, to attack me and drive me insane.

After half an hour I dozed off. I separated from my body and started on my grizzly mission. I flew through the roof and headed down the river. This flying was much better than driving. It usually takes an hour to get to work driving. Flying takes about ten minutes. I knew where the police station was. I drove by it every day on my way to work. In a few minutes I arrived there.

So this is the police station. I walked in the front door. I was nothing more than a shadow in this form so no one would notice. I would only be seen if someone was very closely looking and even then they would just assume their eyes are playing tricks on them. There was a counter up front. It had a glass window which I guess is bullet proof glass. I floated through the door. There was a bunch of desks and computers. It was night so there were not a lot of people here. Let's see. Where are the prisoners kept? Probably on the bottom floor was my guess. I could sense a lot of high emotions coming from the bottom floor. It felt like a mix of hatred and regret. I floated toward the back of the building looking around. I didn't see any holding cells anywhere. I floated into an elevator. OK there is a basement level. I floated down the elevator shaft and through the doors. Here we go. There were bars and metal doors. This is probably it.

I started looking in and out of the holding cells. There was a variety of people in here. I think they were waiting to be sentenced to see what level of prison they are going to. Some people looked like total crap. They looked like they just woke up and were pulled from their home in their pajamas. Some looked very clean cut. It makes me wonder how they got here.

I kept looking then I felt it. Like a vibration on the wind that only I could feel. It was like someone was saying my name over and over again in their mind. That has to be her. I also heard a lot of cuss words thrown in between my name. I slithered across the ground in the direction of the sound. It was in the back corner. There wasn't a lot of light here so that was good for me. Lots of places to hide. This was a single person holding unit. I wonder if she put up a struggle and they put her here. I went through the door. There she was curled up in the corner. She was sitting on the concrete floor with her arms wrapped around her legs. She had a blank expression on her face as she stared at the door. She looked like she was deep in thought. Almost trance like. As soon as I entered I moved across the floor to the shadow under her bed.

"Hello Max. I can feel your presence in my mind. I know you are here somewhere hiding like the coward you are." She said.

I wanted to respond so badly but in this form I am unable to speak. I can do some things but not everything.

"Are you here to kill me? Finish the job you started? I am surprised you didn't have the police man pull out a gun and shoot me right there on the spot."

She just sat there for a few minutes. "So why are you here right now? Why have you not killed me yet?"

In my head I was thinking of the answers but I was unable to communicate them. I tried but she never seemed to acknowledge that I was answering her questions. She sat there in silence thinking. I could feel the gears turning in her mind. She was trying to reason things out. We sat there for quite a long time. She never moved a muscle. Occasionally, I saw her blink. After thirty minutes she spoke again.

"I know why you got here so quickly. I think that you came here to fight me as soon as I fall asleep. You wanted to wait for me to fall asleep and then attack me before I have a chance to attack you. If you waited later you would not have been able to find me. I think that is it. That is pretty clever of me to figure out huh. Bye the way I can hear you laughing under the bed."

I was laughing. Yes, that was very clever. I don't plan to fight you outside you body darling. I plan to enter your mind and cause as much havoc in there as I can. When I am done you won't be the same person.

"Well I am planning to defy you ever chance I get so I am not going to fall asleep until the daytime while you are awake at work. How does that sound? I can hear a sound. It's the sound of your plan crumbling. Hahaha."

Dammit! I thought to myself. She does have a point. That was really the only flaw in my plan. I was counting on her to fall asleep. If she does manage to stay up till five thirty in the morning she will make it. Double Mudder! I started to move around agitated. How can I make her fall asleep? I wasn't sure. I decided to just wait her out. At the first sign of her eyes closing I will be there anxiously waiting in the shadow to strike her down.

She just sat there for the next few hours. It was past mid night. She almost fell asleep a few times. I saw her eyelids start to slowly close over her eyes. You are getting sleepy I kept trying to whisper into her mind. I know she could not hear me but I thought it was odd that every time I said something she immediately shook her head and stood up. She started doing jumping jacks and

388

pushups to stay awake. That was fine with me. Exercise at first might wake you up but it will make you feel more tired later. That's right; exert all your energy so you are more tired. I can't wait for those eyes to shut I thought to myself.

A few more hours passed. It was about four in the morning. This was about the same time yesterday that she tried to kill Jack. She might actually make it. I was starting to think I should leave and call it a night. She is to wound up and determined and most importantly full of rage. I know when I am determined I can outlast anything. Then I saw the first sign that her iron unyielding will was starting to crack. I saw her starting to eye the bed. Her eyes would mostly close and then she would shake her head to wake up. My spring of hope was renewed. That's it. It sure looks warm and comfortable doesn't it? A lot better than lying on the cold floor. Maybe she thought that I had left because I stopped trying to answer her questions or make contact with her. All of a sudden, I knew she was going to get into the bed. I think the long stressful day had done her in. I don't know if she made an actually conscious decision to go lie in the bed or if she was half asleep already and her body was just looking for a soft place to rest her head. She stood up. Her eyes were mostly closed already. "YES GO TO THE BED" I shouted quietly to myself. She walked over and lay down on the bed. I knew she was asleep by the incredibly loud snoring. I waited quietly in anticipation. In a few minutes I knew I would be in her mind and then the real FUN could begin.

Chapter 42

The mind of Nikki. Tuesday July 23.

I awoke from the darkness sitting on top of a snowy hill. A cold breeze blew against my face. My warm breath hung in the air as I breathed. Grey clouds blocked the warmth of the sun. This looked vaguely familiar but I couldn't quite remember where this was.

"Where am I? What are you going to do to me?" I screamed. I tried to move my hands but could not. To my horror I realized they were strapped to the sled.

"Oh no." I Instantly realized where I was. This was the hill I slid down right before I broke through the ice.

"NO… FREE ME…" I screamed until my lungs felt like they were going to burst.

"LET ME GO… FREE ME.." I was hysterical by now. I felt my warm tears stream down my face. The wind started to pick up. I heard humming in the distance. I frantically started to try to free my arms. It was to no avail. I looked to the sky. I knew he was out there and would hear me. I breathed in and yelled until my vocal cords felt strained.

"I swear I will make you pay! I will make you pay!" I felt the words reverberate into my soul. I heard the crunching of snow under boots. He was walking up from behind me. I turned my head as far as I could. He was dressed in all black snow gear.

He came to the front of the sled and kneeled beside me as I cried. His hand came up and I braced for a hit but instead he took his sunglasses off of his face. He looked me in the eyes for a few seconds. I hope he saw how much my soul truly despised him. He had a wicked grin on his face.

"Here we are. So, why did you do it?" Why did you kill him?" He asked me in an even tone.

I looked him right in the eye. "I don't know what you are talking about." I said as defiant as I could.

He grabbed my face and brought his face close to mine. "Listen, don't fuck with me. What made you do it?" Max said.

"Fine. You really want to know?" I said.

"Yes."

"I never wanted anything in my entire life as much as I wanted Ryan to like me. I wanted him to be with me. I wanted to marry him and have his kids. He was in love with that other girl and he was planning to give her a ring. It was too much for my heart to bare."

"So you thought if you killed him it would make things better?"

"If I can't have him no one can. It did make that hole in my heart feel complete again. It did feel better after killing him. I guess, since I knew he wasn't going to be with anyone else ever, it made me feel better."

"I see." Max stood up. He looked around the hill and off into the distance. "It really is beautiful out here. Too bad you will not get to see anything beautiful like this again."

"No...Please..."I said.

"Nikki you have broken one of the most sacred laws of human kind. You have been found guilty of taking a life. As punishment I sentence you to eternal torment. May hell have mercy on your soul." Max said.

"You dare judge me o blackest of souls. You are the master of deceit. You are the fucking devil. Your mind doesn't even bare a resemblance of humanity. In your head you think you are doing justice but you are only destroying everyone around you. Sometimes those people only slightly offended you and you set ruin upon then like a hungry dog. I saw how one of the managers came to your property and said you missed picking up one cigarette butt and you cursed him. When he went back to his property half of it burned down. Or what about when you used you powers to constrict that guys heart till he had a heart attack. Or what about in 2001, when you just got out of college, when you thought the only way you would get a job in your field of study is if everyone in your field was destroyed and you wished for a natural disaster and the next day some people flew some planes into two building." I yelled.

"I can't help destiny. Those were all coincidences. The apartment burning down was from a careless resident dropping a lit cigarette. The guy with the heart attack smoked like a fiend and was unhealthy. The planes flying into the buildings was planned to happen months in advance in another country. Whatever happens is going to happen. Besides where is their God to save them when bad things happen. Why doesn't a higher power step in and save people from certain oblivion?"

"Max... You are the higher power. I don't even know if God exists but I have no doubt that you are much further evolved then the rest of us. You have the power to make all of us jump off a cliff one by one or maybe you can join us on the side of good. Think of all the things we could learn from you. Together we could help fix the world. Shape it to the way we want." I said in desperate plea for a reason for him to not kill me.

Max stood there silently and thought for a second. He was contemplating the situation. Max brought his face within a foot of my face and looked me right in the eyes. "I do actually want a companion. Someone to talk to and help me but sorry to say it is not going to be a piece of shit murderer like yourself. I can see that hot spark of betrayal in your eyes. You would eventually betray me and kill me in my sleep. Do you think I am stupid? You killed your first boyfriend out of jealously. Simple jealously! You tried to kill Jack just because he might talk about something he saw from a memory. That would not even stand up in a court. You meant the world to him. He would have kept his mouth shut till the day he died." Max said. He continued to look me in the eyes for a few moments then he started to move behind me.

393

"No, what are you going to do to me?" I yelled. "I swear on everything I hold sacred I will make you pay. We will meet again." I screamed.

"Not in your lifetime." Max said. Max stood behind me now. He put his arms on my back and started pushing me on the sled down the hill. He ran partly down the hill sending me on my way to oblivion.

"No.." I screamed. The sled was picking up speed now. I was moving much faster then I remember. It felt like I was riding a rocket to my death. Snowflakes flew off the ground and landed on my face. Cold wind was hitting my face. It was exhilarating.

Then I saw it. The lake, the place where I drown before. Events were playing out exactly how they did before. The sled jumped the bank and headed across the ice. The sled came to a stop right in the middle. I knew what was supposed to happen next. I braced myself for the breaking of the ice. I opened my eyes and Ryan was walking across the ice.

"Ryan? Ryan is that you?" I said in disbelief.

"Hi Nikki. I have come here to help you."He said. He reached for my hand. I didn't know what was going on. I was no longer strapped to the sled.

"I am so sorry. I didn't mean to kill you." I said as a fresh wave of tears cascaded down my cheeks.

"I know you didn't. It is ok. I forgive you." He had his arms out and we started to hug each other. His warm embrace was comforting. Our bodies were pressed together. All the memories of him came flooding back. I put my head on his shoulder. My eyes were filled with tears.

"I am so sorry." I said.

"Everything is going to be okay. Now we get to spend eternity together."

"WHAT?" I said. In that same second I heard the crackling of the ice as it gave way and I was engulfed for a second time. The green murky water was frigidly cold. My body tightened up and all my air left my lungs. I watched hopelessly as the last air bubble floated upward. I tried to swim but Ryan was still holding me, pulling me to the bottomless depths. I glanced at him and his eyes flashed blue for a second. I looked up at the hole in the ice I fell through. Light was pouring through the opening. I was getting ready to pass out. I saw Max's shadowy figure standing at the hole. I looked at his face and he was smiling. I knew this was the end as I started to black out. I couldn't help but smile back as I drifted away towards an endless dream.

Chapter 43

The mind of Jack. Saturday July 27.

       I slowly awoke after sleeping for what seemed like days. This was the first time that I slept through the night without waking up and screaming from a nightmare. I still had the dreams of her. I still dreamed that Nikki was drowning in a lake of ice and I would try to save her but I was always too late. She ends up breaking through the ice and the current drags her away. I had dreams about Nikki and me together in the sun. I remember dancing in the sky. Our bodies pressed closely together. I remember what it felt like when we pressed our lips together. The way her mouth fit perfectly into mine. Then I remember, very vividly, her poisoning me right after I rescued her from Max. I wondered if any of that really happen. My memories were starting to fade. Was it all just a dream? I mean, how could I have done half the things I did? I do remember how fun it was to fly. I hope I never forget that. Part of me felt like it had to all just be a wonderful dream. Then why do I feel like my heart was shattered into a hundred pieces when she betrayed me. My feelings for Nikki were real. How could the one I had fallen in love with turn around and stab me in the back?

As I lay there, I heard a lullaby playing in my head. I wasn't hearing it with my ears. It was in my head. It must be Max. I stood up and walked to the balcony to see what it is like outside. I stepped outside. It was going to be a hot one today. The morning sun felt good against my skin. There was a slight breeze. In my mind I heard a lullaby calling me. It was so slight I had to really think about if I was really hearing it or maybe my mind was just making it up.

I headed down to the pool. There was Max stirring the blue waters. In my world he was both the destroyer and the savior. He knew I was here without even turning around.

"You look like a witch stirring the cauldron." I said.

"Hello Jack. I dreamed you would come. I see you recovered, mostly."

"Yes I do feel better. You were right about Nikki. I didn't want to believe it. I am sorry I didn't listen to you. I owe you an apology. I talked to her parents and they said she died that night the police picked her up. She fell asleep in her cell and didn't wake up. I am sure you had something to do with that." I said as Max continued to watch the pool and stir the waters. He was silent for a moment before speaking.

"I know you are probably grieving for her but she died in the arms of the one she truly loved. Jack sorry to tell you this but it wasn't you. It was Ryan. You might have loved her but she didn't love you. I know that is a hard to take. She killed Ryan and she tried to kill you. I know you just want to remember the good times but she had a much darker hidden side that she kept to herself." Max said.

"I know. I just wanted to see the good side of her." I said. I was quiet for a few seconds. I didn't know how I wanted to phrase this so I came right out and said it. "I wanted to ask you something. You don't plan to kill me do you?"

"Well Jack, no I don't plan to kill you. Don't let me catch you doing any out of body adventuring. If I catch you out there I cannot guarantee that I won't attack. Also, don't do anything bad and I won't do anything bad to you. "

"No I don't plan to do that again. I just got caught up in Nikki's plans for revenge. I am sorry all that happened." I said.

"It is no problem. Shit happens. I know you are probably a little heartbroken but I am sure you will meet someone real soon. I bet she might even love you back." Max said.

I wasn't sure what he was talking about. I think he was trying to cheer me up. "Alright. Well Max, take it easy." I said. I was quiet for a minute. "You know, it all seems like a dream. Like it didn't even happen." I said.

Max was silent for a few seconds then he finally spoke. "I don't know what you are talking about." Max said grinning.

I chuckled a little. I turned around and walked back to my apartment. As soon as I walked into the breezeway there was a person carrying a large box in from the other side. She tripped and dropped her boxes. I saw the face from behind the boxes. It was incredibly beautiful. She had long blond hair and her skin was perfect.

I tried to start a conversation. "Hello. Are you ok? Do you need some help?" I said.

"I am ok. My family was supposed to help me move but they have not showed up yet."

"Which one are you moving into?"I said excitedly.

"I am moving into L."

"That is crazy. I live at M. We are going to be neighbors. My name is Jack." I said as I put out my hand for a handshake.

"Are you being funny? My name is Jackie." She giggled as she shook my hand.

"I can help you carry up some of your stuff if you want help. I don't have anything going on."

"Sure that would be wonderful." She kept looking at me. Her face was frozen for a few seconds. "You know this sounds weird but I had a dream that I was going to meet you. The guy in my dreams looked exactly like you. It is like this all happened before."

"Looks like dreams do come true." I picked up some boxes and we started to walk up the stairs together. "Why don't you tell me more about this dream?" I said as we walked up the stairs together.

The End.

www.ingramcontent.com/pod-product-compliance
Lightning Source LLC
Chambersburg PA
CBHW071153250626
47159CB00001B/76